PRAISE FOR
LINDA LAEL MILLER'S
KNIGHTS

"With a few highly original and new twists, Linda Lael Miller follows *Pirates* with another ingenious time-travel romance. . . . Using her many talents and her special storytelling abilities, she spins a magical romance designed to capture the imagination and the heart with wonder."

—*Romantic Times*

"As her readers will expect, Linda Lael Miller whips her fiery characters into yet another clock-bendingly happy ending."

—*Publishers Weekly*

"Charming! *Knights* entertains and enthralls from beginning to end with a clever plot and memorable characters!"

—*The Literary Times*

"Ms. Miller's talent knows no bounds as each story she creates is a superb example of exemplary writing. By the end of one of her masterpieces, the reader will know that not only have they enjoyed the story, but lived intimately with the characters through all their journeys—be it love, joy or pain. Keep it up, Ms. Miller, your stories are just one of the many reasons we love romance."

—*Rendezvous*

"*Knights* is a fun-to-read weaving of elements from a time-travel romance into a magnificent medieval romance. Dane and Gloriana are superb characters deserving the empathy of the audience. Linda Lael Miller's ability to paint a bygone era so vividly that it appears to be more a video than a novel makes this work a one-of-a-kind reading experience."

—*Affaire de Coeur*

RAVE REVIEWS FOR LINDA LAEL MILLER!

LINDA LAEL MILLER "ENCHANTS READERS"
—Romantic Times

"Funny, exciting, and heartwarming . . . another romance that's as wonderful and hot as you'd expect from Linda Lael Miller!"
—Romantic Times, on *Caroline and the Raider*

"Ms. Miller's unique way of tempering sensuality with tenderness in her characters makes them come alive and walk right off the pages and into your heart. . . ."
—Rendezvous, on *Emma and the Outlaw*

"Every novel Linda Lael Miller writes seems even better than the previous ones. She stirs your soul and makes you yearn along with her characters. . . . encompassing every emotion and leaving you breathless."
—Affaire de Coeur, on *Daniel's Bride*

"The love . . . shimmers from the pages just as the sexual tension sizzles. Ms. Miller writes a wonderful story."
—Rendezvous, on *The Legacy*

"Linda Lael Miller continues to prove that she is one of the hottest romance authors writing today. This is a novel filled with passion, mystery, drama, humor, and powerful emotions. Her love scenes sizzle and smolder with sensuality."
—Romantic Times, on *Angelfire*

Books by Linda Lael Miller

Banner O'Brien
Corbin's Fancy
Memory's Embrace
My Darling Melissa
Angelfire
Desire and Destiny
Fletcher's Woman
Lauralee
Moonfire
Wanton Angel
Willow
Princess Annie
The Legacy
Taming Charlotte
Yankee Wife
Daniel's Bride
Lily and the Major
Emma and the Outlaw
Caroline and the Raider
Pirates
Knights
My Outlaw

The Vow
Two Brothers
Springwater
Springwater Seasons series:
   Rachel
   Savannah
   Miranda
   Jessica
A Springwater Christmas
One Wish
The Women of Primrose
Creek series:
   Bridget
   Christy
   Skye
   Megan
Courting Susannah
Springwater Wedding
My Lady Beloved
   (writing as Lael St. James)
My Lady Wawyard
   (writing as Lael St. James)

Linda Lael Miller

My Outlaw

POCKET BOOKS

New York   London   Toronto   Sydney   Singapore

For information regarding special discounts for bulk purchases,
please contact Simon & Schuster Special Sales at
1-800-456-6798 or business@simonandschuster.com

An *Original* Publication of POCKET BOOKS

POCKET BOOKS, a division of Simon & Schuster, Inc.
1230 Avenue of the Americas, New York, NY 10020

ISBN 978-1-4516-1125-0

First Pocket Books printing May 1997

10 9 8 7

POCKET and colophon are registered trademarks of
Simon & Schuster, Inc.

Cover art by Pino Daeni

Printed in the U.S.A.

For my dad, Grady "Skip" Lael,
my favorite cowboy,
and for his wife, pardner, and sidekick, Edith,
with love.

My
Outlaw

❧ PROLOGUE ❧

Redemption, Nevada, 1974

Keighly Barrow was precisely seven years old the first time she saw Darby Elder's image reflected in the dark, wavy mirror of the old ballroom in her grandmother's house, though she didn't know his name then. She was startled by this encounter, being a practical child, but not really frightened.

It was her birthday and there had been a family party, with numerous cousins, colorful balloons and piles of presents, and an enormous cake in the shape of a teddy bear. Keighly was dressed all in ruffles, her long, fair hair brushed to a high shine and held back from her face by a wide satin band. Her favorite gift, a doll that talked when the string in its stomach was pulled, was clasped in her arms.

The other kids thought the ballroom was spooky, with its shrouded furniture and looming chandeliers, its silent harp and ancient, shadowy mirrors. Though the echoing chamber was as clean as the rest of the house, it was private, closed off, as if in sacred tribute to someone or something long gone.

Keighly loved the place, perhaps for the very reasons her cousins did not, and used it as a refuge when she needed a few minutes to herself.

Now, hazel eyes wide, Keighly slipped off the needle-pointed seat of the piano bench and approached the mirrored wall. The boy gaped at her, as if through a giant window, pale under his freckles.

Behind him, Keighly saw a large room with a sawdust floor, a long bar, an old piano. Women in gaudy, low-cut dresses strolled between tables full of cowboys. It was like something out of a western movie, except that the people were far more untidy, and there was no soundtrack.

The boy looked back once, quickly, as if to see if anyone else had noticed Keighly, then turned narrowed eyes back to her. He was about her age, she supposed, and just a little taller. His clothes were odd—he wore knee-length pants, made of some rough fabric, dark stockings, scuffed black boots with broken laces, and a loose, dirty cotton shirt. He had rumpled brown hair and light amber eyes that seemed to sparkle with mischief, even though his expression was solemn just now, and more than a little wary.

Keighly smiled, in spite of the queer, jiggly feeling in the pit of her stomach. "Hello," she said.

He frowned and his mouth moved in a silent response. Tentatively, he raised one grubby hand to the glass. She laid her fingers and palm to his, but felt only the cool smoothness of the mirror against her flesh. A vast sadness overtook her, one she was not capable of understanding, for all that she was one of the brightest children in her school.

They stood like that for a while—Keighly wasn't sure how long—and then, in an instant, the vision vanished. The only reflection Keighly saw was her own, along with the harp that had belonged to her grandmother's sister and all the ghostly furniture.

Keighly was a relatively happy child, the only offspring of intelligent parents who loved her if not each other, and it was, after all, her birthday, an occasion surpassed, in the Barrow family, only by Christmas. Still, she felt an

2

odd, piercing disappointment because the boy was gone. She had no doubt that what she had seen was real.

That night, because her parents were out with friends, it was Keighly's grandmother who came to her room to tuck her into bed. Audrey Barrow was an impressive woman; until her retirement only a year before, she had been a practicing attorney. She had masses of red hair, streaked with gray and always worn in a loose bun at the back of her head, and her eyes were exactly the same shade of hazel as Keighly's own.

They were "kindred spirits," her grandmother liked to say, cut from the same length of cloth.

"The mirror in the ballroom is magic," Keighly announced. With Gram, you just said what you wanted to say, straight out. If you didn't, she'd tell you to speak up and stop beating around the bush.

Gram arched one eyebrow. There were age spots on her skin, and she was pretty wrinkled, but to Keighly she was beautiful. "How so?" she asked.

"I saw a boy in there. And dancing girls. And cowboys."

"Hmmm," said Gram.

"This isn't a story, either," Keighly pointed out, braced for opposition.

"I didn't say it was," replied Gram. She'd come to the house some forty years before, as a bride, according to Keighly's dad. The ballroom had still been in use then, and Gram had danced there, in her wedding dress, with her handsome young husband. Keighly had seen pictures of the celebration, in one of the many photo albums lining the shelves in the study.

"But you didn't say it wasn't a story, either," Keighly replied. She had, after all, been born into a family of lawyers; her mother was an assistant district attorney in Los Angeles, and her dad, the youngest of Gram's four children, had just been made a partner in a large firm, specializing in real estate.

Gram smiled, perhaps a bit wistfully. "No," she conceded, smoothing the lace-trimmed, pink and white gingham coverlet on Keighly's bed. "I didn't." She paused, sighed softly. "I've caught glimpses of things in that mirror myself over the years—just out of the corner of one eye, you understand. It always happened so quickly that I thought it was only my imagination."

"I saw a saloon," Keighly confided. "Like the ones on TV, but dirtier."

Gram hardly batted an eyelash at this news. "This house was built on the site of an establishment called the Blue Garter, according to my research. The ballroom was part of the original building."

Keighly yawned, snuggling down deeper into her pillows, weary from the long, happy day. It was tacitly agreed that what she had seen in the mirror that afternoon would be their secret, hers and Gram's. Both Keighly's mother and father thought she had too much imagination and implied, sometimes, that she used it to liven up the truth.

The following year, Keighly spent the summer with her grandmother, because both her parents were tied up with important cases. As soon as her bags were unpacked and she'd changed into jeans and a T-shirt, Keighly wrote her name on a sheet of paper, backward, and rushed to the ballroom.

The sturdy, raggedy boy appeared almost immediately, as though he'd been waiting for her. He squinted at the tidy letters on the page Keighly held to the glass, bolted to a nearby table, and returned with an old-fashioned slate and a piece of chalk. Hastily, he wrote, Y B R A D, all the letters facing firmly in the wrong direction.

Keighly was puzzled at first, but she quickly translated. Darby.

His name was Darby.

The knowledge filled her with a strange, heady joy.

4

MY OUTLAW

She saw him often after that—almost every day, in fact. Sometimes, to Keighly's alarm, the view was one-sided. Darby would be there, plain as could be, playing cards with women who wore sleazy dresses and funny makeup, or raking the sawdust floor, or wiping down the long bar, but if his gaze strayed toward the mirror, the blank expression in his eyes made it clear that he did not see Keighly at all.

She did not like the feeling of being invisible, especially to Darby Elder. It was almost as though she didn't exist, if he couldn't see her.

That, Keighly told herself firmly, and repeatedly, was nothing but nonsense. Still, it was during that hot, sleepy, slow-moving summer that she first experienced the sensation that would plague her well into adulthood—a disturbing feeling that she was somehow insubstantial, unreal, a mere projection of another, better, stronger Keighly.

Keighly, though troubled, did not confide further in her grandmother or, for that matter, in anyone else. Nor did she mention the boy in the mirror.

That fall, her parents decided to get a divorce. Keighly's mother moved to Paris, to work for a multinational firm, and her father went to Oregon, where he practiced law out of a storefront and lived with a woman named Rainbow, who told fortunes and had four children by a previous marriage.

Keighly was sent to a fancy boarding school in New England, far from her friends and cousins in Los Angeles, and she was suddenly, utterly miserable. The awful feeling that she had no more reality, no more substance, than a shadow wavering on wind-roughened waters went bone-deep and took permanent hold.

When the holidays approached, Keighly refused separate invitations from both her parents and declared that she wanted to go to her grandmother in Redemption instead. A compromise was reached: she spent Thanksgiving in New York, with her mother and an aunt and uncle, and flew to Nevada for Christmas, there to be joined by her father and Rainbow and the kids.

Her grandmother met her plane in Las Vegas, alone, and drove her home to Redemption. Her dad wasn't coming after all, Gram explained carefully, when they stopped for hamburgers and french fries along the way. Rainbow suffered from migraines, and needed to lie in a dark room for a few days.

Keighly didn't let on that she was relieved by the change in plans, but she guessed her grandmother knew. Gram didn't miss very much.

When they arrived at the house Keighly now thought of as home, she found a fourteen-foot blue spruce waiting in the ballroom, still clad in the damp, fragrant chill of the high mountains from which it had come. The handyman, Mr. Kingsley, had strung thousands of tiny fairy lights through its lush branches, but the job of bedecking the tree with priceless ornaments, made and collected over generations, had been saved until Keighly could be there to help.

The following evening, when supper was over and the decorating had been done, Gram teetering atop a high stepladder to do her part, Keighly sat alone in the dark ballroom, gazing at the twinkling lights and shimmering decorations and indulging in a sort of brokenhearted admiration. She would have liked to live in Redemption with Gram until she grew up, but the older woman's health was declining, and there were days when her arthritis kept her in bed.

Nobody seemed to take Keighly's suggestions that she might be helpful, even if she was almost nine years old, very seriously, so she finally stopped making them.

She was reflecting on the fact that she didn't really belong anywhere, and feeling more transparent than ever, when she saw him, just at the edge of her vision. She turned her head quickly, her heart giving a lurch and then swelling with anticipation and relief. Darby was there, gazing in wonder from her to the tree and back again.

He'd grown taller. His hair was longer and somewhat shaggy and there was an angry scrape on his left cheek.

He mouthed her name; she felt his soul tug at hers.

Keighly rose from her chair, crossed the room, and pressed her forehead against the glass, as if to will herself through it, so strong was the pull between them. She laid her hands flat on the mirror's cold surface, barely able to keep herself from squeezing her fingers into fists and pounding at the barrier that separated her from Darby, who did the same. There was no mockery in his motions; only a certain awkward tenderness.

"Darby," Keighly whispered. "Oh, Darby—the world's fallen apart and I'm only a pretend girl—I'm not real at all." She talked on and on, emptying her heart, never moving, and felt better for saying it all, when the emotional storm was over. Even though Darby couldn't hear her, he seemed to understand, to know how sad she felt, and how lonely.

Most important of all, she knew he cared.

They stood like that, touching and yet not touching, for a long time. Then, when Gram came in and flipped on the overhead light, Darby vanished in an instant.

Keighly turned, blinking, half-blinded by the sudden illumination and by her tears. Her grandmother hurried over and drew her tightly into her arms, kissing the top of her head.

"Oh, sweetheart," Gram whispered. "Sweetheart. I'm so sorry, about everything."

Gram didn't ask why Keighly had been leaning against the mirror and crying—she had her own theories, of course—and Keighly didn't attempt to explain, then or ever. It was too private and too precious a thing to share, even with Gram.

Over the coming years, Keighly visited her grandmother whenever she could, and as she grew older, she began to dream vivid, dizzying, breathless dreams about

Darby, whether she was in Redemption or far away, but to her sorrow she saw his image in the mirror less and less often.

When Keighly was twenty, and in art school, her mother was killed in a car crash in Europe. Her father died, only a year later, after a bout of flu, and then, six months after that, her grandmother passed on, too. The house in Redemption was closed, pending settlement of a large and complicated estate.

The mirror became only a mirror, something dark and empty, in a house far away. And Keighly, living in L.A., engaged to a man she should have loved, but didn't, did her best to forget Darby Elder, and all she'd felt for him.

Still, he called to her, waking and sleeping, working or playing, and the longer Keighly stayed away from Redemption, the more ethereal she felt.

❧ CHAPTER ❧

1

Redemption, present day

The elegant old house, emptied by the other heirs of everything except the fixtures, one bed, a few boxes of papers and books, and Great-Aunt Marthe's harp, seemed to yawn around Keighly Barrow as she stood in the entry hall, one suitcase at her side.

She bit her lower lip and held back tears, allowing the mantle of ownership to settle slowly over her. Her emotions were mixed: she had always loved this place, and her experiences here had almost invariably been happy ones. Still, its very emptiness was a painful reminder that her grandmother and parents were dead.

Keighly sighed. She owned a small art gallery in Los Angeles, selling other people's paintings and sculptures, and she and Julian had been dating seriously for five years. She had plenty of money, inherited from her parents and carefully invested. There was no reason to hold on to an enormous old house in the near-ghost town of Redemption, Nevada, fifty miles from anywhere, and yet Keighly had not wanted to give the place up.

The reality was that the mansion was literally falling to ruin; it was time to do something—restore it and put it on the market, turn it into a shelter of some sort, donate it to the local historical society, if there was one . . .

Or move in herself, and pursue her sculpting in peace.

Keighly shook her head. That last idea was out of the question, of course. She had the gallery to consider, a circle of friends . . . and Julian. A successful pediatric surgeon, he could not be expected to abandon a thriving practice and start all over in a town so small that even freight trains didn't pass through.

She felt a mild surge of irritation, and suppressed it quickly. She was thirty years old, after all, and she wanted children. But, that required a husband, which was where Julian came in.

Keighly picked up her suitcase and sighed again. It wasn't that she didn't love him—he was sweet, steady, and even good-looking, if a little on the predictable side. It was just that—well—where was all the wild passion she'd expected to feel? Where was the poetry, the romance?

Where was Darby?

At the foot of the broad stairway leading to the second floor, Keighly glanced toward the tall double doors of the ballroom, which stood slightly ajar, remembering the photographs of her grandparents dancing there, Gram in her wedding dress, Grandfather in his coat and tails.

Oddly, a stray breeze stirred the strings of Aunt Marthe's harp just then, and Keighly thought she heard the notes shape themselves into a brief, merry tune.

Brow puckered in a slight frown, she put the suitcase down again and, after drawing a deep breath and squaring her shoulders, proceeded into the ballroom. She glanced at the harp, a large instrument, once spectacular, like the house, but now fallen into disrepair.

Keighly knew she was stalling. On some level, she'd been thinking about this room and its mirrored wall since the last time she'd visited the house, several years before, when she'd been tempted to sell. In the end, she hadn't had the heart, even though the real-estate market had been booming then and her uncles and cousins had all encouraged her to go for the big bucks.

She hadn't seen Darby during that visit, which shouldn't have surprised her, she supposed. There had been no sign of him the day the memorial service was held for her father, or after her grandmother's funeral, either. His absence had seemed like a betrayal, and deepened her already fathomless grief.

She forced herself across the dusty marble floor and stood directly in front of the mirror, in just the spot where she'd first glimpsed Darby, on her seventh birthday.

Nothing.

Unexpected tears burned in Keighly's eyes. "Where are you?" she asked in a whisper.

The harp's strings stirred, and overhead, the crystal teardrops of the Murano chandelier tinkled a soft, almost mystical response. A sweet shiver danced up Keighly's spine.

She was alone, of course.

She smiled ruefully and turned back to the mirror, almost as an afterthought, and what she saw made her gasp.

There was still no sign of Darby, but the saloon was back, crammed with unsavory-looking types in canvas dusters, battered cowboy hats, and mud-caked boots. Stringy hair and pockmarked faces abounded. On a small stage at one end of the room, three women in scanty costumes and garish makeup performed a suggestive dance, while a diminutive man wearing a derby, garters on his shirtsleeves, and high-water pants with suspenders hammered away at the keys of the same ruin of a piano. A fat, mustachioed barkeeper polished glasses, and other men played cards at various tables, most of them armed with long-barreled pistols in battered holsters.

The tableau was completely silent, and yet Keighly felt the faintest vibrations of sound and energy, as though the scene were just barely beyond the reach of her hearing. The colors were vivid; women moved among the tables serving beer and whiskey, as sleekly bright and colorfully plumed as birds from some undiscovered jungle.

Suddenly, desperately, Keighly wanted to step through the mirror, like Alice, and enter that other world.

She retreated a step, swallowing hard. Her own image, that of a tall, slender blond woman clad in bluejeans, a white cotton shirt, and a lightweight tweed blazer, was hazy and transparent. As though *she* were the ghost, and not the long-dead people on the other side of the glass.

The uncomfortable sense of unreality she so often felt intensified in those moments, making her light-headed.

Holding her breath, Keighly stared through her reflection at the scene beyond.

She took another step back. Instinctively, she knew that the cowboys and the dancing girls and the barkeeper were not specters or hallucinations; they were utterly real, going about their business in their own niche in time, completely unaware of her presence.

Only Darby, she thought with a pang, had ever been able to see her.

Where had he gone?

Keighly dashed at her cheeks with the back of one hand. Maybe he'd died, she thought. What she was seeing was obviously the nineteenth century, and mortality rates had been high there, for everybody. The population was plagued by such killers as typhoid, smallpox, cholera, and consumption, to name only a few. People carried guns, and didn't hesitate to use them.

Of course, they did that in L.A.

She shook her head involuntarily, rejecting the idea that Darby could be dead. In almost the same moment, she made up her mind to have a look at the old part of the local cemetery, a place she had assiduously avoided when visiting her dad's and grandmother's graves. Un-

12

less Darby had left Redemption, never to return—a distinct possibility—there might be a stone or monument bearing his name and the date of his death.

The spectacle in the mirror began to fade, and Keighly leaped forward again, without thought, pressing both her hands to the glass as though to hold on, to stop all those busy strangers from leaving her. A moment later, she moved back again, quickly, and dusted her palms on the thighs of her jeans.

Keighly turned and left the ballroom with as much dignity as she could muster.

Once, she'd visited a psychiatrist in L.A. and told him about the mirror, and he'd diagnosed the phenomenon as an "autogenic hallucination," a condition often associated with migraines. Keighly had explained that she'd never had a headache serious enough to be described as a migraine in her life, only to be handed a prescription for pain pills.

She'd tossed the slip of paper into a trash bin in the lobby of the doctor's office building.

Even now, she didn't question her sanity. Yes, she was a sculptor and therefore an artist—Julian said she was hopelessly right-brained—and she had always had an active imagination. But Darby and the Blue Garter Saloon were not illusions.

Were they?

She was in her old room, studying the naked mattress on the narrow canopy bed with distaste, when the cellular telephone in her purse gave a burbling ring. Knowing the caller was Julian, Keighly hesitated, then pulled the electronic marvel out of her bag and flipped down the mouthpiece.

"Hello, Julian," she said. Had she sounded snappish? She hoped not, because Julian didn't deserve that kind of treatment. He was only being thoughtful. He was *always* being thoughtful, no matter what he said or did.

He chuckled, and she imagined him in the hallway of

Los Angeles' Mercy Hospital, wearing his lab coat and stethoscope over a crisp white shirt and well-pressed trousers. His dark hair would be impeccably combed, no matter how frantic the day had been. Nothing, but nothing, ruffled Dr. Julian Drury, miracle-worker and surgeon extraordinaire.

"I guess I should be grateful you weren't expecting a call from some other man," he said.

Keighly held back a sigh, shoved the fingers of her free hand through her hair. "I'm a one-man woman," she replied, a little flippantly. *If you don't count your weird obsession with Darby Elder,* taunted some part of her brain that usually minded its own business and kept quiet.

"How was the trip, darling?"

"Long," Keighly answered. "I'll feel better once I've had a shower and something to eat." She glanced at her watch—it was nearly four in the afternoon—then at the bed, where her suitcase rested, unopened. Maybe she would check into a motel, just for a few days, until the utilities were turned on and she'd had a chance to buy a cot and some blankets, sheets and pillows. She'd been so anxious to return that she hadn't foreseen the need for secondary lodgings.

Julian would have, of course. He'd have planned ahead. Made reservations.

No, Keighly thought ruefully. The whole trip was a fool's errand to him; he wouldn't have come back at all, if he were in her place.

"Do you know what I think you should do?" he asked, startling her back to attention.

Yes, Keighly reflected, mentally rolling her eyes. Julian meant well, but he could be so pedantic. *You've already told me a thousand times, and now you're going to tell me again. And I'll listen because I want so badly to love you.* "What?" she asked, in a quavering voice.

"Get a good night's sleep, hire a real-estate agent to

14

sell that monstrosity of a house, and then drive straight back to L.A. Your life is here, Keighly. With me."

She was starting to get the kind of headache that called for a buffered pain reliever, and it annoyed her that Julian had referred to her grandmother's home as a "monstrosity," when he'd never even seen it, but she was too tired to debate the matter. "It isn't going to be that simple, Julian," she replied moderately. "The place needs a lot of fixing up and besides, Redemption isn't exactly the crossroads of the nation. People aren't clamoring to buy property here."

"So hire carpenters and painters and leave already," Julian said, with a sort of blithe peevishness. "Give the place to the town for a library or free clinic, blow it up or burn it down. Just get rid of it."

Keighly waited a beat before answering. She hated it when they quarreled, and being so far apart would make it worse. "What do you care if I own one old house in the desert?" she asked, as reasonably as she could. "You have investment property all over the country, after all."

"That's just the point," Julian replied, with tender indulgence. "I have *investments.* Holding on to a rickety old mausoleum in a ghost town is not good resource management, Keighly."

Keighly bit her lower lip. "I think we should talk about this another time."

"When, if not now?"

"Julian, I have a headache. I'm tired and I'm cranky and I'm feeling very unreasonable. That's why I am hanging up now. Pressing the End button. Good-bye, Julian. I'll call you in a few days."

His sigh bounced up to some satellite and back down, into Keighly's ear. She visualized the whole process, and it seemed to take place in slow motion. "I'm sorry, darling. You're right—this is no time to talk about anything important. And I'm being paged, so I'd better go. Get some rest, Keighly."

With that, he was gone.

Irritated with herself, rather than Julian, Keighly switched off the power on the cell phone and tossed it back into her purse. Then, picking up her suitcase again, she left her childhood bedroom and went downstairs to her car. She passed the Shady Lane Motel on the way to the cemetery, and smiled to herself. No concierge floor there, she thought. No room service, and no minibar. But at least the place would be clean, and the VACANCY sign was lit.

Reaching the Redemption Cemetery, Keighly stopped to pay her respects to her father and grandmother before moving on to the weed-filled part of the grounds, where the oldest graves were. Here, there were crooked monuments, weathered crosses, and, occasionally, brass nameplates all but covered in dirt and grass.

Some sites were ringed with white stones or broken bricks, and many had vanished altogether. More than an hour had passed before Keighly found Darby Elder's grave, tucked away in a plot belonging to a family named Kavanagh, and marked with a bronze sundial, half grown over with moss.

It did not surprise her, this tangible proof that a person called Darby Elder had actually lived.

It was the family plot that troubled her.

Maybe, Keighly reasoned, with a strange, deep pang of sorrow, Darby had married a woman of that name. Or perhaps the Kavanaghs had been his mother's people. In either case, she had never heard her grandmother mention that particular clan, and that was odd, since Gram had been an authority on Redemption's colorful history.

She caressed the name with almost reverent fingertips. It was spelled out in large, raised letters, simple and unembellished. Finally, with a sigh, she scraped away the debris in order to read the dates beneath.

Born, 1857. Died, 1887.

Keighly's throat closed over a soft sob, and again tears stung her eyes. It was just plain silly to be kneeling in an overgrown graveyard, mourning a man who'd died over a century before, but there she was.

What would Julian say, if he saw her now?

She smiled a little, despite the sorrow that gripped her, rising awkwardly to her feet, dusting her dirty hands off on her jeans. He'd probably suggest, with a teasing glint in his eyes, that she look into the possibility of having a left-brain transplant, since her own didn't seem to be functioning.

She drove away from the cemetery in a hurry, and stopped at a filling station to wash her hands and face and run a comb through her hair before checking into the Shady Lane Motel. After a consuming a grilled-cheese sandwich from the snack bar in the bowling alley across the street, she went back to her room, bolted the door, took off her clothes, and headed for the shower.

Afterward, she pulled on a cotton nightshirt, brushed her teeth, and fell into bed, attempting to watch television. There was nothing on but syndicated sitcoms and tabloid shows hacking away at tired themes.

Keighly switched off the set and slept, though fitfully, her mind crowded with dreams she would not remember in the morning.

San Miguel, Northern Mexico, 1887

When they finally found Darby Elder, he was playing strip poker with three whores and a corset peddler, and he was losing. Fact was, he'd got down to his drawers and boots, which surprised neither of his exasperated, trail-weary half brothers.

"God damn it, Darby," Will Kavanagh growled, sweeping off his hat and slapping one thigh with it in pure annoyance, "why the hell do you have to put us through this kind of shit? It ain't like we're trying to haul you back for a hangin'."

Darby narrowed his eyes, but did not raise them from

17

his cards. He had a lot at stake. He figured the peddler was bluffing, but there was a devilish twinkle in Maria's dark gaze that said her run of luck was holding. She wasn't going to ask for his boots if he lost.

"What about you, Simon?" he asked, around the cigar clenched between his teeth. "Don't you have a piece to say?"

The eldest of the three, Simon was well read, Eastern-educated, and obviously tired of chasing his father's bastard son all over the west, trying to force an unwanted birthright down his throat.

"If it were up to me," Simon responded, "I'd hang you right here."

Darby laughed and rubbed the stubble of beard covering his jaw. Maria wasn't even fidgeting.

"I'm out," the peddler said, probably unnerved by Will and Simon's unexpected arrival and unkind attitudes. He threw down his cards, picked up his satchel full of samples, from which he'd lost a garter and a lace-trimmed camisole, and fled.

Maria's glance flickered toward Angus Kavanagh's sons and heirs, taking in Will's invariably affable, if disgruntled, personage, and Simon's graceful good looks. A slight smile settled briefly on her lips before she turned her concentration back to the game. The two remaining players, Agnes and Consuela, threw in their hands without giving an explanation.

Maria slid a stack of poker chips into the center of the table. "Call," she said, purring the word, knowing damn well that Darby couldn't match the ante.

He spread out his cards. Three tens and a pair of deuces.

Maria grinned and laid down her hand.

Four of a kind, all jacks.

"Shit," Darby said.

"What an utter waste of time you are," Simon commented.

18

MY OUTLAW

"I love you, too," Darby replied. He still hadn't looked at either of them. Maybe if he waited them out, they'd have a few drinks and then get back on their horses and ride home to Nevada.

Even as he relished the prospect, Darby knew they were about as likely to do that as Maria was to ask for his boots. Before she could say anything, though, Simon tossed a handful of silver coins onto the table in front of her.

"Game's over," he said. "Take your winnings and get out."

Maria looked at the money, a sizable amount from her point of view, then at Darby. With another little smile and a twinkle in her dark eyes, as if pondering the choice, she scooped up the loot, gave the girls the signal to vamoose with a slight inclination of her head, and vanished.

Which left Darby alone with his brothers in the small, private room, wearing only his boots and drawers. He rubbed the back of his neck—the game had been going on for hours and he was tired and sore as hell—and finally turned to face Will and Simon.

Will, blue-eyed, golden-haired, easygoing Will, was leaning against the wall, his brawny arms folded, gazing at the door through which Maria and her little helpers had just disappeared. It wasn't hard to figure out what he was thinking.

Simon, on the other hand, stood like a rooster, his canvas duster pushed back at the sides because his hands were resting on his hips. He had dark hair, long enough to curl over the back of his collar, and strange silver eyes that could pin a man to the wall as surely as a sword's blade. It was said that he resembled his mother, a legendary Tidewater beauty, long-since succumbed to the rigors of settling in the wild west.

Will looked like Angus—or at least, like the youthful image in the portrait of the old man that hung over the

19

fireplace in the big study out at the Triple K—but his temperament was all his own. Angus was about as good-natured as a grizzly with a forked stick up its ass.

Darby sighed and reached for his trousers, which had been tossed onto an extra chair in a corner of the room. As for him, well, he didn't take after anybody in particular.

"You've got to come back," Will said.

Darby hitched up his pants and buttoned the fly. "Like hell I do," he answered.

"The old man is sick," Simon put in. There was something in his voice—weariness, grief—that caught Darby's attention right away.

"What do you mean, he's sick?" Despite it all, he felt a stab of alarm. Somehow, he'd expected Angus to live forever, he guessed. He snubbed out the cheroot in a chipped saucer provided for the purpose.

"Pa wants to see you," Will interjected. He looked pale, under all that trail dirt, and there was no sign of the cussed well-being that usually gave him the look of an overgrown kid up to mischief. "He took to his bed about ten days back. Can't get his breath half the time, and his chest hurts."

Darby snatched up his shirt and turned his back on Angus Kavanagh's legitimate sons to button it. When he spoke, his voice sounded hoarse, though he'd made an effort to avoid that. "Reckon you shouldn't have left him," he said, strapping on his gunbelt and securing the holster to his thigh by a worn strand of rawhide. "What I don't understand is what he wants with me. We've settled all there was to settle, he and I."

He'd barely gotten the words out before he was gripped by the shoulders, whirled around, and flung hard against the wall. The forty-five leaped into his grasp, an automatic response born of years of almost incessant practice, and his hand trembled slightly as he put the pistol away.

Darby and Will had often roughhoused, both as boys

and as men, but it was Simon he faced now, Simon he had nearly shot. His eldest brother, usually not given to violence, stood close enough to gut-shoot, his quicksilver eyes glittering with fury.

"You owe him this much, damn your worthless ass, and if you don't go willingly, I swear to Christ I'll have the undertaker sew you up in a shroud and take you home over the back of a packhorse!"

Home. To Darby, home was the Blue Garter Saloon, his mother's fancy whorehouse. The only thing he missed about the place was the image of that girl he'd seen in the mirrors that lined one wall of the dance hall. He'd thought she was an angel for a long time, with her big, gentle eyes and shining blond hair; now he figured she'd been an illusion, pure and simple. Something imagined by a lonely kid.

But he mourned her all the same.

"You mean back to the Triple K," he said. The meaning of the ranch's name had never eluded him: it stood for the three Kavanaghs, Angus, Will, and Simon. No place for a prostitute's by-blow in that equation.

Simon let out an explosive sigh and thrust a hand through his hair. His black hat rested on the poker table, where Maria's ill-gotten gains had been. "Yes," he said, with exaggerated patience, "that's what I mean."

Will's head was down. "He's dying," he said, in a voice that made Darby want to offer some sort of comfort. The trouble was, there was nothing he could do or say that would change anything. Angus was a big, broad-shouldered man, with a full head of white hair and the stamina of a bull bison, but people got old. An accomplishment in itself, in that part of the country.

"You'd better tell him the rest," Will added, when Darby didn't give in. Didn't speak at all.

"The rest of what?" Darby demanded, narrowing his eyes, jabbing his brother's chest with one finger.

Simon thrust a hand through his hair again. "It's your ma."

"What about her?"

It was Will who answered the question, sounding wearier than ever. "She's dead, Darby—it happened just before Pa fell sick. Some kind of fever." He paused, drew a breath and released it audibly. "I'm sorry."

Rage and something Darby couldn't quite acknowledge as grief surged through him, overrode the effects of the raw Mexican whisky he'd been drinking all day. He slammed both hands into Simon's chest, nearly knocking him off his feet.

Simon did not attempt to defend himself.

"You knew Harmony was dead when you walked in here *and you didn't tell me?*"

"Take it easy," Will pleaded. "It's the sorta news a man has to work up to. You can't just say a thing like that right out—it ain't decent nor kind."

Darby let his hands drop to his sides, turned his head away for a moment. Harmony Elder had been a whore, there was no denying that. She'd also been a good mother, in her no-nonsense way, and proud. She'd built a thriving business and held on to it.

"Something has to be done about the Blue Garter," Simon said quietly. "Even if you won't come to the ranch and see Pa, you ought to settle your mother's affairs."

Darby's eyes burned; he told himself it was because of the haze of cheroot smoke that still filled the little room. He cursed under his breath, and it wasn't because he knew he had to go back to Redemption. He'd promised Harmony a long time ago that, when the time came, he'd see that the terms of her will were carried out.

He neither knew nor cared what those terms were.

"All right," he said. "Just let me get my things and settle up a few accounts."

"Tomorrow is soon enough," Simon said, with uncommon gentleness. He started to lay a hand on Darby's shoulder, then wisely thought better of it and drew back.

MY OUTLAW

"It's fixin' to rain," offered Will, who, unlike Simon, had never bestirred himself to go back East and learn to talk fancy. The younger of Angus Kavanagh's two sons loved the ranch too much to leave it, and Darby didn't blame him. It was a glorious place, the Triple K. Nearly seventy thousand acres of timber and cattle land, with two working silver mines thrown in for good measure. The main house was big, a mansion by Redemption standards, but both Simon and Will had sizable spreads and lived under their own roofs.

Will was married, Simon was a widower with a young daughter.

Darby envied them their homes and families far more than their money, or the paternal love of old man Kavanagh.

"Yeah," Darby agreed belatedly. "It's fixing to rain, all right. You'll want to get beds down the street, at the hotel. It's clean enough, and they set out a decent meal."

"We'll ride north in the morning," said Simon. Though he phrased the words as a statement, Darby knew they really added up to a question.

He nodded.

"You could eat with us," Will said tentatively. He'd always been the peacemaker and, in spite of his efforts not to care, Darby liked him.

"I don't need or want your charity," he said coldly.

"We were expecting you to pay," Simon put in, with a wan grin. "I just gave most of my money to that whore— she was cheating, by the way—and you know Will's Betsey. She never lets him out of her sight with more than two bits in his pocket."

Darby might have smiled, under other circumstances. As it was, the only thing he had to look forward to at that point was the unlikely possibility that he might see Keighly Barrow in the mirror again, once he got back to the Blue Garter.

He'd caught glimpses of Keighly on and off since he

23

was a kid, but she hadn't put in an appearance in several years. Not since before he took up with the Shingler brothers, in fact. She was a fancy of his and nothing more, however much he might have liked for things to be different, and yet the longing to see her again, when it came to him, was a savage ache, rooted somewhere behind his heart.

Even now, with the news still fresh in his ears that his mother had died and the man who had sired him would soon follow, it was Keighly he wanted to turn to for solace.

It had taken Keighly three days to get the lights and water turned on in the old house, and she was sleeping in the ballroom on a cot from the camping department of the hardware store.

She was happier than she'd been in a very long time.

The peace and quiet was blissful, and she might have gone so far as to turn off her cell phone and let the battery go dead if she hadn't known Julian would get upset if he couldn't reach her and either send out a search party or come to fetch her himself.

She didn't want to go anywhere, except maybe to Las Vegas, the nearest city of any size, to buy clay and a new set of sculpting tools. Her hands ached to shape something fresh and new, something born of her own soul.

A desert storm was brewing, complete with thunder and spectacular flashes of lightning, when Julian called. Keighly was standing at the French doors at the far end of the ballroom, eating fast-food chili out of a paper container and watching the spectacle, when the telephone rang.

Reluctantly, she answered. The transmission was crackly, and Julian's voice sounded hollow, as though he were calling from another planet, instead of the next state. At the moment, Keighly was thinking in terms of Pluto.

"Hello," she said, balancing the phone between her shoulder and ear.

"I can hardly hear you!" Julian screamed good-naturedly.

Keighly flinched, forced herself to smile. "There's a storm," she said, and took another bite of chili.

"What did you say?"

She chewed hastily and swallowed. "I said, THERE'S A STORM!"

"When are you coming home?"

Keighly suppressed a sigh. "I don't know," she answered. "I need to stay here for a while, Julian. I can't explain it. I just need to stay."

Julian was silent for so long that Keighly thought they'd been cut off. Then, resignedly, he said, "I'm coming over there."

"No," Keighly said, quickly and with a firmness she usually reserved for cheeky shipping clerks and rude waiters.

"What did you say?"

Lightning sliced the sky and filled the ballroom with light. The harp sang and the chandelier made soft, crystalline music. And then the room was dark.

"I don't want you to come here, Julian," Keighly explained. The house was big and empty, but even with the power off, it wasn't spooky. She felt a strange, expectant buzz in the pit of her stomach, as though something important were about to happen, and strolled over to the mirror.

No sign of Darby or the Blue Garter Saloon.

"Keighly, what's happening here?" Julian asked, sounding baffled. "Are you trying to tell me, by any chance, that you don't want to see me anymore?"

"No!" Keighly said, so vehemently that she was embarrassed. Without Julian, there would be no family, no babies, no house filled with laughter and squabbling and light. "No," she repeated, more circumspectly. "I'm not

25

saying that at all. It's just that—well—it's so quiet here, and Los Angeles is so hectic. It feels marvelous just to take a break from the smog and the freeways."

"And me," Julian said forlornly.

"No," Keighly insisted. But she wasn't so sure this time, and she knew Julian was perceptive enough to discern that, in spite of poor electronic reception.

"Maybe this will be good for both of us." He sounded slightly stiff, distant. She'd hurt his feelings, and she hated herself for it.

"It's not like I'm dating anybody," Keighly pointed out.

Julian made no comment. He'd accused her, during past arguments, of withholding a part of herself from him, and she knew he was thinking of that now. "Call me when you're ready to talk," Julian replied, after a short pause. "You've got my pager number." With that, he disconnected.

Keighly stared at the small receiver in her hand for a few moments, seeing her fantasy children disappear, one by one, from the imaginary family photograph she carried in her head. She almost called Julian back right then, to tell him she was packing her things and returning to L.A. immediately, but something stopped her.

It was the faint sound of a train whistle.

Frowning, Keighly closed the phone and set it aside on a windowsill, along with her plastic spoon and half-finished meal. She waited, listened intently, and, in between claps of thunder, heard the plaintive wail again.

Shaken, she went to her cot, dragged it a few feet nearer to the mirrored wall, and sat down to wait. There was nothing weird about hearing a train whistle, she reflected, her heart thumping against her breastbone, unless you happened to know that the old depot had burned down in 1952 and there weren't any tracks inside of thirty miles.

❧ CHAPTER ❧

2

Although Keighly had intended to keep a vigil, at some point she had fallen asleep, there on the cot in the ballroom, still wearing her jeans, T-shirt, and shoes. She awakened with a jolt, the echo of thunder thrumming in her ears, and stared into the mirror.

Darby was there.

Darby, a gangly boy when she'd last seen him, and now a man in every sense of the word, though scruffy and in need of a shave, not to mention a bath. His tawny hair was long and sun-streaked, tied back like an Indian warrior's, and he seemed at ease in his broad-shouldered body.

Keighly's heart did a tap dance, then spiraled upward to lodge in her throat with a lurch that nearly choked her. She rose slowly from the cot, went to the mirror, and pressed her right palm to the glass.

Darby, wearing a collarless shirt open at the throat, a vest, and a pair of muddy trousers, did the same. There was a six-gun riding low on his right hip, plainly at home there, and he'd tossed a battered hat and an old canvas duster across one of the nearby tables.

For a long time, they just stood there like that,

touching and yet not touching. Neither tried to speak; they knew from past experience that words could not breach the barrier between them. Perhaps their hearts could bridge that gap, or their dreams.

For the moment, it was enough for Keighly just to know that Darby was alive. That he was back from wherever he'd gone.

There was a look of sorrow in his eyes that made her raise her other hand in a fruitless attempt to caress his cheek. Then, suddenly, overwhelmingly self-conscious, she stepped back. Darby, with a slight upward twitch at one corner of his mouth, countered her retreat with an advance, and pressed both palms to the mirror.

Keighly resisted an old, familiar urge to hurl herself at the glass, so great was her need to reach the other side. Tears of frustration and loneliness filled her eyes; she dashed away the first to trickle down her cheek with the back of one wrist.

Then, in a mere blink, Darby disappeared, along with the Blue Garter Saloon, and all Keighly could see was her own forlorn reflection staring back at her, hair sleep-rumpled, eyes puffy and red-rimmed, clothing wrinkled and askew.

She rested her forehead against the surface of the mirror, wondering why her heart was breaking when Julian Drury was so clearly meant for her, and she for him. Julian, after all, was a flesh-and-blood man, capable of making love to her, fathering her children, sharing her dreams. Darby might as well have been a shadow, or a figure made of glass.

And she'd visited his grave that very afternoon.

1887. He'd died in 1887, according to the raised numerals on the sundial marking his final resting place. Her heartbeat quickened again, this time with renewed fear for Darby. She'd just seen him, but what year had that been? Just how imminent was his death—was it a week, a day, an hour away?

MY OUTLAW

Trembling, she turned from the mirror and left the ballroom. Upstairs, she bathed, put on a nightshirt, and brushed her teeth rigorously. When Keighly returned to her cot, she stretched out and closed her eyes, but sleep did not come again.

He'd seen her.

Darby sat alone in his mother's saloon, a glass of whisky untouched before him, staring bleakly at the empty mirror. He had been back in Redemption for less than an hour, and *he'd seen her.*

Recalling the look of tenderness in Keighly's hazel eyes, and her gentle effort to lend comfort, Darby swallowed hard. He ached with weariness and with sorrow, and in those moments he would have given his very soul to close the space between them and take her into his arms. Although he had been with plenty of women in his time, Darby had never experienced the sort of yearning he felt for Keighly.

He sighed. Maybe he would see Keighly again, and maybe he wouldn't. When the last card was dealt, it really didn't matter, because they could never be together. To care for someone you couldn't have was to ask for pain, and there was enough of that near at hand. A man didn't have to go looking for it.

Darby raised his glass to his lips, frowned, and set it down again. In the morning, he would ride out to the Triple K and pay his respects, such as they were, to Angus Kavanagh. Then he'd see his late mother's lawyer, Jack Ryerson, who was as much a thief, in Darby's opinion, as Jesse James or Billy the Kid. The difference was, Ryerson didn't need a gun to pull off a holdup; he could do it with a pen, some ink, and a smarmy smile.

Once Harmony's business was settled, Darby meant to ride out of Redemption and never come back. He'd probably head down to Mexico, play a few more hands of poker with Maria, maybe buy himself a certain little spread he particularly admired with the proceeds from the sale of the Blue Garter and become *el patron.*

He grinned briefly, wryly, at the thought. He and Harmony hadn't parted on the best of terms—he'd fallen in with bad companions before he left town the last time, two years before, and she'd called him an outlaw. For all he knew, she hadn't left him so much as a brass spittoon.

Christ, he missed her. And he sure as hell wished he'd gotten back before it was too late to square things between them. Their last conversation had been a bitter, angry one, and Darby would regret that, he knew, to the end of his days.

Maybe Harmony had been right. Maybe he was no better than an outlaw.

Gentle hands came to rest on Darby's shoulders, and he was startled. He hadn't heard anyone approaching and, for a moment, he almost expected to raise his eyes and see Keighly standing behind him. Instead, it was Oralee, one of Harmony's "girls." She was plain in the first place, Oralee was, and her dyed yellow hair and face paint didn't help. Her skin was scarred by an early case of smallpox and she had skinny legs, but she was a gentle sort and Darby had always liked her.

She began massaging the back of his neck. "You come on upstairs, Darby," Oralee said kindly. "I'll make things better, at least for tonight."

Darby reached back, patted her hand. He normally wouldn't have passed up the opportunity, such as it was, but he was tired that night. Or at least he told himself that was the reason. In truth, he was still a little shaken by Keighly's reappearance. Sleeping with Oralee or any other woman, under the circumstances, would have seemed like a betrayal. "That's a charitable offer, Miss Oralee," he replied, "but I wouldn't be much good to you."

She bent and kissed the top of his head. It was sweet,

that kind of tender warmth, so sweet that it thickened Darby's throat and made the backs of his eyes burn. Her hands lingered lightly on his shoulders. "Your mama was over bein' mad at you when she passed on," she assured him quietly. "She never meant what she said about you bein' an outlaw because you was ridin' with the Shingler brothers and all."

The Shinglers had robbed trains, banks, and stage-coaches during their heyday. While Darby had never been a party to any of those crimes, he wasn't proud of his assocation with them, brief as it was. His reputation in Redemption had never been much anyway, him being the son of a prostitute, and taking up with Duke and Jarvis Shingler hadn't helped matters any. He realized in retrospect that he'd done it mostly to spite Angus.

Darby squeezed the hand he had just patted, then tugged Oralee into the chair next to his. "Will and Simon said Harmony came down with a fever," he said. She'd already been buried, his mother had, somewhere on the Triple K; he would visit the grave before he left, say his fare-thee-wells in private. Again, he wished he'd been a better son to Harmony.

"It took her fast," Oralee replied, with a nod. She reached for Darby's forgotten glass of whisky and sipped. "She didn't suffer overmuch."

Darby closed his eyes for a moment. God in heaven, but he was tired.

"She asked for you, o' course," Oralee confided, refilling the glass. "I won't deny that, even to spare your feelins. She wanted Angus, too, Harmony did, and he came a-callin', big as life."

Darby stared at her. "Angus came here?" Old Man Kavanagh and Harmony had been lovers for years, and everybody knew it, but Darby couldn't recall a time when the high-and-mighty Mr. Kavanagh had set foot in the Blue Garter. He and Harmony had had a little hideaway someplace in the hills; nobody would have dared to follow them, or ask where it was.

Oralee warmed to her subject, wide-eyed and eager. "He brought a fistful of flowers, too. Walked right through this saloon and straight up them stairs." She cocked a thumb over one shoulder to indicate the steps, in case Darby'd forgotten where they were, evidently. "Everybody just got out of his way and stayed out. He sat with poor Harmony for hours—Mabel Ann peeked through the keyhole a couple of times, and she said he was holdin' Harmony's hand, with tears runnin' down his face."

Angus was an intimidating man, with his long strides, his powerful body, his land and money. Or, at least, he had been—if Will and Simon had been telling the truth, old age had finally caught up with him. But Darby felt little or no sympathy for the rancher now. Angus had used Harmony, and he'd been too good to give her his name even when she bore his child.

"I guess he cared for her, in his way," Darby allowed. He nearly choked on the words, though he knew there was an element of truth in them.

"Now they say Mr. Kavanagh is dyin' hisself," Oralee persisted. "Do you think it's because he loved your ma so much he just can't go on without her?"

"I think it's because he's old," Darby said, and felt instant remorse, for Oralee did not deserve sharp words. He thrust himself to his feet. "I'm going to turn in now," he said, reaching for his coat and hat, leaving the open whisky bottle for the bar keep to collect in the morning and the glass for Oralee.

"What's goin' to happen to us now, Darby? Us girls, I mean? You gonna shut up the Blue Garter and move on?"

He paused to lay a hand on her bare shoulder. She was still wearing her dandelion yellow dancing dress, but the strap had slipped down on one side. "I won't leave without making sure you'll be all right," he said quietly. "You can tell the others that."

Oralee sighed. "Thanks, Darby."

32

He nodded and made his way through the dark hallways behind the main saloon, into a small, moonlit nook next to the kitchen. It wasn't a big place, or fancy, but it was private, and well away from the bar. The upstairs rooms, where Oralee and the others plied their trade, were on the other side of the building.

Darby paused, for only then did he grasp the fact that Harmony had tried to shield him, as best she could, from some of the grimmer realities of her livelihood. Then he tossed his hat aside, threw his coat over the back of a chair, and kicked off his boots. The springs creaked when he lay down on the narrow cot next to the wall, hands cupped behind his head, and considered the future.

Fact was, it didn't look very promising. He had nobody now, except for Keighly, the woman in the looking glass, and she was probably a trick of his imagination.

Pure exhaustion made him sleep, and when he awakened, he heard pans crashing around in the kitchen next door, and caught the delicious scents of fresh-brewed coffee and bacon frying. With a wry grin, Darby raised himself from the cot.

He was still wearing his boots, and a glance in the mirror over his bureau made him wince. He looked about as clean, he figured, as the floor of a stagecoach at the end of the route.

Darby went to the door, wrenched it open, about to yell for Tessie, the cook. A black woman with a broad lap and a smile to match, she was already standing there in the corridor before he managed to get her name out of his mouth.

"Look at you," she said, with affectionate contempt. "You ain't sittin' at my table, Darby Elder, or eatin' my victuals, lookin' like that." She waved a capable hand in front of her face and grimaced. "Nor smellin' that way, neither. I'll bring you a plate, 'cause I got a soft spot in my head where you're concerned, and old Burris'll haul in a tub. You got any clean clothes to put on?"

Darby grinned. He was used to Tessie's harangues; she'd been after him about one thing or another for most of his life. She'd also been the one to hold him, when he was little and had bad dreams, and care for him when he took sick. Perhaps most important of all, she'd taken real pains to convince him that it didn't signify what folks said about a person—what mattered was what that person truly was, deep inside. What they did and what they thought and what they said.

"I probably have some trousers and a shirt in the wardrobe, there," he answered, gesturing toward a small burlwood cabinet in the corner of the room.

"Well, open a window," Tessie commanded, but her dark eyes twinkled as she turned to trundle back to the kitchen.

Darby sat on the edge of his bed and consumed the breakfast Tessie brought while Burris, a timid little wet rat of a man who cleaned up in the saloon, lugged in a copper bathtub, followed by seven or eight buckets full of hot water, two at a time. When Burris was gone, and Darby had eaten the eggs, bacon, toasted bread, and fried potatoes and set the plate in the hall, he bolted the door, stripped off his clothes, and climbed into the tub.

It took a good twenty minutes just to soak off the trail dirt, and another fifteen of hard scrubbing until he got down to plain skin, but Darby felt a lot better when he climbed out. There was tepid water in the basin on his bureau, along with a razor, and after sharpening the blade on a strop, he lathered up his jaw and shaved.

The clothes folded on the shelves of the wardrobe were faintly musty, but they were clean. Darby dressed and brushed his wet hair back from his face, then tied it with a rawhide cord. When he reached the kitchen, Tessie was washing dishes.

"You look a whole lot better," she said grudgingly.

Darby chuckled and kissed her cheek. "It's good to be back," he said.

MY OUTLAW

" 'Bout time," Tessie replied.

The words were meant to prick, and they did. "I've got the rest of my life to regret not being here when Ma passed over," he replied quietly, holding up both hands, palms out, in a gesture of peace.

"She knowed you loved her," Tessie said, drying her hands on her apron and raising one to touch his face gently.

Darby wondered about that, would probably *always* wonder. He hoped to God Tessie was right, and some solace lay in the fact that she generally was.

"Was there a proper funeral?" he asked.

Tessie nodded solemnly. Although she worked at the Blue Garter, cooking for Burris and Harmony and a stable of loose women, she was a believer and stood in the back of Redemption's one church every Sunday morning, next to the door. She wasn't allowed to sit down with the others, though whether that was on account of her skin color or her association with the late proprietress of the Blue Garter Saloon, Darby didn't know. He considered it an injustice, either way.

"Mr. Kavanagh, he seen to the burial," she answered, dark eyes luminous with the memory. "It was private doins, though, and he said the words over her himself. Read out of the Good Book, too, and ordered a marble monument from back East."

Darby's throat thickened for a moment. He got a mug down off the shelf and filled it from the coffeepot on the back of the big cookstove, then set the cup aside again. "I hear Angus is doing poorly," he said. He didn't want to face the old man, didn't want to set foot inside that big hollow house that towered a quarter of a mile beyond the main gates of the ranch.

Tessie laid a hand to Darby's upper arm. "You're goin' to pay him a call, aren't you," she said. "That's good, Darby. That's real good."

He sighed. If the idea was so damn wonderful, how

come he'd rather shoot off his toes one at a time than follow through with it? "Yeah," he said. "And I guess I'd best get it over with."

Tessie made a stern face, and she was proficient at it, too, having had much practice over the years, but of course Darby knew what a fraud she was. She was a large woman, but her heart was bigger—so big that its outer boundaries were beyond reach.

"You be kind to that man, Darby Elder. He tried to be a father to you, and you never would let him. You just remember that, 'fore you go a-judgin' how he should have done things!"

Darby didn't answer. He just reached for his hat and left the kitchen by the back door.

His horse, a skinny sorrel he called Ragbone, was across the alley, comfortably ensconced at one of Redemption's four livery stables. Darby had gotten the nag in a single hand of five-card stud, down in Texas. Given the animal's nasty temperament, he wasn't sure whether he'd won the game or lost it.

After giving the stableboy a coin, Darby saddled the gelding and headed resolutely in the direction of the Triple K. He'd say good-bye to Angus, find out where his mother was buried, and pay her a visit, too. Then he'd see the lawyer, Ryerson, and make sure Harmony had provided for Tessie and Oralee and the others, though there was no doubt in his mind that she had.

Though the gates of the Triple K were a good five miles from town, and Darby never pushed Ragbone past a comfortable trot, he had reached his destination long before he was ready to be there.

He rode beneath the high, arched sign and along the short, twisting stretch of track that led to the house.

The silence was unnerving. On the few previous visits he'd made since he was a boy, and those had always been under some sort of duress, the place had been bursting with sound and fury—a smithy, hammering away in

Angus's forge, men breaking saddle horses in the corral, or pitching hay down from the high window of the barn.

Darby squinted and looked around again, then swung down off Ragbone's back and tethered him loosely to one of the hitching rails in front of the house.

The building was three stories high, with shining glass windows and walls of log and mortar. There was a veranda that stretched along the front and around the side, to the kitchen. He'd lived here one summer, when Harmony had to travel to San Francisco on some mysterious business, and he and Will had made a practice of stealing sugar cubes out of the pantry, along with cookies and oranges and whatever else they could grab. Simon, older and wiser, had literally been above all that; he'd spent most of his free time high in the branches of an old oak tree out behind the pump house, reading books about pirates and knights and Arabian sheikhs.

Will and Darby had preferred *being* those things, rather than reading about them, and spent whole days pretending to board ships, storm castle walls, and carry off fair maidens to their tents in the desert.

When the front door of the house swung open, Darby was startled back to the present. Simon stepped out onto the porch, hands braced against the veranda railing as he leaned.

"If it isn't the Prodigal Son," he said. While there was no welcome in his tone or manner, there was no rancor, either. Darby wouldn't have known Simon gave a damn if he returned in time to say good-bye to Angus if the man hadn't searched half of Mexico to find him.

Darby swept off his hat, slapped it against his thigh. "I'll be leaving again as soon as I can," he said, holding Simon's silver gaze. "Is he up to seeing me?"

Simon inclined his head slightly. "He can manage it," he said. With that, he turned and walked back into the house, leaving the door ajar.

Darby followed.

37

They passed through the familiar, shadowy entry hall, the coolest place in the house at the height of a hot summer day. An old longcase clock ticked ponderously on the landing of the stairway. Angus's study, with its looming double doors, was to the right, the main parlor to the left.

Darby felt a peculiar yearning, similar to what Keighly roused in him, but there was no point in putting a name to either emotion. He didn't belong on the Triple K any more than he did at the Blue Garter.

Like a thousand other men roaming the West, he didn't have a real home.

He told himself he didn't want one.

Angus's bedroom was large, taking up the whole back of the house and offering a spectacular view of the timbered foothills and the broad meadow beneath, where his horses and cattle grazed. There was a massive white stone fireplace at one end of the room, the hearth cold and swept clean on this warm summer day.

The old man sat in a wheeled chair, beside one of the windows, a turquoise and black Indian blanket over his lap, his white hair neatly brushed and shining in the refracted sunshine pouring through the glass. He did not turn his head toward Darby and Simon, did not acknowledge their presence at all.

Darby stood just over the threshold, his hat in his hands, and Simon went out, closing the door silently behind him.

A long, stubborn silence settled over the long room. Darby did not move, nor did Angus. Darby figured they might stand that way forever, if somebody didn't say something, and he was just about to give in when his father gestured with one hand.

"Come on over here, boy," Angus said. "Where I can see you."

Darby obeyed the summons, stood a few feet from Angus's chair, turning his hat slowly, around and around, by its brim. "I guess I should thank you," he said gruffly. Grudgingly.

"You should," Angus replied. Darby noticed that the old man's hands, resting uselessly in his lap, were gnarled and twisted. "But I don't reckon you will."

"It was the least you could do, burying my mother."

Angus closed his eyes for a moment, sighed heavily, and then raised his gaze to Darby's face. "You would have had me marry her?"

"Yes," Darby answered.

"That wasn't possible," Angus said. He nodded toward the window seat. "Sit down. It hurts my neck, looking up at you like this."

Darby sat, put his hat aside. "Why wasn't it possible?" he demanded, without raising his voice. "Because she was a whore?"

A flush of crimson rose along Angus's neck to pulse in his jawline. The rest of his face had gone pale as snow. "By God, I'd knock you on your ass for saying that, if I had the strength," the old man seethed. "Harmony Elder was no whore."

"Then why didn't you marry her?"

"I must have asked her a thousand times. She always turned me down."

Darby got up, turned his back, afraid he might give in to his baser instincts and choke Kavanagh to death with his bare hands. "I don't believe that. She loved you."

"Yes," Angus agreed, his voice hoarse with grief. "And those were her grounds for refusing me as a husband. She said it would be the ruin of all of us—her and me and my sons in the bargain." He paused, but before Darby could speak, he went on. "Including you."

Darby recalled schoolyard fistfights, some won and some lost, spawned by his illegitimacy and what his mother did for a living. He'd never forget the way the good women of the town had swept their skirts aside when he passed, the way their daughters had chased him

39

in private and ignored him in public. He'd been an outlaw all his life, after a fashion, simply because he didn't seem to belong anywhere.

"Simon tells me you're dying," Darby said, when he could trust himself to speak.

"Simon," Angus said unflinchingly, "is right."

Darby returned to the window seat again, sat down, and interlocked his fingers, letting his hands dangle between his knees. "I'm sorry," he told the old man. And he meant it.

Angus met his gaze for a long moment, then laid a hand to his once-broad chest in an unconsciously protective gesture. "No need for apologies," he said. "It's this renegade heart of mine, you know. Every once in a while, it just takes to carrying on, like a stallion trying to kick down the corral gate."

Darby's lips curved slightly at the analogy, but the expression was made up of sorrow as well as humor. "Thing like that has to hurt." He didn't know what else to say.

Angus nodded and smiled proudly. To men like him, pain—when coupled with the ability to bear it without complaint—was a badge of honor. "Had to have a wound cauterized with a hot poker one time. That was worse."

There was a brief, difficult silence. "And now you're figuring on dying sometime soon," Darby said at last.

Angus flushed again, insulted. "It isn't like I just decided to do it. I'm an old man—I've lived my life and made my fortune and now it's time to pass everything on down to my sons."

"Will and Simon are good men," Darby said. "They'll make the place pay."

"They need you to help them."

"The hell they do," Darby retorted quietly, keeping his tone even and his countenance friendly. "I'd be a hindrance in every way, and we both know it."

MY OUTLAW

A muscle tightened in Angus's jaw and, for a moment, the aged, domineering Scot looked young again, and vital. "You're a hindrance to yourself, Darby Elder, and nobody else. That god-awful pride will be the end of you yet!"

"I must have inherited it from you," Darby said.

"It isn't all you're inheriting from me," Angus insisted. "One-third of this ranch, including this house, will come down to you."

"I can sell," Darby pointed out, sensing a trap.

"You won't," Angus stated, with utter confidence. "Because your mother rests right here on this land."

Darby wanted to walk out, just walk out and never look back, but he couldn't bring himself to stand. His legs felt brittle as bacon rinds. "You did that on purpose," he accused.

"You're damn right I did," Angus answered, without chagrin.

"I could have her coffin moved." The thought of disturbing her made him ill.

"Where?" Angus challenged. "I guarantee they won't let you lay Harmony to rest in the churchyard. You want her out in the prairie somewhere?"

Darby covered his face with both hands and gave another sigh, full of weariness and frustration. "Damn you, old man," he breathed. "Why are you doing this? Why in God's name won't you just let me ride out of here and forget this miserable place ever existed?"

"Because you're my son," Angus said. "As much as Simon or Will. But maybe I did make a mistake. Maybe you haven't got the guts to handle the kind of land and money we're talking about here. If that's the case, well, hell, it's your problem. Yours and your brothers'. I'm tired and I'm sick and all I want to do is lie down beside Harmony one final time."

Darby wondered why Angus didn't care to be buried next to his first wife, Simon's mother, Lavinia, or his

41

second, Ellen, who had borne Will and died in the process, but it didn't seem right to ask. "I don't want it," he said. "Not the money, not the land."

"How about your mother's final resting place? You want that?"

Darby clenched his teeth for a moment. It was just a plot in the ground, his mother's grave, but it was enough to hold him close by, at least for a while. "You wouldn't allow it to be desecrated," he said.

"You're right," Angus agreed. He was looking worse with every passing moment. "But I'm not going to live very long. And while Will and Simon are both good men, Harmony wasn't their mother. They're not likely to hold that grave in such high esteem as you and I do."

Darby took up his hat and stood. "I need to think about this. I'll be in town a few days, if you want to reach me."

"Wait," Angus said. Slowly, awkwardly, he turned his invalid's chair and wheeled across the room to a bureau. From a top drawer, he took a small red velvet pouch. "This is the betrothal ring I tried to give your mother. She never would wear it, of course, but she asked me to pass it on to you. Said what you needed more than anything else was a woman to love you."

Darby took the pouch and tucked it into the pocket of his vest—Angus was in no shape for further argument—and for some reason Keighly, the woman in the looking glass, came to mind. He'd give the ring to Will or Simon, he vowed silently, after the old man was gone. There was no use in working Kavanagh into a state now.

"Thanks," he muttered.

"Help me get into bed," Angus commanded. "I'm feeling poorly."

Darby raised his father out of the chair, supporting him by draping one of the old man's arms over his shoulders. He got him to the bedside and covered him when he'd stretched out on the plump mattress. "You want the doctor?"

Angus shook his head. "Hell, no. That old sawbones doesn't know any more about mending sick people than I do about the backside of the moon."

"I'll be back," Darby said, starting toward the door. He paused there, one hand on the knob, and looked over his shoulder at the emanciated figure lying on the bed.

Angus smiled. "That's good," he replied, and closed his eyes.

Simon was waiting at the bottom of the stairs, leaning indolently against the fancy newel post, as if he didn't have anything better to do. "Well?"

"It was the same as always," Darby said. "We got nowhere."

Simon thrust a hand through his hair and suppressed what portended to be a mighty sigh. "Come on," he told his youngest brother. "I'll show you where Harmony's grave is."

There was a temporary stone on the top of a small knoll behind the house. A fence encircled the plot, to keep cattle and horses away, and fresh wildflowers were strewn from one end of the mound to the other. Overhead, the Nevada sky was cloudless, and so blue that Darby's weary heart caught.

Simon slapped him on the shoulder and left without a word.

Darby stood holding his hat, his eyes burning. Because there were no words for what he was feeling, he didn't speak, but simply let the grief wash over him, in great, crushing waves, hoping that somehow Harmony knew he'd loved her, and that he was sorry for a great many things.

He wasn't sure how much time had passed when he finally left Harmony's graveside and returned to the hitching post in front of the house to collect his horse. He touched his hat brim and nodded to Simon as he rode out.

His mind should have been on his upcoming appointment with the lawyer, Ryerson, he supposed, or maybe fixed on memories of his mother. Instead, Darby found himself thinking about the woman in the mirror, and wondering how he could reach her.

❧ CHAPTER ❧

3

Julian did not call Keighly, and she returned the favor.

Instead of worrying about the relationship, she threw herself into getting the house in shape, hiring a local contracting company to make rudimentary repairs, such as changing the locks on all the doors and windows, nailing down a loose floorboard here and there, and replacing the screens on the summer porch.

Keighly didn't want to leave Redemption—perhaps it was that one tantalizing glimpse of Darby that held her—so she telephoned various stores in Las Vegas and placed orders for a refrigerator, a small microwave oven, and a supply of clay and sculpting tools. She got a library card and checked out a stack of books, bought groceries at the local supermarket, and returned to the big, lonely house to wait, as patiently as she could, for a glimpse of Darby.

Jack Ryerson was sitting, with his feet on the surface of his desk, when Darby walked into his office without pausing to consult the blustering clerk in the high celluloid collar who stood guard at the door. The minion followed on Darby's heels, muttering protests.

"It's all right, Clyde," Ryerson said, with a wave of one hand. "Some clients have manners and some don't. Elder here happens to fall into the second category."

Clyde went out, scowling, and closed the door behind him. Darby wondered if the little weasel thought he couldn't see his shape, pressed against the frosted glass panel, a listening shadow.

"Let's get this over with," Darby said. "You know why I'm here."

Feet planted firmly on the floor now, the lawyer took a cigar from a painted tin box on his desk and bit off the end. He offered one to Darby, with a gesture, and Darby shook his head, pulling up a chair.

With an elaborate amount of puffing and blowing, the lawyer lighted his cigar and settled back in his seat. "Your mother left a considerable estate," he said, after a long time. "Burris and the barkeep are pretty much on their own—Harmony figures they've already stolen their share. Generous provisions were made for the cook and all the girls. Doc Bellkin checks 'em all once every seven days to make sure they aren't diseased, and Harmony wanted that to continue."

Darby sighed. "I don't plan to run the Blue Garter," he said. "I'm selling out as soon as I can. Moving on." He felt a brief, poignant regret, saying the words aloud. He'd miss Tessie and Oralee and some of the others. But mostly, he hated leaving Keighly's image behind, trapped in that mirror.

Ryerson indulged himself in a long sigh and a smirk that made Darby want to catch the bastard by the throat and see how many teeth he could dislodge with one punch. "You won't be able to do that," he said, "unless you're willing to forfeit everything and see that old Negro woman and a whole passel of soiled doves tossed out with no place to go."

Darby leaned forward. Before, he'd been bored and impatient; now he was suddenly alert. "You just said

46

they'd all be taken care of under the terms of Harmony's will," he snapped.

"So I did," Ryerson responded, making a steeple of his beringed fingers under his chin and settling back in the chair with a creak of metal and wood. He was enjoying this, the son of a bitch. "What I hadn't gotten around to mentioning yet was the stipulation."

The hairs stood upright on the back of Darby's neck, and something coiled in the pit of his stomach. He knew he was teetering on the brink of a trap, and the nature of the snare was just beginning to come clear. "Let me see the will," he said, almost growling the words. "Now."

Ryerson produced a thick, folded document from the inside pocket of his waistcoat and tossed it across the desk.

Frowning, Darby broke the fancy wax seal and snapped his mother's last will and testament open with the flick of one wrist. While he had never been good in school—he'd spent more time fighting than learning—he'd consumed most of the books in Angus's library and inherited his mother's skill with numbers, so he pretty much had the gist of the situation in a matter of seconds.

Harmony had left him the Blue Garter, along with various plots of land, two sizable bank accounts, one in Redemption and one on deposit in San Francisco, and all her personal belongings. The hitch was, in order to claim the legacy, he must also accept his birthright as one of Angus Kavanagh's sons. If he failed to do so, Tessie and the girls would have to make their way in the world as best they could, and the remainder of the estate would go to Harmony's half-brother, an easterner named Stuart Mainwaring, who had long since disowned her.

Darby clenched his jaw.

"Looks like you'll have to give up outlawing and make a solid citizen of yourself," Ryerson said. Either way, he was going to get his fee; he could afford to goad Harmony Elder's bastard son and unwilling heir—at least, where the will was concerned.

Darby gave the lawyer a scathing look. He'd never been an outlaw, but he was damned if he'd explain anything to this boot-licking sidewinder.

"I'm caught all right," Darby said, after a few moments of poisonous silence, during which he glared the smartass grin right off Ryerson's face. And for now, it did seem that he was trapped. However, there was nothing to stop him from collecting his bequest, agreeing to Angus's demands, and setting Tessie and Harmony's brightly plumed flock up in decent circumstances. Once the dust had settled, he'd simply saddle old Ragbone and ride out for parts undecided upon.

When Angus had passed over, Darby suspected Will and Simon wouldn't be so eager to bring their prodigal half-brother back into the fold. In fact, they'd probably be more than happy to see him sign over his share of the family holdings and say good-bye for the last time.

"Sign here," Ryerson said, pushing a single sheet of heavy paper, a bottle of ink, and a pen across the surface of the desk in one easy motion.

Darby read the statement, saw immediately why Ryerson had been so eager to complete their business. He was to receive a substantial bonus for "persuading" Miss Harmony Elder's heir to accede to her demands, payable from estate funds as soon as Darby's signature had been obtained.

He hesitated only a moment before signing. While Oralee and the other girls would probably have landed on their feet, so to speak, Tessie was an old woman, alone, for all practical intents and purposes, in a hostile world. Darby didn't even want to speculate on what would happen to her if she was turned out of her little room in the back of the Blue Garter Saloon, penniless except for whatever pittance she might have managed to save over the years.

"Excellent," Ryerson said. "As of right now, you have access to your dear late mother's assets."

Darby thought he detected a snide note to Ryerson's

reference to Harmony, but he was too irritated at the moment to rise to her defense. She'd finally gotten her way, making him beholden to Angus Kavanagh, and love her though he had, he would not soon forgive the betrayal. It was painfully obvious that, in the end, Angus's wishes had meant more to her than those of her son.

He pushed back his chair, collected his copy of the will, along with several bank books and other accoutrements of inheritance and, without a word to Ryerson, turned to leave the office. Clyde barely managed to trundle away from the frosted glass door before Darby rammed it open.

Full of a curious mixture of anger and sorrow, Darby unhitched Ragbone and rode down the street to the Blue Garter. Burris was waiting out front; he took the reins and scuttled away to put the gelding up in the livery stable around back of the saloon.

The Blue Garter was doing a rousing midday business, and cowboys, gamblers, general no-accounts, and bad women called a cacophony of greetings to Darby as he entered. He ignored all of them and strode over to his usual table, which by good fortune happened to be empty, and sat down, facing the mirror.

To his utter astonishment, he could see Keighly clearly, though she did not seem to be aware of his presence. She was lying on her side on a cot, her odd, manlike clothes rumpled, tousled hair tumbling over the high curve of her cheekbone, eyes closed in sleep. Although her coloring was fair, her lashes lay dark and thick against her skin.

Darby was so stunned that he couldn't move. He waited for the vision to vanish, but it didn't. His own reflection was less substantial than Keighly's, transparent and smoky, barely solid enough to be called a shadow.

Oralee came up behind him, laid her hands on his

shoulders. He knew her by her scent; the mirror did not show her image.

"What do you see in there?" he asked, his voice rough as rust. He didn't dare look around or even blink.

"In where, honey?" Oralee asked, bending to kiss the top of his head. She was not overly bright, which accounted for a great many things.

"In the looking glass," Darby ground out, with all the patience he could manage. "What do you see?"

"You, sweetie," Oralee said tenderly. She was starting to sound just the least bit worried. "You and me and a whole saloon full of people."

Darby leaned forward. Keighly. She was sleeping. He willed her to wake up, look at him with those magical, soothing eyes. Even more than that, he wanted to touch her, talk with her, hear her laugh. Did she sound breathy when she spoke, like Oralee? Husky and brisk, as his mother had, or gentle but firm, like Tessie?

She didn't move, but she didn't fade away, either.

"Get me a drink," Darby said, not unkindly, his eyes never shifting from the panels of silvered glass before him.

Oralee hurried to obey, and returned shortly with a bottle.

"You visited Mr. Kavanagh this mornin'," Oralee said. "How was he?"

"I don't care to chat just now," Darby replied, as gently as possible, without sparing Oralee so much as a glance. "Angus is still among the living."

"Maybe I'd better get Doc Bellkin," she suggested, at great length. "For you, I mean. You don't seem right, Darby. Just starin' into the mirror like that. You might be ailin' yourself."

"Go away," Darby said, with neither rancor nor interest. As he looked on, Keighly stirred in her sleep; one shapely breast rose, its peak visible through the thin white fabric of her shirt.

His mouth went dry.

MY OUTLAW

"But, Darby—" Oralee protested.

"Just go," he told her coolly.

The sensation of being watched brought Keighly slowly out of the gloomy, dreamless depths of her slumber. She'd stretched out on the cot after an afternoon of conferring with carpenters, plumbers, painters, and paperers, at about two o'clock, hoping for a short rest. That had obviously turned into a full-scale, knock-out nap, and she was groggy as she sat up.

The ballroom was dark, except for a light burning in the hallway, but a glow came from the mirror.

Keighly saw the kerosene lamp shining in the middle of the rough-hewn saloon table before she looked at Darby, who was sitting there, a drink beside him, apparently untouched. He was leaning forward, his handsome, Westerner's face beard-stubbled and frowning. Except for him, the Blue Garter appeared to be empty.

Hastily, Keighly grabbed up a tablet she'd kept on hand for just this purpose, having laboriously printed out a backward question earlier in the day. The words Darby would see were "What year is it, where you are?"

He bent and wrote in the sawdust at his feet. "1887. There?"

Keighly's heart was thudding painfully in her throat, the image of his gravestone fresh in her mind, but she managed to scrawl a reply on the bottom of the tablet page. Then, quickly, she flipped to the next, penned, "I want to come to you."

He closed his eyes for a moment, mouthed his answer. "I want that, too." But his expression was hopeless.

"I'm going to find a way," Keighly wrote. "I swear it."

Only in the moments following, when Darby's reflection had finally disappeared, did she wonder what had prompted her to make such a promise, when she had no means of fulfilling it.

51

The next morning, she was at the door of Redemption's one-room library when the door was unlocked for the day's business.

"Finished already?" asked the librarian, Miss Pierce, who had lived in Redemption all her life and known Keighly's grandparents well. Keighly set the books she'd borrowed the day before yesterday on the return desk and nodded. "Quick reader," said Miss Pierce approvingly. "Audrey was like that, too. Smart as a whip. She read right through our stacks before she was out of grammar school, and we had to borrow books from other libraries just to keep up with her."

Keighly acknowledged the compliment with a slight smile. "I was wondering if you keep old records—births and deaths, things like that?" Redemption was too small to have a courthouse or even a newspaper, though there had once been a flourishing weekly, according to Gram.

Miss Pierce beamed. "We have a microfilm machine—secondhand, of course—with maybe a hundred copies of the *Trumpet* recorded. Was there someone in particular you wanted to know about?"

Keighly cleared her throat. "A man named Darby Elder. He died in 1887, and was buried here in Redemption—"

"Right in with the Kavanagh clan," Miss Pierce interrupted, with cheery disapproval. She bent toward Keighly and dropped her voice to a whisper, although, as far as Keighly could tell, the place was empty except for the two of them. "His mother was a madam!"

Keighly tried to look shocked, but of course Miss Pierce's announcement came as no surprise. Darby had told her a lot about himself over the years, though not verbally, of course. He just hadn't happened to mention that he was going to die in 1887, or how.

"I'd—I'd like to know what happened to him."

"No need to look on the microfilm," said the librarian, sounding somewhat disappointed. "We've got journals, kept by Simon Kavanagh's daughter, Etta Lee. Quite a little writer, she was. That ranch is still in the Kavanagh family, too. One of them, I think her name was Francine Stephens, came in just last week and made photocopies of everything we had with regards to her people."

That precluded asking to borrow Etta Lee Kavanagh's journals; if Miss Pierce hadn't loaned them to a relative of the author, she probably wouldn't let Keighly take them out of the library either. "Do you know where Ms. Stephens is staying?" Keighly asked. She was itching to read the journals, but something in her gut told her that the ramifications of Francine's visit to Redemption might be important ones.

Miss Pierce's already blinding smile brightened to high-beam. "Why, right in the old Triple K ranch house, dear. I think it's lovely, the way you children have come back to our little town, restoring important houses to their proper grandeur."

"Is that what she's doing? Renovating the main house on the Triple K?"

Miss Pierce nodded. "Isn't it wonderful? She works in Chicago—or was it New York? She's an executive of some sort. She wants the ranch for a vacation home. Says maybe she'll raise a few horses there, too—that's in her blood, you know."

Keighly made a mental note to pay a call on Ms. Stephens and then asked to see Etta Lee's diaries. Miss Pierce brought them, a musty little stack of hardbound books coming loose from their bindings, and Keighly turned the pages carefully, smiling here and there as she read chronicles typical of a young girl, whatever her century. Would she *ever* be pretty? Did Jimmy Wilson wink at *her* during spelling practice, or had the flirtation, God forbid, been directed at Molly Robbins, instead, since Molly sat right beside her?

There was discouragingly little information about the workings of the Triple K Ranch, let alone its occupants, or one Darby Elder, the illegitimate son of Etta Lee's grandfather, Angus. She wrote that she wished her father, Simon, would remarry, because then maybe he might be at home more, and expressed deep affection for her uncle Will and aunt Betsey, with whom she often stayed.

Keighly's stomach was grumbling—and the library was about to close for the day—when she finally ran across a reference to Darby, who must have been, to young Etta Lee, a shadowy and questionable figure at best. No doubt, given Victorian sensibilities concerning such matters, she had not heard a great deal about this second uncle and the circumstances of his birth.

Etta Lee had not entered a date at the top of the vellum journal page as she usually did, but had simply begun to write. *Papa and Uncle Will have gone to town, even though it is after midnight, and I am here alone, except for Gloria, Grandfather's cook. I heard Uncle Will say Darby Elder got himself shot, at the Blue Garter Saloon . . . I don't know what poor Keighly will do without him. . . .*

Keighly could not breathe or move.

The news about Darby's shooting was terrible enough, but seeing her own name written by the hand of a long-dead girl stunned her into a state of suspended animation.

It was Miss Pierce, bless her heart, who brought her around. She put a hand, light as a bird's claw, on Keighly's shoulder and set a cup of steaming tea in front of her. "Are you all right, dear? You look wretched—pale as Aunt Hortense's nightdress. Here—drink this right away."

Keighly used both hands to raise the mug to her lips, trembling so violently that Miss Pierce discreetly moved the Kavanagh journals to a safe place nearby. Etta Lee's words echoed relentlessly in Keighly's head.

. . . got himself shot . . . don't know what poor Keighly will do . . .

. . . poor Keighly . . .

MY OUTLAW

It could be coincidence, of course, but the name was unusual.

Keighly took a sip of tea. Dear God, was it possible? Had she—*would* she—manage somehow to cross over into Darby's world?

"Do you feel better?" Miss Pierce asked anxiously.

Keighly managed a nod, started to get to her feet so the librarian could lock up and go home, and toppled right back into her chair again. "I—I know you want to leave for the day—"

"Nonsense," said Miss Pierce. "There's no one there waiting except for my cat, Milton, and he isn't much of a worrier."

Keighly smiled tentatively, full of appreciation. She was oddly shaken, and did not want to be alone. Not yet. "Have you ever heard my name before, Miss Pierce?" she asked.

"You used to come in for Nancy Drew books, when you were spending time with your grandmother," Miss Pierce recalled, in a tone of proud pleasantry. "And I recall that you read *Jane Eyre* at least half a dozen times in one summer."

"Was there ever someone else called Keighly, or perhaps a family by that name?"

Miss Pierce, keeper of the literary flame, pursed her lips and thought hard. "I don't recall it, dear," she said, after a considerable interval had passed. "However, I will be happy to research the matter as best I can and give you a call with the results."

Keighly glanced longingly toward the stack of journals, now resting on top of a bookcase stuffed with ancient reference volumes. "I know it's past closing time," she said quickly, awkwardly, "but if I could just make a few photocopies of one of the journals—?"

"I'm sorry, dear," Miss Pierce said firmly. "That will be impossible, tonight at least. Our machine is old, you know, and it requires quite a long time to warm up properly. Unfortunately, I've already switched it off."

Keighly nodded. She would return in the morning, have another look at the diaries. The only question was, how was she supposed to get through the rest of this night without knowing whether or not Etta Lee had made other references to her? Even worse, Keighly would be left to wonder why Darby was shot, and by whom. Whether he had suffered, whether he had lingered a long time, or died immediately.

For a moment, she thought she was going to throw up.

"You just take the books," Miss Pierce said, in a whisper. "You have fine, honorable blood in your veins and it isn't like you're a stranger. I'll need them back first thing tomorrow, though. If that Ms. Stephens should come in wanting another look at them, I'd be hard put to explain where they were."

Keighly almost flung her arms around the little woman and hugged her in gratitude, but she didn't wish to alarm Miss Pierce, who was a bit on the timid side, so she contained herself. "I promise I'll be careful," she said.

Keighly finished her tea and she and Miss Pierce walked out of the library together. The sounds of a small-town summer evening were all around them—kids being called in to supper, sprinklers coming on to spray diamonds onto thirsty lawns and flowerbeds, the ghost of an intrepid moon, there to give the dying sun fair warning of day's end.

"Thank you," Keighly said, when they stood together on the bumpy sidewalk, Miss Pierce having carefully, reverently, locked the library door. "For everything."

Miss Pierce patted her hand. "I don't know what it is you're looking for," she said, "but if you ever need to confide in someone, I can be trusted." With that, the small, dignified woman started off toward her pristine cottage of a house, which stood at the end of that same street, in the shade of a weeping willow tree.

Keighly set the journals carefully on the passenger seat of her car, then went around to the driver's side and climbed in. She stopped at the supermarket for bread and cheese, planning to have a grilled sandwich for supper and then spend the evening reading Etta Lee's diaries. When she got home, however, she was surprised and irritated to see Julian's white Jaguar parked out front.

He was standing in the newly mown front lawn, chatting amiably with the painter's helper, who had been scraping the shingles in preparation for a fresh coat of white paint. The apprentice was listening politely while he knelt, putting away his tools.

"What are you doing here?" Keighly asked, hurrying up the sidewalk. She wished she'd been a little more diplomatic, but the question was out of her mouth so quickly that it might have asked itself.

"I thought you'd be glad to see me," Julian replied, sounding stricken. The painters' helper was studiously not listening as he hurried away, toolbox in hand.

Keighly took a deep breath, let it out. "I thought we agreed that you'd stay in California until I gave the word," she said, in a voice that was still a bit taut, for all her effort to moderate her tones. She was holding her grocery bag in one arm, Etta Lee's journals in the other.

Julian sighed. He looked spectacular in his white cotton shirt and tailored black slacks, as spotless as his car. How had he managed that, she wondered—driving all the way from Los Angeles to Redemption, Nevada, without getting his Jag dusty?

"At least let me buy you dinner," he said. "I won't even ask to stay here—I already have a room at the local motel." He paused to suppress a shudder and didn't quite succeed. "Be reasonable, Keighly. We really need to talk."

Looking at him, Keighly thought of the beautiful, smart, talented babies they might have made together, and felt infinitely sad. As much as she wanted babies, beautiful or otherwise, she couldn't have them with Julian. It was unfair to encourage him when, deep in her heart, she knew she was wasting his time as well as her own. She'd been fooling herself, and him, for far too long.

She patted the grocery bag. "I've got the makings of grilled-cheese sandwiches here," she said. "Come in. I'll make supper, and we'll say what needs to be said."

He caught hold of her arm as she started up the sidewalk toward the porch, stopped her. "Keighly, I'm sorry. I should have called—"

Keighly worked up a welcoming smile. She'd dated this man for five years and he was a very good friend, even if she didn't love him. . . . "It's okay," she said, dreading the moment when she'd have to tell him she wanted to call off their engagement. "Come in, Julian— you must be hungry."

They'd eaten their sandwiches and talked, awkwardly, about unimportant things, when Julian brought up the topic of the hour. "Keighly, is it over between us?"

Keighly blinked back tears. Saying good-bye was hard, even when it was the right thing to do. Sitting at the newly purchased table in her grandmother's kitchen, she pulled off the expensive diamond ring Julian had given her. "Yeah," she said. "It's over."

"Why?"

It was such a reasonable question, and so difficult to answer. "Because I don't love you, Julian," Keighly answered, as gently as she could. "And because you don't love me."

He took the ring, though hesitantly, and dropped it into the pocket of his slacks. Keighly knew he kept small change in there, and a spare battery for his pager. Why, she wondered, did irrelevant facts so often come to mind at such moments?

"I see," Julian said.

She wanted to touch him, to say she was sorry for hurting him, but she couldn't speak. She just sat there, biting her lower lip, her eyes brimming with tears.

"I don't think I can discuss this intelligently just now," he said presently, rising to his feet. Keighly almost wished he would get angry, yell, throw things. She would have felt less like a heartless monster. "I'm going back to L.A."

With that, Julian turned and walked out of the kitchen.

Keighly followed him to the front door, her face wet and her chin trembling. "Good-bye, Julian" was all she could make herself say.

He kissed her forehead. "Good-bye," he said hoarsely, and then he walked away, and Keighly closed the door. She wanted to slide down the panel onto her haunches and weep inconsolably, not just for Julian and the pain she'd caused him, but for her never-to-be-born children. Then, when she'd recovered her emotional equilibrium, she went back into the kitchen. After setting Etta Lee's journals to one side and splashing her face repeatedly at the sink, she made herself a cup of hot tea, sugary and strong the way she liked it, and proceeded to the ballroom, books in hand.

The mirror was blank, and Keighly stood with her forehead resting against the glass for a long time, feeling lonelier than ever.

Finally, she sat down on the edge of the cot and began reading the diaries again. There wasn't another mention of the name Keighly, or of Darby Elder, for that matter. Deeply disappointed, Keighly took a bath and went to bed, but with a difference. She carried the cot upstairs and slept in her old room.

If she'd stayed in the ballroom again, she would not have rested.

First thing the next morning, after a shower and light breakfast, Keighly put on khaki slacks, a short-sleeved cotton print blouse, sneakers, and some lip gloss. Then she got into her car and, after returning the Kavanagh journals to Miss Pierce at the library, as promised, drove out of town, toward the old Triple K Ranch. She hadn't been near the place since she was a child, and it had been boarded up then, with all the horses gone from the fieldstone stables and all the furniture either sold, in storage, or under tarps. Her grandmother hadn't told her much about the Kavanagh family, except to say that those members who'd survived the First World War had gone on to make their homes in other parts of the country.

Now, like Keighly's own place in Redemption, the main ranch house at the Triple K was bustling with contractors and their various apprentices. A young woman with lively gray eyes and dark hair pulled back into a French braid came out onto the wide veranda to greet her—Francine Stephens, no doubt.

"I'm Keighly Barrow," Keighly said, approaching the steps and holding out one hand in greeting.

Francine smiled, but she also paled slightly, and Keighly noticed that her fingers tightened a little on the railing of the still-gracious porch. "So it's true, then," she murmured.

Keighly felt a combination of excitement, as though she were about to embark on some magnificent quest, and plain, ordinary fear. "What's true?" she asked, stopping on the walk.

"I'm sorry," Francine said softly, "I didn't mean to be rude. My name, as you've probably guessed, is Francine Stephens. Angus Kavanagh was my great-great-great-grandfather, give or take a great or two. Come in, and we'll talk."

Following her hostess up the steps, Keighly was already dealing with yet another odd sensation. The place felt familiar, though she never been inside.

"This is spooky," she said, without meaning to utter the words aloud.

"You don't know the half of it," Francine answered. "Wait until I show you what I found in the attic."

❧ CHAPTER ❧

4

Inside the ranch house, the feeling of recognition grew stronger; Keighly knew without asking that the study was on the right, the main parlor on the left, the kitchen in back. Upstairs, the master bedroom ran the length of the structure, and there was a white rock fireplace at one end. Her heart was beating so fast that she thought it would give out from sheer exhaustion—or excitement.

She found her voice, which had deserted her the instant she stepped over the threshold and into the foyer of Angus Kavanagh's rough-hewn mansion. "How did you know I was coming?"

Francine, apparently headed for the attic, was already halfway up the main staircase. She paused, more composed now, and turned to favor Keighly with a reassuring smile. "That part wasn't magic. Miss Pierce called and told me you were on your way. And that you were interested in the Kavanagh family."

Keighly paused for a moment, one hand resting on the newel post, then followed her hostess's lead. The steady *thwack-thwack-thwack* of hammers echoed all around them. "What about the remark you made on the veranda—I think you said, 'wait till you see what I found in the attic'?"

They walked along the corridor of the second floor and Francine started up another set of stairs, narrower and steeper than the broad ones they'd just climbed. "A lot of the old family stuff has either been sold off, divided between my brother Michael and me, or just thrown away. But there were some trunks and crates left behind in the attic, and I discovered some interesting things inside."

The trapdoor stood gaping at the top of the steps. Francine entered the attic, and Keighly was close behind her. The large room was shot through with bars of golden, dust-flecked light, and the air was dry and vaguely musty.

The first object to catch Keighly's attention was a large sculpture, chiseled from plain granite. It was an amazingly intricate depiction of a horse and rider, traveling at full speed over rocky ground, perhaps twenty-four inches tall at its highest point. The sight of it brought unaccountable tears to her eyes and, once again, that frightening sense of foreknowledge. She'd seen this piece before, and yet she hadn't, *couldn't* have.

She knelt beside it, touched the smooth, beautifully detailed sculpture with trembling fingertips. Even in that dim light, she could make out the rider as Darby.

"How—?" Keighly croaked, and could say no more.

Francine, a complete stranger until a few minutes before, crouched beside her on the dusty plank floor. "It was packed in a crate, otherwise Michael would surely have sold it a long time ago. Look at the artist's mark, and the date."

Next to the horse's left rear hoof was her personal insignia, a simple K etched into the stone, followed by the year 1887.

Keighly raised one hand to her throat and gasped, and Francine laid a steadying hand to her shoulder. "There's more," she said gently. "Would you like me to get you some water before I show you the rest of it?"

Examining the sculpture, Keighly ran both hands over

its varied surfaces, like a blind person memorizing a beloved face, stunned to the core of her soul. "It can't be—" She couldn't quite manage the last word, "mine."

Francine stood. "I'll get the water. Try to stay calm, okay?"

Keighly didn't speak, could not look away from the statue, or lift her hands from it. She'd seen visions in the ballroom mirror since she was a child—a peculiar situation by anyone's standards—and yet this experience came as a real shock.

Presently, Francine returned. Keighly had composed herself a little by then, but she was still shaken. She had sculpted this piece with her own hands, in honor of Darby, she had no doubt of that, yet she could not remember doing so. And she had never worked with such stone, even in art school.

"It's yours, isn't it?" Francine asked gently, handing her a glass as she nodded toward the sculpture.

"It can't be," Keighly whispered. "And yet—"

And yet it was. This phenomenon was as real as Darby's image in the ballroom mirrors of her grandmother's house.

Keighly gulped down some water and fought to compose herself. "That is my mark," she admitted at last. "But how did you connect it with me? I mean, I'm not exactly well known."

Instead of answering verbally, Francine moved to one of the heavy wooden chests nearby and raised the lid. From inside, she took a thick leather-bound book that might have been either a scrapbook or a journal.

It was, as it happened, a combination of the two, and tucked in between the first two pages was an old sepia daguerreotype, a wedding picture showing a man seated and a woman standing behind him, with one hand resting on his shoulder.

Keighly gasped, for the image of the bride was undeniably her own—not even an ancestress could have resembled her so perfectly. She wore a long gown of ivory silk, trimmed with lace, and an old-fashioned veil. The groom, of course, was Darby, scrubbed and barbered, breathtakingly good-looking in his dark suit.

Although both their facial expressions were serious, in keeping with Victorian custom, smiles twinkled in their eyes and played around their mouths.

"Oh, my God," Keighly whispered. *I did—I will go back.*

Francine grasped Keighly's arm and seated her on one of the other trunks just before her knees would have given out. She took the glass of water and set it within reach, on top of another crate.

"Look on the back," she said quietly.

Keighly turned the photograph over, saw her own handwriting, impossibly faded. *Darby Elder and Keighly Barrow Elder on their wedding day. May 5, 1887. Redemption, Nevada.*

She made a sudden sobbing sound, though from joy or despair or both she did not know, and bent double, clutching the precious photograph, careful even in her terrible confusion not to do it harm. Then she began to weep, rocking back and forth on the trunk's lid.

Francine returned the photograph to the scrapbook and sat cross-legged on the filthy floor, heedless of her clean jeans and classic cotton chambray shirt. "Keighly is an unusual name," she said softly. "I suppose I could have heard it somewhere before, but I don't think so. First there was the mention in Etta Lee's journals. Then Miss Pierce called to say you had an interest in the Kavanagh family and she wondered if I could help. This morning I came up here with the electrician, looking for the circuit board, and there was all this stuff. I should have been doing other things, but I was curious. I found the sculpture first, and then the scrapbook, and I jumped to a few conclusions."

Keighly sniffled and dried her cheeks with the back of one hand. She felt like a fool—or a lunatic. "I'd appreciate it if you'd share them with me. The conclusions, I mean. Because right now, I'm really at a loss."

Francine reached for the glass of water she'd set aside earlier and held it out to Keighly. "Who could blame you? And the worst part is, I haven't told you everything. There's a dress in that trunk—the one you were wearing in the wedding picture. And several other things that are probably pretty personal."

Keighly's throat constricted, and she felt dizzy, as though she might faint. She didn't speak, but waited for Francine to go on.

"Tell me the truth," Francine said, clasping one of Keighly's hands. "You can trust me, I swear. Are you a time-traveler?"

Swallowing hard, Keighly nodded her head, then shook it, then murmured miserably, "I don't know." She studied Francine's upturned face carefully. "And why should I trust you? We're strangers."

"Because I think we can be friends" was Francine's frank reply. "Maybe we're even related."

Keighly's eyes widened as the ramifications of that began to unfold in her beleaguered mind. "You are awfully accepting of this whole situation—"

Francine's smile was reassuringly sane. "I've always been interested in all things mysterious," she said.

"Convenient," Keighly answered, "because right now I really need a friend. You really don't think I'm crazy?"

"No," Francine said. "Whatever is happening here, Keighly, it's a purely natural phenomenon. Nature doesn't break her own laws. There are a lot of facets to reality, and we don't begin to understand the world we live in, much less the human mind and all its undiscovered faculties. For all we know, time travel is a mere shift of consciousness."

"You sound like you really believe—"

"Don't you?" Francine asked. "Listen, this is a lot to absorb, all at once, so here's my suggestion. I'll have somebody from the carpentry crew drop the trunk and the sculpture off at your place in town. That way, you can go through the things inside in private, at your own pace—provided, of course, that you want to look at all."

Keighly nodded. She wanted that, all right. In fact, it was all she could do not to spring up, hurl back the lid of the trunk from which Francine had taken the scrapbook, and rifle through the contents at a maniacal pace. What stopped her was the knowledge that her new friend was right—she needed solitude for the task. "Thank you," she said.

"In the meantime," Francine went on, "we'll go downstairs, have some tea, and get to know each other."

They sat in the ranch house's big kitchen, apparently the first room to be finished, for it sported new cabinets, a dishwasher, and one of those fancy refrigerators with double stainless-steel doors.

"Are you going to spend a lot of time here?" Keighly asked, in an effort to distract herself from the trunk and its contents, the statue of Darby, the wedding picture.

Francine smiled. "I hope so. I run an advertising firm in Chicago, and I'm flirting with burnout. I was divorced last year, and I have a thirteen-year-old son who prefers to live with his father in Vermont."

Keighly felt a stab of sympathy, as well as admiration. "Is it difficult? Being separated from your child?"

"I miss Tony, of course," Francine replied frankly. "But he's going through one of those chest-beating, hyper-hormone phases and for the time being he really is better off with Geoff. What about you? Is there a significant other in the picture?"

An unfortunate choice of words, Keighly thought, with grim amusement. She had never loved any man, she realized in that moment, except for the phantom in the mirror. Now, it seemed, the two worlds were beginning to overlap. . . .

She caught herself, brought her mind forcibly back to the conversation. "I was engaged for five years—to a pediatric surgeon in L.A. I still have an art gallery there."

MY OUTLAW

"No children?"

Keighly shook her head. "That's one of the great disappointments of my life."

Francine refilled their teacups without speaking, and then one of the workmen came in and asked for instructions about the delivery of the trunk. Keighly gave directions, and the carpenter's apprentice promised to stop by sometime that afternoon.

"You're still young," Francine said, when they were alone again, picking up the topic exactly where they'd left off. "There's no reason you couldn't have a houseful of children, if that's what you want."

"You need a man for that," Keighly pointed out. "Call me old-fashioned, but the high-tech methods aren't for me."

Francine laughed. "Well," she said. "I guess that figures."

They'd come full circle then, back to the mystery.

Keighly let out a long sigh. "Why were you so quick to suggest the possibility of time travel earlier?" she asked. "I'd think that would be exactly the kind of thing a successful, hardheaded businesswoman would scoff at."

She could just imagine Julian's reaction, if she told him. Pity, probably. And certainly professional concern.

"Who says I'm hardheaded?" Francine retorted good-naturedly. "Creativity is my business, and I have to keep an open mind. In fact, the older and more experienced I get, the more sure I am that practically anything is possible."

"You really think people can just disappear into another century?" Keighly's heart was beating fast again. She knew what Francine thought, she was just asking because she so hoped it was true, because she wanted to be with Darby, had wanted that since the first time she'd seen him, on her seventh birthday.

Francine shrugged. "Who knows? That stuff in your trunk is certainly evidence that *something* out of the ordinary is going on. And I've done a lot of reading on the

67

subjects of regressive hypnotherapy, parallel dimensions, time warps, all of that kind of stuff. There are documented cases, Keighly, of people vanishing into thin air, in front of reliable witnesses."

Keighly considered telling Francine about the mirrored wall at home, and the many times she'd seen Darby's reflection there, but there had been enough weird revelations for one day. Maybe she'd confide the secret later, and maybe not.

"What about parallel lives?" she ventured, thinking of her own feelings of being somehow unreal, like a figure in a dream. "Could a person live in two places—two time periods, I mean—at once?"

Francine looked intrigued, though Keighly had no doubt she'd thought the subject over before. She was obviously a curious woman, innately sensible, and yet fascinated with the supernatural. "That's an interesting concept," she replied. "I suspect that the real answers to questions like that are a matter of perception, rather than any arbitrary set of cosmic rules. We already know for a fact that what we see and hear and generally sense, as human beings, is only a fragment, a shadow, of reality. The full truth is probably far beyond our ability to comprehend, at this point in our development, anyway."

Keighly was overwhelmed, swamped with confusion. "At least if I disappear," she said, knowing even as she spoke the words that she sounded like a madwoman, "one person in this world will know where I went."

Francine patted her hand again. "You're very shaken, and that's certainly understandable. Look, maybe you should call somebody to come and provide moral support for a day or two—a sister, a friend?"

Keighly shook her head. She had no sister, of course, and her friends were all busy with their own families, careers, lives in general. They couldn't be expected to drop everything and rush to her aid. Besides, she reflected grimly, she wasn't that close to any of them. She'd devoted most of her attention to Julian for most of the last five years, and her other relationships had suffered as a consequence.

"I'll be all right," she said. "I should get back, though. Prepare myself for going through that trunk."

Francine got up, scribbled a number on a page from a small notepad, and handed it to Keighly. "Don't hesitate to call if you need somebody to talk to," she said.

Keighly was inordinately touched. It was a simple gesture, and yet she couldn't think of anyone else in her life who would have made such an offer without a lot of qualifications. "Thanks," she replied, and stood.

Francine walked Keighly back out to the car, probably making sure she wasn't too overwrought to drive, although she was too polite to say so outright. Keighly murmured more thanks and drove resolutely away.

She was determined to think this latest development in the strange saga of Keighly Barrow through in a logical and sensible fashion. It gave her comfort to recall Francine's theories—that such occurrences as she'd been experiencing were probably not supernatural at all, but simply one of the myriad propensities of the brain.

Nevertheless, as soon as she got home, Keighly took a couple of aspirin and marched into the ballroom, hoping to find Darby waiting for her in the mirror, even though she knew it wasn't going to happen.

And it didn't. The glass was dark and, except for the reflections of herself, her grandmother's exquisite chandeliers, the old harp, and the bare marble floors, quite empty.

In the echoing kitchen, Keighly made a substantial lunch of pasta and salad and ate it, in an effort to arm herself for what might prove to be a difficult afternoon. She tried to take a nap, but sleep was impossible, and even from her room upstairs, she could hear the soft whispers of the harp as drafts in the old house flowed between the strings.

The trunk was delivered at 3:15, by two of Francine's workmen. She had them put it in the front parlor, rather than the ballroom. They hoisted the sculpture onto the mantelpiece, as requested, and Keighly gave them each a tip and practically pushed them back out the door.

Then she was alone with the trunk, with all the remnants of a life she couldn't remember living.

She raised the lid of the undecorated pinewood chest, only half hearing the sounds of her own workmen, pounding and sawing in various parts of the house. On top lay the scrapbook, from which Francine had taken the wedding photo.

Keighly laid the thick album aside, for the time being, and began the search, though whether for her past, her future, or simply a grand delusion, she could not begin to guess.

She found the gown and veil first, carefully wrapped in tissue paper and cheesecloth and tied with faded blue ribbon. Francine had obviously taken great care to put everything back just as she'd found it.

After caressing the heavy silk, which smelled of time and, very faintly, of lavender perfume, Keighly laid those items to one side and dug deeper. She came across an old rag doll, with an embroidered smile and buttons for eyes, and clutched it briefly to her chest, trying to grasp memories as elusive as fireflies. Had the people in that wedding photograph—surely herself and Darby, though that seemed impossible—had a child?

Keighly closed her eyes in longing and frustration, but tears seeped through anyway. Maybe there were pictures in the scrapbook.

Holding the doll tenderly in the crook of one arm, Keighly returned to the volume and opened it carefully. The pages were of heavy vellum, discolored and mustysmelling and infinitely precious.

Leaf by leaf, she went through the book. Pressed flowers—a nosegay of violets. A program for a play in Chicago, tickets to a circus in San Francisco, both dated 1890. A photograph of a beautiful but sorrowful little girl, resembling Francine to an amazing degree.

MY OUTLAW

Keighly guessed before she turned the picture over to read the notation on the back that this was not her own child, and her suspicions were confirmed. *Etta Lee Kavanagh,* someone had written. 1889.

She set the daguerreotype aside for Francine and proceeded through the pages. There were poems, in handwriting she did not recognize, something that might have been a bookmark, a cross woven of human hair. Keighly put that down with a shudder and moved on. Newspaper articles, three of them, chronicling the shooting death of Darby Elder.

Keighly felt as though the breath had been knocked out of her. She couldn't read the articles, not yet—but marked their place with a finger to come back to.

In the final pages were more photographic likenesses.

Herself, with a young boy of six or seven at her side, her eyes full of sorrow. Weeping silently, Keighly turned the picture over and saw her own faded writing once again. *Garrett and myself, 1893, five months before he perished of the scarlet fever.*

Keighly put down the scrapbook, ran to the nearest bathroom, and threw up.

Then she forced herself back to the scrapbook. There were still the articles concerning Darby's death, and the pages she had not examined. She had to know what had happened, no matter how painful it was.

Further on, there were more pictures. Herself, once again dressed for a wedding, though this time her gown was not white but some dark color, and her hair was pulled back from her face in a severe fashion. The groom—she had no clue who he was—was a big man, handsome in a refined, nineteenth-century way, with his dark mustache and long hair. He wore a silver badge on the breast of his suit and a faintly smug smile.

Keighly's image was one of resignation, acceptance, but certainly not joy. There were no words written on the back of the photo to explain anything. Further on, there were more images—children, two good-looking, dark-haired boys and a girl, fair like Keighly. All three were solemn, but plainly healthy and intelligent, well cared for and well loved.

She stared at the picture for a long time, trying desperately to remember them. Their names were not inscribed on the back, as young Garrett's had been.

Keighly finished the scrapbook; there were no more photos, no more names. That was at once a relief and a disappointment.

She was trembling, clasping the doll again.

She put it down gently, out of harm's way, and dug deeper into the chest. A wooden pull-toy, a hand-carved horse—somehow she knew it had been Garrett's. A small, hinged silver box containing two locks of hair wrapped in fragile, time-yellowed paper. Darby's, no doubt, and Garrett's.

Fresh tears brimmed in Keighly's eyes. She was ashamed that she felt such grief for Darby and the son they had almost certainly conceived together, and no emotion at all, except curiosity, toward the other children and their father. Her second husband, she supposed. A man she did not know.

The last item in the trunk was a large Bible, bound in heavily tooled leather. Inside, again in Keighly's own hand, was the date of her marriage to Darby, followed a notation that he'd died a short time later. Her vision blurred; she could barely read the neat, curving letters. Garrett's birth, and then his death. Another marriage, this time to one of the Kavanaghs—Simon, the eldest son. Etta Lee's father.

After the wedding were listed the births of the three children she had seen in the photographs. William Angus. Joshua. Francine.

Francine? Had Keighly named her daughter for a woman who would not be born for almost a century?

It was too much to absorb.

Keighly put everything, save the gown and veil, back into the trunk, very carefully, one item at a time. Then she went upstairs to her room, lay down on her cot, and fell asleep, holding the fragile gown in her arms.

When she awakened, hours later, the room was filled with starlight and the cool glow of the moon. It took her a few moments to get her bearings, several more to realize that the sound she heard was the fey, lilting song of a harp.

The tiny hairs stood up on her arms and nape, her heart thundered against her rib cage, and her breath was shallow and quick, but Keighly wasn't afraid.

No, what she felt was pure excitement.

She could not have explained why she did what she did then, but then nothing in her life truly made sense anyway. Like a graceful sleepwalker, Keighly rose from the bed, stripped off the clothes she had lain down in, and donned the whispery, elegant dress she had worn for Darby on their wedding day. She pinned her hair up quickly, leaving tendrils around her neck and at her temples, and slipped downstairs, barefoot, drawn by the enchanting, magical music of the harp.

The ballroom was aglow, but at a glance Keighly saw that Aunt Marthe's harp stood silent in its usual place near the dais; the tender refrain came from another, newer version of what appeared to be the same instrument, but it was inside the mirror.

Darby was there, handsomely if not richly dressed, in a dark suit and pristine white shirt with a black string tie. She did not know where the harp music came from, for except for him, the Blue Garter was empty.

Perhaps because of all she had learned that day, Keighly wanted more than ever to be with Darby, but there was a spell in the air, and she felt no sense of desperation or urgency. She reveled in the look of purely masculine appreciation he gave her, and for the moment it was enough that she could see him.

Keighly began to turn in slow, charmed steps, as though bewitched.

Darby rose and came to stand close to the glass, both

hands pressed to it, watching her, beckoning her, willing her to come to him.

And she knew that she would, for she had seen the evidence. As heartbreaking as some of it was—Darby's death, and then Garrett's, followed by what logic told her was a loveless marriage to Simon Kavanagh—she was eager to obey his summons. However short her time with him might be, she sensed that she would find, in his arms, in his heart, in his smile, a happiness more complete than most people were ever blessed to know. She coveted every precious moment of it.

The music ceased, the harpist faded away into the shadows, and she and Darby stood face-to-face before the mirror, as they had on other occasions, their gazes linked, their hands touching.

A strange buzzing sound filled Keighly's ears, and she felt her knees weaken, as though she might tumble into unconsciousness, perhaps even death, at any moment. She saw stars racing toward her at warp speed, and then her vision vanished and it seemed that her heartbeat stopped. She felt herself topple forward, but after that, all awareness deserted her.

When she awakened, she was in Darby's arms, and he was carrying her along a dark, narrow corridor.

At first, of course, Keighly thought she was dreaming. Then she realized that she had indeed passed through the looking glass, that Darby was solid and real.

"What happened?" she whispered. "How—?"

He carried her into a small room and laid her on a moon-washed bed before answering. His voice was a whisper, but his white teeth flashed in a triumphant grin.

"I'll be damned if I know how it happened, and I sure as hell wouldn't want to try to explain it to anybody else, but you swooned, Keighly. And for a moment, it was as though the glass in that mirror had turned to water. You literally fell into my arms."

His voice sounded just as she had always thought it

would. She stared at him, hardly able to believe she was with him at last, that she truly wasn't asleep.

Darby approached the bed, crouched beside it, took her hand in a grasp more reverent than lustful. At the same time, he stroked her hair, her forehead, the line of her cheeks and jaw. The moonlight glinted in his gold-streaked hair. "You're real," he marveled, in a hoarse whisper. "I was afraid I'd just imagined you—hell, maybe that's what I'm doing now."

His touch was light, making no demands, and yet the passage of his fingertips sent fire surging through Keighly's blood. She had loved him since she was seven, wanted him since puberty. And now she was lying on his bed, and he was caressing her, and time was passing all too quickly. With every beat of his heart, with every breath, Darby was drawing nearer to his own death.

She put her hands on either side of his face. "Kiss me," she said, with tenderness as well as passion.

He smiled, bent his head, and tasted her lips with his, as though he were sampling the wine of the gods, forbidden and unutterably sweet.

Keighly trembled as Darby deepened the kiss, running the tip of his tongue around the edges of her mouth so lightly that she moaned, needing firmer contact. He nibbled at her lower lip and then, finally—*finally*—conquered her in earnest, shaping her mouth to his, plunging his tongue deep within. They sparred, and Darby's hand came to rest upon Keighly's right breast, the nipple puckered hard beneath the fabric, seeking the roughened flesh of his palm.

She would gladly have given herself to him, then and there, but Darby finally drew back with a gasp, and his hand slid off her rib cage to rest in the curve of her waist.

He laughed. "You're real, all right."

"Make love to me," Keighly said. With Julian, she'd sought excuses not to be intimate, but with this man, she was shameless. Need ached in every part of her, soul as well as body, and she felt a strange constriction, as though she would not be able to breathe until Darby Elder had given her release.

"If I didn't know better," Darby teased, "I might think you weren't a lady."

Keighly recalled the newspaper articles, describing Darby's death, and wondered if by being there she could change the course of events somehow. Perhaps if they left Redemption, she and Darby, he would live and their son, Garrett, might escape the scarlet fever that would otherwise take his young life.

"It's not like we're strangers," she reasoned softly. He was wearing a string tie, and she undid it with awkward, persistent motions of her fingers.

Darby groaned. "Keighly." There was a warning in his voice, but not much conviction.

She tossed the tie aside and pushed his fancy jacket back off his shoulders, down his arms. "Do you want me or not?" she teased. She was on the edge of weeping, because life was so brief, so magical, so precious.

"Damn it, Keighly, you know I do," Darby answered, with gruff impatience.

She left off undressing him to open the buttons of her own bodice. Underneath she was still wearing the front-catch bra she'd put on in the twentieth century.

"This isn't proper," Darby protested, but his eyes were on her fingers, and when she opened the bra and her breasts spilled free in the moonlight, he drew in a sharp breath. "Keighly, we're not married." He sounded downright feeble by then.

Keighly put her hands behind Darby's head and drew him down to a waiting nipple. "Is that a proposal?"

"Yes," he ground out, after only the briefest hesitation. Then he took her offering in greedy earnest.

❦ CHAPTER ❦

5

The pleasure of Darby's mouth upon her flesh in such an intimate way was sharp and sudden and so keen that Keighly arched upon her lover's narrow bed, gasping, her eyes open wide in joyous amazement.

Darby smoothed away the bra and the delicate bodice of her timeworn wedding gown, then made slow circles on her bare stomach with the palm of his hand. He had calluses, but they only added to the nearly unbearable piquancy of his caresses.

Keighly entwined her fingers in Darby's thick hair, felt the faintest roughness of a new beard against her skin as she pressed him close.

But he raised his head from her nipple, looked deep into her eyes. "Don't you think there might be a few things we should talk about, Keighly," he asked in a low, gruff voice, "before we go doing something we might regret?"

She blushed hotly, embarrassed and a little indignant. What did he think of her? He must have seen her high color, even in the dim light, for he chuckled. "Have I insulted you, darlin'?"

Keighly bit her lower lip, still dizzy, resisting a wild and somewhat juvenile urge to grasp the sides of her bodice

77

and pull them closed over her swollen breasts. Aching heat still pooled between her legs, tormenting her, driving her to assuage a fulfillment she was too proud to seek further. "Actually," she whispered, "yes."

He kissed her mouth just lightly but over and over, until her lips pulsed with the same need as her nipples. "We're strangers," he reminded her when, after some time, he deigned to respond. "Born on opposite sides of the mirror. To my way of thinking, that's a matter that needs talking about."

Awkwardly, she closed her bra, fastened a few strategically placed buttons on the dress, and sat up. "We are not strangers," she protested, and though she spoke calmly, she trembled with furious frustration. "I have known you since I was seven years old, Darby Elder."

Darby scooted her over and stretched out on the bed beside her, leaving her hardly any room. She was, in fact, pressed between his body and the wall, both of which seemed equally hard. He crossed his booted feet at the ankles, apparently heedless of the mud he might leave on the coverlet, and clasped her hand tightly in his.

"It isn't that I don't want you," he said. "God knows, I do. I'll even go as far as to say I feel certain tender sentiments toward you."

Was he saying he loved her? Keighly was afraid to ask. She let her head rest against his shoulder, glad just to be there, beside him, dazed by the experience of moving through time, and still faintly chagrined that she'd immediately made a fool of herself. She did not allow herself to think about the tragedies that lay ahead, only the happiness.

When they'd both been silent for a while—Keighly was measuring time in heartbeats now—Darby went on. "What's happening to us?" he asked. "All those times I saw you in the mirror—even though I couldn't hear your voice, it was as though I knew your thoughts." He paused, smiled. "Even when you didn't write them out for me. Do you know you tuck your upper lip between your teeth when you're printing backwards?"

Keighly unlaced her fingers from his only long enough to slip her arm around his elbow and gave a wistful smile. "I had to concentrate," she said. "As for what's going on here—I don't understand it any better than you do." *But I've seen your grave. I know we'll be married, and I'll bear you a son called Garrett, and he'll die of scarlet fever.*

"Tell me about your world," Darby said comfortably.

She hesitated. She wanted to give him an accurate picture of the future, but it was hard to decide where to start, and how to achieve a fair balance between the positive features of the late twentieth century and the negative.

"They've made a lot of strides in medicine," she said, her voice a little unsteady because the unborn Garrett, her baby, immediately came to mind again. She swallowed, blinked back tears. If only he could be born in the future. "Children can be inoculated against a lot of diseases that are fatal now."

"Did the Rebs rise up again and make a success of the Confederacy?"

Keighly shook her head. "No. The U.S. is still all one country, from the east coast to the west, and Hawaii and Alaska are states as well." It seemed odd to be having such a conversation, when they'd been on the verge of making love only minutes before. In fact, Keighly's senses were still thrumming with thwarted desire. "We've fought some wars—two really major ones, involving the whole world, and several that were pretty unpopular."

"Seems to me," Darby reasoned, squeezing her hand, "all wars ought to be unpopular."

"Yeah," Keighly agreed, wholeheartedly. "But they still seem to hold a certain fascination for some people. Mostly politicians."

"I was hoping they'd changed."

"Not a bit," Keighly replied. "If anything, they're worse than ever."

Darby sighed. "Any interesting inventions?"

Keighly was overwhelmed at the prospect of covering *that* subject. "You wouldn't believe it. Machines that think. Automobiles—er, horseless carriages—that travel over a hundred miles an hour. Spaceships called 'shuttles' that can take off like an airplane, orbit the earth, and land again—"

"An airplane? You mean a flying machine?"

"People travel all over the world in a matter of hours," she said, with a nod, enjoying the wonder she saw in Darby's face, the interest that glittered in his eyes.

"Have you ridden in one?" he asked.

Keighly was touched by the note of astonishment in his voice. "Lots of times."

"What's it like?"

She wished with all her heart that she could show him, take him to the future with her, where they would be safe. But was her time really any more secure than 1887? She thought of international terrorism, of crime, more prevalent and more sophisticated than it had been in the nineteenth century, of new diseases and air pollution and income taxes and the disintegration of the family unit.

"What's flying like?" she asked, with a swallow, after taking a moment to remember his question. "To tell you the truth, it's a little scary for me, taking off and landing, anyway. The seats are comfortable enough, and they show movies."

"Movies?"

Keighly was beginning to get a headache. Sheer overload. "Films. They've figured out how to make photographs move in sequence, so it looks like real life. Color and everything."

Darby was silent, apparently absorbing this revelation. "Sounds mighty hectic to me," he said.

She nodded again, opened her mouth wide in an involuntary yawn. "Things happen fast there," she said. "If there's a disaster on the other side of the world, like an earthquake or a flood, you hear about it within minutes. In fact, you *see* it. And there are so many things to remember."

Darby rose from the bed, got a collarless shirt from a chest, and brought it to her. "Put this on and get some sleep. We'll work out what to do in the morning."

"Do?" Keighly echoed, with another yawn.

He chuckled. "There'll be some explaining called for," he told her, pulling her gently to her feet, divesting her of the fragile gown with the same innocent efficiency he would afford a sleepy child. He buttoned her into the shirt and drew the covers back. "Folks will want to know where you came from, for one thing. And that's going to require some fast talking, because hereabouts, everybody knows who came in on the train or the stagecoach. Not to mention when, why, and what they were wearing."

Keighly frowned slightly as she gazed at the wedding dress she'd taken from Francine's trunk that very day. It was draped over a chair back now, its folds interlaced with moonlight and shadow, and somehow the sight disturbed her, though she could not think why.

"Ummm," she said, half-asleep already. "We'll say you found me wandering in the desert—"

Darby undressed, lay down beside her again, and drew her into his arms. Her head fit comfortably in the curve of his neck. "Don't you leave me," he said, just as she tumbled into a deep slumber.

When Keighly awakened, she was afraid to open her eyes, afraid the whole thing was a dream. She would be lying on the cot in her bedroom at her grandmother's house, she knew, still clad in the old wedding dress and as far from Darby as ever.

The smell of strong coffee teased her nostrils.

"Wake up," Darby said, in good-natured reprimand. "Half the day's gone already."

Keighly looked at him—he was wearing trousers, boots, a long-sleeved undershirt with buttons up the front, and suspenders. His glossy hair lay unbound around his shoulders, and in one hand he carried a steaming mug. His mouth tilted upward on one side, in a half grin.

Joy and relief surged into Keighly like a flash flood into a gully. It was real—*he* was real. Suddenly her throat was constricted, and she swallowed hard in an effort to force it open. Her hands shook a little as she reached out to accept the coffee with a murmured "Thanks."

Darby bent, kissed her forehead. "You can't stay here," he said.

"Some welcome," Keighly responded, taking a sip of the stout brew. It was pungent indeed, not at all like the refined stuff she bought at the supermarket, but she liked it for its substance. God knew, there was probably enough caffeine in it to keep her spread-eagled on the ceiling for a month.

"It isn't proper," Darby said. "Bad enough that you spent the night in my room. I won't have folks saying you're sullied."

"I hate to tell you this," Keighly answered, after another cautious sip of high-octane java, "but it's too late. I'm—sullied."

He narrowed his eyes.

Keighly proceeded to explain. "Where I come from, extramarital sex is all too common. If you were expecting me to be a virgin, you're in for a sad surprise."

Darby's scowl gave way to a grin. A rather lascivious one, as a matter of fact. "You might have confided that information last night, Miss Barrow. It would have been pertinent."

Keighly was feeling a bit light-headed, and not just from the realization that she'd stepped through a mirror into another time in history, either. The consuming desire she'd felt the night before was still very much in evidence, in the tingling heaviness of her breasts, the odd hypersensitivity of her flesh and the small, secret ache between her thighs. She felt color rush to her cheeks. "I thought virginity mattered to men of your time," she said.

82

Darby laughed, low and husky. "I reckon under certain circumstances, it does," he replied. "But I wouldn't have held myself a gentleman if I'd just gone ahead and deflowered you without making sure you weren't saving yourself for a husband."

I never wanted any husband but you, Keighly thought, but of course she dared not utter her true thoughts aloud, not yet. She couldn't bring herself to tell Darby all that lay ahead, though she supposed the time would come when she no longer had a choice.

In any case, she hadn't given up hope of changing the future. Forewarned, as the old saying went, was forearmed. Perhaps there were things she could do to alter the course of events at least a little.

"You're saying that you would have made love to me last night if you'd known I wasn't—that I'd—?" Keighly realized she was sputtering, but couldn't seem to stop herself, and Darby stopped the rush of words by grasping her chin in his hand and running the hard pad of his thumb over her lips.

Fresh wanting burst inside her, splintering into shards that pierced her everywhere.

"I'm saying," he answered, husky-voiced, "that I would have made you buck like a spring mare under me. Everybody from here to the border would've heard you holler."

The audacity of his statement, coupled with the unassailable truth of it, came as a fresh shock to Keighly. "You don't lack for nerve, Mr. Elder," she said, flushing hotter than before. "If I believed in violence of any sort, I would surely slap you, and take complete satisfaction in doing so!"

He chuckled, caught her wrists gently in his hands, and pulled her firmly against his chest. "Behave yourself," he warned. "If you don't, I'll have you here and now, and you'll have no choice but to go out there and face a townful of people who know you've been well had."

Keighly tried to will her wanting away, but Darby's

teasing, arrogant words had only made it worse. Her heart was pounding and, as she looked up into his rugged, handsome face, she knew he must be able to feel its rapid beat through the thick wall of his own chest. Surely all she felt was plain in her face; she had waited all her adult life for this one man, had never really expected to experience his embrace outside her most intimate fantasies. And now they were together, and only she knew just how fleeting the time they shared might be.

"Have me, then," she said, with a slight lift of her chin. "And damn whoever hears and all they choose to think."

Keighly had not meant to taunt Darby—it had simply not occurred to her in the heat of her own need—but something in her words caused him to groan softly and drop his mouth to hers, covering it hungrily, conquering and then plundering. Still holding her wrists, he pressed her hands against the small of her back and deepened the kiss until she sagged against him, utterly lost. In those moments, there was no past, no present, and no future, but only Darby and herself and the terrible, unrelenting desire that had seized them both.

Keighly truly believed that she would die if Darby did not make her his, then and there, and for always. She was shocked by the sheer power of her conviction; it pervaded every muscle, every cell, of her body, like some fever born in the darkest regions of the soul.

Without breaking the kiss, Darby began unbuttoning the shirt he had garbed Keighly in the night before. She whimpered when she felt his hands on her breasts, first claiming and weighing their fullness, then chafing the already-taut nipples with gentle but demanding thumbs. When he had her squirming against him, he pulled back with a mingled chuckle and gasp and reached out for the wooden chair over which Keighly's age-crumpled wedding gown still lay.

Darby tossed the dress none-too-gently onto the cot where they had slept.

"No question of our lying down together on that bed,"

he said, with a smile twinkling in his eyes. "Half the county would hear the springs squeaking, and I'll have problems enough just keeping you from yelling."

Keighly knew that remark would incense her later, when she had the time and breath to think about it sensibly, but for the moment all she could think of was this joining that had been destined to happen from the moment she'd become aware of herself as a woman. "God in heaven, Darby, I couldn't want you more if you were air and I were suffocating," she whispered, at great cost to her pride.

"Don't you think I feel the same way?" he asked gently.

Then he slipped the shirt off her shoulders, leaving her to stand bare before him, and slowly undressed himself, starting by sliding his suspenders down. Then he kicked off his boots, pulled his collarless shirt from the waistband of his trousers . . . Keighly watched his every move in fascination.

Finally, when he was as naked as Adam in the Garden, his erection already magnificent against his hard midsection, he sat down on the chair and drew Keighly to him, causing her to sit astraddle of his lap. He stroked her back with light motions of his hands—a gunslinger's hands, according to the articles Keighly had found in the trunk from the Triple K—while admiring her breasts.

"All this time," he confided gruffly, "I've been afraid you were just somebody I invented in my mind."

Keighly tensed with pleasure as he bent his head, teased one nipple into ready obedience with light passages of his tongue. "You're right, you know," she managed to murmur, but she wasn't talking about being a figment of Darby's imagination. "I'm going to yell like crazy. I won't be able to help it."

All around them, beyond the walls of the little room, were sounds of people moving about—someone clattering pots and kettles together in a nearby kitchen, men calling to each other, the clomp-clomp of horses' hooves in the streets.

"I'll do all I can to protect your reputation," Darby promised, just before he took the tip of her breast full into his mouth and began to suckle in earnest.

Keighly bit her lower lip to keep from shouting for plain joy, and arched her back to give her lover ready access. Meanwhile, Darby ran one finger, ever so lightly, up and down the small channel of her spine, heightening her pleasure to nearly unbearable levels by that simple caress alone.

She threw her head back, felt Darby's staff pressed between their bellies, hard and huge, pulsing with the instinctual need to be within her. He turned to her other breast, and savored it, as though it were some rare confection that would soon melt away.

Keighly locked her fingers in Darby's hair and began to move upon his lap, urging him to conquer her. He had not been far wrong, she thought dizzily, in comparing her to a spring mare earlier; her body had taken itself over, flung off all the usual constraints of her mind, and she was in a frenzy to surrender. The encounter was far more than simple lust, however; it was a primitive mating ceremony, not only urged but demanded by some force she could not begin to understand. But neither could this be called lovemaking, because it exceeded that, too. Mere words could not encompass what was happening in that tiny room; it was more cosmic than physical, threatening to consume them both from within, like some internal nova.

She buried her face in Darby's neck, almost sobbing with desperation, vaguely aware that she was wet with perspiration from the top of her head to the soles of her feet. Tendrils of her hair stuck to her cheek as Darby soothed and stroked her, all the while murmuring words that only made her more frantic.

Finally, he kissed her, deeply and thoroughly, and he kept his mouth over hers while he reached down to arrange himself at the aching portal of her body.

Although her lids were closed, Keighly felt her eyes roll back as Darby entered her in one long, slow stroke, and she nearly lost consciousness in those first moments, so fierce was the bliss of being connected with this man at last. He caught her cries of welcome as she uttered them, and swallowed them with his own.

Resting his hands on her now-slippery hips, and still kissing her, making love to her as much with his tongue as with his member, Darby guided Keighly up and down the length of him, at an excruciating pace, leisurely and calculated to wring the last quiver of sensation from every entrance and every withdrawal.

Keighly tried to move faster, but Darby restrained her, made her keep to the steady, measured rhythm he had established. When the first pinnacle seized her, she broke away from the kiss, and hurled her head back, an involuntary groan of ancient triumph rising from deep within her, where the climax itself had burst open to unfold like a rose made of light.

Darby raised a hand and closed it over Keighly's mouth just in time. As she buckled upon him, repeatedly, flung from one violent spasm of pleasure to another, he finally began to lose control as well. He delved deep, thrusting his hips upward again and again, kissing Keighly once more, holding her prisoner even as he set her free, stifling the hoarse sobs of amazement and rapture that rose to her throat, time after time, with his lips and tongue.

The final peak was reached simultaneously, but the descent was slow and treacherous. Darby and Keighly clung together, Keighly's head resting on Darby's shoulder, and occasionally she stiffened, with a little cry, as another, smaller orgasm caught her by surprise. Darby supported her with a hand to the curve of her back all the while, at the same time slipping a finger between the folds of her femininity to fondle the tiny nubbin of flesh hidden there and intensify her responses almost beyond bearing.

At long last, it was over, and Keighly, healthy all her life, felt faint with exertion. Darby kissed her neck, and the upper roundings of her breasts, not with passion but with reverence. Then he raised her slowly off him, and stood, carrying her to the narrow bed where they had passed the night. He laid her down, hidden parts of her still thrumming with residual ecstasy, and covered her with an old quilt.

Keighly was only half aware of sounds around her as she drifted into a blissful sleep—she heard wagons and horses from the street, a blacksmith's hammer ringing against an anvil somewhere nearby, and Darby gathering his scattered clothes. The last thing she was aware of was the clunking noise of a closing door.

She knew something was wrong—very wrong—even before she opened her eyes. There was a difference in the very substance of the air, a heaviness made of strange noises and sorrow.

Keighly resisted full consciousness; she did not want her suspicion confirmed—that she'd been dreaming all along. That she was alone.

Tears seeped between her lashes and tickled their way over her temples. "Darby," she whispered, though she was certain, even as she spoke, that he wouldn't, couldn't answer. After a long time spent working up her courage, Keighly opened her eyes.

She lay alone on the cot in her grandmother's ballroom, naked except for a half-discarded blanket, which lay askew across her middle. There was no sign of the wedding gown.

Outside, a car horn blared, and Keighly slowly sat up, confused. Her body still reverberated with the satiation of Darby's lovemaking, and there were other signs, too. Her nipples were ultrasensitive, and she felt his seed on her inner thighs.

With an anguished sob, Keighly turned toward the mirror, hoping to see Darby there and, at the same time, hoping he wouldn't appear. The surface was smooth, catching the afternoon sunshine and casting back only her own reflection.

Somehow, she had slipped back through a veil no thicker than a coat of silver paint on glass, yet at least a century across. She had been with Darby—there was no doubt of that—but now they were parted again.

Keighly buried her face in her hands, plunging splayed fingers into her rumpled hair. What were the rules governing tumbles through the looking glass? she wondered, her bare shoulders moving as she wept in silence and frustration. Lewis Carroll had neglected to mention them in any of his *Alice* stories.

Presently, when Keighly had recovered the necessary composure, she got up, wrapping the blanket around her sari-style, in a halfhearted attempt at decency, and made her way upstairs. Standing under a hot shower, she wondered if her doomed child, and Darby's, had already been conceived. Perhaps even now, poor little Garrett was growing in her womb.

Keighly let her forehead rest against the tiled walls of the shower stall and closed her eyes against another bout of panic. She reminded herself that even if she was indeed pregnant, the twentieth century had its advantages where such things were concerned. If Garrett were born here, in this time, he would be virtually immune to the disease that was destined to kill him.

I have to be strong, Keighly told herself. *I have to think.*

But even as she gave herself those commands, her knees folded, and she slid down the wall, palms against the tiles, head down. The water beat at her shoulders and the back of her neck as she struggled for control.

Julian would have said she was having a mental breakdown, that Darby was an invention of her troubled and lonely mind, but she knew that wasn't the case. And there was one other person who knew, too—Francine Stephens.

Heartened, Keighly managed to raise herself off the floor of the shower, turn off the spigots, get out, and dry off. By rote, she went into her room, got a bra and panties, jeans and a T-shirt from her suitcase. She dressed, rushed back into the bathroom and threw up once, then splashed her face with cold water, brushed her teeth, and combed her wet hair, leaving it to dry as it would.

Then, shivering but determined, she took herself downstairs, collected her purse and keys, and left the house. In her car, she put on sunglasses, to protect her eyes against the bright light. She remembered very little of the drive to the Triple K, and Francine was waiting on the porch when she pulled up, as though she'd sensed Keighly's imminent arrival. There were workmen everywhere, as before, but they paid little or no attention to the newcomer.

"Something's happened," Francine said, coming down the steps and the walk to take Keighly firmly by one arm and escort her toward the house. "My God, Keighly—you look so pale!"

"I saw Darby," Keighly murmured. "I was with him."

Francine hustled her friend through the front door and into the study. She had obviously been working there, for the large Italianate desk was littered with papers and pens, and the ice in a tall glass of tea had yet to melt.

Carefully, Francine closed the study off from the rest of the house.

"Sit down," she said, in a gentle voice.

Keighly had been standing stiffly in the center of the room. Only when she'd noticed the desk had she realized that she was interrupting Francine's day. "I should have called," she fretted, and started toward the towering study doors.

"Keighly," Francine said, her tone quiet but insistent.

There was one other chair in the vast room, a ladderback affair with a needlepointed seat. Keighly collapsed into it, remembered her sunglasses, and tentatively removed them.

"You certainly look like hell," Francine announced, going to a little table behind the desk and pouring two glasses of something that was probably alcoholic. From where she sat, Keighly couldn't see what it was, and in point of fact, she didn't care. Just then, she wouldn't have refused a shot of antifreeze.

"Thanks," Keighly said, and managed a wry smile. Her hand shook when she accepted the cordial; it was Anisette, judging by its licorice-like scent.

"For the drink or the comment on your appearance?" Francine asked, with an answering smile, before taking her place behind the expensive desk.

"For the drink," Keighly responded. "I already knew what I looked like."

"You said you were with Darby."

Keighly took a restorative sip of the liqueur. "Yes," she said, after a long moment. "And it's true. I was. I didn't want to come back."

"I might have guessed that much," Francine observed gently. "Go on. Tell me about it. Or, at least, those parts you feel like sharing."

She wanted to cry again, and took almost a full minute to regain control. "After I left here," she began, when she dared speak, "I went home. The contents of the trunks were very revealing—I learned some things I probably would have been happier not knowing." Briefly, haltingly, Keighly told her friend about Darby's fate, and that of their unborn son, Garrett. "I don't know why I put on the wedding dress," she went on, following another period of shattered silence, "maybe I wanted to feel close to Darby, maybe I just wanted to see if it would fit. But I was wearing that gown when I went into the ballroom, and I saw Darby in the glass—" She stopped again, unable, for several seconds, to continue. "I stumbled through—he described it best by saying it was as if the mirror had turned to water. I spent the night in Darby's arms, and when we woke up, we—we made love. I was exhausted afterward, and I remember that he tucked me into bed and left the room."

"And after that?" Francine prompted, when Keighly had been silent for a very long time.

A tear slipped down Keighly's cheek. Now that she knew what it was to be with Darby, not just sexually but in the ordinary, everyday sense, the future looked so bleak that she wasn't sure she could face it. "I fell asleep. And when I woke up, I knew I'd come back to the twentieth century. It had something to do with that damned dress."

"Why do you say that?" Francine asked, raising one eyebrow.

Keighly sniffled. "It's just a feeling," she confessed. "I can't explain it any more than I can the other stuff. People don't see other people, other times, in mirrors. They don't fall in love with reflections, and cross over into a different century."

"Apparently they do," Francine countered quietly.

Keighly pushed the fingers of both hands through her hair, taking no further heed of the way she looked. "I can't get over it. That you believe me, I mean."

Francine smiled. "We're friends, or at least I'd like to think we are. Besides, you don't seem like the hysterical type to me."

"I want to go back to Darby," Keighly said then, simply and quietly. There was a hairline fracture in her words, though she tried to maintain her dignity. "Francine— suppose I'm already pregnant?"

The words seemed to echo in the room, even though they were softly spoken.

"Suppose you are? It would be far better to give birth in the here and now, for you and for the baby, whether or not you manage to return to Darby."

Keighly set her drink aside, unfinished, and pressed the fingertips of both hands to her temples. "I've got to go back, Francine, no matter what," she whispered. "I might be able to stop Darby from being killed."

There was another pause. "And you might not," Francine replied quietly.

❧ CHAPTER ❧

6

She was gone.

The first realization of that was like a mule kick to the belly. For several agonized moments, Darby stood frozen in the doorway of his room at the Blue Garter, unable to believe the evidence of his own eyes: Keighly had vanished.

The tattered wedding dress was still draped over the foot of the bed.

Perhaps, he thought, in his desperation, she had simply gotten tired of waiting for him to return and gone exploring, but instinctively he knew she hadn't done that. She couldn't have gone out stark naked and besides, if all she'd said was true, and he had no reason to doubt it, given that he himself had seen her image in the saloon mirror a dozen times over the years, his world was alien to her. While Keighly was obviously courageous, she was also practical, and he didn't think she'd venture out alone until she was a little more familiar with the way things were done.

He dropped the parcels he carried onto the still-mussed cot, where he had left Keighly dozing only a little over an hour before. The things he'd bought for her to wear, shoes and fussy underthings that had made the mistress of the general store raise an eyebrow, frocks and skirts and shirtwaists, were all useless now. It didn't even matter if he'd guessed the sizes right.

He closed the door tightly behind him, just as he had so often closed his heart in the past, to so many other things—the taunts of his schoolmates, not being Angus Kavanagh's rightful son, like Will and Simon, knowing he was called an outlaw and, finally, losing his mother. This latest loss was in some ways worse than all the others, for until last night Darby had hardly dared to believe that Keighly might truly be real.

Now, he could have no doubts. He had made love to her; his body and soul still pulsed with the sweet revelations she had wrought in him. No specter, born of his imagination, could have invaded the very core of his being the way she had done; only a flesh-and-blood woman possessed that kind of power, that kind of magic.

Darby whirled back to the door, grasped the knob, and stopped himself just as he would have wrenched the thing open and gone into the hall shouting Keighly's name. He let his forehead rest against the wooden panel and shut his eyes, fighting the tears he had not let himself shed even at Harmony's graveside. He needed to think, decide what to do, figure out how the hell he was going to manage to go on without Keighly.

He would not have admitted as much to her, even if she'd been standing before him—and that was his greatest wish—but he supposed he already loved Keighly. Maybe he had since she was a little girl, swinging her feet from the seat of an ornate chair and clasping a doll in both arms. She'd been surprised but not scared that day—he'd been able to tell from her expression and the fact that she didn't turn tail and run. For his part, he'd been so stunned he'd forgotten to breathe and damn near suffocated, and when he had gotten his wind back, he'd nearly yelled with fear. Especially when he'd realized that no one else could see her but him.

Now, Darby drew deep, slow draughts of air until he felt calmer. In careful, measured motions, as though he were performing some sacred ritual, he folded the gown, tucking the betrothal ring Angus had given him under the lace bodice, and placed them both on the shelf of his wardrobe.

Then he squared his shoulders, crossed the room to the door, and went out.

The first person he encountered when he got as far as the saloon was Oralee. She was wearing the yellow dress again—her personal favorite—and she grinned when she saw him.

"You got to settle a bet," she said, slinking over and slipping her arm through his. "We all know you had a woman in your room last night. We just can't figure out who it was."

Darby glanced toward the mirror, despite himself. As he had expected, there was no sign of Keighly, but she'd taken him by surprise before, and hopes such as he cherished died hard.

"It's none of your damn business who it was," he answered good-naturedly. Then he worked up a slight smile and chucked the whore's chin. "Just tell 'em it was you, darlin'," he said, in a low, confidential voice.

Oralee laughed delightedly and swatted her thigh. "That'll put a stop to Maggie's braggin'. She's got a fly up her nose these days 'cause she's Simon Kavanagh's favorite—he brought her a comb from Denver."

Like father, like son, Darby thought. Angus had had Harmony Elder for a plaything, and now there was Maggie for Simon. Next time he saw his half-brother, he'd remind him that the women at the Blue Garter were people, not objects created for his use, and their sentiments shouldn't be trifled with. In the meantime, he was consumed by a need to escape the fact that he'd lost Keighly after only just finding her. It was almost unbearable, being inside, standing still.

Darby needed to be riding fast, working hard, or throwing punches at something or someone, in order to regain some semblance of composure. He felt as though he'd turn inside out if he had to stay in one place much longer.

He put the smiling Oralee gently away from him, planted a tender kiss on her forehead for pure show. She knew the gesture was meant for the edification of the crowd and played to it by laying a hand to his cheek.

"Thanks, Darby," she said in a fond, mischievous voice. Then she turned in a rustling swirl of faded yellow skirts and pranced back to join the others who lined the bar, watching out of the corners of their eyes, sipping stout coffee and gossiping among themselves. Generally, their services weren't called for before late afternoon, and half of the women didn't even bother to rise from their beds until the sun was high.

Darby couldn't blame them, though he wondered if they didn't want a change of scene once in a while.

Reminded that they depended on him now that Harmony was gone, Darby felt the renewed weight of responsibility, along with everything else. He had to take action where these women were concerned, though he hadn't decided just what to do. He'd suspended every other concern when Keighly tumbled through the mirror into his arms the night before, and some essence of her still saturated his brain, in the way of strong drink, and throbbed within him like a tandem heartbeat.

With one more surreptitious glance at the looking glass, Darby put on his hat, collected his gunbelt from behind the bar, and strapped it on as he went out for the second time into the bright midmorning sunshine. Now he had far more reason to stay in Redemption than the conditions of Harmony's will, for his only hope of finding Keighly again was to remain there. When the Blue Garter closed at two in the morning, he meant to draw up a chair, sit down in front of that mirror, and wait for her. One thing was for damn sure: if she came through again, he was going to make certain they got as far from that spooky hunk of glass as they could, in the shortest possible time.

Toward that end, Darby took himself over to the livery stable where he'd left Ragbone the day before, after visiting Angus and then paying his respects at his mother's final resting place. He had money now, thanks to Harmony, and he meant to get a better, faster horse, just in case the opportunity to snatch Keighly up and squire her off to safety happened to present itself.

A corner of his mouth lifted in a shadow of a smile as, briefly, he thought of himself and Will, as boys, pretending to be Knights of the Round Table.

He swept off his hat just long enough to wipe his forehead on the sleeve of his shirt. Truth of it was, he'd be lucky if he ever saw Keighly again at all, let alone got to make her his wife and hold her in his arms every night until he died. He'd never been especially lucky, except at cards, and even that was a rarity.

Darby was dickering with Ned Feeny over a spirited black gelding, just in from the Triple K and only half broken to ride, when Will rode up on a sorrel with a white patch on its chest. The younger of Angus's legitimate sons greeted Darby by sweeping off his weathered hat.

"I don't know why you'd want to pay good money for horseflesh," he said cheerfully, swinging down from a well-worn saddle, "when you've got a whole herd of the critters to choose from out at the ranch."

Darby tightened his jaw and ignored the remark. "How's Angus this morning?" he asked, though he knew the answer already. Will, far closer to his father than Simon had ever been, would not have been grinning the way he was if the old man weren't feeling better. No doubt the news that Harmony's bastard had complied with the stipulations of her will by agreeing to accept his birthright had already reached him. Not much happened in Redemption that didn't get back to the Kavanaghs, one way or another, and Darby's capitulation would have been special news.

"He's wondering when to expect you. Had the house-keeper make a room ready and everything."

Darby suppressed a sigh. It wasn't Will's fault that their father and everybody else in the world seemed to be dead-set on running his life for him. An easygoing sort, Will was happy most of the time, no matter what anybody else around him might be doing. It was one trait among many that Darby had always admired in him.

"I'll buy my own horse," he said flatly. Miss Gloria, Angus's housekeeper, might have made a room ready with dispatch, but it wasn't so easy to come up with an answer. Not where the subject of taking up residence at the Triple K was concerned.

Will frowned, but his eyes showed puzzlement, rather than irritation. That was another thing about him—he was usually slow to anger, just like the Good Book said. God help the man who got in his way, though, once he'd finally worked himself into a lather about something.

"Ryerson said you signed papers in his office, agreeing to the terms of your mother's will. And that means taking on your share of the Triple K."

Darby gave Feeny a twenty-dollar gold piece, and the livery owner handed over the gelding's reins. "I signed them, all right," Darby said. He swung up onto the horse's bare back, felt the animal quiver beneath him, powerful legs stiffened and set wide apart in a stubborn stance, eyes rolling.

"Hold on," Will said, with one of his luminous, dimpled grins, watching the animal appreciatively. "He may be just one horse, but he's about to head in six directions, pretty much all at once."

"Easy," Darby told the beast. Indeed, he felt and understood its barely restrained fury, the ferocious energy of its wildness and its fear, in every cell and fiber of his own being. "We're going to be partners, you and me. No need for you to go flinging me over the fence just to humiliate me in front of my little brother."

MY OUTLAW

"I ain't your little brother," Will pointed out, still beaming. "I was born a full year before you were."

The gelding was trembling with rage now, its hide glistening and wet, like ebony after a rain. "Jesus, Joseph, and Mary," Darby growled, "will you just shut your mouth? I'm a little too busy for a chat just now, in case you haven't taken notice of the fact."

Feeny had to put in his two bits, now that he'd tucked the gold piece into his vest pocket. "Will's right," he said, with relish. "Thatun's about to turn his belly to the sky, and when he comes down again, he's goin' to grind you right into the manure."

Darby spat a curse, under his breath, rightly guessing that the last of the gelding's internal restraints had just snapped. The creature had made up its mind, and Will and Feeny were right—he would either throw his rider over the roof of the Blue Garter or tear himself right down the middle in the trying.

The black took a leap and then exploded in midair, like a star made of darkness and rage. He flung his head and knocked out the top rail of the corral fence with both hind legs before bending himself into a curve any sidewinder would have been proud to execute.

Will gave a whoop of glee, for he was a true rancher, not a gentleman farmer like Simon, and he loved a good fight, especially when one of the opponents was a half-wild horse. Darby held on with both legs, both hands, and all his formidable determination, while the gelding went every way but belly-up, and a couple of times he nearly managed that, too.

Every bone in Darby's body was jarred, every muscle clenched. His eyes were gritty with dust, his throat parched. Sweat drenched his formerly clean clothes and his hat was long since stomped into the dust and manure of Feeny's corral, but he stayed mounted, even spurring the gelding lightly with the heels of his boots every now and then. The horse was lathered now, and snorting, flanks and withers bunched, eyes showing only white.

All of it came as a tremendous relief. However brief, however uncomfortable, the ordeal was a distraction, all a man in Darby's situation could ask for.

Will hollered again, with a combination of joy and admiration, though Darby couldn't tell and didn't care whether the latter was directed at him or the horse. He just wanted to stay on, because crashing through a fence or against Feeny's stable wall would mean profound embarrassment, not to mention a few cracked ribs.

Finally, after a small group of spectators had gathered, the gelding reached the end of his rebellion, for the moment at least, and stood still, his magnificent head down, his great lungs ballooning with air. Darby patted the sleek black neck in a comradely way and quietly complimented the animal. The long battle was over, for today anyway, though the war itself might continue for some time. The gelding still needed to be broken to a saddle, and the introduction of that particular accoutrement was bound to foster another disagreement.

In the meantime, Darby sat the beast's bare back calmly, murmuring words of comfort and conciliation. The great creature nickered and tossed his head, and his jet-colored mane stuck to his neck in places, for he was as saturated with sweat as Darby, and maybe as sore in the bargain, though Darby doubted that.

"Got to give him a good name," Will observed. He'd recovered Darby's hat from the ordure of the corral and was now carrying it thoughtfully toward him, as though it were a helm of armor instead of a piece of leather stomped in horseshit. "A mount like that deserves to be called something special."

"His name's Destry," Darby answered, holding the reins loosely in one hand now, and stroking the horse's shuddering withers.

Will beamed his approval, standing nearby now, with Darby's ruined hat in one hand and his own on his head, pushed back. They'd played a chess tournament or two when they were young, though Simon had usually come out the winner, and the knight, mounted upon a destry, had always been Darby's favorite piece. "You handled him real well," he said. "You'll be a credit to the Triple K."

Darby swung a leg over Destry's neck and slid gracefully to the ground. He managed to hide the flash of pain that surged from the balls of his feet to his nape; he'd done too much drinking, card-playing, and whoring in recent years, and not enough honest work, but he'd have taken Ned Feeny for a bride before admitting he was out of shape. Come nightfall, he'd be requiring a bottle of liniment for the ache on one side of his hide, and a fifth of whisky for the one on the other. Maybe more, if he hadn't figured out a way to deal with losing Keighly, or found her again.

"You promised to take up your rightful place on the Triple K when you signed the papers in Ryerson's office," Will pointed out, taking Destry's reins and giving the animal a salutary pat of his own. Darby thrust splayed fingers through his hair with one hand, and flung the hat his half-brother held out aside with the other. If he hadn't, he might have punched Will for reminding him of something he preferred to forget.

"Damn it, Will, I know that," he snapped. "You don't need to keep deviling me about it!"

Will regarded Darby in silence for a while, a certain glint in his otherwise guileless eyes being the only hint that he was just as annoyed, despite his inborn good spirits. Maybe, Darby thought with wry amusement, he wasn't the only one who wanted to thrash somebody.

"Angus is watching the road for you," Will said, at long last. His smile was as bright as always, but his eyes were hard. "He's dying. And by God, Darby, you'll go to him if I have to braid your innards into a rope and drag you there by it."

Darby's chuckle was low and bitter. "You have a colorful way of making yourself understood, brother."

"Long as I get my point across," Will replied. He sounded like Simon, and Darby began to wonder if he'd underestimated him.

"That gelding ain't gonna take to no saddle," Feeny put in. He was known for a great many things, was Feeny, but social grace wasn't among them. He spat as both Will and Darby looked at him, having forgotten he was there. "Poor old slab of dogmeat you call Ragbone ain't fit to be seen on the Triple K. He'll die of mortification, amongst all that fine horseflesh."

"Saddle him," Darby said, just to be obstinate. After the round with Destry, which was only the first of several, he was more than willing to ride a nag. And if Ragbone stood out on the Triple K, a thorn among roses, so much the better.

Muttering, Feeny turned and went into the barn to obey.

"You say Angus is watching the road for me," Darby said, when they were alone again. "Why doesn't that old man ever give up?"

"He didn't get where he is by giving up," Will replied easily. "Besides, I could ask the same question of you. All we're trying to do here is give you what's rightfully yours. A man'd think, from the way you act, that we wanted to force you into a coffin with an ugly woman and nail down the lid."

Darby couldn't bring himself to say that he had his pride, that going to Angus now, after all these years of wanting to be made legitimate and keeping it to himself, seemed like groveling. "I never wanted his charity or yours."

"Blast it," Will said, that light flaring in his eyes again. "How many times do I have to explain?"

Darby had to laugh at the thought of Will being the explainer, the keeper of wisdom and champion of reason among the three of them. Those singular and sanguine tasks had always been Simon's. He slapped Will's shoulder as Feeny brought old Ragbone out of the livery stable. The horse looked something the worse for wear, and so did Feeny.

Will gave the animal a rueful assessment. "You got a heart at all, brother, you'll put that pitiful creature out to pasture as soon as we get to the Triple K and never trouble him to carry anything heavier than a fly or two."

Darby did have a heart, though he'd often wished, over the years, that he hadn't. A second look at Ragbone decided him; Will was right. "Better give me another horse after all," Darby said to Feeny. Muttering that nobody ever listened to him, Feeny turned and lumbered back into the stable, leaving Ragbone nearby with his reins dangling. The small crowd of onlookers had vanished meanwhile.

Gently, Darby removed the saddle from the worn-out gelding's back and held it in both hands as he waited for the stable keeper to return. Will, ever charitable, stroked Ragbone with one big hand and promised him a meadowful of sweet grass and all the oats and clumps of sugar one horse could want.

Darby was both amused and touched, though of course he didn't say so. "How's Betsey?" he asked instead.

"Reckon you'll have to see for yourself. She's expecting you to come to our place for supper tonight."

"Knowing you, she's probably expecting something else, too."

Will's ingenuous face shone. "Due in February," he said. Thanks to him, there was no lack of heirs for the Kavanagh fortunes—he and Betsey had four young sons, at last count, and Simon's girl, Etta Lee, was to inherit an equal share. Not for the first time, Darby wondered why they wanted to be bothered with him and whatever questionable progeny he might produce.

Fact was, they did want him, and there was no way out of the situation, for the time being at least, if he was to stay around Redemption and wait for Keighly to return, let alone keep Oralee and the girls from being turned out into an even harsher world than the one they already knew.

So it was that Darby acquiesced, and rode with Will to the Triple K that morning, still wearing his grimy, sweat-stained clothes, leading Ragbone behind him on a slack line.

"I think you should spend the night here," Francine told Keighly. "You are obviously distraught and, besides, I could use a little female company. I haven't got anybody else to talk to, otherwise, besides the carpenters and plumbers."

Keighly dredged up a tremulous smile. She had never been afraid of her grandmother's magnificent house, and that hadn't changed. However, she *was* troubled, and Francine's presence would be reassuring. "If it won't be any trouble—"

"What trouble could it be?" Francine asked, heading for the double doors. "Come on—I'll show you where your room is, and then we'll have a light lunch. After that, I suggest a short nap on the screened sunporch. The workmen are pounding on the opposite side of the house today."

Keighly rose, tottering, out of her chair. That old, disconcerting sensation was back. She felt so weak, so insubstantial, as though she were merely a version of herself, hardly more than a reflection. She had always been strong, mentally and physically, no matter what she was facing, and this deep-seated fragility worried her.

"What you need," Francine went on, escorting her friend up the stairs by a light grasp on one elbow, "is to put this whole question of time travel out of your head for a while. You can bet your subconscious is trying hard enough to sort through it all without your conscious mind fussing and fretting and getting in the way."

Keighly put a hand to her forehead; she felt oddly dizzy, diluted, as though she were in two places at once, and had left the better part of herself somewhere else. But that wasn't possible, of course. Slipping through a mirror into another time, or dimension, or realm of consciousness, was hard enough to comprehend. Anything beyond that was simply too much to grasp.

Francine's hold tightened. "Keighly," she said firmly. "Are you all right?"

Keighly drew a deep breath and let it out slowly. The workmen were plying their trade on the sunporch after all. "Yes—considering."

Francine led Keighly toward the main staircase.

They entered a room at the far right end of the hall, spacious but not overly large. There was something familiar about it, some nuance that quickened Keighly's flagging senses for a moment. She raised her head, looked around, recognizing nothing and yet understanding that this room was, or had been, important in some way.

Francine was looking at her closely. "Do you want to leave? Good heavens, you look *dreadful*. Every bit of color is gone from your face!"

Keighly put a hand to her forehead. "This room—?"

"I don't know much about it," Francine said. "The large suite overlooking the meadow belonged to Angus Kavanagh, not surprisingly. This may have been the quarters of one of his sons, or simply a guest chamber. People didn't often visit in those days, but when they did, they stayed for months. Even years."

Keighly's heart constricted. *Darby.*

She forced another smile. "I promise to be gone by tomorrow," she said.

Francine squeezed her hand. "No hurry. Shall I bring you anything? Water or tea? Aspirin, perhaps?"

Keighly shook her head. She just wanted to be alone, to assemble her thoughts, to try to understand why she was falling apart all of the sudden, after being a relatively solid and responsible citizen for so long. She focused her attention on the room itself, groping for the reason that it had stirred her memory.

There was a double bed beneath the windows, obviously new, and the walls had been freshly painted and papered in muted blues. The impression that she knew the place faded gradually, replaced by a fierce headache and an attack of nausea that promised to become violent if she didn't lie down soon.

She kicked off her shoes and stretched out on the bed, and Francine left her, closing the door softly as she went.

Keighly lay staring up at the ceiling. Maybe the best thing to do was to go back to L.A., if not to Julian, and try to forget all about Darby Elder and his strange, parallel world.

She turned restlessly onto her side. As if it were that easy, especially after he'd made love to her. That experience had changed her forever, and there was no sense in pretending she could simply walk away and go on as if nothing had happened.

Plenty had happened, and damn it, it was real. Darby, the Blue Garter Saloon, the narrow cot on which she'd lain with him, sheltered in his arms, throughout the night. Everything had been genuine.

Tears pooled along her lashes. Darby was both her blessing and her curse—she loved him in a way that most people only dream of loving another person, and yet she might never see him again. Even though there was evidence—the items in the trunk at home in Redemption—to indicate that she would return to the nineteenth century, that he would die of a gunshot wound, that their child, too, was destined to perish of a cruel and unnecessary illness.

Knowing those things, maybe it wasn't right to go back. Their son could not die of scarlet fever if he wasn't born in a century where such maladies flourished, if he wasn't born at all, and Darby too might avoid his fate if Keighly left him alone.

MY OUTLAW

That was it. She would spend the night here, with Francine, as agreed. In the morning, she'd fetch her things from the house in town, get into her car, and head back to L.A. If she worked hard, refurbishing the gallery, starting a new sculpture of her own, she would eventually forget what had happened here, in this dusty little Nevada town.

Except that she would *never* forget.

Some deep instinct insisted she was already pregnant, that events had begun to move inexorably toward some ultimate climax, like a great stone tearing loose from its bed of pebbles on a mountain slope. There was, she was certain, no returning to the days of innocence, when Darby had merely been a figure in a mirror.

She knew too well that he was a man, that he needed her, and that she needed him. Destiny would have its way, for good or ill, and she and Darby were no more than pawns in its grasp.

She closed her eyes, emitting a great sigh, convinced to the very marrow of her bones that she was too upset to sleep. Yet unconsciousness swallowed her almost instantly, a great, dark beast with a vast and soundless void behind its throat.

The merry tinkle of a piano tune awakened her, something simple and sprightly.

Keighly rolled onto her back and stretched, listening intently. The room was dark, except for the light of the moon and stars, and beyond the music and the low murmur of voices, beyond the sturdy walls of the house, lay a profound silence. A wolf or coyote howled somewhere in the hills, and Keighly reminded herself, with a slight smile, that Francine lived in the country.

Her eyes widened a little as full wakefulness overlook her.

Downstairs, the din increased. These were men talking, and children running about, laughing and calling to each other. The pianist pounded on the keys with renewed gusto, in order to be heard, no doubt, over the rising tide of noise.

Keighly realized she was holding her breath. It was the television set, of course. Francine was watching some program with a large and rowdy cast.

She got up slowly, listening. "Francine?" she called softly, knowing it was impossible for the other woman to hear her from downstairs, especially with the bedroom door closed and the TV playing.

Keighly went to the door and opened it, heard it creak on its hinges. She felt for the light switch, because the hallway was so dark, but failed to find it. Stepping back over the threshold, she frowned, looking for a lamp.

In the glow of the moon, she could see that the bed she'd arisen from a few moments ago was not the one she'd stretched out on in the afternoon. The wallpaper, too, was different, she thought, squinting. Large, ugly cabbage roses covered it, like splotches of blood in the gloom.

Keighly raised a hand to her mouth to stifle a cry. It had happened again, this time without the aid of the mirror in her grandmother's ballroom. She had traveled back in time, but to what decade? Was it the same day, or would Darby be a little boy when she found him, or long since dead and buried?

Her knees threatened to give out, and she eased her way back to the bed, where she sat down heavily. The springs creaked and the sound seemed to echo.

Any moment now, some member of a previous generation of Kavanaghs would come racing up the stairs to fling the door open, soon to be followed by all the others, demanding to know who she was and what she was doing in their house. And Keighly hadn't the faintest idea what she would say to them.

She was still trying to sort out the situation for herself.

Bile surged into the back of her throat when she heard footsteps on bare wooden stairs. Someone had heard her. She would be arrested, dragged off to jail or an insane asylum, if she wasn't shot for trespassing. . . .

108

MY OUTLAW

The door opened, and Keighly squeezed her eyes shut, searching her mind for a convincing lie.

"Keighly?" The voice was male, and familiar. Hoarse with what sounded like a mingling of hope and disbelief. "Is that you?"

Tears of relief trickled down her cheeks and, for a long moment, she couldn't speak. The figure in the doorway was Darby, and he knew her. "Yes," she said, her voice trembling.

He was across the room in a stride or two, and had gathered her up into his arms, crushing her against his chest as if to impress her image upon his skin. His fingers plunged into her hair and as he tilted her head back to look down into her face, she saw his amber eyes glitter in the partial darkness, like those of some magnificent, predatory animal.

"What happened?" he rasped. "How did you get here? I thought the mirror—"

"You thought the mirror was the only way," Keighly finished for him, beginning to smile even though her face was wet with tears. "Obviously, it isn't, because I'm definitely back."

He gave her a quick, smacking kiss. "This time I'm not going to let you leave my side," he said.

"I didn't do it on purpose," Keighly replied, a little impatient.

He kissed her again, on the forehead, and chuckled. "Now all we've got to do is figure out how to explain your sudden appearance in an upstairs bedroom of Angus Kavanagh's house."

Keighly touched his lips with the tip of one index finger. "First tell me how long I've been away. Didn't we share your cot at the Blue Garter last night, and make love this morning?"

Darby stared at her for a brief interval, as if astounded, then shook his head. "No, darlin'," he said. "You've been gone two weeks."

109

"Two weeks," Keighly breathed. For her, less than twenty-four hours had passed. A possibility she hadn't considered before occurred to her then. "What planet is this?" she asked.

He laughed this time, making no effort to keep his voice down. "Earth," he answered presently. "You from somewhere else?"

❧ CHAPTER ❧
7

Keighly looked down at her very modern clothes—jeans and a cotton shirt. And, she realized for the first time, she was barefoot.

"What *are* we going to tell people?" she asked, but she wasn't really concerned.

Darby grasped her hand, tugging her toward the door of the bedroom. "Nothing, while you're wearing that getup. We'll sneak out the back way and I'll bring my horse around from the barn in a few minutes. I've got some stuff I bought for you back at the Blue Garter. You can change there."

Keighly was so happy to be with Darby again that she didn't let herself think beyond that. After a separation of truly cosmic proportions, details weren't important.

They made their way stealthily down a rear staircase—the house had not changed in terms of structure from the version Francine inhabited, though of course the furnishings and decorations were vastly different—and out the kitchen door. Keighly stood in pitch darkness on the step, waiting for Darby, who had almost immediately disappeared into the gloom.

Only minutes later, she heard a horse whinny, and then Darby was there, mounted on a steed straight out of a fairy tale. Black as night, the creature snorted and tossed its head, causing bridle fittings to jingle.

"Darby?" a man's voice called from inside. "You out there?"

"Hurry," Darby said, bending down and extending a hand to Keighly. "Simon is the last person I want to run into right now."

Simon Kavanagh, whom she would one day marry, unless she managed to alter history and keep the man she loved alive and well. A chill tripped down Keighly's spine even as she took Darby's arm and allowed him to swing her, movie-cowboy-style, up onto the horse behind him.

She put her arms around Darby's hard waist as the animal bolted away into the deepest shadows of the night, able somehow to make its way. They had put the house well behind them when the clouds that covered the moon moved aside, spilling silver light over the land.

The horse—Keighly recognized it now from the sculpture Francine had found in the attic of the modern Kavanagh mansion—moved at an easy canter. A gelding she recalled, with the name of . . .

Destry. How, she wondered immediately, did she know that?

"Did you mention this horse to me when we were together last?" she asked, raising her voice a little to be heard over Destry's hooves on the hard-packed dirt road and the fresh wind rising from the desert.

Darby sounded jubilant, like a man who has just found gold after many years of fruitless mining. "No," he replied. "I bought him right after you disappeared."

Then somewhere in my mind, I remembered him. That's the only possible explanation. "I guess women aren't the only ones who shop when they're depressed," Keighly observed aloud. She was, after all, in a certain degree of shock, even though this was what she had wanted, to be back with Darby.

"What?"

"Never mind," Keighly answered, with a slight smile,

112

and held him tighter. He smelled of starch and sunshine, bay rum and man. She let her cheek rest between his shoulder blades, where his long hair was bound back, and was truly content for the first time since they'd made love—that morning for her, two weeks ago for Darby.

She didn't try to sort it all out, not then.

Redemption was larger than it would be in the twentieth century, full of bluster and commerce. The Blue Garter Saloon was doing a rousing business, which was probably only one of the reasons they entered from the back.

They might have reached Darby's room undiscovered if a large black woman hadn't come around a corner, carrying a lamp. She wore a snow white nightdress, and her hair was tied up in rags. Her eyes narrowed suspiciously at the sight of Keighly, then went wide again as she took in her jeans and shirt and comparatively short hair.

"Land sakes," the stranger gasped. "You aren't a man—" She leaned in a little closer, glaring at Keighly. "—are you?"

Keighly was stricken dumb; even in her nightie, with a crown of white rags on her head, this woman had presence, an air of natural authority that only the unwise and unwary would ignore.

It was Darby who answered, first with a chuckle, then by saying, "I haven't changed *that* much since I left here, Tessie."

Keighly, who prided herself on being female, was now recovered enough to feel nettled by Tessie's implication. "I most certainly am not a man," she said.

"Then you must be the one that was carryin' on like the damned hollerin' from the heart of hell, in Mr. Darby's room a couple weeks back. I don't care what that silly Oralee says, it weren't her."

Keighly blushed and looked away. A reply did not come readily to mind. "Who is Oralee?" she whispered to Darby.

113

"Was everybody in this place listening at the keyhole?" Darby demanded of Tessie. Keighly might not have been there at all for all the notice he paid her, except that he was still holding her hand, his fingers intertwined with hers.

"Nobody had to do that," Tessie retorted, her nose an inch from Darby's. "It was downright scandalous, too, Darby Elder!"

In one deft motion, Darby opened the door of his room, shoved Keighly over the threshold, and closed her away from him. Out in the hallway, the argument resumed.

Keighly had no desire to take part in the debate. She started to sit on the chair where she and Darby had made love, then bolted back to her feet as though the seat were hot and began to pace. She was taking things one moment at a time, not trying to think, just biting her lip and waiting.

After a while, the confrontation between Darby and Tessie, whoever she was, came to an abrupt if dramatic finish. The door opened a crack and Keighly heard Darby's voice.

"You decent?"

Keighly laughed softly. "You'd probably prefer it if I weren't."

Darby came in, grinning. "I was hoping, that's all."

"Who was that woman out there? She scared the hell out of me."

Darby chuckled, bolting the door. "That was Tessie. She likes to mother me some, and if she could heckle me back onto the straight and narrow path, she'd do it, I reckon."

He paused to kiss Keighly, his hands light on her shoulders, then went to the chest at the foot of his bed and started pulling out parcels wrapped in brown paper and tied with string. "Here," he said. "I went through the tortures of the damned buying these gewgaws, so I hope they suit."

Keighly was touched, especially when she opened the

114

first package and found a lace-trimmed camisole and matching drawers inside. For a man like Darby to make such a purchase would truly have been an ordeal. "They'll suit," she said, strangling a little on the words, because she wanted to cry.

All of the garments fit well enough, and when she had laid the last of three dresses aside, Keighly stood before Darby in petticoats and the pretty camisole.

Darby was looking at her as though he wanted to strip her bare, and the truth was, she wanted the same thing, but it wasn't going to happen. Not when, according to Tessie, everybody in the building had heard her "carrying on" the last time.

"Who's Oralee?" she asked, taking a step back and nearly toppling over onto the cot on her back.

Darby grinned in the flood of moonlight from the window. His teeth were as white and perfect as the devil's own. "Just one of the girls who works upstairs," he said. "I had to have some explanation for the ruckus in here, so Oralee very kindly took the blame. You ought to be grateful."

Keighly tugged awkwardly at the top of the camisole, thinking it was too low and revealing. "Well, I'm not," she said, hoping he couldn't see that she was flushed. With her luck, his vision was probably as good as that of his horse. "Grateful, I mean."

He chuckled and held out his arms, and she couldn't resist. She moved into his embrace, and her eyes filled with tears of relief, of joy, and the knowledge of what lay ahead, both bitter and sweet.

"We can't make love here," she said, without much conviction, her head resting against Darby's chest. Through his shirt, she felt his heart pounding out hard, steady, regular beats.

His grin touched her like the warmth of a candle's flame and shimmered in his voice. "We're about to," he replied. "There are less likely places, you know."

"But if everybody heard—"

115

"You'll just have to try to be quiet."

Keighly balled up a fist and struck him on one shoulder, but not very hard. "I wasn't working alone, if you recall," she pointed out.

He laughed and lowered his head to kiss her and, in that moment, she was lost. With no thought of the past and future, which were all turned around for her anyway, Keighly gave herself up to this man and all she felt for him.

Darby plundered her gently with his tongue, and Keighly met him stroke for stroke, but there was never any doubt of who would dominate. In this one facet of their relationship, he was her master, her teacher, and she had no wish to change that, ever.

Still kissing her, Darby slipped his hands under the straps of her camisole and tugged it down, freeing her bare breasts. Then, drawing back a little way, he admired her bounty, held each mound of plump flesh in his palms, chafed each nipple with the pads of his thumbs.

Keighly gasped and at the same time curved her back, offering herself.

"So beautiful," Darby said. "I can almost believe you're a nymph from some Greek fable, or a goddess gone astray of Mount Olympus." He made a circle around the peak of Keighly's right breast with his fingertips.

"Fancy talk for a cowboy," she managed, after a little whimper.

"Somebody tell you cowboys can't talk fancy?" he asked, and then bent to take slow suckle at the morsel he had so carefully prepared.

Keighly couldn't hold back a low, throaty cry. She plunged her fingers into Darby's hair, and held him close to her even as she faced the certainty that the pleasure was too much to bear, and would be the end of her.

"I haven't—oh, God—known any cowboys—"

"That's good," Darby said, between brief, delicious bouts of savoring her. "If I have my way, you won't know another man after me. Not like this."

116

Sorrow brushed against the edges of Keighly's passion, for she had seen what lay ahead, but she resisted, would not allow the rapture of being with Darby again to be poisoned. She'd save him somehow, as well as their child, and never give herself to Simon Kavanagh or anyone else in marriage.

In fact, as far as she was concerned, she and Darby were already man and wife. The exchange of vows would be a mere formality, for they had already melded into one flesh and one spirit. In all times and dimensions, Keighly belonged to Darby, and he to her.

He continued to ravish her breasts, which swelled with delight under his attentions, and Keighly flung her head back in full surrender. When he laid her down on the cot, she barely noticed, let alone offered a protest.

"God help me," Darby whispered against her throat, "I don't care who hears us. Tell me to stop and I will, but I swear I'll be half killed if you do."

Keighly drew her petticoats up around her waist; helped awkwardly as Darby removed her drawers. "Does this mean you aren't going to torture me with an hour of foreplay?"

"I'll ask what the hell 'foreplay' is later," Darby answered gruffly, nibbling at her earlobe now, even as he unbuttoned his trousers with the other hand. "And I hardly think 'torture' is the proper word, though you've been known to scream like somebody in the dungeons."

She arched her back; he found and entered her with a frustrating lack of hurry. Her nails moved over the hard, knotted muscles of his shoulders, his ribs, his waist and buttocks. "Damn it, Darby," she moaned, *"faster."*

"Not for anything," he replied, and took her at his own measured pace, skillfully and with a thoroughness that left her so spent that she could barely breathe.

When it was over, Darby covered her face with light, nibbling kisses.

"Don't you dare tell anybody you were with Oralee," she said, when the capacity for speech had returned to

117

her, sometime later. "I don't care what it does to my reputation."

He laughed. "I guess it won't matter," he said. "You marry me, and you won't have any reputation to speak of, anyway."

Keighly felt her eyes go wide. "Are you asking me to be your wife?"

"I'm telling you that if you don't stand up in front of a preacher with me, I'll have to carry you off to the mountains and make you live with me in sin."

"With you," Keighly teased, wriggling beneath him once and draping her arms loosely around his neck, "sin has its good side." They were still joined, and Darby groaned, low in his throat.

Then he kissed her, not like before, but briefly, and with an affection that stirred something small and sore in her heart. "Yes or no," he said. "And if you refuse me, I'll tell everybody you're a man."

Now it was Keighly who laughed. "Wouldn't that be harmful to your reputation?"

"Mine? It couldn't be worse," he replied, and kissed her again, this time in earnest.

Keighly was almost afraid to open her eyes when she felt the heat of the morning sun on her face, for fear of finding herself back in the twentieth century, in Francine's guest room. It was the scent and substance of Darby, lying next to her, half wrapped around her, that gave her the courage to look.

He was still asleep, his lashes uncommonly thick where they lay against his tanned flesh, his jaw stubbled with a new beard. One side of his mouth curved upward, ever so slightly, in an nearly undetectable grin. His hair was unbound, so manly in an untamed sort of way, and shimmering in the sunlight.

A rush of love went through Keighly as she admired him, sweeping her breath before it, knocking her pulse out of its comfortable meter so that it raced for a few seconds. *Let me stay with him,* she prayed silently. *Even if I can't change things, let me stay and love Darby Elder, as much as I can, for as long as I can.*

Darby stirred, opened his eyes. "If you'd vanished, I would never have forgiven you," he said.

She snuggled closer, which wasn't hard since they were sharing a bed barely wide enough for one. "Not much you could have done about it," she replied.

"You are a saucy minx," he remarked.

She tucked her head under his chin, as contented as she had ever wished to be. "When it comes to sex," she said forthrightly, "you are definitely in charge. However, I feel I must tell you that women of my time are not dutiful little mice who obey their husbands' every command."

Darby chuckled. "When were women *ever* 'dutiful little mice who obey their husbands' every command'?" he countered.

"You have a point, insofar as it goes," Keighly allowed, snuggling. "Nevertheless, nineteenth-century females are not permitted to vote. They are the legal chattel of their spouses, with no more rights than a man's horse, or his dog."

He drew the sheet down, uncovering her breasts. Brushing them lightly with the backs of his fingers. "Ummm," he said.

Keighly shivered with pleasure and at the same time tried her hardest not to lose control. "I must have your—your promise, Darby, that you won't—oh, dear heaven—that you won't try to subjugate me."

He was poised over her now, looking down into her eyes. Into her very soul. "You have my word," he said clearly. "Outside any room with a bed in it, my love, you'll be your own woman."

Darby went out, presently, and returned with food and the promise of a bathtub full of hot water. Keighly ate ravenously and looked forward to bathing and dressing in standard nineteenth-century clothing.

"It's a good thing you didn't buy me a corset," she commented, thinking of Victorian fashions, when they'd both eaten and Darby had dragged in a tub big enough for about three-quarters of an average person, "because I wouldn't have worn it."

"You don't need one," Darby said.

"You wonderful man. Keep up that flattery and I'll be putty in your hands."

He grinned from the doorway, on his way out again, presumably for hot water. "You're already putty in my hands," he observed, closing the door just before the sweet roll Keighly tossed would have struck him in the head. When he was gone, she got off the bed, still smiling, and peered at her image in the small shaving mirror over the bureau.

She looked as happy as she felt—her cheeks glowed, her eyes shone.

Half an hour later, she was up to her chin in hot water and soapsuds.

Darby sat astraddle of the wooden chair, his arms draped across his back, watching Keighly and trying to assess his feelings. He was in most respects a practical man, but where this woman was concerned, he felt like a hotheaded kid—just the thought of any other man looking at her, let alone seeing her like this, made him half crazy.

He sighed. He'd get nothing done for being riled if he fretted every time somebody laid eyes on his woman. Keighly was beautiful, like an angel given to mischief, and any man with decent eyesight would want to look his fill.

"You don't belong in a place like this," he said thoughtfully, studying her with frank and undeniably brazen admiration. "You ought to be reigning in some castle— lady of the manor."

120

"All right. You build me a castle, and I'll reign in it."
Keighly sank deeper into the water, so that the suds
floated just beneath her chin. Her eyes, green in the
moonlight, looked almost gray in the sunshine, and were
full of impudence. "Are we still getting married, or have
you thought up some excuse to get out of it?"

"We'll say the words today if you want to," he said.
"Personally, I'd like to ride down to San Miguel first. I
have friends there, and there's a *hacienda* I've always
wanted to buy."

Keighly's brow creased into a slight frown as she
regarded him. "San Miguel," she repeated, in an odd tone
that couldn't be described as either a question or a
comment.

"We can't stay here," he told her. He would be firm
about that if he had to, even though he meant to honor his
vow not to dominate her anywhere except in bed. He was
glad he didn't aspire to control Keighly, for he suspected
it was an impossible goal.

"You're worried that I'll vanish again," she said, in a
slightly more normal voice, holding out the soap and a
wet cloth.

Darby knelt beside the tub, lathered the soap, and
began to wash her back. It was the first time he'd done
this, although he felt as though they'd performed this very
ritual a thousand times before, so familiar were the
motions. "Aren't you? You don't want to go back, do you,
Keighly?"

She hesitated just long enough to stop his heartbeat for
a moment.

"Keighly?" he pressed.

She turned her head, looked up at him with tear-filled
eyes. "Not unless you go with me," she said, at long last,
and in barely more than a whisper.

Darby dropped the cloth and took her chin in his hand.
"What is it? What do you know about me, about us?"

Keighly wouldn't tell him. She just stared into his face,
her teeth sinking into her lower lip.

121

"Damn it," he muttered, after another interlude of silence. "You *do* know something."

She nodded. The tears were flowing now; he wiped them away with the sides of his thumbs and gathered her into his arms, heedless of the fact that she was soapy and wet and thus soaked the front of his shirt.

"Maybe going there, to Mexico I mean, will make a difference," she murmured. "Only let's never come back. Let's never, never come back—"

He took her head in his hands, his gaze searching her eyes, scouring deep. Suddenly he knew that whether they went to San Miguel or stayed in Redemption, fate would be served. Judging from the grief he saw in the face of Keighly Barrow, his intended wife, there was much pain ahead, as well as happiness.

"I love you," he said. He had never spoken those words to another woman and, he knew, he never would. They belonged to Keighly alone.

She rose onto her knees in the water, still weeping, her arms around his neck now. "And I love you, Darby Elder."

"Where'd she come from?" Will asked, that evening, inspecting Keighly with an appreciative eye as she stood beside Darby in the main entry of the Kavanagh house. Will liked women, that was no secret, but he was a faithful husband; Betsey, being his match in nearly every way, would have shot him between the eyes if he hadn't been.

Darby sighed. As he'd expected, everybody wanted to know who Keighly was and how she'd gotten to Redemption without coming in on the stagecoach or the train, but he was getting tired of spinning yarns. "She rode in on her own," he said. "She and I are old friends, and she was looking for me."

Will frowned. "She doesn't look like she's spent much time on a horse. And she ain't sunburnt."

"All right," Darby said, exasperated, "she came out of

122

the mirror. Just stepped right through from the other side."

Will laughed and slapped Darby on the back with such force that he nearly lost his balance. "You got an imagination," he said. "But then, you always did."

Just then Simon came out of the study and stopped in his bootprints at the sight of Keighly. She was standing nervously at the base of the stairs, one gloved hand resting on the newel post, looking beautiful and all wrong for her surroundings, at one and the same time. Her dress was yellow calico, long-sleeved and high at the neck.

She hadn't wanted to come back to the Triple K; she was afraid the house would swallow her. Darby knew, though he couldn't have said how, that nothing like that was going to happen. It was the mirror at the Blue Garter they had to watch out for, the saloon itself, maybe even the town of Redemption. The ranch, for tonight at least, was a safe place.

"Simon," Darby said easily, while his half-brother stared with rare ill manners at Keighly. "I would like to introduce the woman I mean to marry. Miss Keighly Barrow."

The words broke whatever spell Simon was under; he turned his silver gaze to Darby briefly, then smiled at Keighly. "You'll pardon me for gaping, I hope," he said, with a gentlemanly bow. "It's just that I've never seen anyone quite so lovely in my life."

"Except maybe Maggie, over at the Blue Garter," Darby put in.

Simon favored him with a brief glare before turning his cultivated charm on Keighly again. Only then did Darby notice that she'd turned pale and indeed looked as though her knees would buckle.

So, Darby concluded silently, and with resignation, the future she feared so much included Simon. He moved quickly to her side, put a supporting but not possessive arm around her waist.

123

"I thought it was customary to invite a lady to sit down," Darby said, ushering an uneasy and silent Keighly into the seldom-used parlor and seating her on a silk-upholstered fainting couch. "What's happened to your manners, Simon? And yours, Will, if you ever had any?"

Will and Simon exchanged a look, Simon raising one dark brow.

"Pa's real anxious to meet you, Miss Keighly," Will said, with one of his boyish, glowing smiles. "To tell you the truth, we'd all about given up hope that Darby here would ever amount to anything."

Darby laughed at that, and Simon had a wry expression in his eyes.

"A first encounter with our father sometimes calls for a drink," Simon said to Keighly, who seemed to be rallying a little now that she'd had a chance to catch her breath. "We keep sherry, for our rare lady visitors."

Keighly wet her lips with the tip of her tongue, causing a grinding sensation deep in Darby's loins by that simple and innocent gesture, then shook her head. "No, thank you," she said. "I understand Mr. Kavanagh is quite ill."

"He's confined to his room," Simon said. "And he hates it."

Neither Will nor Darby offered a comment. A bedroom without a woman in it was good for one of two things—sleeping or dying.

"I wouldn't want to impose," Keighly replied. She wasn't kidding, Darby thought. She looked ready to bolt for the door.

"He'll horsewhip all three of us if we let you leave here before he gets a look at you," Will boomed, with no apparent fear of the lash.

"True enough," agreed a deeper voice, from the parlor doorway.

Everyone turned to see Angus standing there, leaning on a cane and neatly clad in trousers, a white shirt, polished boots, and a satin smoking jacket. His white hair

1·24

gleamed in the lamplight and, even in his illness, Darby thought, the old man was still imposing, still impressive as all hell.

Angus smiled at Keighly and, for the first time in his life, Darby understood, at least partially, what Harmony had seen in her longtime paramour. Here was a man who genuinely loved and respected women, in a way that few men did, and it came as a revelation to his illegitimate son.

With great dignity, Angus made his way to where Keighly sat, and she had the courtesy and good sense not to rise out of deference. Reaching her, he held out a hand, and she laid her palm on his. He bent and lightly kissed her knuckles. Simon's suave ways, then, were not invented, but inherited.

"I must confess that I have despaired over my youngest son's manner of living," Angus said, standing straight and tall again. His eyes were shining. "Now I see that I need not have worried, for Darby's taste in women is clearly impeccable."

Keighly blushed and inclined her head in thanks, but did not speak.

"It seems to me," Darby said, addressing his father, "that none of us have known each other as well as we thought we did."

Angus's gaze moved to Darby, full of rough, quiet affection. "Perhaps you're right," he agreed, and the unspoken implication was that he had always understood his third son and had confidence in him.

Simon managed somehow to usher Angus to a chair, without appearing to do so. He knew how to handle the old man's formidable pride, a knack neither Will nor Darby had ever mastered, much to their detriment.

"Brandy?" Simon asked, already at the liquor cabinet, pouring the blend Angus favored.

The patriarch nodded, but it was Keighly he was watching. He knew there was something different about her, Darby could tell—he was an astute man, was Angus Kavanagh—though of course there was no way he could have guessed the remarkable truth.

"I don't recall seeing you around Redemption, my dear," he said. Darby started to speak, but Angus silenced him with one upraised hand. "I was speaking to your intended," he pointed out smoothly and without rancor.

"I'm from California," Keighly said, almost primly. She looked at Darby and fluttered her eyelashes. He wondered if he was going to regret promising not to interfere with her independence after they were married. "I've been—traveling."

"You're a very long way from home," Simon observed, handing his father a snifter and perching on the arm of a nearby chair.

Keighly smiled demurely, and Darby knew she wasn't trying to charm Simon. She was teasing *him,* and he would have his revenge later, when they were alone. "You have no idea how far," she said.

"And yet how close," Darby felt compelled to point out.

She agreed quickly, and sweetly. "Quite true. Life is one big paradox."

"Tell us," Simon said smoothly, "exactly where did you encounter our illustrious brother, Miss—er—"

Keighly didn't miss a beat. "Barrow," she reminded him, though Darby knew she suspected Simon hadn't forgotten in the first place. "Keighly Barrow. Darby and I are old friends, actually. We met when we were children. I was passing through town, so to speak, with my family."

Simon pondered the revelation in silence.

Will, who had left Betsey at home that evening, because one of their boys was sick from eating green apples, felt compelled to join the conversation. It had never mattered to Will whether or not he had anything pertinent to say; he was just inclined to be sociable. "There were lots of wagon trains going through back then," he said.

Angus, Darby noticed, was still studying Keighly's face.

It was almost as if he recognized her from somewhere, although that was patently impossible.

"I understand the wedding is to be held in San Miguel," Angus said.

Keighly looked to Darby to explain, and he didn't know what to say. Angus was dying, and there was a new accord between them, however tenuous. How could he refuse to be married in Redemption, so that his father, estranged from him these many years, might attend?

"Darby seems to have a fascination with San Miguel," Simon remarked, going back to the liquor cabinet, this time for himself. He returned with a glass of whisky.

"We've changed our minds," Keighly blurted out. Her color was high and her eyes flashed with fierce decision. "We're not going anywhere. Not—not yet."

Darby stared at her but did not attempt to counter Keighly's announcement, because in his heart, he knew she was right to insist on staying. It would be cowardly to leave now, whatever differences he and Angus might have.

She tossed a pleading look in his direction and wet her lips again. "There are things that need to be worked out," she said, with fetching bravado.

"You have not only chosen a beautiful woman for your wife," Angus told Darby, "but a compassionate, intelligent one, as well. You are to be congratulated."

Darby cleared his throat. "I'm glad you think so," he said.

Will gave him a hearty slap on the back. "Nothing like a first-class female to bring a man to his senses," he said.

"It didn't work with you," Simon commented mildly, but there was a grin lurking in his eyes.

Darby loosened his collar, which suddenly seemed too tight, even though he wasn't wearing a tie and he'd left the top two buttons of his shirt unfastened. He shot a look at Simon, who looked intrigued. "Keighly and I won't be living in this house," Darby said gruffly. "The Culverson place is up for sale—six hundred and forty good acres and a cabin. We'll buy that."

She looked both relieved and fearful. Good God in heaven, but she was beautiful, too splendid for such a low and dusty place as earth. Her gaze locked with Darby's and much was communicated between them in those few seconds—all the dangers, all the hopes, all the secrets that were theirs alone.

She mouthed two words to Darby. "Thank you." Then, turning her dazzling smile on Angus, she said, "But we'd like to hold the ceremony here at the Triple K, if that's all right with you, Mr. Kavanagh. I know you've been ill—"

Angus set aside his glass and then took both Keighly's hands in his, and Darby knew his father had just gained an important ally. "You have quite restored me," Angus said graciously. "I can't think of anything that would please me more than a wedding."

❧ CHAPTER ❧
8

In that same house, but a century in the future, Francine Stephens opened the door to the room that she now suspected had been, at some point, Darby's. She was not really surprised to find Keighly gone, the imprint of her slender body still on the bedclothes, her shoes on the floor, where she'd kicked them off. All the same, it was not an everyday experience to have someone vanish into thin air under one's own roof, and Francine leaned back against the doorjamb for a few moments to catch her breath.

It was all true, then, Francine thought, marveling. If she hadn't seen the wedding photograph, the marvelous sculpture of Darby and his horse, indeed if she hadn't seen Keighly's face as she related her experiences, she wouldn't have believed such a thing could happen. As it was, she knew she would not find Keighly at the house in Redemption if she got into her car and drove there, knew she would not find her anywhere on earth. In this present moment, Keighly Barrow Elder did not even exist, except as remains in some long-buried coffin.

Francine's throat tightened. Then she gently closed the door, went back down the stairs, keeping her hand lightly on the bannister rail lest her watery knees let her fall, and fetched her purse and keys from the table in the hall-way.

She headed toward Redemption, leaving the workmen to the gathering of their tools, the day's labors finished, and parked outside the cemetery. Heart pounding, tears burning unshed behind her eyes, Francine passed the newer graves for the ones of her own family—Angus Kavanagh's clan.

Except that Angus was buried on the Triple K, next to a stone bearing the name Harmony.

Darby's grave was marked with a sundial, the weeds cleared away by Keighly's own hand only a day or so before. Francine knelt in the soft, dry grass and began to search nearby for another marker.

Finally, she found what she was looking for, but well away from Darby's final resting place, next to Simon's. Now the tears Francine had withheld finally spilled over. *Keighly Elder Kavanagh,* the simple marble stone read, *Beloved wife and mother, much and grievously mourned.* There was no month and day of death, but the dates were most telling, to anyone who cared to look. *Born, 1967. Died, 1910.*

Someone had known the truth—Simon, perhaps, or one of their children. Or had Keighly ordered the stone herself, in advance of her death? If so, Francine knew that the marker was, in a sense, a message to her, a sort of verification that this miracle, this wondrous tragedy, had indeed taken place.

Francine dried her cheeks with the back of one hand and got to her feet. A brief search revealed that some of Keighly and Simon's children were buried nearby, having lived to ripe old ages, but there was no stone for Garrett Elder, the son Keighly had born to Darby.

That proved nothing, of course. He might well have passed away somewhere other than Redemption.

Stumbling only a little, Francine went back to her car, sat until she had stopped shaking, then drove to the town's one and only supermarket and bought a disposable camera. Returning, she took several shots of Keighly's monument, and two or three of Darby's as well, then wound the film to its end and brought the whole thing back to the store to be developed.

Driving slowly because her head was spinning with all the myriad and largely incomprehensible implications of what had happened, she returned to her large, empty house. The workmen were gone for the day, but the desert sun was still dazzlingly bright.

Alone in the newly remodeled kitchen, Francine made a simple green salad, not having the wits to assemble anything more complicated, and sat down to eat. She nibbled, tasting little or nothing, and ate only because she knew she needed nourishment. Later, if Keighly didn't reappear, she would surely be called upon to explain where her friend had gone, most likely to the police, since Keighly's car was still in the driveway, but for the moment that was the least of Francine's concerns.

Keighly had wanted to go back to Darby, and attempt to circumvent his fate, along with that of their unborn child, Garrett. The photographs Francine had taken that day of two separate gravestones might eventually tell, she theorized, her head beginning to ache, whether or not her friend's mission had been successful.

If it was, the dates on the stones themselves would very probably be different from the ones she'd captured on film that same afternoon. So too might the letters and other things in Keighly's trunk, but investigating, at this point, would be an intrusion. Francine would wait, anxious though she was, because there was nothing else she could do.

"Aren't you angry?" Keighly asked, when Darby escorted her outside, after dinner with his father and brothers, and helped her into the waiting buggy.

"Because you changed the whole course of my life with

a single sentence?" Darby asked, though his tone indicated that he didn't expect an answer. "No, Keighly, I'm not angry. You're right, after all. There comes a time when a man has to stop running and face what's his to deal with."

The rig creaked as he climbed up beside her and took the reins. The vehicle belonged to the livery-stable owner, a man named Ned Feeny, and Darby had paid for its use.

"You need to make things right with your father," she said. "I don't see how you can be completely happy until you do."

"I'm afraid there's more to it than that," Darby said and, with a flick of the reins, they were moving, drawn through the moonlit night by a single gray horse, also Mr. Feeny's.

Keighly thought of the kindly invitation Angus had drawn her aside to issue, after dinner. Her future father-in-law had asked her to stay with them at the ranch, until the wedding, diplomatically suggesting that the Blue Garter wasn't a "comfortable" place for a lady. She'd refused, though politely, but she hadn't told him the real reason, which was that she was afraid of being wrenched through time again, and away from Darby.

"More?" she asked belatedly. "Besides the fact that I won't be born for almost a hundred years, you mean?"

"Yeah, besides that," Darby answered, not looking at her.

"Are you going to tell me about it?"

"Yes," he said.

"When?" Keighly prompted, when a lengthy silence had fallen between them.

"When I can think how to explain it," Darby replied at last. Then, in a tone that said he wouldn't be persuaded to discuss the matter further, he changed the subject. "Angus was right, saying you shouldn't stay at the Blue Garter, Keighly. I'm taking you to the hotel."

"Will you come with me?"

MY OUTLAW

Darby chuckled. "No, ma'am," he said. "From now on, we're doing things right and proper."

Heads turned, half an hour later, when Darby Elder walked into the tiny, rustic lobby of the American Hotel, wearing a fancy suit and escorting a lady.

Keighly felt herself coloring as they underwent the scrutiny of the few travelers seated beside glowing oil lamps, pretending to read their newspapers, and she raised her chin a notch.

At the desk, Darby arranged for a single room, paid the amazingly low cost, and turned the registration book to Keighly. The skinny mail clerk, watching her in fascination, handed her a quill pen.

She dipped the point in the ink provided and wrote her name with a flourish.

Darby did not kiss her good night, and while she was disappointed by that, she understood. Things were different in the nineteenth century; he was treating her like a lady, trying to protect whatever might remain of her reputation.

"I would appreciate it," Darby said to the clerk, sliding a coin that amounted to half the cost of the room across the counter, "if you would see Miss Barrow safely to her door."

The boy, Adam's apple bobbing, nodded and scooped up the coin. "Yes, sir, Mr. Elder," he said, rounding the desk so fast that he almost tripped over his feet.

"Good night," Darby told Keighly, so formally that she was surprised he didn't shake her hand. If it hadn't been for the spark of mischief in his eyes, she would have been worried.

The clerk escorted Keighly upstairs and opened the door of room number seven. He lit a lamp on the table just inside and subsided back into the hall again with a muttered "Good evening." Keighly thanked him, took the key, and closed the door again, immediately locking it.

The room was small, but very clean, with a narrow bed, a washstand with a pitcher and bowl, and a tall cabinet

133

for clothing. It was only then that Keighly realized she didn't have a nightgown, a toothbrush, or a change of underwear.

With a sigh of resignation, she went to the window and pulled aside the lace curtain.

Darby was standing in the center of the street, like some kind of western Romeo waiting for his Juliet. At her appearance, he swept off his hat, executed a deep bow, and then turned and walked away.

She missed him already.

Three days later, after several harried visits to the Culverson place to sweep down cobwebs and direct the placement of the furniture Angus had insisted on donating and a lot of frantic planning, Darby and Keighly were married. Father Ambrose, a young priest who ran an Indian mission nearby, performed the ceremony, and Tessie, Oralee, and a number of the other women from the Blue Garter were in prominent attendance.

Keighly wore a long-sleeved gown of crisp ecru linen, with a bib of lace. Because it was not the dress she had seen in her wedding photograph, and been wearing on her first visit to the nineteenth century, she was lulled into a tenuous sense of security. Perhaps, she reflected happily, humming as she fussed with her broad-brimmed hat in front of Angus's parlor mirror, the expected course of events had already been altered. Darby would live, and Garrett, too, if indeed the child would exist at all.

A child conceived on a different night would be a different child, she reasoned. Although she wanted with all her soul to avoid the experience of losing her son, not to mention her husband, Keighly felt a swift, deep sadness pierce her heart nonetheless. Even if Garrett was never born, and thus could never die, she would always know he had been meant to be her child, and Darby's, and in her way she would mourn.

She drew a deep breath and let it out slowly. She must

concentrate on what *could* be changed and let go of what couldn't, though she had no illusions that the task would be easy.

"You are exceedingly beautiful," a polite voice observed from behind her. "My brother is a most fortunate man."

Seeing Simon's dark and handsome countenance reflected in the mirror, beside her own, Keighly repressed a shiver and turned, attempting to smile. Simon was not an evil man, after all, but a very good one, intelligent, charming, and handsome, and it wasn't his fault that he might one day court her and persuade her to be his wife.

She wondered fleetingly what would make her agree to the marriage, should she fail to prevent Darby's death and find herself a widow. Loneliness, perhaps? Financial need? It was difficult, with so few conveniences, just to manage ordinary tasks in the nineteenth century. Maybe doing so with a broken heart was simply too much.

"Thank you," she said, acknowledging Simon's compliment at some length.

Like everyone else, he was dressed for the wedding, which had taken place in the small garden beyond the French doors of the parlor. Angus's cook and housekeeper, Gloria, an elderly Indian woman with a singing voice like that of an angel, had been preparing for the occasion night and day since the marriage had been announced.

"It was kind of you to be married here," said Simon. "Being present means a great deal to my father."

Keighly wished Darby were beside her, but he was off somewhere, surrounded by well-wishers. Will's children were running through the house, noisy as wild ponies, while Betsey, a blithe, lively woman, helped Gloria in the kitchen. Simon's adolescent daughter, Etta Lee, sat dreamily in the garden, on a marble bench.

"But you still don't trust me," Keighly said, in response to Simon's remark about her charity. "Do you?"

He smiled benignly. "Let's just say there's something

odd about all of this—something I can't quite put my finger on. My father senses it too, you know."

"Maybe you're both imagining things," Keighly suggested.

"And maybe we're not," Simon replied. His tone was not unfriendly, merely matter-of-fact. "Fancy has always been Darby's province, and Will's. Pa and I are not given to fey thoughts."

"Too bad," Keighly said, thinking of the lonely little girl seated in the garden, a big bow in her hair and her hands primly folded in her lap. The child's solemn nature and separateness tugged at her heart; it would have been much better, in Keighly's opinion, if Etta Lee were in the thick of things, making a racket with Will and Betsey's boys. "A little magic makes life more interesting, as a general rule, and commonplace troubles easier to bear."

Simon executed a small bow, more an elegant inclination of his head, really. "And what about the deeper sorrows?" he inquired. "How shall we bear those?"

Keighly was at a loss to answer, not knowing quite what he meant. She was about to ask when Betsey arrived, having gathered her tribe and shushed its members into an unwilling and no doubt temporary semblance of order. "Don't monopolize the bride, Simon Kavanagh," she said, taking Keighly's hand. "There are people she ought to meet."

Darby returned just as Betsey began squiring Keighly from one group of Angus's friends to another. Here, in the decorated garden of the Kavanaghs' impressive house, it did not seem to matter that Darby was the son of a prostitute and Keighly herself had not only appeared out of nowhere, but spent time within the walls of the Blue Garter Saloon. They were warmly congratulated and invited to come to supper, once the honeymoon was over.

It was a fleeting, lovely afternoon, bathed in sunshine and the mingled scents of carefully nurtured flowers. Keighly had been aware only of Darby, herself, and the priest during the actual ceremony, but when she had been pronounced to be Darby's wife, and he her husband, she had turned, beaming, to toss the bouquet to Etta Lee.

A look of such transcendent happiness wreathed the child's face that Keighly's joy, already beyond containing, was multiplied many times over. Etta Lee raised the delicate flowers to her nose for a moment, then crept close to Keighly and tugged at her skirts.

"I'll press them for you, Keighly," she said politely. "So you'll always have a pretty remembrance."

Keighly had felt another chill then for, although the child had not meant her statement to be ominous, the new Mrs. Elder was recalling a nosegay, dried to paper-thin fragility and tucked away in the crumbling vellum pages of a scrapbook. That incredibly delicate, faded spray had been—would someday be—these very flowers, so carefully selected to bring color and joy to her wedding day.

"Is something wrong?" Etta Lee had asked, her gaze worried and wide.

Keighly had bent and kissed the child resoundingly on the forehead. "No, sweetheart," she'd said. "Everything is just fine."

Once the introductions had been made—Keighly knew she wouldn't remember a single name—she sought out Etta Lee again. Darby had told her that the little girl played the piano. "Perhaps you wouldn't mind making some music for us," she said gently.

Etta Lee's face shone once more, as luminous and open as Will's. Her nod was eager. "You'll want something merry, of course," she said breathlessly. "I'll see to it right away. I've placed your wedding flowers in one of Grandfather's heavy books."

"Thank you," Keighly said, and Etta Lee hurried off.

"Poor little thing," said Betsey, standing beside Keighly with a glass of punch in one gloved hand. "Lord knows I do my best for her, but I've got my own brood and there are only so many hours in the day."

"How old was Etta Lee when her mother died?"

"Just a baby. Simon tries, you know, but he's only a man."

Keighly felt momentary tears sting her eyes. She'd been desperately lonely after her parents divorced, and she thought she understood how Etta Lee felt. "Why hasn't he remarried?"

"He's got a cussed streak in him, just like his pa and his two brothers," Betsey said, with another sigh. Then she went dashing off to chase one of her boys, who was running through the crowd waving a pair of drawers over his head like a flag.

Darby was nearby, talking with Will and the priest, who was evidently a friend. As music began to drift through the open French doors, Keighly looked to one side and saw that Simon was there.

"Etta Lee is the image of her mother," he said, clearly aware that his daughter had been the subject of Keighly and Betsey's concerned conversation. Like most of the other guests, he carried a glass of rum punch, from which he took the occasional well-mannered sip.

Keighly wasn't drinking, because she suspected she was pregnant, and the members of her new husband's family had stopped offering her alcohol after the first few refusals.

"Then your wife must have been beautiful indeed," Keighly said.

"Oh, yes," Simon replied, in a low voice, his eyes fixed on something far away. Perhaps he was recalling the day of his own marriage, though Keighly could not read his emotions. "Kathleen was lovely."

Just then, Darby slipped his arm through Keighly's, and kissed her soundly on the cheek. When he spoke to Simon, his voice was gentle and, at the same time, wry. "She was too pretty for the likes of you," he said.

"Amen," agreed Will, who had tagged along.

Simon smiled, though with a touch of sadness. "Yes," he allowed. "Kathleen was my superior in every way."

The gathering was definitely swelling. "It is a day for

138

happy subjects," Angus put in, with brusque good humor. He'd gathered strength, according to Darby, ever since his introduction to Keighly, and now looked very dapper in his best suit and highly polished boots. No one doubted that he was seriously ill, though. He'd wanted to witness this day, this wedding, and had rallied accordingly. "We need not speak of poor Kathleen."

Inside the parlor, Etta Lee went on playing. The tune was sweet and cheerful, and a bittersweet warmth pooled in the bottom of Keighly's heart. Another sign, she reflected privately, that her suspicions were right—she was already carrying Darby's child. She had never been one to cry easily in her old life, beyond the mirror, but this existence was more real somehow, more fundamental, more textured, more meaningful in every way.

Here, even if she was afraid or sad, she was also solid. Real.

Events and people touched her far more deeply, in this place and time. She was more vulnerable than ever, she could not deny that, but she was also more alive. It was rather like being the survivor of some dread disease or near-fatal accident, suddenly and newly aware of the keen blueness of the sky, the fragrant caress of the breeze, the value of laughter, the poignant intensity of true love. Every heartbeat was precious, every breath and smile.

"What happened to her?" she asked Darby, hours later, after cake and dancing and punch and a great deal of Etta Lee's stalwart piano-playing, when they were in a room at the American Hotel. "Kathleen Kavanagh, I mean."

Darby undid his string tie and tossed it aside with an expression of pure relief. "Kathleen," he reflected, with a long sigh, remembering. "She was born in Boston, and Simon met her there while he was in college."

"Did she like living on a ranch?"

"I suppose," Darby said. "She loved Simon so much, I think she would have lived in a chicken coop or a hayloft, if it meant they could be together."

"What did you think of her?"

"I hardly knew Kathleen. She and I did have something in common, though. Her mother was a governess in an important household, seduced by her employer and forced to raise the resultant daughter on the charity of the church."

Keighly was taken by surprise. "I guess I thought she would be the sort of woman who's been written about in the social pages all her life."

Darby shook his head. "All that came after she married Simon."

Keighly was stalling, but it wasn't because she didn't want to make love with Darby. She was just enjoying the anticipation, and she could see that he knew, and was playing the same game.

"And then?" she prompted.

"And then she died, giving birth to twin sons."

"The children?" Keighly asked, holding her breath, instinctively pressing one hand to her abdomen and thus revealing far more than she had intended. "What happened to them?"

"They were stillborn," Darby told her. "Simon, normally the most sensible of men, was drunk for a solid year. If Angus hadn't loosened his teeth one fine day and told him to stop feeling sorry for himself and look after his motherless daughter, he might still be pouring bourbon down his throat."

Keighly flinched. "Is that how Angus disciplined his sons? With violence?"

Darby crossed the small room, touched her cheek. "No," he said, with a tender smile. "It isn't. He was probably the only man within a hundred miles of Redemption who never took a razor strop to his boys—he doesn't believe in that approach. Which isn't to say there weren't plenty of people who thought he should whup all three of us twice a day."

"You've disliked him all this time," Keighly said, unpinning her hat and laying it aside on a pretty table with a top done in delicate marquetry. "Why?"

140

"Not because he ever tanned my hide," Darby confessed. He was plainly impatient with the delay, and wanted to move on to other business, but Keighly was a part of the family now and she was curious about its history. "I guess I always wanted Angus to ride into town, collect my mother from the Blue Garter Saloon, and marry her in front of everybody. I wanted to be as much his son as Will or Simon."

"But you *are—*"

Darby laid a finger to her mouth and shook his head. "I was the bastard, the spawn of a whore," he said quietly, without bitterness or a trace of self-pity. He was merely reasonable. "I was the one who had to defend my mother's honor, such as it was, every single day of my life."

She slipped her arms around his neck and pressed her forehead to the base of his throat. "Oh, Darby—"

He caught her hand gently in his, stroked her palm with his fingers. "Don't fret over me, Mrs. Elder. All that matters is right now, and as of this moment, I'm a happy man."

Looking up into Darby's pale amber eyes, Keighly believed him. The past really *didn't* matter to him just then, and if he wasn't mourning his difficult childhood, for the moment at least, so why should she? Perhaps Darby too had undergone some kind of personal epiphany that day, as she had done, and felt the same aching reverence for the present moment.

She slipped her arms around his neck. "I think you ought to kiss me, Mr. Elder."

He laughed. "That's one request I'll be glad to indulge."

He took her mouth then, and Keighly was half drunk by the time he withdrew, and turned her deftly toward the bed.

She felt another stab of alarm. "Suppose the bed creaks?"

Darby laughed and laid a finger to her lips. "I guarantee you'll be past caring if it does." He bent, kissed her in a way that promised she would forget her name before the night was over. "Now, darlin', I think we should go ahead and have ourselves a wedding night."

He swept Keighly off her feet and into his arms in grand cavalier fashion and carried her to the bed. There, tenderly, taking his time, he undressed her, stroking and admiring and nibbling at each part of her as he uncovered it. He shed his own clothes, when Keighly pleaded with him to make love to her, and only then did he blow out the lamp.

The ranch Darby had bought was a nice piece of land, and although Will had told her, somewhat smugly, that it bordered the Triple K, Keighly didn't let on that she knew. It was important to Darby to have something of his own, and she understood and sympathized.

"Now that we've got this place," Keighly said, standing in the middle of the living room—more properly the parlor—with its beamed ceiling and natural rock fireplace, "what are we going to do with it?"

Darby laughed. He was wearing regular clothes again, his wedding suit packed away, along with Keighly's special dress, in a trunk. "We're going to raise cattle and horses, Mrs. Elder," he answered, "and a whole crop of kids, I hope."

Keighly looked around briefly before meeting her husband's gaze again. The cabin was reasonably large, with a kitchen and three bedrooms, though of course there was no indoor bathroom. Until she could get the plumbing concept across, they would have to use the privy out back.

"I'd like a dozen," she said. "Kids, I mean."

Darby came and took her into his arms, shaking his head. "Weren't you paying attention yesterday, Mrs. Elder, when Will and Betsey's boys were running wild?"

She smiled. "I think they're wonderful."

He kissed her. "Do you, now? And what do you think of me?"

142

Keighly pretended to consider her reply very carefully before, at length, she answered. "I think I've always loved you," she said seriously, "and that I always will."

For a moment, his eyes were troubled. He knotted his fingers with hers and raised them to his mouth, brushing a light kiss over her knuckles. "For better or for worse?"

Keighly felt the brief, keen touch of fear, just behind her heart. "For richer or for poorer," she replied, as a confirmation. But other words echoed in the silence, words she had hardly thought about as she spoke them, only the day before, at their wedding.

Until death do us part.

❧ CHAPTER ❧
9

Keighly's first few weeks as a wife were idyllic. At night—and whenever they got the chance in the daytime—she and Darby made love, and each exchange was a melding of their souls, as well as their bodies. Some encounters were playful, others were almost desperately passionate, and still others were so sweetly poignant that Keighly wept for the joy of being who she was, where she was, with the man she loved more than life.

Despite the frequent interludes of lovemaking, those days just following the wedding were busy ones. Darby had reluctantly accepted a hundred head of horses from Angus, and he planned to ride to Mexico, in the near future, to buy a hundred more. He was up with the sun every morning, pulling on his clothes in the half-light and heading outside to make sure the workmen he'd hired were out of their bedrolls and ready to continue shoring up the old barn. The Culversons, he liked to remark, with great pride, had really let the place go to hell.

Guilt invariably drove Keighly from between the smooth linen sheets soon after she heard the kitchen door close behind Darby. He worked twice as hard as any of his men, and he couldn't be expected to mend fences and unload hay and crawl around on the barn roof without breakfast.

Betsey, who was proving to be a very good friend as well as a thoughtful sister-in-law, had taught Keighly how to pump water at the well behind the house, to chop kindling, and to build a fire in the wood-burning stove in the kitchen. Keighly had figured out the cooking on her own, and after a few flaming pancakes and scorched attempts at fried chicken, she got the hang of using cast-iron skillets and pots to make a meal.

She discovered right away that everything was at least ten times as difficult in the nineteenth century as in the latter part of the twentieth. Washing clothes was a major enterprise, backbreaking labor that took a whole day, and by the time the tub had been dragged out into the yard and water had been heated and carried, soap added and the scrubbing done, Keighly thought she would collapse.

Of course she couldn't. Everything had to be pegged to the line Darby and Will had so cheerfully erected for the purpose, and no matter how early she started, the laundry was never dry until late afternoon, when it was past time to be thinking of supper. Wash day was followed inexorably by ironing day, a sweaty process of heating flat irons on the cookstove and wielding them while they were hot.

On top of that, there was daily cleaning, an endless round of meals and dishwashing, and Darby dragging her outside by the hand every other hour to see some new addition to their growing menagerie of farm animals—the cow, the accompanying calf, the prize bull, the sow.

Keighly was exhausted every night when, after she and Darby had made love, she fell asleep in his arms, her head resting on his shoulder.

She had never, at any time in her life, been happier.

Then, inevitably, came the moonless night when some sound or feeling awakened her, and she opened her eyes, fearing at first that she'd gone back to the modern world again. But there was Darby standing at the bedroom window, a figure made of flesh and shadow, hands braced on the sill, gazing out.

Her heart clenched with relief at the sight of him, then again, with worry.

"Darby?"

"Go back to sleep, darlin'," he said gruffly, without turning around.

Keighly raised herself onto her elbows, blinking. She was terribly afraid, though she couldn't have said why. All she knew was that her fear had nothing to do with her propensity for spontaneous zapping from one century to another. "What's the matter?"

Darby sighed. "I can't sleep."

"That's obvious," Keighly said, fear disguising itself in her voice as annoyance. "And now I can't either, so you might as well start talking."

He chuckled, but there was no humor in the sound. "You are one contentious woman," he said, coming back to the bed, sitting on its edge, just out of reach.

Keighly made a good-naturedly contemptuous noise and propped both their pillows behind her. "I think I'm being pretty docile. After all, where I come from, the work I do around this place would be considered slave labor. You don't see me rebelling, do you?"

Darby leaned toward Keighly, cupped her face in his palm. Then, too soon, his hand fell away, and he shoved splayed fingers through his beautiful, savage hair. "You'll have help directly," he said. "Father Ambrose suggested a woman and her boy—they've been living at the mission and they need a place."

Hard as it was, washing and cooking and cleaning, Keighly wasn't sure she wanted another woman under-foot. The house was hers, hers and Darby's, and she was surprised to find that she was almost as territorial about the structure as she was about the man.

"I wasn't complaining," she said quietly.

"I know you weren't," Darby replied, bending to kiss her forehead. "But I won't see you wear yourself out like

146

some hardscrabble farmer's wife. I'd crawl to Angus and beg him for his pocket change before I let that happen."

"I love you," Keighly told him, scooting forward far enough that she could stroke his hair with one hand. "How long has it been since I told you that?"

"About two hours, I suppose," Darby answered, and his teeth flashed in a grin. "Course you didn't say it gentle like that. You had both heels dug into the mattress and your head flung back and—"

"It won't work, Darby," Keighly interrupted firmly. "I'm your wife and I love you and I demand that you tell me what's bothering you. You've been putting me off long enough."

He glanced toward the window, as if he might be considering making a bid for escape. "I'm not like Simon and Will, Keighly," he said, after a long time. Although she couldn't see him very clearly, she knew his expression was grim. "I spent some time on the Triple K, it's true, but mostly I lived in the Blue Garter Saloon while I was growing up. I got in trouble a lot. And when I was seventeen, I took off for the first time, got into more trouble, and generally refined my skills as a no-account drifter. I came back eventually, out of plain loneliness, I reckon, and did everything I could to get a rise out of Angus. He spent half his time threatening to horsewhip me and the other half trying to talk some sense into my head.

"I wasn't having any of that. Nothing Harmony or Angus said got through, and the only thing that mattered to me—the only thing, Keighly—was seeing your image in that mirror. As long as I could get a glimpse of you once in a while, I was all right. But then you went away, or vanished, or something, and I couldn't stand it. I rode out again, with a couple of outlaws who'd been drinking and whoring at the Blue Garter, and Harmony and I exchanged hard words before I went." He paused, took an unsteady breath, and clasped Keighly's hand tightly in his. "Turned out, the Shingler brothers knew more about trouble than I did—they robbed a bank while I was riding with them, and shot the teller in cold blood."

Keighly's stomach turned over. "Oh, God, Darby. Were you—?"

He shook his head, as if desperate to stem damning words before she could utter them. "No, darlin'. I wasn't there, and fortunately for me, the local sheriff knew I wasn't, because he'd thrown me into jail the night before for disturbing the peace, and I was still behind bars when Duke and Jarvis held up the bank. The clerk was alone when it happened—he gave them the money and they still killed him, the bastards."

Keighly covered her face with both hands for a long moment, fingers splayed so that she could see Darby between them. Such violence was one thing in a shoot-'em-up on late-night television and another entirely when it had really happened.

"What did you do then?" she asked, lowering her hands now to fiddle with the edge of the top sheet.

"I served my time—fifteen days—and then I got on my horse and rode out. I was in Mexico until Will and Simon found me there and told me about my mother, and about Angus."

Keighly put her arms around Darby, drew him down beside her on the bed. "Were you an outlaw then?"

"No," he said, settling into her embrace. "But I was a saddle bum, and that's not much better, in most people's eyes."

"That's ridiculous. Our wedding was packed with guests, townspeople and other ranchers and their families, and they all treated us as though we belonged."

Darby laid an idle hand over her breast, though the electricity in his fingertips warned that he would not be idle long. "They were there for two reasons, Keighly— one, they're all beholden to Angus in some way and, scandalous though the circumstances of my birth might be, I'm his son. And two, they were curious about you. There hasn't been a bride in the family for a long time;

MY OUTLAW

Betsey was a raised on a farm outside Redemption and sat two desks over from Will the whole time they were in school, and poor Kathleen turned out to be delicate, and died before anybody outside the family knew much about her."

The mention of Kathleen reminded Keighly of Simon, and how she was slated, by fate, to marry him one day, after Darby was dead. A chill moved through her, and she held her husband more tightly, as if to protect him.

"For all your talking, Darby Elder, you haven't told me what you were worrying about, standing there at that window."

"You are the most damnably stubborn woman."

"True. So you might as well tell me what's troubling you."

He was quiet for a long time—so long that Keighly thought he was going to dodge the issue again, whatever it was, and leave her outside his feelings.

"I'm not through with the Shingler brothers," he said, at last. "They were caught and sentenced to hang a month after the robbery and murder, and they're sure to know I told the sheriff where they were likely to hide out."

Keighly felt fear settle, cold and sharp, into the very marrow of her bones. "Did you? Tell, I mean?"

"Hell, yes," Darby answered. "They killed a man, after all. They were brought in and tried and sent to prison to be hanged. Along the way, some of their friends must have come along, because the sheriff and his deputy were both shot and the Shinglers haven't been seen since."

Keighly's heart was hammering. "Surely they've forgotten you."

"They haven't forgotten any more than I have, Keighly. It would be naive to think they had."

"Is that why you wanted to go to Mexico? You hoped we could avoid them?"

"Partly, yes," Darby admitted, gathering her very close. "And there was another reason, too. I'm scared as hell that somehow you're going to be taken away from me

149

again. I'm vulnerable, Keighly, in a way I've never been before."

She kissed the hard, cool flesh of his shoulder. "Me, too," she said. "I guess that's the price of really loving somebody. And you know what? It's still a bargain."

He turned over to look down into her face, his hair brushing her cheek. "I agree," he said, and lowered his mouth to hers.

The next morning, Father Ambrose brought Manuela, a slender, ageless woman who might have been in her twenties or her fifties, and her young son, Pablo, to meet Keighly. She was in the kitchen, attempting to press one of Darby's shirts, when they arrived.

"Come in and sit down," Keighly said, beaming, genuinely pleased to have company. In the bright light of day, with work to do and her body still thrumming pleasantly from Darby's lovemaking in the middle of the night, the world seemed a safe and reasonable place to her, and she was in a cheerful mood.

Father Ambrose, about thirty and very handsome, wore a monk's robe, sandals, and a rope belt. He smiled and then spoke quietly to Manuela, who looked as though she might bolt and run. She was clutching a cloth bundle, probably containing all her belongings, in both arms.

When the guests were seated at the round oak table, a donation from Simon, and Keighly had poured coffee for Father Ambrose and Manuela and milk for Pablo, she sat down to join them.

"Manuela lost her husband six months ago," Father Ambrose said quietly. "She had a position as a cook in town for a while, but lost the job when the family decided to move back East. She and Pablo have been staying at the mission—Pablo here is one of the best students in our little school—but Manuela is anxious to earn her own way."

"I can work too," Pablo piped up eagerly. He was a

beautiful child, about eight years old, with luminous dark eyes and a wealth of springy black hair. "I can feed horses and cows and pigs. I am very strong, like a man."

Keighly smiled at him. "I can see that," she said. "I'm sure we could come up with plenty of chores for you—after school, of course."

Manuela looked at Keighly with slightly less reserve than before, but she still did not speak.

"They don't require much," Father Ambrose said, with a sort of fond hopefulness. "Just a room, a small salary, and their food."

Keighly fixed her gaze on Manuela. "I'm sure I'll be wondering what I've done without you before the day is out," she said. "The work is pretty hard, but it shouldn't be so bad if we share it between us."

Manuela's brown eyes flashed with pride, then softened. She spoke for the first time. "Thank you," she said.

Pablo gave a little cry of glee, excused himself, and shot out through the back door.

Father Ambrose laughed. "He's anxious to work with the horses," he explained.

Keighly went to the window, a little alarmed. After all, the horses in the corral, selected to be broken to ride, were wild, and they were dangerous.

"Don't worry," the priest said, pushing back his chair. "Darby will look after the boy."

Sure enough, even as Father Ambrose spoke the words, Darby was climbing the corral fence, crossing the yard, offering his hand to Pablo, one man greeting another.

"I'll show you where you'll be sleeping," Keighly said to Manuela. There was a small lean-to on the side of the house opposite the master bedroom, outfitted with two cots with crude straw mattresses, a chest of drawers, and a washstand.

Standing in the doorway, Keighly thought of the guest room in her apartment in twentieth-century L.A., with its shining brass bed, bright yellow coverlet, and ruffled pillow shams, its pale carpet and cheery pastel wallpaper, and she blushed.

"It's not much—"

Manuela's creamy brown skin seemed translucent. She put her bundle on one of the beds and tentatively pulled open one of the bureau drawers in that time-honored way of women getting to know a new place.

Even in the face of the other woman's obvious pleasure, Keighly felt compelled to assuage any doubts she might have.

"We'll fix it up as best we can, of course—new curtains, decent mattresses, a rug—"

"It is fine," Manuela said, looking her straight in the eye. "Now, you must show me the work you want me to do."

Father Ambrose was waiting politely in the kitchen when they returned. "If everything is settled, I'll be getting back to the mission," he said. Evidently, the three had walked the five miles between the little compound and the ranch house, because Keighly had seen no sign of horses or a wagon. He shook Keighly's hand. "Thank you, Mrs. Elder."

Keighly liked the sound of her married name, and didn't ask him to call her by her first. She'd get around to that later, she expected, when they had become better friends.

"I'm grateful to you," she replied.

When Father Ambrose had gone, taking Pablo with him because school was in session that day, Keighly took Manuela on a tour of the house. Even though Keighly and Betsey had worked hard to make the place livable before the wedding, there was still a great deal to do. Manuela soon proved herself a person of initiative and set about washing down the dusty interior walls with soap and hot water.

After the noonday meal, which Darby ate sitting on the back step, with Keighly perched beside him, because he was filthy from head to foot from breaking horses, Betsey arrived in her small buggy, drawn by a sturdy pair of mares, one brown, the other a black and white pinto.

"I'm going over to look in on Angus," she called to Keighly, approaching the house and giving Darby a laughing wide berth as he passed her on the way back to the corral. "Want to come along?"

Keighly nodded. "I'd like that," she said, and it was true. She cared deeply about Angus. Still, it gave her a pang to know that the house was already being run without her, for all practical intents and purposes. Manuela had stopped her wall-washing long enough to make lunch, and by now she'd finished the dishes. "Just let me freshen up a little."

Betsey waited while Keighly dashed to the bedroom to splash tepid water on her face, smooth her hair, and check her practical gingham dress. When she got back to the kitchen, Betsey was chatting amiably with Manuela, who was already setting out the ingredients for a huge supper.

The ranch hands, who had cooked for themselves over a campfire, would now, by Darby's decree, be taking their evening meal in the house.

"I feel as if I'm exploiting her," Keighly confided, when she and Betsey were in the buggy and driving down the rutted track toward the Triple K ranch house, several miles away.

Betsey gave her sister-in-law a wry look. "Manuela is thrilled to be making her own way again—she told me that herself. Furthermore, Mrs. Elder, I think your concerns are a little less benevolent than you'd like me to think. You don't like another woman doing for Darby."

Keighly opened her mouth to protest, but before she could get a word out, Betsey went on.

"It's all right," she said, smiling. "I'm the same way about my Will. Or at least I was, until those boys of ours were born, one right after the other. Then I was mighty glad to have young Sally Quill to help me now and again, even if she is a foolish little thing. Keighly, Darby hired Manuela because he loves you, because he doesn't want you working yourself to death."

"I know," Keighly said deflatedly, looking down at her hands.

Betsey shook her head, her pretty face still alight with amusement. "Land sakes, woman—stop feeling guilty and enjoy being fussed over. Soon enough, you'll have a houseful of kids, like Will and me, and even though I know that's what you both want, and it'll certainly make your lives richer, things won't be quite the same."

Keighly thought of the mirror in the Blue Garter Saloon, and of all Darby had told her in the night, about the Shingler brothers, and she felt such a bittersweet yearning to grow old with her husband that hot tears sprang to her eyes.

Betsey spotted them and nodded knowingly. "You're in the same sweet fix as I am, I do believe," she said, and touched her middle, as if to confer a blessing on her and Will's fifth child, growing within. "A woman gets emotional when she's in the family way."

Keighly bit her lower lip. She couldn't think about the very real possibility that she herself was already carrying a son, Garrett; she had enough to worry about, between the prospects of an unseen time warp looming somewhere ahead and the two outlaws who might be plotting even then to hunt Darby down and kill him.

"It must be unbelievably painful, having a baby here," she commented, before she'd thought the words through.

Betsey looked at her oddly. " 'Here'? I don't reckon it hurts any more in Nevada than it does anywhere else."

Keighly tried to smile. She'd been comparing childbirth conditions in the nineteenth century to those of the twentieth, but of course she couldn't say so. "Tell me what it's like."

"I called Will Kavanagh three kinds of a devil and promised to run him through with a pitchfork if he ever came near me again, but then the baby would get himself born and I'd look at him and I'd look at Will and since I was already in love with the little one, I figured I might as well go right on loving Will, too." Betsey sighed. "I do hope this one will be a girl, though. I would dearly love a girl."

"I hope so, too," Keighly said. For all that they'd been born in different centuries, and thus different worlds, she liked Betsey, saw her as the sister she'd longed for but never had. "Will you come and help me, Betsey, when and if my time comes?"

Betsey elbowed her lightly and smiled. "Your time will certainly come, Mrs. Elder, you being married to a man with the same blood in him as my husband's got. And, yes, I'll be there, along with Dr. Bellkin from town. Darby won't be any use at all, you know."

Keighly laughed at the thought of the dither Darby would be in when things got down to brass tacks. "You're right," she said. "He won't."

When they arrived at the ranch house, Betsey and Keighly found Angus sitting on the screened sunporch in his wheeled chair, reading a well-thumbed book on the history of Greece. He was plainly delighted to see his daughters-in-law and, looking at him, Keighly's spirits lifted.

Angus seemed stronger, despite the chair. His color was good and there was a sparkle of delighted mischief in his eyes.

They visited for an hour. Betsey told Angus all her four boys' latest exploits, and he laughed with hearty appreciation. Keighly related what was going on at the ranch— how Darby was breaking horses and Manuela and Pablo had come to live with them.

Angus patted her hand, just before she and Betsey rose to take their leave. "You're the best thing that ever happened to that son of mine," he said. "I'm so grateful that you came along."

Impulsively, Keighly kissed Angus's weathered old cheek. "I want you to be here, on this veranda, to listen to stories about Darby's and my children, when our turn comes," she said.

He smiled. "I'll do my best," he promised.

When Betsey dropped Keighly off at home, Darby was in their bedroom, up to his neck in a tubful of steaming water. A thin cigar stuck out of his mouth at a jaunty angle.

Keighly felt a sharp stab of envy—Manuela had probably prepared the bath for him—and in the next instant, chagrin. This was no way to begin a marriage.

"How is Angus?" Darby asked.

"For a man who pretends not to like his father," Keighly replied, bending to kiss the top of his head and wrinkling her nose at the cigar, "you seem awfully concerned about his health, Mr. Elder. It just so happens that he's looking much better."

Darby grinned, clamping the smoke between his teeth. "I think he fancies you, that old man. If he was forty years younger, I'd have to fight him for your hand."

"If he was forty years younger," Keighly answered, hoisting the sticky window to let out some of the smoke, "you wouldn't be born yet, and neither would I."

Darby drew on his cigar and blew a shifting miasma into the steamy air above the tub. "I think you fancy him, too," he teased.

"You're right," Keighly said, jerking the offending cheroot out of his hand and dunking it with a sizzle into the bathwater. That done, she tossed it out the window. "I think Angus is a wonderful man. I wish my father had been half so strong."

Darby had been about to issue a protest regarding his discarded cigar, but instead his look of aggrieved annoyance quickly gave way to another of those lethal, knee-melting smiles of his. This one was downright devilish.

"Why don't you take off your clothes, Mrs. Elder, and climb into the tub with me?"

"Because we aren't alone in this house, for one reason. And because you've been rolling in mud, and worse, all day long, for another."

"If we have to be alone for you to share a bath with me, darlin', Manuela and the boy will have to go back to the mission. As for your second reason, I have no answer to that. I had to rinse off in the creek before I was fit for a tub."

Keighly sat down on the edge of the bed. "I don't want Manuela and Pablo to leave. They need us, and we need them."

"Darlin', I wasn't serious," Darby said, reaching for a towel.

"I'm a little jealous of Manuela," she confessed. "I don't like the idea of someone else looking after you."

He stood and Keighly, despite her resolution to conduct herself with Victorian decorum, at least for the time being, watched him in admiring fascination. She ached, suddenly, to sculpt again, to fashion an image of Darby that would outlive them both.

"I'll be faithful to you," he said quietly.

She wanted to touch him, not only as a wife, but as an artist learning her subject. She longed to run her hands over the hard muscles of his thighs, the ridged wall of his belly, the depth and width of his powerful shoulders. He was so magnificent that he nearly took her breath away.

She made herself look up, into his eyes. "I love you, Darby," she said. "I love you so much that I can't imagine ever caring more, but every day I wake up and find out that I do."

He came to her then, without a word, still damp from the bath, and eased her back onto the bed.

Keighly offered no protest as Darby opened the bodice of her dress, reached inside to caress her breasts as he took her mouth with his. Somehow, he managed to divest her of most of her clothes without breaking off his tender assault on her senses, and soon he was inside her.

She lay beneath him, transported, undulating wildly, clasping the rails of the headboard in perspiring hands, while he took her to a new place, a height they had never scaled before.

When it was over, they lay still for a long time, entwined, watching the light change at the window.

That night, Keighly hummed as she helped Manuela serve a supper of trout, fried potatoes, and carrots from the array of canned goods Angus's housekeeper, Gloria, had provided. Darby talked about breaking horses and herding cattle with the other men, but every once in a while, his gaze locked with Keighly's, and the kitchen seemed charged with lightning.

❧ CHAPTER ❧

10

Keighly knew she was lying beside Darby, knew she was sleeping, and yet the dream was too vivid to be a mere state of mind.

She stood in the moon-washed cemetery of modern-day Redemption, the hem of her cotton nightgown fluttering against her bare ankles, the grass cool and wet under the soles of her feet. Before her was a familiar grave, fitted with a sundial instead of a headstone, and the name and date inscribed there were plainly written in a blend of starlight and shadow.

Darby Elder. 1857–1887. Cherished husband.

A cool breeze rippled through Keighly's hair, and she knelt, pulled away the grass that had begun to obscure the marker. *Cherished husband,* she thought, as tears slipped down her face. Those words, truer than any others could have been, had not been there when she'd first seen the grave. She must have added them herself.

She got shakily to her feet. It was cold in the graveyard; the chill seemed to emanate from inside her own soul, rather than the darkness of the night and the icy silver glow of the moon.

"Darby," she whispered, like a witch uttering a desperation incantation. "Darby—"

Keighly awoke with a wrenching sensation, sitting bolt upright in bed and gasping for breath. Her body was drenched in sweat.

Beside her, Darby stirred. "Darlin'—?"

She murmured senseless words, meant, by their tone, to comfort, and he settled into the depths of sleep again.

Keighly waited until she was sure Darby would not wake up, then slipped from the bed, pulled on a wrapper, and crept out into the kitchen. In the twentieth century, she would have popped a cup of water into the microwave oven and brewed some herbal tea to settle her nerves, but it wasn't so easy here. She didn't dare take a drink, being fairly certain she was pregnant, so she simply lit a single lantern and sat, trembling, at the table, her hands clasped in her lap.

Manuela approached so quietly that when she appeared at Keighly's elbow, Keighly started and gave a little cry.

"You are sick, Mrs. Elder?" Manuela asked.

Keighly shook her head. She was so upset by the dream, by the reminder that nothing had changed where Darby's fate was concerned, that she could not speak.

Manuela went to the stove, added wood to the banked fire, and put a kettle on to boil. While she waited for the water to heat, she assembled the ingredients for tea, never saying another word the whole time.

It was only when she brought the crockery teapot and a cup to the table that she ran her eyes over Keighly's Victorian nightgown.

"Did you fall, Mrs. Elder?" she asked. "Perhaps you went outside and stumbled in the darkness?"

Keighly looked down at herself, and gave an anguished, disbelieving cry, hardly more audible than an indrawn breath, at what she saw. The pristine cotton of her gown, bought as part of her trousseau, was stained with grass and dirt. But she had not left the house since after supper, when she'd carried the dishpan out back to empty it in the yard.

"Mrs. Elder?" Manuela prompted.

160

Keighly shook her head, afraid to speak again lest she disturb some tenuous balance and inadvertently send herself away again, into that other time.

Manuela filled Keighly's teacup and added sugar, as she had seen Keighly do at supper. Then, gently, she slid the brew toward her. "Drink. You will feel better."

Using both hands, and shivering so violently that she feared she would spill hot tea all over herself, Keighly raised the mug to her lips and took a few sips. Manuela left the kitchen for a few minutes, and returned with a blanket, which she wrapped around Keighly's unsteady shoulders.

"I will call Mr. Elder," the housekeeper said.

"No!" Keighly choked out. "No—please—don't."

Manuela frowned. "But he is your husband—"

"I'll be all right," Keighly said, with as much conviction as she could manage, given the fact that she'd just traveled through time in her sleep. "Please—Mr. Elder works very hard. He needs to rest." She bit her lower lip, hoping the minor pain would bring the real world back into clear focus. She could still feel the dewy chill of the grass, the cool night wind, the heartache.

Looking up at Manuela's face, Keighly saw that some explanation was still needed. The woman was frowning.

"I was probably just sleepwalking," Keighly said lamely. It was an understatement of epic proportions, of course, but it wasn't truly a lie, and it would probably ease Manuela's concern. "Do go back to bed—I'll be fine."

Manuela hesitated, then returned to the room she shared with her young son. Keighly finished her tea, blew out the kitchen lamp, and went back to the master bedroom. There, she pulled off her damp, soiled nightgown and replaced it with a fresh one. Then, after wadding the discarded one up and shoving it to the back of a drawer, she crawled into bed beside her sleeping husband.

Or, at least, she'd thought he was sleeping.

161

"What was that all about?" he asked.

"What?"

He turned onto his side, made a sleepy, sigh-like sound, wholly masculine. "Stop it, Keighly. You know damn well what I meant."

"I had a bad dream," she said, nestling closer to him, hoping he would drop that particular line of questioning.

"Must have been bad," he replied, "if you had to change clothes after it."

Keighly's face burned in the darkness. "Something happened."

"Yeah, I'd guessed that." Darby cupped her chin in his hand, turned her so that the thin moonlight illuminated her face. "I'm listening, Mrs. Elder."

Keighly could hardly protest, when she'd made him tell her about his experience with the Shingler brothers just the night before. "I think I—well, I was just lying here sleeping—"

He waited in companionable silence.

"I think I went forward in time. It seemed that I was dreaming, and yet I knew I wasn't—"

"What happened?"

She eased herself out of his embrace, slipped out of bed, and recovered the dirty nightgown from its hiding place. Darby sat up and struck a wooden match to light the lamp on the bedside table, blinking in the flickering glow.

Keighly showed him the mud and grass stains on the gown.

He scrubbed his face with one hand and yawned. "You could have been walking in your sleep, couldn't you? Maybe you took a spill on your way back from the privy or something."

It would have been so easy to let that interpretation stand; after all, it was the most obvious, most sensible one, and Manuela had already raised it as a possibility. In the end, though, Keighly couldn't bring herself to mislead him.

"No, Darby," she said. "I never left the house. I didn't even leave the bed."

He was silent for a long time. Then he tossed the gown aside and flung back the covers, patting the mattress. "I'd just as soon hear the rest of this with both my arms around you real tight," he said.

Keighly joined him, her vision slightly blurred, and he leaned over her to put out the lamp.

"Tell me," he said.

Keighly swallowed hard, sniffled once. "I was in the cemetery, in Redemption. I was—I was looking at your tombstone."

Darby gave a low whistle through his teeth. She'd heard him use a shriller version to get his men's attention when they were working with the horses. "So that's it," he said.

Keighly squirmed closer to him, even though they were already touching in a dozen places. "Yes."

"Don't hold out on me, Keighly. I can tell there's more. And it doesn't take an eastern education to guess that you didn't care much for one of the dates you read on that marker."

She closed her eyes tightly, and helpless tears of frustration and grief squeezed through her lashes. She had thought she was protecting Darby by not telling him what she knew about the future, but now she realized that she'd been unfair. Of course he had a right to know it all. There might be things he could do to change his fate, things she hadn't even considered.

"It said you died this year, Darby," she made herself say. "Eighteen eighty-seven." After that, in careful, halting words, she told him about the chest in Francine Stephens's attic, about the newspaper clippings and the sculpture. She even told him about Garrett.

All she kept back was the knowledge that she was destined, if Darby died, to marry his brother, Simon.

He listened to everything without speaking or even flinching, his breathing so deep and steady and even that, except for the occasional reassuring tightening of his embrace, she would have thought he'd fallen asleep.

When the flow of tortured words stopped, and Keighly lay there trembling and spent from the telling, too grief-stricken even to cry, Darby turned onto his back and rolled Keighly smoothly onto his stomach. He held her backside in both hands, his grasp possessive, and for all that her face was in shadow, he seemed to look not only into her eyes, but into her very soul.

"Listen to me," he said. "Everybody dies, Keighly, some sooner, and some later. Maybe we can change things, and maybe we can't, but I'll tell you one thing we're not going to do—we're not going to waste a moment of the time we have together. Whether that's five minutes or fifty years."

She buried her face in his neck. "I hope I die before you," she murmured wretchedly, raising her head to look into his eyes again. "I'm selfish, Darby. I don't want to face the pain of being left behind. I don't want to have to mourn, to make do with memories—"

"Then I guess you shouldn't have gotten yourself born in the first place," Darby scolded gently. He sighed, wound a finger loosely in her hair. "Fact is, you're not the only selfish one, though, because I feel pretty much the same way—I'd a lot rather die than lose you."

"Let's go away—to Europe or Mexico or Canada—"

He kissed her lightly on the mouth to silence her. "No, Keighly. We already decided not to run, remember? You still want to take a trip on New Year's Day, 1888, then we'll pack our bags and head out. In the meantime, we're going to stay at the table and play the cards we've been dealt."

"You're right," Keighly said ruefully. "God, I hate it that you're right."

He began to flex his hands over the firm flesh of her buttocks, at the same time easing the hem of her night-

164

gown upward. "Now, to get back to my philosophy on making the most of every moment—"

The following morning, restless and out of a job because of Manuela's efficiency, Keighly decided to search the surrounding countryside for a piece of rock to sculpt. She'd bought chisels and a small hammer at the general store the previous week, when she had gone to town with Darby to buy supplies for the ranch.

That day, some of the cattle were being rounded up for branding, and Darby was mounted on Destry, the black gelding he rode so fluidly. Looking at them, man and beast, racing across the flatland to head off a stray heifer, Keighly was stopped in her tracks by the magnificent picture they made.

This moment, she knew, had been, and was, the inspiration for the sculpture of Darby and the gelding Francine would find in her attic in a little over a century. This, whether they circumvented fate or not, was how she wanted to remember the man she loved.

After collecting her emotions, Keighly went on, and found a sizable chunk of granite that would work very well for the purpose she had in mind. The question was, how could she get it back to the ranch house?

She was pondering that when she heard hoofbeats and looked up to see Darby riding toward her at a canter. He swept off his battered hat when he reached her and, grinning, nodded his head. He was as clear-eyed and full of mischief as ever. "Morning, Mrs. Elder," he said. "Did I happen to mention that there are snakes out here, and a lot of them live under rocks?"

Keighly looked at the stone she'd chosen for the sculpture and flinched ever so slightly. "I should have remembered that," she said. "Gram used to warn me about it when I was a kid."

Darby bent and offered Keighly his leather-gloved

hand, at the same time slipping his left foot out of the stirrup. Keighly let him swing her up behind him, even though it was awkward, since she was wearing a calico dress and petticoats.

"If you're going to wander around by yourself, you'd better learn to shoot," Darby said, turning in the worn saddle to look at her. There was no reprimand in his expression or in his tone; he was simply stating what he saw as a fact. He replaced his hat and pulled it low over his brow, surveying the flat horizon from the shadow beneath the brim, and Keighly knew he was thinking about the Shinglers. "I'll start teaching you directly after supper."

She laid her cheek against the sun-warmed, sweat-dampened spot between his shoulder blades. His shirt smelled of hard work and, vaguely, of soap and fresh air. "I came out here to find some stone for sculpting," she told him. "I want that big one, right there."

She pointed, and Darby followed the gesture. "You would," he said, with a note of cheerful resignation. "Maybe between the seven of us, the boys and I can drag the damn thing home."

In the end, he managed the task himself, with help from Will and Simon. They levered the rock onto a sledge, employing an old plow Darby had found in the barn, and used a team of two horses, borrowed from a couple of the workmen, to haul it back to the house.

Keighly had them leave the stone in the yard; it could be carried inside, she said, after she'd chiseled away those pieces that weren't part of the sculpture. She set immediately to work, kneeling in the grass, with Pablo and Etta Lee both hovering nearby, watching in fascination.

"Do you mean there's something inside it?" Etta Lee asked. She was clad in a blue and white checked pinafore and her dark hair was plaited into two thick braids, neatly tied with ribbons. Like Pablo, she attended the mission school, and Simon had brought both children to the ranch

166

when he went to collect his daughter after class was dismissed.

Pablo narrowed his eyes and peered at the stone, obviously trying to discern an image.

Keighly smiled. "Yes," she said. "Your uncle Darby is inside, and so is his horse, Destry."

"How long till they come out?" Pablo wanted to know.

She shrugged. "That depends," she answered. "Granite is very hard. It might take a long time to finish the piece."

The sun was riding lower in the sky, since it was late afternoon, but it was still hot and Keighly was conscious of tendrils of hair sticking to her nape. When a shadow fell over her, she thought it was Darby and raised her face with a ready smile.

Instead, Simon stood there, looking uncertain. "Come along now, Etta Lee," he said to his daughter. "We'd best be getting home."

Etta Lee was not a petulant child, but her lower lip protruded just slightly and she started to protest.

"I was hoping you and Etta Lee might stay for supper," Keighly said. It wasn't Simon's fault that he might figure in her future, and besides, she would do whatever she could, within reason, to foster better relations between Darby and his family. "Manuela is making fried chicken, and there really is plenty."

Simon looked reluctant but, at the same time, Keighly could tell he wanted to give in. Etta Lee was fairly jumping up and down.

"Please, Papa," she pleaded. "I want to be here when Uncle Darby and Destry come out of the stone!"

Keighly laughed and reached out to hug the child close against her side with one arm, but she was looking at Simon. "I told them it might take months."

Simon crouched and laid one hand to the rock, feeling its surface. He looked very serious for a moment, then met Keighly's gaze and smiled. "You've made quite a difference to all of us," he said quietly. "I appreciate it."

She didn't know what to say—even "thank you" would sound too self-satisfied.

"Can we stay, Papa?" Etta Lee demanded. "Please, please?"

"Yes," Simon said, hoisting himself to his feet with a sigh that was more drama than exertion, since he was, like Darby, a well built and very fit man. "I fear I'll get no peace if I refuse."

"And no fried chicken," Pablo put in.

Simon and Keighly both laughed.

"And no fried chicken," Simon confirmed.

Supper was a happy, hectic affair, what with all the workmen, Simon and Etta Lee, Darby and Keighly and Pablo and Manuela all in attendance. Will had gone home to Betsey and the boys, after helping to move the stone.

When the meal was over, Darby announced that he meant to teach his wife to shoot, while there was still some daylight left. He fetched a rifle from the rack on the living-room wall and sifted a handful of shells into his shirt pocket as he came back into the kitchen.

Manuela was doing the dishes, the cowboys had gone out to their improvised camp behind the barn, and Pablo and Etta Lee were working at their lessons on the newly cleared kitchen table. Simon joined Keighly and Darby for the shooting lesson.

The Culversons had stored numerous mismatched bottles in the barn, among other things, and Darby carried out a crateful, setting the first one on the top of a fence post, well away from everyone and everything.

Simon stood watching silently as Darby showed Keighly how to hold the rifle, how to take aim and fire. He would also teach her to dismantle, clean, and reassemble it, he explained, but for the moment he wanted her to get used to the weight and the recoil.

Keighly's first shot went well wide of the dusty blue medicine bottle on the fence post, setting a flock of birds to flight.

MY OUTLAW

In the twentieth century, Keighly would have refused to touch a gun or even have one in the house. Here, she was a willing, if not exactly eager, pupil.

After fifteen minutes of concentrated effort, she'd exhausted all the ammunition and never come close to hitting the bottle. Darby took the rifle from her and handed it to Simon.

Then, in a move so quick it was over before Keighly could credit that she'd seen it, Darby drew his own gun, a .45, and splintered the vial in a single shot.

The exhibition should have reassured Keighly—Darby Elder was definitely a man who could take care of himself—but instead it sent a shiver spiraling down her spine. Were the Shingler brothers as fast—or faster?

Simon cleared his throat as Darby turned away from the improvised shooting range. "I came out here to tell you something," he said, to his brother.

Despite fresh alarm, Keighly started to move away, so that Darby and Simon could have privacy, but Darby caught hold of her arm and stayed her.

"What?" he asked.

"It's nothing to worry about," Simon said. "I just thought you should hear it from me, that's all. Marshal Pratt turned in his badge to the mayor and the town council today. They asked me to take his place and I accepted."

Keighly was as shaken as she had been the night before, after her unscheduled visit to the future. In the family picture she'd found in Francine's trunk, of herself and Simon and their several children, he had been wearing a star-shaped badge. Fate had just scored another point, and she couldn't tell Darby about it without breaking the news that she would one day become his brother's wife.

Darby's reaction to Simon's announcement surprised her, even as she reeled from this newest blow. "God damn it, Simon," he rasped, "you're a rancher, not a lawman. Do you want to get yourself killed?"

Simon gave a ragged sigh. "I'm not a rancher, Darby," he argued reasonably. "Not like you and Pa and Will, anyway. I'm a gentleman farmer, raising fancy horses for money I don't need."

"What about Etta Lee?" Darby demanded, casting an eloquent glance toward the house, where the setting sun played on the window glass in dazzling oranges and crimsons and golds. "Isn't it enough that she lost her mother? Does she have to lose you, too?"

Simon's smile was sad and rueful. "If I didn't know better, I'd get the idea you gave a damn what happens to me," he said.

Darby swore, wrenched the rifle out of his brother's hands, and stormed off toward the house.

"Well," Simon said, watching him go, "that certainly went well."

Keighly had recovered her composure enough to slip her arm through her brother-in-law's as they slowly followed Darby. "He's afraid for you, Simon," she said. "Surely you understand that."

Simon's handsome face tightened, just briefly. "Yes," he said. There was anger in his voice, but no bitterness. "Will and Pa and I have been afraid for him since he was ten years old. It's about time he found out how it feels."

"Things were different for him," Keighly pointed out, taking care to shape the words gently.

Simon merely looked grim.

In the kitchen, Darby was leaning against the sink, drinking from an enameled mug of hot coffee. It was one of the mysteries of the universe—never mind time travel and magic mirrors—how he could consume the amount of caffeine he did and still sleep like a fallen log at night.

Simon and Darby exchanged unfriendly looks, but Simon's voice was kind as he spoke to his daughter.

"We'll be leaving now, Etta Lee," he said. "Gather your things."

Etta Lee obeyed without argument this time, though

she seemed blissfully unaware of the scorching glare her father and uncle were tossing back and forth over her head. She stuffed her slate and spelling primer into a canvas bag and looked up at Keighly with a bright smile.

"Thank you, Aunt Keighly, for a very nice supper." In the instant it took for the child to turn her gaze to Darby, his whole countenance softened. Keighly thought, with a constricted throat, what a good father her husband would make, provided he lived long enough. "And thank you, too, Uncle Darby."

The ingenuousness of the grin Darby bestowed on his only niece fairly broke Keighly's heart. "You're welcome here anytime, missy. Anytime at all." He raised his gaze to Simon's face. "Think about what you've got, brother."

Simon simply added his own thanks to his daughter's, said good night, and left. Their wagon could be heard rattling away through the thickening twilight.

Manuela had herded Pablo off to their room, so Keighly and Darby were alone in the kitchen.

"You were a little hard on Simon, don't you think?" Keighly asked. "It says a lot, that he wanted to come here and tell you in person that he'd decided to take the marshal's job."

Darby tossed the dregs of his coffee into the sink and set the cup down with a thunk. He folded his arms across his chest, and his gaze was far away. "I wish I'd taken it better, Keighly. All my life I've wanted what I thought about things to matter—especially to Simon. When he finally shows that it does, I lose my head."

Keighly put her arms around him. "All you have to do is go and see Simon and tell him you're on his side. When that's done, you'll both feel better."

He kissed her forehead and changed the subject.

"By the way," he said, "you're a lousy shot."

Keighly laughed. "Thanks," she said.

That night, as every night, they made love. And that night, as every night, it was wonderful, but when Darby slept, satisfied and worn out from a long day of very hard work, Keighly lay sleepless in his arms, afraid to close her eyes.

Afraid of being catapulted back to the twentieth century, or any other time where Darby Elder did not exist.

It struck her, as she lay there, that during the day it was remarkably easy to forget the truth, which was that she might very well be in the nineteenth century on some sort of cosmic sufferance. While the sun was shining, and there was work to do, she barely gave a thought to the tenuous nature of her situation, unless something forced her to consider it. She was too busy living, too busy loving Darby.

Still, Keighly reasoned, as coolly as she could, it was very dangerous to forget. As it was, her other life seemed like a distant memory most of the time, and it wasn't hard to imagine being absorbed into the texture of the nineteenth century and putting everything else out of her mind.

That was a luxury she could not afford, for if she didn't remember, she wouldn't be vigilant. And vigilance was vital, if she and Darby were both to survive the coming months.

After an hour of lying there, wide awake, Keighly got up and left the bedroom, just as she had done the night before. This time, instead of taking refuge to the kitchen, she went to the desk where Darby kept stock lists and various ledgers where investments were recorded. She lit a lamp and rifled the drawers until she found an unused volume, which she appropriated for a journal.

Taking ink and a pen, Keighly opened the appropriated ledger book, dated the top right-hand corner of the first page, and began to write. She started by describing her and Darby's initial encounter, through the mirror in her grandmother's ballroom when she was seven. She described every episode she could remember, in as much detail as possible, and was about to write about falling through the mirror and into Darby's arms when exhaustion finally overtook her and she was forced to put the project away. She brought the journal to the bedroom with her, and slipped it into the drawer in the nightstand.

This time, Darby didn't awaken, but when she got back into bed, he enfolded her in his arms and murmured her name.

"Hold me tightly," she whispered, cuddling close. "Hold me very, very tightly." Then, because she could no longer hold out against it, fear it though she did, Keighly succumbed to a deep sleep.

❧ CHAPTER ❧

11

"I'm not going," Darby announced, even as Keighly fiddled with his string tie the following Sunday morning. Simon was being sworn in as the new marshal, at a casual ceremony to be held in town, after church.

Keighly didn't even pause. "You are," she said. "You gave me your word last night and it's too late to back out now."

"Last night you were—we were—" Darby actually colored slightly. "I agreed under duress," he finished.

"Nevertheless," Keighly responded cheerfully, "you promised." She brushed his shoulders, powerful and taut under the spotless cloth of his best coat.

Darby was frowning as he escorted Keighly outside. Even after he'd helped her into the buggy one of the men had hitched up at her request and climbed into the seat to take the reins, he didn't say anything.

Keighly couldn't bear the silence. "Your refusing to attend the ceremony won't make Simon change his mind about being marshal," she said, as they headed along the rutted, twisting track that would take them to Will and Betsey's place, four miles from their own. Angus would be the only member of the family not to be there, and he was staying away only because he was still too ill to make the journey.

Darby gave Keighly a look of mock sternness and then grinned somewhat sheepishly. "I can't work out, Mrs. Elder, whether you are a good influence on me or a bad one."

"A good one," Keighly assured him confidently, smoothing her skirts and then slipping her arm through his. She'd been working hard on her sculpture for the past few days and had made no more terrifying shifts between centuries, and she was quite content, all things considered.

Darby's expression turned serious again as he gazed, unseeing, at the road. "Doesn't it worry you, Simon serving as marshal? He's all Etta Lee's got, and he's the firstborn. If anything happened to him, what do you suppose it would do to Angus?"

Keighly laid her head against Darby's shoulder for a moment, in an effort to lend some simple comfort. "I don't like the situation, either," she confessed. "But I can understand Simon wanting to do something he considers important. Besides, it isn't our business how he lives his life, is it? I doubt you'd welcome any such interference in yours, Darby Elder."

"He should consider Etta Lee and Angus," Darby insisted.

"Etta Lee would be devastated if Simon was hurt or killed; we all would. But she isn't alone in the world—she has you and me, and Will and Betsey, and her very devoted grandfather. And Simon can't live to please Angus any more than you ever could."

Darby rolled his eyes. "It's a wonder to me that there are so few female lawyers," he said, with fond irony. "God knows, nobody can frame an argument quite like a woman."

Keighly smiled, though any reference to the future always brought an ache to her heart. "I feel duty bound to

175

tell you, Mr. Elder, that in the twentieth century, there will be a great many women practicing law. Also medicine."

Darby was quiet for a long while. The buggy rocked and jostled on its primitive springs and the single horse, a shaggy gray mare from Triple K stock, nickered and tossed its head every now and then.

"Is it a better place?" Darby asked. "The world you came from, I mean."

Keighly couldn't bring herself to lie, even though it might have been kinder. "In many ways, it is, yes."

"Do you ever wish you were back there?"

"No," Keighly said immediately. That was one she didn't need to think about.

"Would you still feel that way if I wasn't here, though?" Darby pressed. This was, evidently, a morning for personal dilemmas and hard questions.

Keighly ran the tip of her tongue over her lips, something she often did when she was thinking. Then, reluctantly, she shook her head. She couldn't make herself speak.

Darby held the reins in one hand and linked the fingers of the other with Keighly's. "If something happens to me," he said, "I want your word that you'll go back."

She swallowed hard. "It isn't like the noon train, Darby," she said, with some difficulty. "I can't just show up at the station, buy a ticket, and get on board."

Darby squeezed her hand. "Isn't there a chance that this is—well—some kind of skill or power, that you just haven't learned to control yet?"

Keighly had never considered the possibility that the process might be in any way voluntary, and she doubted the theory, but it did strike a certain faint note far within her.

"What makes you think that?" she countered.

Darby shrugged. "It seems to me that most things that happen to us are the result of some choice or decision we've made, or some action we've taken, even when they seem like an accident."

Keighly reflected on that until they came within sight of Will and Betsey's sprawling frame house. The wagon was hitched to a team of four horses and as Darby and Keighly approached, the front door flew open and a stream of boys spilled out, calling raucous greetings.

Will was right behind them, dressed up in his best suit. He waved with his hat and then herded his sons toward the wagon, hoisting them up one by one. Betsey stepped outside, dressed in a lovely rose-colored dress and carrying a large basket, which Will took from her and brought to Darby's side of the buggy.

"Betsey made up a picnic," he said, grinning. "You'd better keep it with you, though, or these boys will have it eaten before we get to town."

Darby laughed and tucked the basket behind the seat. Wonderful aromas rose from it. "You ought to feed them once in a while, Will."

"Hell," Will countered, beaming proudly, "they eat more than all the locusts in the Old Testament as it is."

"Will," Betsey called sweetly, from her place beside the Kavanagh wagon, "we'll be late if we dally any longer."

Will lowered his voice to a conspiratorial tone. "I'd just as soon miss church anyhow," he confided. "I don't suppose you could manage a broken axle along the way?"

Darby pulled off his hat and whacked Will with it, laughing again. "The suggestion of an irretrievable sinner if ever I've heard one."

Keighly took the hat—he'd forgotten it wasn't the battered one he wore to break horses and herd cattle evidently—and straightened it. She tried to look missish and prim, though she knew her eyes were sparkling. "A two-hour sermon will be good for both your souls," she said.

Will and Darby groaned in unison.

The church in Redemption was crowded, and Darby caused a stir right away by first ushering Keighly to a seat at the front, then going back to the doorway and taking Tessie by the arm. He half-dragged the black woman up the aisle and pinned her into the pew by taking a seat at the end and stretching his legs.

While Tessie fumed and fussed under her breath, Darby looked smug and teased her with the occasional wink.

Keighly, seated on Tessie's other side, thought she had never loved her husband more.

The sermon was indeed long, though not quite two hours, and by the time it was over, Keighly was feeling smothered. The air in the small church was close and hot, and the pews, made of rough-hewn wood, were hard.

When the final prayer was said, Tessie slammed her drawstring bag into Darby's stomach and pushed past him to trundle down the aisle and out into the sunshine. He followed her, after a mischievous glance at Keighly, and she was right behind him.

Outside, under a specially planted oak tree, her dress dappled with leaf shadows, stood Tessie. For all her show of irritation, her dark eyes glimmered with affection even as she shook a finger under Darby's nose.

"You've just got no sense at all," she scolded. "No sense at all!"

Darby folded his arms and grinned down at her. "Forgive me," he said. "I was overcome by passion."

She swatted him with her bag again, then laughed and looked at Keighly as if seeking an ally. "You gone and married the devil's second cousin, miss," she said.

"Until today, I thought you'd left town without saying good-bye," Darby told his old friend. He was no longer teasing, Keighly could tell, although his manner was still pleasant. "If you're looking for work, you could help Manuela at our place."

"I put up with you long as I'm going to, mister," Tessie said. Then she patted the now-tamed handbag. "I got me a ticket in here. I'm going home to Missouri to live with my sister. Between the money you gave me and her cabin and little piece of land, we'll get by just fine."

"I'm glad for you," Darby said, and leaned forward to kiss her forehead.

The old woman started to protest, then gave up and with a small cry, wrapped her arms around him, and held him tightly for a moment. There were tears in her eyes when she drew back and looked up into his face. "You be careful, Darby Elder. You got a nice wife now, and a real home. You give Mr. Kavanagh a chance, you hear me? It's what your mama wanted."

Darby squeezed her hands, but Keighly noticed that he didn't make any promises. "You were always kind to me, Tessie," he said. "I thank you for it."

Tessie dabbed at her eyes with a wadded handkerchief, plucked from the sleeve of her dress. Then she waved one hand at Darby in tender dismissal, gave Keighly a nod of farewell, and turned to hurry off down the road.

Darby watched her go.

Keighly slipped an arm around his waist. "Know something? I not only love you, Mr. Elder, I like you, too. You're all right."

He looked down at her, kissed the tip of her nose, then turned and squired her back into the milling congregation, many of whom were probably discussing Darby Elder's latest impropriety.

Will collected the picnic basket from the back of Darby's buggy and Betsey spread a blanket in a grassy spot on the church grounds and soon began filling plates for her boys and for Etta Lee. Simon, looking very much the competent lawman, had joined them, using a block of weathered wood for a chair. It was he who waved Darby and Keighly over.

The swearing-in would take place on the front steps of the church, after everyone had consumed their picnic lunches. Simon, according to Betsey, would be expected to make a short speech.

"Why didn't you invite Tessie to come and eat with us?" Betsey demanded of Darby, when the children had gobbled their food and raced off to chase each other all over the churchyard, mingling with a flock of other kids and whooping like a war party.

"She would have refused," Darby answered, with plain regret. He'd taken off his suit coat and hung it over the top rail of the split-rail fence surrounding the church property. He'd shed his tie well before that, and he looked especially good, Keighly thought, in his white collarless shirt and simple vest, black trousers and polished boots. The gunbelt he normally wore was tucked under the seat of the buggy.

Simon had given up his seat for Keighly, while Will brought a wooden crate from the wagon for Betsey to sit on. They held their plates of sliced ham and bean salad and sweet-potato pie in their laps.

"At least you've given the fine folks of Redemption something new to talk about," Betsey said, grinning at Darby with frank approval. It didn't need saying that she was referring to his bringing Tessie to the front of the church to hear the service.

"They've come to expect it of me," he replied.

Keighly had a sense of sweet contentment as she sat there, near this man she cherished, gathered in by these people who had become her family. If only she could hold on to it, make time stop, however briefly, so that she could savor it all a little longer. Memorize the sounds of their voices, the blue-upon-blue of the sky, the scent of the summer grass.

Tears burned in her eyes and, as luck would have it, Darby spotted them instantly.

He dropped to one knee before her, setting his plate aside. "Keighly? What is it, darlin'?"

She sniffled. "I'm just so happy!" she wailed, and at that they all laughed, though fondly.

Will, seated on the edge of the blanket, reached over

180

and slapped Darby on the back. "Congratulations, brother," he said. "I know all the signs, and I think it's safe to say you're going to be a father."

Darby's face was transformed by the idea. "Keighly—is that—is that possible?"

More communal amusement followed that question, and this time Keighly joined in.

"Of course it's possible," she said, wiping her eyes and snuffling even as she laughed. Her period was weeks late, and she had other symptoms, too.

"But do you think it's true?" Darby pressed, his eyes shining. He held one of Keighly's hands in both of his.

She nodded. "Yes," she answered.

At that, Darby got to his feet, bringing Keighly with him. Hands on her waist, he gave a loud shout of celebration and spun her around and around, right in the middle of the church picnic. Keighly clung to his neck and gave herself up to joy, even though she knew it might soon become sorrow.

Simon's swearing-in was a suitably solemn moment, despite Darby and Keighly's capering a few minutes before. When he had accepted the star-shaped badge and promised, with his hand resting on a Bible, to uphold the laws of the state and of the nation to the best of his ability, Simon offered a speech.

It was short and sincere, and when it was over, the citizens of Redemption cheered and tripped over each other to shake his hand. Will and Darby shouted the loudest, and they were the first to offer their congratulations, but Keighly had watched them closely during the ceremony. Their faces, similar in profile, had been grim, and their misgivings plain to see.

Only Betsey and Keighly herself took notice.

"We'd best be getting these children home," Betsey said softly, linking her arm with Will's, when the festivities were calming down. "You go and ask Simon if Etta Lee can spend the night with us, since he'll probably want to stay in town and get settled into his office."

Will nodded and walked away. Darby had already been dispatched to round up his nephews, and he was approaching through the bright afternoon sunshine with one boy squirming and giggling under each arm.

He flung them up into the back of the Kavanagh wagon with an exaggerated grunt of effort. "Now stay put, you polecats," he said, to their delight.

Then he came toward Betsey, dusting his hands together after a job well done. "There're Samuel and Nathan," he said. "I'm afraid Angus and Billy are on the roof of the outhouse. They refuse to come down."

"Maybe they'll fall through," Betsey said, but her eyes were sparkling.

Etta Lee came shyly to Darby's side and tugged at his sleeve. "You could help me into the wagon if you want to, Uncle Darby," she said.

He leaned down, cupped her little face in his hands, and planted a smacking kiss on her forehead. "So I could, princess," he said. "And so I will. Maybe you'll have a civilizing influence on those hooligan cousins of yours." With that, he lifted his niece up to join the boys, but his motions were as gentle as if the child were made of the most gossamer glass.

By the time Darby and Keighly arrived home, twilight was gathering. Darby headed for the barn to see to some chores, and Keighly went into the house, feeling contented and very tired.

Manuela was preparing a light supper—it had been a long time since lunch, but Keighly was still surprised to realize that she was hungry—and Father Ambrose was there, seated at the table.

Keighly liked the man, and greeted him with genuine pleasure.

MY OUTLAW

"How was Simon's swearing-in?" the priest asked, after he'd risen from his chair.

"Fine," Keighly said. She was a little confused, because Father Ambrose had performed her and Darby's wedding ceremony, and yet neither Darby nor any of the other members of his family seemed to be Catholic. "Practically everyone in town must have been there."

The priest smiled, as if he'd read her thoughts, and sat down again. "Simon will be a good marshal, I think. He's strong, and honest, and he has plenty of courage."

Keighly sighed. Now that it was getting dark, she felt uneasy, not only for herself, but for Darby and for Simon and for Angus. For all of them. "Darby and Will are worried," she admitted. She had tacitly offered to help with the cooking, only to have Manuela shake her head, so she joined their visitor at the table.

"I know," Father Ambrose said gently.

Keighly bit her lip because suddenly she needed to cry and she wasn't about to give in to the impulse. Manuela lit a lamp and set it between them without a word.

"My child—" the priest began.

In the middle of his sentence, the door opened and Darby came in.

"Hello, Ambrose," he said cheerfully, going to the bureau, where Manuela had left a basin of water, a bar of soap, and a towel, and beginning to wash his hands.

"Darby," Ambrose replied, with a nod.

Father Ambrose stayed for the meal, and blessed the food before they ate. After the dishes were cleared, Keighly left her husband and the priest discussing the price of cattle to go into the bedroom, undress, wash, and topple into bed.

She didn't hear Darby come to bed, but he was there when she awakened in the night and heard the lonely cry of a wolf or coyote, far off in the distance. The sound made her sad, and she snuggled closer to Darby, her back to his chest, his wild, soft hair tickling her cheek.

Maybe he'd been right that morning in the buggy, she

reflected, when he'd said she might have a choice whether to leave the nineteenth century, or stay. Just in case, Keighly concentrated all her will on a single thought: growing old with Darby Elder.

The following morning, Pablo returned from school at a little after ten, riding Father Ambrose's brown donkey. Keighly was busy with her sculpture, while Manuela did wash nearby. Darby and the other men were on the range, branding cattle.

"Why are you not in school?" Manuela asked sternly, as her son slid down off the donkey's back and tethered it to one end of the clothesline.

"Father Ambrose sent me home," he answered, glancing from his mother's face to Keighly's and back again. "He said to stay put, because there is scarlet fever on one of the homesteads. And he gave me this note for Mr. Elder."

Keighly, who had abandoned the sculpture at Pablo's appearance, took the note the child offered and read it aloud. " 'The Reaneys have scarlet fever. Their place is the one on Dennison Creek. Please send Dr. Bellkin as soon as possible and warn Will and Simon to keep their children at home.' "

Scarlet fever, the disease that was destined to take one of her own children from her one day. Keighly felt sick, and swayed slightly on her feet, one hand pressed to her abdomen in an unconscious, protective gesture. "My God," she whispered, and turned blindly toward the part of the range where she knew Darby was working. "My God."

Manuela caught her, put a firm arm around her waist, and issued a crisp order to her son. "Mr. Elder is there," she said, pointing to the distant glow of a branding fire. "Go and get him."

Pablo untied the donkey and climbed onto its back again, while Manuela guided Keighly into the house.

184

"No medicine," Keighly fretted, thinking of the Reaneys, the first to be struck by scarlet fever. Would there be others? Suppose Etta Lee fell ill, or one or more of Will and Betsey's boys? "What good is getting the doctor when there's no medicine?"

"You must calm yourself," Manuela said, when they reached the front parlor, a room seldom used because their lives were so busy, so full. "It is not good, this worrying."

Keighly sat in the rocking chair, one hand over her mouth, struggling to control her emotions. Manuela was right; getting upset would be a mistake, and yet Keighly wondered how long she could hold back the rising tide of panic she felt.

Presently, Manuela left her. Keighly rocked vigorously, battling hysterical fear, and when she heard a clatter in the kitchen, she knew Darby had come. Before she could rise from the chair, he was in the parlor, striding toward her, covered in dirt and soot and sweat from head to foot.

"I need a promise from you, Keighly," he said, bending before her, putting his hands on the armrests of her chair and stilling her frantic rocking. "You've got to stay right here, with Manuela, no matter what. Will you do that?"

She nodded, somewhat numbly, resisting an urge to grasp one of Darby's hands and cling. "You—you'll be careful?"

"I've had scarlet fever, darlin'," Darby said gently. "I won't get it again."

Keighly tried to think whether she'd been vaccinated against the fever as a child. Some diseases, like smallpox, had been so nearly eradicated in the late twentieth century, at least in the Western world, that inoculations were not longer necessary. Which ones was she, and thus their unborn baby, safe from?

"I love you" was all she said, but she saw by the look in Darby's eyes that it was enough.

She went back to the yard when he'd gone, back to her

sculpture, and worked furiously, desperately, until the sun was going and the muscles in her arms ached with weariness.

At supper time, Darby had still not returned, and Keighly ate the bread and cheese and sliced apples Manuela put before her because she knew she should, but she tasted nothing.

It was past ten when Darby came home, and full dark. He looked tired enough to drop, standing in the yard, when Keighly went out to greet him.

"The Reaneys?" Keighly asked, from the step, where she stood, holding a lantern aloft.

"Five little ones," Darby said quietly. "Four of them gone."

Keighly clapped her free hand over her mouth, but not in time to stifle the moan of despair the announcement had wrung from her.

"The doctor couldn't help?" she asked, after a short and terrible struggle.

"It was too late. And it took me most of the day to find him in the first place. Turns out there are other cases, and the doc already had his hands full dealing with those."

She set the lamp down on the step, started toward him.

"Don't," he said, holding up one hand.

Keighly froze. "But you told me—"

"I told you I've had scarlet fever," Darby interrupted. His voice was at once gentle and absolutely intractable. "But I was in the Reaney cabin after I left Simon's place, and Will's—Doc Bellkin needed help and I was the only one around to lend a hand. I could be carrying the disease, Keighly."

For the thousandth time, Keighly tried to remember her childhood vaccination program, but it was impossible. "H-How will we know?"

"Doc Bellkin said to wait until the epidemic runs its course," Darby answered, and Keighly's heart sank.

She could endure anything, she believed, as long as she

could be with Darby. "Will and Betsey's boys, and Etta Lee—"

"All well, so far," Darby answered. "Betsey's got Etta Lee with her and Will."

Keighly nodded. "I didn't expect this," she said.

"No one did," Darby responded kindly, but he sounded weary enough to drop. "Good night, darlin'. Try to get some rest."

With that, he turned and walked away from her, toward the barn.

Keighly did not expect to sleep that night, but she did, and soundly. Dreamlessly.

In the morning, through the kitchen window, she saw Darby crouched by the cowboys' campfire, drinking coffee from a metal mug. He was close enough that she could make out the strain in his face and the bits of straw clinging to his filthy clothes, and yet she dared not go to him.

The feeling was frighteningly like being on one side of the ballroom mirror, while Darby was on the other.

Keighly went no further than her sculpture, and that was a blessed distraction, keeping her occupied through the long days that followed. At night, when she couldn't sleep, which was often, she worked on the journal, writing out a detailed account of her experience so far.

Word came from the Triple K that Angus was still on the mend, and from Will and Betsey's place that young Samuel had come down with the fever. They'd closed off part of the house and Betsey was nursing the boy herself.

Keighly was wild with anxiety when Darby stood twenty feet from her in the yard and told her the news. She began to sob and hurled her chisels, one by one, into the high grass.

"Stop it," Darby commanded.

"What if he dies?" Keighly cried. "What if Samuel dies? And what about the baby Betsey is carrying?"

"Those are questions I can't answer," Darby said, with

stark, simple honesty. "But whatever happens, Will and Betsey will go on, because that's the kind of people they are. You're not doing anyone any good, Keighly, least of all yourself and our baby, by working up a state."

Keighly knew he was right, but that didn't make it any easier. She was fairly swamped with despair; she had been such a romantic fool, loving the nineteenth century the way she had. She'd overlooked scarlet fever, and small-pox, and diphtheria and a thousand other terrors that lurked here.

"I hate this place," she said woodenly. "I hate it."

For a few moments, Darby's own sorrow lay bare in his face. Then, without a word of either reassurance or reprimand, he turned and walked slowly away, and never once looked back.

❦ CHAPTER ❦
12

The old feeling was back. It seemed to Keighly that she was fading, by degrees, becoming somehow less present with every passing day, less tangible. At times, she looked into the mirror over the bedroom bureau and was half surprised to see her image reflected there.

Day after day, night after night, Darby kept his distance. Keighly missed him savagely, but she knew their forced separation wasn't the reason for the disconcerting sensation that she was slowly vanishing. God knew, she loved the man with every ounce of passion she possessed, but she was a whole person in her own right, with a much-wanted baby growing in her womb, and even the suggestion that she was pining away from yearning would have infuriated her.

For three and a half weeks, scarlet fever raged through Redemption and all the surrounding ranches and homesteads. Then one night Angus himself came to call, driving a smart black surrey pulled by a team of four fine bay horses, with old Doc Bellkin perched beside him on the seat.

Keighly went out into the yard to meet them, not knowing whether to be hopeful or afraid. Ever since she had met Angus Kavanagh, he'd been an invalid, however reluctant, and now here he was in a surrey. Darby, Keighly saw, had come out of the barn, to which he had exiled himself in order to protect Keighly and Manuela and Pablo.

Her heart gave a painful turn at the sight of her husband, keeping his distance like a leper, but she managed a tentative smile for Angus and the doctor.

"If you bring news," she said, "I hope it's good."

The doctor, a middle-aged man with bags under his sorrowful eyes and a sparse thatch of unkempt white hair, looked weary enough to fall out of the surrey into a heap.

"Young Samuel is on the mend," Angus said, making his voice carry, so that Darby could hear, too. "The worst seems to be over now; Doc Bellkin will examine you all to make sure there's no trouble here."

Doc Bellkin climbed carefully down and fetched his medical bag from one of the rear seats. The poor man's fatigue was so evident that Keighly nearly ran over to offer physical support.

"I'll have a look at that young rascal over there, first off," the doctor said, inclining his head toward Darby. "Seems to me he had the fever, though, back when he was in knee-pants." He glanced up at Angus, both for confirmation of the remark and out of concern for a patient. "You going to be all right?"

"A cup of hot coffee with some brandy in it would solve all my problems," Angus said, heartily. Like the doctor, he looked tired, and Keighly couldn't help rushing over and hovering a little while her father-in-law secured the reins to the brake lever and climbed slowly and carefully down to stand beside her. "How are you, Keighly?" he asked. "How is my son?"

She linked her arm with his, casually so he wouldn't think she expected him to lean on her, and ushered him toward the kitchen. Manuela, with her usual silent efficiency, had already put the coffeepot on the stove.

"I—I'm fine," Keighly said, stretching the truth just a

little. How could she explain that she'd been feeling a little transparent lately, and thought her time-travel visa might be expiring? "And I don't know about Darby. We haven't communicated, except to shout things across the yard. Is it your fault he's so stubborn?"

Angus chuckled. "Partly," he said. "His mother, God rest her, had a will like a Roman general."

They proceeded through the kitchen to the parlor. Keighly's thoughts were fragmented, for while she was attentive to Angus, she was also very much aware that, at last, she would hear Darby laugh, feel his arms around her, share their bed with him again.

She blushed and averted her head for a moment, making a great business of sitting down on the horsehair sofa, smoothing and arranging her skirts.

Angus, who walked with the aid of a cane, lowered himself into the rocking chair and emitted a loud sigh. He was an active man, strong and able all his life, and Keighly could see that resigning himself to frail health was difficult.

"Blast this old body of mine," he said. "Should have been me that perished, instead of all those little children."

Keighly's rising happiness was stemmed by the reminder. "But Samuel, and the other boys—"

Angus met her gaze squarely. "Samuel's lost his hearing," he said. "But he's alive. That's the important thing, damn it. The lad's alive."

Tears gathered in Keighly's lower lashes; she blinked them back, sniffled, and raised her head. "How is Betsey?"

"Tuckered out," Angus answered, in his frank, unvarnished way. "She's been looking after Samuel day and night, of course. Even when Will tried to spell her, she wouldn't leave the boy's bedside. She's resting, though, and I've sent Gloria over to help Will with the family."

Keighly dabbed at one eye, and then the other, with the back of one hand. "And as for you, Angus Kavanagh," she began, changing the subject with determined good cheer, "you look as though you might not be planning to leave us after all."

"I thought losing Harmony would kill me," he said gruffly, looking more like a bereaved schoolboy, in that moment, than a tough, experienced rancher well into his sixties. "I guess, in some ways, I wanted to die, so I could go to her. Then I started thinking what she'd say to me, if she was here, and I knew she'd call me an old fool and tell me to straighten up. After that, I just started getting stronger, a little a time."

Keighly saw a movement out of the corner of her eye and noticed Darby standing in the doorway. From the expression on his face, it was plain that he'd heard his father's reference to Harmony, and been touched by it.

"Doc Bellkin wants to see you, darlin'," Darby said to Keighly. His voice, like Angus's, was a bit on the hoarse side. His bright eyes seemed to devour her as she stood.

She rose, crossed to him, gave him her hands. It was so good to touch him again, even if he did need barbering and a good scrubbing.

He kissed her lightly on the mouth, and though he didn't tell her aloud that he'd missed her, his expression was eloquent indeed.

Keighly felt a leap of pleasure, anticipating the moment when they could be alone, and smiled at him. "Entertain your father," she said quietly. "Manuela will bring the coffee in when it's ready."

He nodded and let her hands go, and as she joined the doctor in the kitchen, she heard her husband and father-in-law talking in low voices.

Manuela put coffee and the attendant paraphernalia onto a tray, along with a plate of molasses cookies, and followed Darby. She and Pablo had both been pronounced healthy, and the boy was outside, running wildly about in the sunshine and whooping with the singular joy of freedom after a long confinement.

"Let's have a look at you," Dr. Bellkin said, indicating

192

a chair at the table and putting his stethoscope in place. "Rumor is, you're in the family way."

Keighly was amazed at first, but then she realized that she and Darby had made quite a scene over the news, on the day of Simon's swearing in. It probably hadn't been hard to guess what all the excitement was about.

"Yes," she said. "I believe I am."

The aging physician listened to her heart, looked at her throat, checked her reflexes and her eyes and ears.

"You look a mite tired, Mrs. Elder."

Keighly urged him into a chair and poured him a large mug of coffee from the pot on the back of the stove. She wished she could confide the truth about how she felt, that it was as if she was leaving that world cell by cell, breath by breath, but of course she didn't dare.

"Everybody's been under a strain these past few weeks," she hedged, setting the mug down in front of the doctor. "Especially you."

He sighed and gratefully ladled a hefty dose of sugar into it, never bothering to stir, and when he drank, it was with an appreciative slurping sound that amused Keighly, rather than offending her. "I wouldn't know what to do with a night's rest if I got one," he said presently. He gave a chortle of laughter. "Hell, I haven't slept more than four hours at a time in thirty years."

Keighly thought, for the first time in a long while, of Julian. She wondered what he would think of Dr. Bellkin, and his primitive but sincere ways. No doubt each of them could learn a great deal from the other.

"It's miraculous, how much better Angus seems."

Dr. Bellkin looked at her in silence for a few moments, as if gauging her ability to absorb what he was about to say. And that alone told Keighly all she needed to know, even before he spoke.

"Angus is not so well as he'd like everyone to believe, Mrs. Elder. He is a very sick man." The doctor took another noisy sip of his coffee. "Still," he continued, in

193

good time, "I wouldn't like him to sit at home with a lap rug over his legs. He's had good reason to rally, after all: his family was threatened."

Keighly interlinked her fingers. "We do need him. All of us."

"I know," Dr. Bellkin said. "And he needs those boys of his—all three of them. You want to do your father-in-law a real kindness, Mrs. Elder, you make sure that husband of yours irons some things out with Angus. It's there to do, and they've got to get on with it while there's still time."

Keighly glanced toward the parlor, where she could hear Angus and Darby talking, then back at the doctor. Manuela had returned to the kitchen and was working silently at the sink, peeling potatoes.

"But things have never been better between them—"

"That's where you're wrong," Dr. Bellkin said, with tired resolution. "Darby's treating the old man with kid gloves, because of his bad health, but deep inside he's still mad as a shaved cat. As for Angus, he'd like to throttle Darby for playing the Prodigal Son all these years, wasting time they could have spent together. If Angus passes on before they have it out, it's going to be a bad thing for everybody."

Keighly was overwhelmed, and thrust her fingers through her hair. There were so many worries—the growing conviction that she was destined to go back to the future again, or even just dissolve into oblivion, the desperate fears of Darby's being killed, and the danger of her child being born, only to perish at a young age from scarlet fever.

"I don't know what to do," she said miserably.

The doctor squeezed her hand and smiled. "You've already worked quite a change in this family. Besides, it isn't your task to fix them. You just need to be here, like Betsey is. The main strength of this outfit isn't in muscle, or land, or cattle or money. It's in the womenfolk—you, Mrs. Elder, and Betsey Kavanagh."

194

Keighly was moved, for all her many uncertainties and fears—Darby was still doomed to be shot, as far as she knew, and her child was threatened. In fact, all her children, should she be lucky enough to bear them, here or in the future, would face perils she didn't like to think about. The late twentieth century, after all, was no less threatening than the nineteenth; it was only cleaner and technically more advanced.

"Now," said Dr. Bellkin, when Keighly didn't—couldn't—speak. "I'm going to finish this coffee and take myself home for an hour's nap."

"Won't you stay and have supper?"

"I won't," replied the doctor, cheerfully but firmly, "and neither will Angus, if I have to drag him out of here by his ears."

Keighly laughed at that, and Darby joined in, from the parlor doorway, where he stood gripping the doorjamb on either side with steady, callused hands.

"No need for that, Doc," Darby said. "Angus is ready to leave right now."

Angus stumped up behind his son and edged him subtly aside. "I am indeed. Gloria has promised to send over peach cobbler to go with my evening meal and I won't risk missing it."

At that, a round of good-byes were exchanged, and Angus and the doctor took their leave. Manuela went outside, carrying two metal buckets, and left Keighly and Darby standing in their kitchen, facing each other.

"You need a bath," Keighly managed, after a long time.

Darby chuckled. "I imagine that's what Manuela is about, filling those buckets. Will you wash my back, Mrs. Elder?"

Keighly smiled. "Will you wash mine?" she countered.

Darby looked down at his clothes, and when he raised his head again, his expression was one of almost comical disappointment. "I'll have to fall into the creek at least once before I'll be fit for a regular bathtub," he lamented.

"I expect you'd better get started, then," Keighly said,

"because when that bath is ready, I intend to climb into it, whether you're already there or not."

Darby's Adam's apple moved visibly as he swallowed. He started to say something, stopped himself, and bolted out of the house with hardly more decorum than Pablo had shown, when he'd been turned loose earlier.

Keighly helped Manuela to heat and carry water, at least as much as Manuela would allow her to, and made sure the tub was set squarely in the middle of the bedroom floor. When it was full and steaming and fragrant with the special salts Keighly had sprinkled in, Manuela left and Keighly began stripping off her clothes.

She was down to her drawers and stockings when Darby opened the door and came in. His hair was wet and in attractive disarray, and he'd exchanged his dirty clothes for temporary garb that was only slightly cleaner. Standing just over the threshold and staring at Keighly the way he did, he looked as stricken and awkward as a virgin bridegroom.

"I thought, sometimes, that this night would never come," he confessed, his throat working again as Keighly began to untie the ribbons of her drawers.

"So did I," she answered.

Darby kicked off his boots, one by one, and then began shedding his clothes. His eyes never left Keighly as he peeled away his socks, tossed aside his shirt, stepped out of his trousers. Keighly tried not to look at his erection, but her gaze kept straying back.

"I'm not sure I have the self-control to take my time with this, Mrs. Elder," he said, walking toward her.

She didn't move, didn't speak. She simply watched him.

Reaching the bathtub, Darby stepped into it and stood facing Keighly, his hands resting lightly on her hips. He bent his head to hers and kissed her, softly at first, but with growing command.

Keighly put both arms around his neck and stood on

196

tiptoe, to respond as completely as she could. When the kiss ended at last, she felt as though her muscles and bones had become part of the bathwater. Her body, long denied the completion it craved, would brook no dalliance; she was as fully ready to take Darby inside her as if he'd spent an hour arousing her.

He understood, must have felt the same way.

"Would it hurt you, Keighly," he asked, looking so deep into her eyes that she could feel parts of her melting under the heat of his scrutiny, "if I had you now—right now?"

She could only shake her head. Her throat was thick with emotion, her mind dizzy. The intense physical need was almost painful in its urgency.

With a groan, Darby drew Keighly close and kissed her again, this time with such thoroughness that she was utterly lost. At the same time, he raised her off her feet, his hands grasping her waist, and set her unerringly on his staff.

Keighly put her legs around him and threw her head back with a soft, throaty cry of anguished welcome. He conquered her by inches, despite his earlier assertion that he could not wait long to have her, and she entwined her hands in his hair and took his mouth in a frantic kiss.

The need doubled and redoubled, and neither Darby nor Keighly showed the other so much as a moment's quarter. In the end, Darby got out of the bath, carrying Keighly with him, and pressed her hard against the wall of their bedroom.

"Yes," she gasped insensibly, "yes—"

Darby drove into her, every stroke more powerful than the last, as heedless as she was of the rest of the world. They climaxed at the same time, their cries confined within a desperate kiss, their sleek young bodies moist with exertion.

Somehow, Darby managed to hold them both up until he'd gotten his breath. Then he took Keighly back to the tub and lowered her, and himself, into the cooling water.

They were still joined as they knelt, their foreheads touching. Keighly's heart was pounding, and she laid her palm against Darby's chest and found that his was, too.

In a few moments, Darby drew back, his smile rueful and more than a little shy. "I'm sorry, Keighly."

"For what?" He'd just given her an orgasm that might have been measured on the Richter scale. What could he possibly regret about that?

A slight flush glowed at the base of his neck. "The wall—you're a lady and—"

Keighly smiled up him, tracing his lower lip with the tip of an index finger. "I don't want to be a lady, Darby," she said. "Not when we're making love."

He nibbled at her mouth and, incredibly, she felt him stirring inside her, growing strong and exquisitely hard again. "All the same," he muttered, "I think we'll use the bed this time. There's not so much danger of breaking it."

Keighly laughed, but when Darby kissed his way down the length of her neck and over her collarbone to take her nipple hungrily into his mouth, she gasped. "I'm not so—so sure about that," she replied.

After breakfast, and the morning chores, Darby hitched up the buggy and he and Keighly set out for Will and Betsey's place. Keighly had brought along a small valise, just in case Betsey needed her to stay for a few days and help out with the children and the house. Will did his share—as a husband and father he was definitely ahead of his time—but he had a ranch to run.

When they arrived, Simon was there, his badge pinned to his coat, standing on the veranda smoking a cheroot. He looked thinner than when Keighly had seen him last, and he was pale, but then all of them were probably a little the worse for wear.

He greeted Keighly with a gentlemanly nod and extended a hand to Darby, who responded in kind.

198

MY OUTLAW

"Have you seen Angus?" Darby asked, pausing on the step while Keighly advanced toward the door.

"Yes," Simon answered. "He's been to my place, as well as yours and Will's. He shouldn't be out gallivanting all over the countryside—he isn't fit for it."

Keighly looked back over one shoulder and saw Darby's jawline tighten just as the front door swung open and Betsey spoke.

"Oh, Keighly, it's so good to see you!"

Keighly turned back to greet her sister-in-law, aware that Simon and Darby were arguing now, though they were doing it quietly. Even politely.

Betsey had shadows under her eyes, and the strain of the vigil with Samuel showed plainly in her face and countenance, but she smiled and embraced Keighly with genuine happiness. Keighly returned her hug.

"How are you?"

Betsey pulled her into the house. "I feel like I could sleep for a month," she said. "Of course as soon as I closed my eyes, the boys would dismantle the whole place, board by board. Come and have a cup of tea with me. I've been perishing for the company of another female."

In Betsey's spacious, no-nonsense parlor, Keighly took a seat, as commanded, and waited quietly while her sister-in-law vanished into the kitchen. She'd protested that she was perfectly capable of brewing tea for the both of them, but Betsey wouldn't hear of a guest doing such a thing. Which didn't bode well, Keighly supposed, for her chances of wangling an invitation to stay a few days to cook, clean, and wipe noses.

Before Betsey returned, Samuel came in, clad in flannel pajamas and dragging an old baby blanket. He was perhaps five years old, with Will's golden hair and ingenuous features, and the scarlet fever had left him frightfully pale and rail thin.

Knowing that he couldn't hear, Keighly ached with despair, though she did not allow her sympathy to show in her face. She simply held her arms out to him. He came

199

to her, climbed into her lap, and rested his head against her bosom.

"Simon claims there's a sign language we can learn, and teach to Samuel," Betsey said, when she returned fifteen minutes later and found them still sitting together, in silent, peaceful accord. She sounded as though she was trying to convince herself that everything would be all right, as well as Keighly, and there was a brittle note in her voice that tore at Keighly's heart.

"Yes," Keighly said, stroking Samuel's soft, gossamer hair. They were all fortunate that the child had survived—so many hadn't—but it was still a tragedy that he'd lost his hearing, still something that would need grieving over. Working through.

Betsey began to cry suddenly, softly. "I'm sorry," she sobbed, nearly spilling the tray she carried before managing to set it down on a table. "I'm just so tired—"

Samuel, sensing his mother's distress, looked up with wide eyes.

"Of course you are," Keighly said gently. "Let me stay and help you for a few days, Betsey."

The little boy wriggled off Keighly's lap and ran to his mother, tugging at her skirts until she drew him into her arms and held him tightly for a few moments, reassuring him. Only when he'd retrieved his blanket and gone back to bed did Betsey look at Keighly and shake her head.

"I appreciate your offer, Keighly," she said, "but I've got to refuse it. In the first place, you belong with your own husband, in your own home. And in the second, the sooner we get on with things here, the better off we're all going to be."

Keighly knew better than to argue; the look in Betsey's eyes said she wasn't going to give in and any attempt to persuade her would be viewed as an intrusion. "Simon and Darby are bickering out there on the porch," she said instead, after pouring coffee from Betsey's pretty china pot into a matching cup. "Do you know what it's about?"

"The marshal's job, I imagine. They're never more than

a hairsbreadth from a fist fight anyhow, the three of them, no matter how good a face they put on things."

Keighly knew Will, Simon, and Darby had their differences, serious ones, but she had never thought the peace between them was quite so tenuous as all that. "Why?" she asked, pained. "Why are they so angry with each other?"

Betsey added generous portions of sugar and cream to her coffee and savored a small sip before answering. "I think a lot of it's just got to do with being male, though it's true there's been a lot to be tense about lately. They've all got a share in the blame, though. Simon is real territorial and kind of holier-than-thou, being the eldest and having that fancy education. Will acts easygoing most of the time, but he's sensitive because he knows most people think of Simon as the smart brother and Darby as the daring one, and he wonders where that leaves him. As for Darby, well, you'd know better than I do, but of course he's always regarded himself as an outsider, no matter what Angus or anybody else did or said to convince him otherwise. And he still thinks that, I reckon, in some corner of his mind."

Keighly nodded glumly. "Doc Bellkin told me yesterday that he thinks Angus and Darby still have a lot to settle, too. He also warned me that Angus's recovery might not last."

Before Betsey could reply to that, Will came down the stairs, carrying one of the boys on his back. He frowned as he set the child down—this one was Nathan, Keighly thought—and rushed toward the door.

"Will, what—?" Betsey began, but her husband paid her no mind.

Meanwhile, the low, angry murmur outside had escalated alarmingly.

"Damn it, if you two want to knock each other's heads off, then go out in the orchard or behind the barn!" Will barked. "There are women present, in case you idiots have forgotten, and kids, too!"

Keighly shot to her feet, but Betsey caught her eye and shook her head.

"Don't mix into this, Keighly," she warned. "You'll only delay things if you do that."

"But what if they hurt each other?"

Calmly, without so much as a tremor, Betsey reached out for the coffeepot and refilled her cup. She added the same generous amounts of cream and sugar and stirred with unhurried swirls of the spoon. "Let them," she said simply. "They're grown men. If they haven't any more sense than to black each others' eyes and bloody each others' noses, let them suffer the consequences."

Keighly stared at her sister-in-law in horrified admiration. Betsey's attitude was a practical one, but it couldn't have been easy to arrive at in a world where women were taught that their men's problems were their own, and they were duty bound, as good and loyal wives, to solve those problems or die in the attempt.

Young Angus, the eldest of the Kavanagh boys, burst in through the front door, his blue eyes round, his face radiant with delight. "Mama!" he cried. "Pa's fighting with Uncle Simon and Uncle Darby!"

"Ninnies," Betsey said. "I hope they had the good sense to take off their gunbelts."

Keighly nearly choked on her coffee, and might have bolted for the door to intervene if Betsey hadn't fixed her in place with another look.

"They did," Angus confirmed. "They hung them on the fence. Uncle Simon took off his coat and threw it over a branch."

Betsey merely shook her head.

Some fifteen minutes had passed, by the clock on the parlor mantel, when Will came in, looking battered and sheepish, his lip bleeding and one side of his jaw swollen to twice its normal size.

"You've set a fine example for these boys, Will Kavanagh," Betsey said, without raising her voice. "Don't think for one moment that I'm going to sit up half the night mixing you headache powders and salving your wounds."

Keighly was alarmed by Will's appearance, and could not longer resist going outside to find out what condition Darby was in. He and Simon were bent over the pump in the sideyard, splashing their faces and the backs of their necks with cold water.

Darby had a split lip and bloody knuckles, and Simon's right eye was disappearing into a large, blue-green bruise. They had apparently vented their anger, for although they weren't exactly chummy, neither was the air thrumming with hostility like before.

"What purpose," Keighly began stiffly, "did that serve?"

Darby looked as though the question surprised him. "It made us feel better," he explained. Keighly was still trying to comprehend how that could possibly be the case, when all three of them looked like they'd been thrown into an empty cement mixer on high speed, Simon put his arm around Darby's shoulders and they started toward the house, looking for Will.

❧ CHAPTER ❧

13

Unlike the philosophical Betsey, Keighly could not so easily reconcile herself to the idea that brothers will brawl, now and then—even grown-up ones. She did not say a word to Darby all the way back to their own ranch house, that afternoon, and she found it too painful to look at him, with the cut on his mouth and the open skin on his knuckles.

It was still midafternoon when they arrived, and Keighly noticed that Darby set his teeth slightly as he climbed down from the rig. She hoped he was good and sore. He reached up to help her and their gazes finally met.

Darby's expression was maddeningly unapologetic. "I have work to do, Keighly," he said. "I don't intend to stand here all afternoon waiting for you to get out of the buggy."

She raised her chin slightly. "By all means," she said, "don't hang around. I hardly need your help, do I?"

"You're going to have it," Darby replied. His amber eyes darkened and flashed. He held out one hand.

Keighly glared at it for a moment, then gave in with a sigh and let Darby assist her. "Come inside," she said coolly. "Those cuts need some attention."

He grinned. "Will that get your over your pet, Mrs. Elder?"

"No," Keighly said succinctly. "I am furious with you. You acted like a fool today, and so did both your brothers."

Darby sighed, sounding resigned, and led the way into the house.

There, Pablo was slogging through a chapter of his reading primer at the kitchen table, while Manuela stirred something savory-smelling at the stove.

Pablo gave a low whistle at the sight of Darby's enormous lip. "What happened?" he asked.

"He got into a fight," Keighly said, making slight banging noises as she got the iodine out of the pantry and set it down on the table.

"You must have lost," Pablo remarked, looking at Darby with fascinated sympathy.

Darby laughed. "Oh, I lost all right," he said, glancing at Keighly's annoyed face, "but not in the way one might think."

Manuela put the lid back onto the soup and quietly sent Pablo outside to feed the chickens. When the boy had gone, the housekeeper excused herself and left the room to busy herself in some other part of the house.

"Sit down," Keighly said to her husband. She took clean cloth from a drawer in the side table and shook the brown bottle of iodine.

With a sort of glum good humor, Darby pulled back a chair and sank into it. "I suppose you want me to apologize?" he said.

"I don't care if you do or not." Keighly sat next to him, soaked a corner of the cloth with medicine, and dabbed none too gently at the cut on Darby's lower lip.

He bellowed a swear word, bolted to his feet, and had to be shamed back into the chair with a pointed look.

"Give me your right hand," Keighly said.

Darby did so, but hesitantly. His jaw was clamped

down hard and Keighly knew it was all he could do to keep from closing his eyes. "Do we have to do this?"

"Yes," she answered.

"You're enjoying it," Darby accused, wincing slightly as Keighly treated each of his knuckles to a generous dousing in iodine.

Keighly smiled and gestured for him to present his left hand. "I'm insulted," she said sweetly, "that you would accuse me of such a thing."

Darby gasped when the ministrations continued. "Damn it, Keighly—"

"Yes?"

"That hurts!"

"Pity," Keighly said, with an utter lack of conviction.

Darby glowered, leaning toward her, sort of nursing his most recently treated hand against his middle. "You are beginning to make me mad," he warned.

Keighly raised her eyebrows. "What happens when you get angry?" she asked conversationally. "I mean, at someone besides your own brothers, who are just as ornery as you are?"

He stood and then bent over her, so that his nose as an inch from hers. "I'll tell you what I do," he said. "I yell!"

She batted her lashes. "I'm relieved to hear you won't be using your fists," she said, and her tone, while mild, was also acidic.

Color surged into Darby's handsome face and then receded. "I've never struck a woman in my life!" he hissed.

"That's very reassuring," Keighly answered.

"You are trying to piss me off," Darby complained, "and it's working!"

"Then I think you ought to slam out of here and sulk," she said.

Darby stared at her for a few moments, his breath fanning over her face. Then, suddenly, he laughed. "Damned if you haven't left me without a single option," he said. He dropped to one knee beside her chair, a mischievous supplicant with a fat lip. "Come on, Keighly, forgive me. Please?"

She sighed. He was almost irresistible when he looked like that, but she couldn't let him know just how effective his ingenuousness was, for fear he'd use it whenever he wanted to get around her.

"Of course I'll forgive you," she said. "But I despise violence."

"What happened between my brothers and me today wasn't violence, darlin'," Darby replied. "It was horse-play."

Keighly's mouth twitched at one corner, though she did her best to stay mad. "Did you really lose?" she asked.

Darby smoothed a lock of her hair back from her forehead. "Of course not," he said. "You saw Will and Simon. I'd say I held my own." He rose, with a little grimace. "Now, as much as I'd like to stay inside fostering the peace, I've got work to do. We'll take up your shooting lessons again, right after supper."

Keighly swallowed. She hated looking at guns, let alone aiming and firing them, but in that time and place it was a necessary skill. "Yes," she said. "After supper."

While Darby joined his men on the range, where they were branding, Keighly worked on her sculpture. Although it probably looked shapeless to everyone else, she could clearly see the image of Darby and his horse, Destry, emerging from the stone.

Manuela served stew for supper, with delicious dumplings and canned green beans from the general store. Darby and the men ate outside, because they were all so dirty, and Keighly joined them, seating herself beside her husband on the back step. The ranch hands were in a cheerful state of mind; now that the quarantine was over, it was safe for them to go to town, and they meant to spend the evening at the Blue Garter.

"I thought you closed the saloon down," Keighly said quietly, taking Darby's empty bowl and stacking it with her own.

"I didn't close it," Darby said, unconcerned. "I sold it. Oralee and a few of the others are running it until the new owner gets here."

Keighly looked at the bowls in her hands. "I see." She didn't like knowing the place existed, not because she feared Darby would patronize it, but because of the mirror. Lately, she'd felt as though she were being sucked toward that murky glass, like a star being pulled into a black hole.

When she would have risen to go back inside the house, Darby clasped her wrist gently and prevented it. He spoke in a low voice, and Keighly knew none of the men could hear. "You're afraid," he said.

Keighly nodded. She knew she should tell him, then and there, that she felt herself slipping away from him, from the nineteenth century, but she couldn't. Not yet, not when they'd been apart for so long because of the scarlet fever.

He took the dishes from her. "It's been a long time since you came back, Keighly," he reasoned. "Doesn't it seem likely that you're here for good?"

"I hope so," she said softly.

"Let's get on with those lessons." With that, Darby went into the house. He came out a few minutes later, checking the cylinder of his .45 as he descended the steps.

Keighly waited for him in the yard, the evening breeze tousling her hair. Even though it was an age of violence, she wished poignantly that she'd been born in the nine-teenth century, and need have no fear of leaving it, of leaving this man.

It was no comfort to remind herself that the pictures and newspaper clippings and other such things in that trunk in her house in modern-day Redemption indicated that she would live out her life as a Victorian, for as far as she knew, Darby's fate had not changed. Besides, there was that sensation of being torn away, piece by minute piece.

Keighly's shooting was better that evening—perhaps it

was using the pistol instead of an unwieldy rife—and the evening after, too. Darby said she had a talent for it.

Keighly didn't feel proud.

The next morning, she was chiseling away at the sculpture, and Darby was in the corral, breaking yet another horse to ride, when a vaguely familiar woman with dyed yellow hair, garish makeup, and a tacky ruffled dress of cheap red silk drove a buggy into the yard at top speed.

Darby, who had just been thrown, scrambled over the corral fence and sprinted toward the dusty rig.

Feeling both jealous and alarmed, Keighly put down her tools, rose, and shook the stone dust out of her skirts. Darby and the woman—Keighly now remembered her as one of the more unconventional guests at their wedding—were talking earnestly, although Keighly couldn't hear what they were saying.

Without a word to his wife, Darby bolted back toward the barn.

"I'm Keighly Elder," Keighly said, without a smile, standing beside the buggy and extending an introductory hand to the woman.

"I know" was the reply. "My name's Oralee, and I work at the Blue Garter."

Keighly refrained from saying she might have guessed where Oralee was employed. There was no reason to be unkind. Before she could find the words to ask what business the visitor had, Darby came out of the barn again, leading Destry. He swung up into the saddle, said something to the men in the corral, and trotted over to Keighly.

"What is it?" she asked, shading her eyes from the sun with one hand as she looked up at him. Her heart was in her throat, and her stomach trembled with dread.

"Simon may be in trouble," he answered, and he seemed like a stranger in those moments, so remote and quiet was his tone. "Oralee, you go and tell Will what you've told me."

She nodded. "Be careful," she begged.

Darby glanced at Keighly once more, then rode out.

Keighly took a few steps after him before she realized the futility of trying to catch up with a determined man on horseback. Without saying anything more, Oralee slapped down the reins and started for Will and Betsey's place.

Terrified, Keighly hugged herself. Obviously, there was something dangerous happening in town, and Darby meant to ride right into the middle of it. This might be the day, the horrible day, that her husband would be killed.

Keighly couldn't just stay at home and wait for news, even though most people would have said that was the sane and sensible thing to do. She needed to know what was going on, moment by moment.

With help from Pablo—and ignoring the polite, worried protests of the ranch hands—Keighly saddled a mare she often rode, a dapple-gray called Tillie, and headed for Redemption as fast as the little horse would go. They traveled overland, so as not to encounter Will on the main road; Keighly didn't want to waste so much as a second arguing.

It was more than half an hour before Keighly arrived in town; Tillie had a mind of her own and would only go so fast, no matter how her mistress pleaded, spurred, or threatened.

The main street, usually bustling with wagons and horses and pedestrians, was ominously still and empty. Pale faces peered over the sills of the dirty front windows of the Blue Garter Saloon, and the shades of the assay office and the general store were drawn. The door of the marshal's office, now Simon's domain, stood open, creaking on its hinges as a dry breeze sent it slowly inward.

Keighly's heart was doing double-time. She dismounted and tied Tillie to a hitching rail. Where were Darby and Simon? Where was everyone else?

"Psst!" someone hissed, from the Blue Garter. "Mrs. Elder! Mrs. Elder!"

Keighly started across the street. At that moment, the doors of the bank burst open, and the still air seemed to explode with gunshots.

She dived behind a horse trough, as she'd seen people do in old movies, and crouched there, half sick with fear.

Two men fairly flew out of the bank, both shooting, aiming their pistols at some target overhead, probably on the roof of the building across the street.

Taffeta rustled as someone dashed up to crouch beside Keighly. In a sidelong glance, Keighly saw that it was Oralee, the woman who had come to the ranch in such a panic to fetch Darby.

"Are you loco?" Oralee hissed. "You might have been shot!"

Keighly's attention was back on the action. One of the gunmen fell in the street; the other hesitated, then snatched the saddlebags from his companion's hand and, still firing, made a dash for an alleyway. Within moments, Keighly heard the hammering of a horse's hooves as the outlaw made his escape.

Keighly started to stand, Oralee jerked her back down again.

"You just stay put!" she snapped. "This ain't over until Darby and the marshall say it is!"

Keighly drew a series of deep breaths, trying to think. The fallen bandit still lay in the middle of the road, bleeding in the dirt. She ached to see Darby, to know that he was all right. She stood again and this time Oralee couldn't hold her back.

She hurried down the sidewalk, the heels of her heavy Victorian shoes thumping on the wooden planks. The sound was muffled by the roar of blood in her ears. "Darby," she whispered, frantic, as she ran. "Darby—"

Then, suddenly, she saw him. He was on the lowest part of the roof of Jack Ryerson's law office, holding an inert Simon beneath the arms. Two or three men had materialized on the ground beneath.

"Let him down easy," one of them said, and Keighly, in

a daze, recognized Will, looking up, arms extended. "Real easy, Darby."

"How bad is he hurt?" another man asked.

"One of you get Doc Bellkin!" Darby shouted. His shirt was covered with blood, his hair had come loose from the leather thong that usually bound it. All in all, he looked like a savage, capable of doing murder with his bare hands, and Keighly felt a deeper fear than any she'd known before when he jumped down from the roof and strode purposefully toward the man sprawled, motionless, in the street. He was still carrying his .45.

Keighly held her breath, watching, unable to cry out.

"Jarvis Shingler," Darby said, for the benefit of hidden onlookers, holstering the gun and reaching out to find the pulse at the base of the man's neck. He paused a moment or two, then shook his head.

In the meantime, someone went into the bank to investigate, came out again quickly. "Horace is all right," the man announced. "Just scared, that's all."

Keighly stood grasping one of the rough-hewn hitching rails, watching her husband. Even then, Simon was being carried up the steps to Doc Bellkin's office by four men. He was pale, unmoving, and Keighly felt tears sting her eyes. She didn't want to be Simon's wife, ever, but she certainly hadn't hoped to be spared the decision by his untimely death.

Darby was about to follow the others when he noticed Keighly. Behind him, another man bent to drag Jarvis Shingler's body out of the road and up onto the sidewalk on the opposite side.

"Keighly," Darby said. Her name seemed to scrape against his throat, so hoarsely did he utter it.

She didn't care if he was angry. He was alive, miraculously alive; that was all that mattered. "Are you all right?"

Darby looked down at his bloody shirt. "Yes," he said.

"What happened?" Keighly didn't quite dare approach

him, though she was fairly devouring him with her eyes. She'd been so sure he'd be killed, so terribly sure.

His tone and manner remained distant. "Duke and Jarvis Shingler made up their minds to hold up the bank. Simon got word of it earlier in the day." Darby flung an unreadable look toward Dr. Bellkin's office, where his eldest brother had been taken only moments before. "I guess he wanted to be a hero. If it hadn't been for Oralee, neither Will nor I would have known what a goddamned fool he really is."

Keighly was horrified by what had happened to her brother-in-law, and to Jarvis Shingler, but what mattered most was that Darby hadn't been hurt. "Will he—will Simon die?"

Darby regarded her for a few seconds, his hands on his hips. The stains from the iodine she'd applied to his knuckles were still plainly visible, and the swelling in his lip had gone down only slightly. "I don't know," he said. "There was so much blood, I couldn't tell how bad he was hurt. I don't appreciate your coming here, Keighly. You should have stayed home, where there were people to look after you."

She was already moving toward the doctor's office, unable to bear Darby castigating her for following him to town. Under the circumstances, she hadn't been able to help it. Furthermore, she knew he would have done the same thing, had the situation been reversed.

The two men who had helped Will carry Simon to Dr. Bellkin's office came down the steps, looking grim. Keighly passed them without pausing, with Darby right behind her.

Inside the shadowy office, she found the aged doctor busy stanching the blood from a wound in Simon's shoulder.

"Missed his heart by about an inch and a quarter, I'd guess," the physician said, without looking up.

Simon was mercifully unconscious, and pale as death.

Will stood at the foot of the table on which his brother lay, and his coloring was hardly any better.

"Is there something I can do to help?" Keighly asked. She was speaking to the doctor, but it was her husband who answered.

"Yes," Darby said, with a quietness she wouldn't have dared to defy. "You can sit down in that chair by the door and stay the hell out of the way."

Keighly's throat tightened painfully, and she wanted to cry, but she didn't. It didn't matter just then that her pride was in tatters and her feelings were hurt. Simon might well be fighting for his life, and the last thing the doctor, Will, or Darby needed was to be distracted from what must be done.

Doc Bellkin picked up a gleaming, pronged instrument and began probing Simon's wound. Simon, half awake now, moaned and writhed on the table.

"Hold him still," the doctor said, without raising his eyes from the task. His hands and forearms, like Darby's shirt, were covered in Simon's blood. "I don't have a lot of room to spare in here. Can't have him trying to jump off the table or something."

Immediately, Will laid his hands to Simon's legs, while Darby gripped his brother's arms firmly.

Simon clenched his teeth and gasped, trying to arch his back, but Will and Darby had rendered him virtually immobile.

Bile scalded the back of Keighly's throat as she sat there, unable to look away or even blink, and yet absolutely horrified by what she was seeing.

"Can't you give him something for the pain?" Will demanded once, when it got particularly bad.

"No," Doc Bellkin said matter-of-factly, "I can't. Simon's in shock and if I dosed him with morphine, I might just stop his heart." The doctor had not looked at Keighly once, but he spoke to her some minutes later. "You get the fire going, Mrs. Elder. Make it nice and hot."

Keighly broke out in a sweat all over, afraid to think

why a fire might be needed on a warm summer day, but she did as she was told. Her movements were awkward, and she made several false starts, but Manuela had trained her fairly well, and soon she had a blaze going in the little potbellied stove in the corner.

"Now put a poker in to heat," the doctor commanded.

Keighly swallowed, to keep from throwing up and, screaming inside the whole time, took a poker from the rack beside the stove and shoved it into the flames. Then, trembling, she made her way back to her chair and sat down heavily.

Darby was bent low, still holding Simon in an escapable grasp, but speaking close to his brother's ear. "You remember that time when you took Callie Abbot to the Saturday-night dance and then spent all your time with Susie Masters, and to get back at you, Callie told her pa you were the one who put a stick of dynamite down the Baptists' privy on the fourth of July?"

Simon made a sound that was half an anguished sob and half a chuckle.

"Turned out it was really old Will here?" Darby went on.

"It wasn't either," Will argued, exchanging a desperate, conspiratorial look with the storyteller. "It was you, Darby. You're the one who—"

"And you damn near got yourself horsewhipped for it, remember?" Darby was talking faster now. The tale went on and on, senseless and convoluted and gaining speed with every breath Darby drew.

Doc Bellkin left the examining table to bend down and look into the open belly of the stove, where the poker was beginning to glow, and Keighly wanted to scream, wanted to flee or at least close her eyes, but she couldn't move.

"Go on, Keighly," Darby said, with brisk gentleness, never glancing in her direction. "Get out of here, right now."

She wanted to obey, she wanted to so much, but the

muscles in her legs, like her vocal cords, were frozen with fear.

"Hold him," Doc Bellkin warned, using a wadded towel to grasp the end of the hot poker and pull it from the fire.

Both Darby's face and Will's gleamed with sweat.

"God in heaven," Will murmured.

Darby talked faster still, his voice like a runaway freight train hurtling along shaky track. Keighly stopped trying to listen to what he said, stopped trying to move or even to breathe.

There was a terrible hissing sound, and Simon shrieked once, from the depths of his diaphragm, the sound echoing off the ceiling of the cramped, shoddy little office. The scent of scorched flesh roiled in the air, and Keighly gagged, one hand clasped over her mouth.

Tears slipped down both Darby's and Will's faces, when Simon lay still, gasping.

"It's over now," Darby said to his brother. "It's over."

Dr. Bellkin put the poker away, examined the wound he had just cauterized, and calmly crossed the room to where Keighly sat. He handed her a metal basin, and she promptly retched.

Darby knelt beside her, smoothing back her hair, waiting for the storm of sickness to pass. When it had, he calmly held the basin while she rinsed her mouth with water Will thoughtfully provided.

"All right now?" Darby asked, laying the cool cloth the doctor had brought on the back of her neck.

She started to nod, then gave a great, wailing sob instead.

"Better take Mrs. Elder home," Doc Bellkin said, from somewhere in the pounding blur.

Darby stood and stroked Keighly's hair. "What about Simon?" he asked.

"I mean to keep him here where I can watch him for a day or two," the doctor answered.

MY OUTLAW

"My daughter—" Simon said weakly. Doc Bellkin was carefully applying a dressing to his wound.

"We'll look after her," Will said, in the tone of one swearing a blood oath.

Darby raised Keighly out of her chair and lifted her easily into his arms. She could smell Simon's blood on his shirt, and the stench of cauterized flesh lingered. "Come by my place after you've seen to Etta Lee," he said to Will. "We have some business to take care of, you and I."

Keighly was stricken and dazed, but she felt a fresh stab of horror as she realized what Darby was talking about. One of the Shingler brothers had been killed, but the other had gotten away.

"He shouldn't be too hard to find," Will replied, by way of agreement.

"No," Keighly whispered, but she knew no one was listening.

Darby's horse was tied up in the space between the general store and the law office. He lifted Keighly into the saddle and then mounted behind her, keeping her safe within the strong circle of his arms. The mare was still tethered at the end of the street, where she'd left it, across from the Blue Garter.

A woman in a parrot-green dress came out of the saloon, crossed the street, led Tillie over, and handed the reins up to Darby.

"Thanks, Babe," he said.

Keighly came out of her shock-induced stupor just far enough to mutter, "That had better be her nickname."

Darby gave a low, throaty chuckle, though not surprisingly there wasn't a lot of mirth in the sound. He didn't say anything for a long while, and when he did, his tone was entirely serious. "You could have been killed today," he said.

She let her head fall back against his shoulder, her eyes closed against the afternoon sunshine. "So could you," she replied. "Don't lecture me, Darby. It's bad enough,

217

just knowing what Simon went through. I don't think I could bear being chewed out on top of that."

It seemed that Darby's embrace tightened for just a moment, but Keighly couldn't be sure. He'd been angry with her when he'd first seen her, standing there on the sidewalk in Redemption, and even though he'd had good reason, the cold look in his eyes had hurt her very deeply.

"All right," Darby agreed, and she heard his weariness and his pain, and remembered how he had tried to distract Simon, during Dr. Bellkin's barbaric but probably necessary treatment. "No lectures."

"You were furious with me."

"Yes," he answered bluntly. "Fact is, I would have liked to throttle you."

She closed her eyes, longing to curl up in their bed in a fetal position and sleep too deeply to dream. "I know," she said. "I think that would have hurt less than the look on your face when you saw me."

He bent his head, kissed the side of her neck. "I apologize for that," he said. "I looked at you, and I saw you in my mind, with a bullet in you, bleeding the way Simon was bleeding. Getting mad was all that kept me from falling apart."

Keighly's heart softened, and she began to cry again, softly at first, and then wretchedly. Darby did not try to stop her.

When they arrived home, he eased her down from the horse before dismounting himself. He took Keighly into the house while Manuela stared at his bloody shirt in horror.

"You'll be careful?" Keighly pleaded, as Darby undressed her, like a child, and tucked her into bed in her camisole and drawers. She knew she couldn't stop him from going with Will to hunt down the second bank robber; they would find the man if it took the rest of their lives, if for no other reason than that he'd shot Simon.

Darby kissed her forehead. "Of course I will," he said. "I want to come back to you." With that, he stripped off his soiled shirt and brought another one out of the wardrobe. Mentally, Keighly could tell, he was already far away.

❧ CHAPTER ❧
14

Keighly slept fitfully, tossing and turning, starting awake from terrible dreams that fled like ghosts into the depths of her mind the instant she opened her eyes. In between these nightmares and attacks of restlessness, she lapsed into states of slumber so profound that she might have been in a trance.

She awakened at dawn the following morning, trembling and sick, and climbed resolutely out of bed. She felt no more substantial than an image projected onto a fine mist, but her greatest concern just then was not herself, or even the child she carried. No, as Keighly found fresh underthings and donned a practical calico dress, it was Darby she was fretting about.

Darby who, with Will, had gone after an outlaw named Duke Shingler.

She recalled, as she brushed her teeth and combed her hair, all her husband had told her about the Shingler brothers. They'd been thieves, cold-blooded murderers, believing they had cause to avenge themselves against Darby.

Now, one of them was dead, after a shoot-out on the main street of Redemption, and the surviving brother was bound to be lusting for blood.

MY OUTLAW

Please, she told Darby mentally, as she made her way through the dim house toward the kitchen, *be careful.*

She had breakfast well under way when Manuela came out of the lean-to bedroom, yawning. Seeing Keighly, she smiled warmly, but with concern.

"Are you feeling better, Mrs. Elder?"

"Please call me Keighly."

Manuela looked both pleased and reluctant, but nodded her agreement. Keighly had already pumped water and carried it in, and there was hot coffee brewing on the stove.

"Rain today, I think," Manuela said, standing at one of the windows and gazing outward.

"Yes," Keighly agreed. She'd felt the chill in the air when she went out to the springhouse, had seen the dark clouds suppressing the dawn light. The ranch hands had risen before her, and their cooking fire was already blazing when she left the house. "I was thinking we should have one of the men hitch up the buggy and drive Pablo to school."

Manuela helped herself to coffee and then returned to her vigil at the window. In the distance, lightning streaked across the still-black sky, and thunder seemed to shake the very roof over their heads. "Mr. Elder said to keep him home and give him his lessons here," she said. "No doubt Father Ambrose will come to see how we are, and I will ask him which lessons Pablo should be doing."

Keighly had made enough oatmeal and toasted bread for all of them, and she began setting the table. "What other orders did Mr. Elder leave?" she asked evenly.

Manuela turned to face her. "The men are to stand guard, and you and I are to remain close to the house, no matter what. He made that part very plain."

Keighly sighed but said nothing. She'd hated being confined during the quarantine, and she hated it now, but there was no point in rebelling for rebellion's sake.

She spent the morning bringing her journal up to date. That afternoon, the storm moved on, leaving a land blooming with brilliantly colored desert wildflowers in its wake.

Keighly dutifully practiced her shooting, managing to hit seven bottles out of ten on the first try, then rewarded herself by going back to her sculpture. The work absorbed her so completely that when Pablo came to tell her that supper was ready, she was startled to realize so much time had passed.

The ranch hands ate their roast chicken, mashed potatoes, biscuits, and boiled dandelion greens hungrily, then took themselves off to their camp. They'd moved their bedrolls into the barn, for there were signs that the rain would return.

Keighly would not be dissuaded from doing the dishes, since Manuela had prepared the meal, and afterward the two women sat companionably at the table, while Pablo worked at sums on his slate. Keighly read a book she'd borrowed from Betsey, a comical melodrama in which the heroine suffered the torments of the damned because she'd fallen in love with an Unsuitable Man. Manuela oversaw Pablo's mathematical labors with touching attentiveness, silently forming the names of the numerals with her lips as he wrote them.

It was midnight when Keighly forced herself into the empty bedroom she had shared so happily with Darby, undressed, and put on a nightgown. After washing her teeth, she drew back the covers and slipped between them, straining to turn down the wick in the lamp until the light winked out.

Only then, in the darkness, did she allow herself to weep.

Darby. She could not stop thinking of him, imagining him wounded like Simon, and suffering unbelievable pain or, even worse, sprawled dead on the ground, like Jarvis Shingler. Was he lying in the rain somewhere, even then?

She was exhausted, emotionally and physically, but somehow she slept.

The next morning, Keighly grimly loaded the .38 pistol Darby had left for her, set a row of six bottles on a sawhorse, and picked them off one after another.

Then, because it made her feel as if she was actually doing something to help Darby and Will, she reloaded, aligned a half-dozen cracked fruit jars in place of the bottles, and splintered those, too. It was perversely satisfying to see them fly apart in dusky, greenish shards.

"Was this Darby's idea?" inquired a voice from behind her.

Keighly turned, holding the empty .38 at her side, and saw Father Ambrose standing there, looking for all the world like a medieval monk in his long robes and rope belt. The only thing he lacked was tonsured hair; his was dark and luxuriously thick.

"Yes," she said, but she was not inclined toward a conversation about the pros and cons of firearms. Although Ambrose had been a frequent guest at the ranch, he was still a priest, and priests were often bearers of bad tidings. "Has something happened?"

Ambrose was quick to reassure her. "No, Mrs. Elder. Simon is recovering at the main ranch house; he's in considerable pain but there's no infection and, as Angus says, sometimes it hurts to heal."

"And Angus himself?" Keighly had not forgotten the doctor's warning that her father-in-law was by no means out of danger. "I'm sure all this has been a shock to him."

Ambrose smiled wanly. "It has, of course. But he's been thundering from one end of the house to the other, mad as a singed rattler because he isn't thirty years younger and can't go out and help Will and Darby hunt Shingler down."

Keighly linked her arm companionably with the priest's, tucking the pistol, a not-so-romantic gift from Darby before his departure, into the pocket of her pinafore-style apron. "I know how Angus feels, though obviously it isn't age that presents a problem in my case.

223

No matter what happens, I'd rather be with Darby than here, waiting and wondering."

"Mrs. Kavanagh said essentially the same thing about Will, when I called on her earlier today." He patted her hand. "Tell me, how is Pablo doing with his studies?"

"Manuela sits him down with his slate and schoolbooks every night, and both of us help him as much as we can."

Ambrose sighed. "I'm afraid education is a catch-as-catch-can proposition out here, even in the best of times. I try to keep the mission school going, but it seems there is one problem after another."

Keighly and Father Ambrose sat on the back step, outside the kitchen, because the weather was too brassy-bright to stay inside. Darby's men were busy with the horses, and Manuela was taking down the wash she'd pegged on the line earlier in the day. Pablo, no doubt having spotted his teacher, was conspicuously absent.

"Have you known the Kavanaghs a long time?"

"Ten years," Ambrose replied. "Simon and I went to school together, you see, back in Boston."

"Simon wanted to be a priest?" Keighly asked, astounded.

Ambrose laughed. "No. Simon was born a Presbyterian. My father sent me to read law, hoping I would change my mind about seminary, marry, and give him a flock of grandchildren. He was disappointed."

"But you and Simon remained friends."

"Yes."

Keighly's lower lip trembled; she intertwined her fingers and fixed her gaze on the scene in the corral, where two of Darby's men were attempting to calm a rearing young stallion, just brought in from the range. "I was there, in the doctor's office, when—when—"

"When Simon's wound was cleaned and cauterized?" Ambrose prompted gently. "That must have been awful."

"It was worse for Simon than anyone, of course," Keighly said. "But the smell, the way he cried out—" Her voice drifted away with the breeze.

"Simon told me that Will and Darby got him through it."

"They were so strong," Keighly replied, thick-throated, with a nod and a sniffle. "You should have seen them. Either one of them would have traded places with Simon in a second, if they could have, in order to spare him the ordeal. And these are the same men who had barely finished pummeling each other with their fists in Betsey's orchard."

"Things are complicated, where those three are concerned."

Keighly was silent for a time, scanning the horizon. She was wishing, pure and simple, that Darby would come riding in, in need of bath and barbering, saddle-sore and weary, but whole, well, alive, with the quest for Duke Jarvis behind him forever.

The distance was empty, like some huge reflection of Keighly's own soul.

She longed, suddenly, to confide in Father Ambrose, to tell him about the mirror in the Blue Garter Saloon, her forays through time, her terrible fear of vanishing into that other world, but in the end she did not dare.

"Will you stay to supper?" she said, instead.

Father Ambrose sighed and shook his head. "I've got to get back to the mission," he replied, rising. His gaze had found Keighly's half-finished sculpture, standing just a few feet away, in the yard. He went over to examine it, his smile full of cheerful admiration when he looked at Keighly, who had joined him, hands clasped behind her back. "This is wonderful," he enthused.

Keighly felt shy, as well as frankly pleased. "There are times when I hate myself for ever starting it," she confessed. "Now that it's smaller and a bit more manageable, I'll have some of the men carry it into the parlor. The front windows get the northern light."

"Marvelous," Father Ambrose said. "Perhaps, one day, you will do some small piece for our mission. The Virgin, perhaps, or one of the saints."

Keighly was intrigued by the possibility; talk of her art kept her mind off her problems, as did the act of work itself. "Perhaps," she said.

Ambrose looked chagrined. "I've been presumptuous," he told her. "Everyone will want to buy your sculptures, once this has been seen. I am sorry."

Amused, Keighly folded her arms. "I doubt that you could be described as 'presumptuous,' Father, but you are most definitely a flatterer."

"One of the numerous sins against which I struggle," Ambrose admitted, and although he was grinning, a blush pinkened his suntanned cheeks.

After that, he went into the house to see Pablo, who had been cornered there by Manuela, to view the boy's homework.

Keighly left them to it and went over to the men standing at the corral fence, watching another cowboy attempt to ride that same temperamental stallion they'd been working with earlier. She thought, with a certain smug pride, that they'd best leave the task for when Darby came home.

Her smile vanished. If he came home.

The reminder that he might never return to her, or be brought to her tied up in a shroud made of blankets and draped over his saddle, struck her like a bucketful of mountain spring water.

The man Darby had left in charge, a wiry-looking man with skin like dried chamois hide and wise eyes, greeted her with a touch to the brim of his hat and "Mrs. Elder."

"Hello, Mr. Otis," she said, a little embarrassed by the deference. Almost every night, this man and his five colleagues took their suppers in her kitchen, and yet she didn't know any of their given names. Darby always referred to them by their surnames.

"What can I do for you, ma'am?" Otis asked. However kind he might be, however respectful, Keighly knew that Darby's orders took precedence over any request she might make. If she wanted to leave the ranch unaccompanied, for instance, she would almost certainly meet with no end of polite but intractable resistance.

Keighly turned and pointed toward the statue. "My sculpture," she said. "I'd like it carried into the parlor and set on the heavy table in front of the northern window, please."

Otis smiled, revealing several missing teeth. "We'll miss seeing it in the yard, the boys and me," he told her. "But as soon as I've got two men cleaned up and fit to set foot in a lady's parlor, the job will be done."

Keighly thanked him and went back to the house, where Ambrose was just taking his leave at the back door. Manuela had given him part of the crumbly cinnamon cake she'd made for dessert to take home, and he carried it bundled in a checkered napkin.

When the priest had gone, Keighly hurried into the parlor to set the big oaken table in just the right position, so that she could get maximum exposure to the light when she began working again.

As promised, two of the men hoisted the sculpture off the ground and carried it inside, through the seldom-used front door. Seeing the piece in place, Keighly was glad she had made the decision to bring it in. Manuela was predicting more rain, maybe days of the stuff, and being forced to stay inside, her hands aching to sculpt, would have been unbearable for Keighly.

Supper was a less boisterous affair than it was when Darby was home, even though all the ranch hands were present as usual, and their quiet decorum only made Keighly miss him more.

That night, when the dishes were done and she'd finished reading the borrowed novel, Keighly was more at a loss than ever. It was too dark to work on the sculpture; she'd reached a point where lamplight alone would not be enough. She stood at the darkened parlor window, gazing out over the dark range, full of loneliness and longing.

In those minutes, the pull of the mirror in the Blue Garter Saloon was so strong as to be frightening. Even

227

though she knew better, Keighly considered sneaking out of the house and setting off for town on foot, confronting her mystical nemesis once and for all, perhaps to break its spell.

She would take her pistol from its locked case in the desk drawer, where she'd put it away earlier, make her way to the Blue Garter Saloon, and simply shatter the mirror into splinters. . . .

Keighly shook herself mentally. A fine fantasy, she thought, but someone was bound to stop her before she'd managed to fire six rounds into the wall of glass that was the Blue Garter's pride and joy. Whoever was filling in for Simon would arrest her and throw her into jail, and eventually the hated mirror would be replaced anyway, and quite possibly present the very same threat.

Manuela spoke from the doorway behind her. "Good night, Mrs.—Keighly."

"Good night," Keighly responded, turning to smile at the woman. She and Manuela weren't exactly friends yet—Manuela was too careful for that—but they were making progress.

Manuela retired, carrying her lamp, and the house settled, and then was quiet, as though it had only been waiting for its keeper to find repose before it, too, took its rest.

Keighly turned back to the window, letting her forehead rest against the cool glass, and, as she had done since he rode out, simply waited for Darby to return.

A fire crackled in a small circle of stones, and Darby and Will's bedrolls lay close by it. They were fully dressed, their gunbelts strapped on and their .45s loaded, even when they slept.

Now, Darby assessed the night sky with a scowl. He and Will had been hunting Shingler for the better part of two days and nights. At first, the trail had been hot, but it had dwindled with time, and they hadn't turned up any trace of him for more than twenty-four hours. The whole situation was making him uneasy.

"You don't suppose that s.o.b. would double back, do you?" Will asked. He lay with his hat over his face and his hands behind his head, using his saddle for a pillow. Destry and Will's mount, Shadrach, were hobbled nearby. "Might go after Simon, thinking it was him that shot Jarvis."

Darby sighed. He'd spent many a night sleeping on the ground in his life, and he'd usually been able to quiet his mind by studying the patterns of stars overhead. Marriage had made him soft, he figured, because he missed Keighly so much he couldn't concentrate on constellations; he wanted to lie beside her in their warm, clean bed. He wanted . . .

"It's a possibility," Darby said brusquely, responding to Will's theory. "Simon's safe enough, on the Triple K."

"You worried about Keighly?"

"Hell, yes," Darby admitted. "I've got five good men working for me, but things can always go wrong, and if Duke's got any idea how much I care for Keighly, then she's in danger." He was wide awake, and at the same time as bone-tired as he'd ever been in his life. "What about Betsey and the kids?"

"My men are looking after them," Will said, but he didn't sound satisfied with the arrangement. "Shall we start back tomorrow?" he asked.

Darby threw off his blanket and reached for his boots. "Tonight," he said. "Remember, we're two days out of Redemption."

Will was into his boots and on his feet almost as quickly as Darby. "Surely Shingler wouldn't be fool enough to go back there, with half the town watching for him."

Darby was removing the hobbles from Destry's forelegs. "I rode with Jarvis and Duke," he said, as he flung a saddle blanket onto the animal's back, followed by the

229

saddle itself. "Duke's the eldest—he was protective of Jarvis, even though the two of them fought like a couple of tomcats sealed in a five-gallon drum. He's had one too many neat whiskies, too—part of his brain is probably rotted away."

Will whistled with annoyance, kicked dirt over the campfire, and swung up onto his gelding's back. "Damn it all to hell," he muttered. "If that bastard has been planning this from the first, I'm going to feel like every kind of fool."

"If he's been planning that, brother," Darby replied, reining Destry in a southwesterly direction, toward home, "feeling like fools is going to be the least of our problems."

The storm rolled in at midmorning, forcing Keighly to put aside her sculpting tools because the light was poor. She had barely washed the stone dust from her hands when Mr. Otis knocked at the back door.

He was clad in a slicker and, behind him, Keighly could see the other men, similarly attired and mounted. Thunder rumbled under the low-hanging sky like some sort of cosmic threat, and the wind was rising. In the distance, lightning clawed the ground with jagged gold fingers.

Otis touched his hat brim by way of greeting. "One of the men went out to see to the cattle, ma'am," he said. "They're a little spooked by the weather, and we'd best drive them into that ravine on the Triple K before they stampede and hurt themselves. We'll be back here as soon as we can, but in the meantime, Mrs. Elder, I'll ask you to keep to the house."

Keighly nodded, and two enormous fronts collided overhead with deafening force. The saddled horses in the yard danced and nickered in fear, eyes rolling white, and their riders made no effort to calm them, perhaps knowing it would be futile.

She closed the door and threw the bolt, then went to the

front and did the same. Pablo was afraid of the storm, but sat manfully at the kitchen table, trying to pretend he was enjoying it. Manuela calmly rolled dough for peach-preserve pies.

Keighly paced, unnerved by the thunder and her own worries, which had very little to do with lightning, frightened cattle, or outlaws at large. She lighted all the lamps against the gloom, made coffee, then promptly poured the first cupful down the sink.

Darby had been gone for so long now—three days? Four? She couldn't be sure. She didn't sleep at night, except in five- or ten-minute catnaps, and even though she tried to make herself eat, her throat seemed swollen shut, and she could barely force food past it. All she did with any consistency was work and worry.

It seemed that the torrential rain and the knock at the back door came almost simultaneously. Keighly, sitting in the dark parlor in the rocking chair, felt her heart leap with mingled pleasure and relief.

Of course, Darby had returned, and found the door barred against him. She hurried through the house while the wind howled around its sturdy corners and the rain made a sound like raging fire on the roof.

Keighly drew back the bolt and flung open the door, gasping as the wet, chilly wind buffeted her. The man standing on the step wore a long canvas duster and a sodden hat pulled down low over his face, and Keighly did not stop to think that he was a stranger; all she noticed then was that he wasn't Darby.

"Name's Mitchell," the man said, putting his hand against the door when Keighly would have closed it, at least partially, against the weather. "I'm the new hand over at the Triple K."

Keighly's disappointment still had her off balance, as did her lack of sleep and the days and nights of loneliness and fear just past. "The Triple K?" she echoed. "Is Mr. Kavanagh all right?"

"I'm afraid not, missus," Mr. Mitchell said, easing past Keighly and into the dark kitchen. "That's why I'm here, you see. You're wanted at the big house, if you can get away. Mr. Kavanagh's been taken with the pneumonia. It's this sorry weather, I reckon."

Keighly, fully dressed, was already taking her hooded cloak down from the row of pegs beside the door. "Will you please saddle the gray mare you'll find in the barn while I gather my things and write a note to let Manuela know where I've gone?"

"No need," Mr. Mitchell said politely, still standing in the open doorway, letting in the rain and leaving mud on the floor. "I've brought a buggy."

"I'm sure it's too muddy for such a small rig," Keighly began. "Surely we'd make better time on horseback."

"The roads are fine," Mitchell insisted. He looked around. "I expected to find guards here, like we've got over at the Triple K. Where is everybody?"

"Our cattle were frightened by the lightning," Keighly answered distractedly, as she scrawled a quick note on Pablo's school slate. "They had to be driven out of the open, into a more sheltered area."

"Best hurry, ma'am. Mr. Kavanagh was in a bad way when I left, and he asked for you."

Keighly steeled herself to lose Angus, whom she had begun to think of as a father. "Has someone gone for the doctor?"

"Oh, yes, ma'am" was the hasty answer. In the light of the lantern she'd lit to write Manuela's note, Keighly saw that Mitchell was handsome, in a too-boyish sort of way. "The doctor ought to get there just about the time we do. I imagine he'll appreciate having you around to lend a hand."

Keighly raised the hood of her cloak and walked bravely out into the downpour. There seemed to be no air to breathe, only water, and for one terrible moment she thought she would actually drown.

Mr. Mitchell took her arm and hustled her through the

wet grass, and she could see so little that she wondered how they would find their way to the Triple K, where Angus lay, fevered and perhaps dying.

There was no buggy, only a single horse, shuddering in the rain.

Keighly stopped, dug in her heels, and tried to pull her arm free of Mitchell's hold. "Let me go!" she yelled, and she knew the man standing beside her could barely hear her for the wind. There was no hope that Manuela would, far away and behind the thick walls of the log house. "Who are you?"

He shoved a small pistol, perhaps a derringer, under her ribs. "Don't you know?" he shouted back. "Think about it, Mrs. Darby Elder. I believe your husband might have told you a few things about me."

Keighly would have struggled under other circumstances, but the gun ruled out that idea right away. Not only would she be killed if the pistol went off, but so would the precious child she carried.

Duke Shingler, she thought miserably. God in heaven, what an idiot she'd been, opening the door that way, believing his story, letting him into the house. She was just lucky he hadn't murdered all of them, Pablo and Manuela as well as herself.

She let him hoist her onto the horse, sat rigid while he climbed up behind her and, with one hand, unwrapped the reins from around the saddlehorn. The animal took some prodding to move, wet and cold as it was, but a few ferocious jabs of Shingler's boot heels sent it lunging into the darkness.

As they rode, Keighly tried to console herself with the one bright spot in the whole situation: Angus wasn't dying, that had been a lie.

She wondered, with shock-induced calm, if Shingler meant to rape her, as well as kill her. She had no doubt at all that he had taken her as a tool of revenge against Darby, and he would almost certainly use her as bait, in order to draw his old enemy into some inescapable trap.

That was the worst thing of all, knowing that she herself might be the instrument of Darby's destruction. She, whose love for him could not be contained within a single lifetime, or even an eternity, was probably the unwilling siren destined to lure Darby onto the shoals.

She had known, somehow, that it would end like this.

The horse labored through the mud and over the slippery grass, and the rain did not abate. Keighly was soaked to the skin, and she didn't care. A blaze had been kindled within her at some point in the ordeal; it was burning away the weakening sensation she'd endured for weeks, and leaving a tempered determination in its place.

She wasn't surprised, although she supposed she should have been, when instead of heading for some hideout in the hills, Shingler chose to ride right into the center of town instead. The place was battened down against the storm; there were no lights in any of the windows, no horses or wagons in the road.

Shingler reined in his mount in front of the Blue Garter Saloon and jumped deftly to the ground, then held up one hand for Keighly. His teeth flashed in a grin, and she felt a fresh surge of fear.

"Come along, Mrs. Elder," he said, lifting her to the ground. "We have to get you out of those wet clothes, don't we?"

❧ CHAPTER ❧

15

Dr. Julian Drury could not stay away from Redemption, Nevada, even though he was certain now that he no longer loved Keighly Barrow. Time and distance had given him a measure of perspective, and now he knew she'd been right to put an end to their relationship.

Still, something was obviously amiss. He hadn't been able to reach her by telephone, and none of her friends in L.A. had heard from her, nor had Molly and Peter, the college students who worked with her at the gallery. While Keighly might have avoided contacting him, because of the breakup, it wasn't at all like her to leave everyone else in her life high and dry as well.

As busy as Julian was with his practice, and as determined to get on with his life, he had not been able to put the situation out of his mind for more than a few moments at a time.

He supposed it was possible—likely, even—that Keighly had met someone else. If she had gone off with another man, of her own free will, all well and good. He wished her every happiness. But she might have been kidnapped, even murdered; cases like that were in the headlines and on the evening news with grim regularity.

So, with his stomach in knots, Julian flew to Las Vegas on a hot autumn day, rented a car, and drove to Redemption, where he went straight to Keighly's house. The renovations were finished, he gathered, after standing in a flowerbed and peering into one of the rear windows, but there was no sign that anyone lived within those stately walls.

"You lookin' for somebody, mister?"

Julian started at the childish voice and turned to see a boy standing behind him, about ten years old, with freckles and glossy, mud-brown hair. "Yes, as a matter of fact," he replied. He made it a practice to speak to children in the same tone he used with adults; as a pediatric surgeon, he genuinely liked them and had great respect their resilience. "I'm Dr. Drury, a friend of Keighly Barrow's. Have you seen her lately?"

The boy shook his head, watching Julian intently. Keeping his distance. Strangers were an oddity in a small town, and suspect—as they should be. "Tim Felder did, when he was putting up the drywall. Said you could look right through her."

Julian was the least superstitious of men, but he felt something quiver and unfurl in the pit of his stomach all the same. "That's probably nonsense, wouldn't you say?" he asked, tucking his hands into the pockets of his tailor-made slacks. With them, he wore loafers and a blue-and-white pin-striped shirt, open at the throat. "People aren't transparent, after all. What's your name?"

"Bobby," the lad answered, then quickly amended it to "Bob."

Julian's alarm heightened subtly, not because of the boy, but because he was remembering an impression he'd often had of Keighly—that she was somehow absent, even when she was beside him. That he'd somehow *created* her, like some half-imaginary playmate, not by any godlike ability, but because he'd needed and wanted her so much.

He knew now that he'd needed and wanted her for all

the wrong reasons. Keighly, the dreamy one of the pair, had wised up first.

"Well, Bob," Julian said, as evenly as he could, "I'm going inside and have a look around."

"You got a key?"

In spite of his worries, which were looming larger by the second, Julian smiled at Bobby's practicality. "I know where Ms. Barrow usually hides them," he replied. Then he turned and headed toward the back porch.

True to form, Keighly had left the shiny new keys in the tray of a flowerpot. Dead geraniums leaned over the pot's rim, brown and decaying.

Julian shook his head as he opened the door. How many times had he asked her, begged her, to be more careful?

Inside, the large house seemed to thrum with something more than silence and less than sound. Julian felt his heartbeat quicken, as though he might round a corner at any moment and find Keighly standing there—or wafting by, like a ghost. Unseeing, unhearing . . .

God, he thought. *Don't let her be dead. And if she is, let her not have suffered.*

"Keighly?" he called.

There was no answer; he had hoped for one, of course, but not really expected to get it.

Methodically, for it was Julian's nature to be methodical, he began to search the house. He started in the cellar and worked his way through every room between there and the attic.

He found no sign of Keighly, though her clothes were still in the closet of an upstairs bedroom, and there was a trunk in the study, full of musty remnants of some ancestor. In that same room, a magnificent sculpture of a man on a running horse graced the mantel top, and Julian was somehow stricken at the sight of it.

Keighly had been sculpting again—the style was unmistakably hers—and the most profound, moving love pulsed in every curve and crevice of the piece. It was only when Julian took a closer look, and actually touched the statue, that he realized it couldn't possibly be Keighly's work. The form was time-smoothed and mellow in color—only a great many years could have produced such a distinctive patina. Raw stone would have been just that—raw.

Frowning, Julian turned away from the piece and stared, unseeing, at the trunk. It was then that he heard the sound from the ballroom—a place he had already explored—just the faintest stirring of untuned harp strings and a tinkling of crystal, probably from the chandelier.

"Keighly?" he called, for perhaps the dozenth time, and scrambled toward the ballroom with uncharacteristic awkwardness.

He saw her just as he reached the threshold—saw her and, at the same time, did *not* see her.

Keighly. She was standing in the center of the room, near the ancient harp. She wore a Victorian-style dress, calico he supposed, with a cape over that, and she was as wet as if she'd just been baptized in a river.

Julian could see through her as clearly as if she were only an image on a photographic negative. She did not seem to be aware of him; her chin was high and her eyes flashed with temper, despite the bedraggled state of her clothes and hair. She was looking at someone with utter hatred, although there was no hint of another person in the room.

"Keighly," Julian whispered.

She didn't respond. Her hair was longer than it had been when he'd seen her last, tumbling down her straight back in wet curls.

"Keighly," Julian said again, and realized he was weeping. He had no doubt that he was really seeing her— he was a man who trusted his own senses, and they had never failed him at any time. He wasn't prone to hallucinations or fancies, nor was he one to see ghosts.

238

Until now, of course.

His worst fear was confirmed as he stood there, staring, trying to assimilate the evidence his brain could not deny. Keighly was dead, and for some reason she was haunting this house. Or was she haunting him?

"Oh, God," Julian sobbed, struggling to regain his composure. He started toward her, stopped. *"Keighly,"* he pleaded, once again, but she didn't look at him, didn't hear.

He simply stood staring and, finally, she vanished in the proverbial blink of an eye.

Julian roused himself, went into the guest bathroom on the ground floor, and splashed his face with cold water. That done, he walked out to the rental car, fetched his medical bag and his valise, and returned to the house. He shaved and showered and, by the time he'd done those things, he was composed again.

Calm, reasonable, sensible.

Julian picked up the telephone and ordered a pizza for dinner. Then, resolute, he drew a comfortable chair into the ballroom and sat down to keep his personal vigil.

He wasn't going anywhere until he understood what had happened to Keighly.

The interior of the Blue Garter was as dark and clammy as a tomb. Keighly did her best not to shiver in her rain-soaked dress and cloak while the outlaw lighted first one lantern, then another.

"Where is everyone?" she asked, glancing up at the shadowy second story, where various prostitutes supposedly plied their trade.

Duke grinned. It threw Keighly that he was so good-looking; she wouldn't have expected a man with a soul as vile as his to resemble an overgrown choirboy, but he did. "Oh, the girls are here, all right—the ones that didn't move on after Darby sold the place, that is. It's just that they know better than to interfere."

Bile burned the back of Keighly's throat. Oralee hadn't minded interfering the day of the bank robbery and Simon's shooting; she'd rushed out of the Blue Garter and tried, in her own way, to protect Keighly.

Was Oralee all right, or had Duke Shingler silenced her and the others in some terrible way?

He strolled behind the bar and poured himself a drink from one of the array of bottles lined up on a shelf behind it. "I believe I suggested that you get out of those wet clothes, Mrs. Elder," he said.

Keighly had never hated anyone before, but in those moments she truly believed she hated Duke Shingler. He'd shot Simon, and he planned to kill Darby, as well. She was damned if he'd have the pleasure of humiliating her in the bargain.

"Go to hell, Mr. Shingler," she said, putting a slight, mocking emphasis on the 'Mr.'

A door opened and closed upstairs; both Keighly and Duke looked up.

"You mess in this," Duke called out, "and I'll kill every last one of you. Won't make no never mind to me."

Silence.

Keighly closed her eyes for a moment and prayed that whoever had made that sound had the courage to help her. All it would take would be a moment's distraction, and she could hide in the shadows, find a way to defend herself or sneak out of the saloon.

Duke savored a few sips of his drink, obviously thinking. His .45 lay on the bar, a gleaming evil. Keighly yearned to close her hands around it; she was a good shot, thanks to all her practicing. And hadn't Darby himself said she had a talent?

"On second thought," he shouted to the women upstairs, "one of you toss down a dress. I don't want my prize here to take a chill and die before I get any use out of her."

Less than a minute passed—Keighly measured it by her own loud heartbeat—and then a blue silk dress, seemingly constructed mostly of ruffles, floated down from the ceiling to land, billowing, on a pool table.

Shingler picked up the .45 and gestured with the long barrel. "Put that on," he said. "Right now."

"You'll have to shoot me first," Keighly said. She wasn't at all sure he wouldn't do it, but at that point she didn't care. Behind her loomed the mirror, a thin veil between one century and the next, but she didn't consider trying to escape through it.

The outlaw chuckled, set his glass down with a hard thump, and poured more whiskey. "If you think I wouldn't put a bullet in a woman," he said, "you don't know as much about me as I thought. Step behind the piano if that's what you have to do, but get rid of those wet clothes."

Keighly figured the chance to change with something to shield her was probably going to be the only stroke of luck she got all night, so she might as well make use of it. She did as she was told, terrified all the while that Duke would come and drag her out, stark naked, but he was still behind the bar when she'd exchanged her own things for the blue silk.

The bodice of the gown was too tight, the armpits were stained, and the ruffled skirts were limp and frayed, but Duke seemed pleased by the picture she presented.

"You know, that was always one thing about Darby—he had fine taste in women. Oh, yes—he'll come after you, all right."

Keighly drew a deep breath, released it slowly. Basic stress management. "He won't," she said. "He's probably miles away, chasing after you."

Duke laughed and shook his head. "No, Mrs. Elder. Darby might have tracked me for a day or two, but when the trail vanished, he started back here." He paused, took more whisky. "No, ma'am. He'll be here. Probably before sunrise."

"He'll go to the ranch first."

Shingler smiled indulgently. "You're wrong," he said

confidently. "The game started right here, in this saloon, and this is where it has to end. Darby knows that as well as I do."

"You don't think he's stupid enough to walk into this place and let you shoot him?" Keighly retorted, placing her hands on her hips. She was hardly any warmer in the borrowed dress than she had been in her rain-soaked one, but she supposed that was because of the fear. And the neckline.

"I think he'd do anything if he thought it would give you a chance to survive," Shingler replied. "Why don't you come on over here and have some whisky with me? Might warm you up."

"Thanks," Keighly said, operating on bravado and desperation, "but no thanks. Was it you who shot Darby's brother Simon, or was it your brother?"

It had been a mistake to mention Jarvis Shingler, the dead man. Duke's face contorted for a moment, and his hand clenched convulsively on the handle of the .45.

"It was me," he sneered. "I was aiming for Elder, but I missed."

Keighly's heart thundered in her ears. She knew it probably wasn't safe to push Shingler, and yet some strange, strong instinct compelled her to do it. "Darby didn't miss, though, did he?" she asked softly. "He shot Jarvis through the heart."

A terrible, hoarse sob, made up of fury as well as sorrow, erupted from Duke's throat. "Shut up!" he roared, pointing the .45 in Keighly's direction.

Fire burst from the barrel, and the report was loud enough to scare a corpse out of a chalk outline. Keighly waited to be struck—the unseen bullet seemed to cross the room in slow motion—but instead a bottle on the poker table beside her splintered into a glittering fragments, and a slow stain spread over the faded felt. No sound indicated that the mirror had been hit.

Keighly didn't speak. She couldn't have, even if she'd dared.

MY OUTLAW

"You're going to drink with me," Duke said, suddenly and frighteningly calm. He sheathed the .45 in its holster, picked up the glass and what remained of the whisky he'd appropriated, and started toward her. "Have a seat at that table, there." He pointed with the bottle. "No, wait. You can sit on my lap."

Keighly closed her eyes briefly. Her fear was rising, but so was the feeling of strength that had come over her earlier, when she first realized that she, Darby, and their unborn baby were all in terrible danger.

There was a chance, she thought, just the merest hint of a chance, that if she did as Shingler wanted, she could get the .45 from his holster. The drunker he became, the better her opportunities would be.

He hauled back a chair and sank onto it, his eyes mocking Keighly, challenging her to resist his command. He patted one thigh.

Keighly wet her lips with the tip of her tongue, so filled with revulsion that she could barely think, let alone move, and made herself approach him, made herself stand beside his chair.

Shingler took her wrist in a painful grasp and yanked her down onto his lap. "Did Darby ever tell you that he hooked up with Jarvis and me right here in this saloon, sugar? Oh, his old mama, she didn't like that one bit. Told him we weren't fit to ride with. Can you imagine that? A whore's whelp, too good for us? Hell, she was never even married, was Harmony—Elder was just a made-up name."

Keighly wanted Darby to be far away, yearned for it, but some sense told her that he was nearby and getting closer by the moment. Duke's trap was going to spring.

"I'm talking to you," Duke scolded.

"Yes," Keighly said quietly, and with hard-won dignity. Elder might be a "made-up" name, but it was hers, and she was proud of it. "Darby told me he met you here."

Duke filled his glass. How many drinks had he put away by now? Five, six? Keighly had lost count, but it seemed reasonable to hope that his reflexes were at least starting to slow down.

"Worst mistake of my life, taking that sidewinder in the way I did. 'Fore he killed Jarvis—couple of years back— old Darby sold us out to the law. After all we did for him, he helped them bring us in." Duke's glazed eyes glittered ominously, fixed, for the moment, on something terrible and far away. Then he smiled, and that was even more frightening. "Course, we had friends, Jarvis and me, and they met us along the road, 'tween Virginia City, where we was tried, and the state prison. From that day to this, we was free."

"They murdered the men assigned to guard you," Keighly said evenly.

Duke nodded, threw back another drink, and poured more. This time, he held the glass to Keighly's lips. "Drink," he ordered.

"Sorry," Keighly said. Out of the corner of her eye, she saw a flicker of shadow, and the fine hairs on her nape stood up. "I took the pledge."

Duke laughed, and it was a horrible sound. "You are one cussed female," he said. "Time somebody straightened you out."

Keighly lunged for the .45 in that moment, hoping to disarm him before he could draw, but he was too quick for her, and a whole lot soberer than she'd dared to hope. He flung her to the floor with a hard motion of his arm and, in almost in the same moment, got to his feet and whirled, the pistol steady in his hand.

Darby had probably entered the saloon by a rear entrance, and now he stood a few feet from the mirror, as wet with rain as Keighly had been earlier.

"Mistake," he said to Shingler, in a voice as cold as a tombstone in winter, and though he didn't so much as look at Keighly, all three of them knew what he meant. He had seen the outlaw hurl his wife to the floor.

Keighly didn't try to rise. She sat with her hands behind her in the filthy sawdust, like a broad jumper who's just

244

made a landing, her gaze fixed on her husband. His pistol was still in its holster, on his hip, but he held a rifle in both hands, and his right index finger was already looped through the trigger guard.

"No," Keighly said. The word seemed to echo, as though she'd shouted it into a tunnel.

Duke kicked at her, and that was when the world came apart.

Keighly dove forward, both arms flung out, in an attempt to throw Shingler off balance before he could shoot Darby, and missed completely. In the same moment, Darby fired, and as Duke Shingler fell, his .45 went off.

Before Keighly looked, she knew.

Darby had been hit.

Keighly screamed and scrambled toward her husband.

A crimson pattern of blood marked the front of Darby's shirt as he toppled backward, into the mirror. Through the glass and into the darkness on the other side.

"Darby!" Keighly shrieked, trying to follow, but the mirror, though badly cracked, was solid and impenetrable.

Both hands pressed to the cool, uneven surface, her dress covered in Duke Shingler's blood, Keighly slid slowly to her knees, sobbing and screaming at the same time.

Stunned, Julian Drury watched as the mirror, which had turned itself into an violent old West tableau only moments before, buckled like crystal, bubbling still-fluid from a glassblower's pipe, and then spilled inward in a shower of tinkling splinters. The cowboy, the man Keighly had tried so desperately to save, landed on the dusty marble floor at Julian's feet, and the looking glass was suddenly flat again, cracked but otherwise intact.

Keighly was on the other side, wearing a bloodstained dress and screaming soundlessly, both hands pressed to what remained of the reflective surface. The expression on her face was one of the purest agony, and it so twisted Julian's heart, watching her crumple to the floor, that, for a moment, he was actually breathless. Ever the doctor, he had automatically squatted beside the fallen man, who was bleeding copiously from a wound Julian had yet to locate, and his hands were groping for the source of the hot crimson flow even as he watched Keighly fade, by degrees, into nothing more than cracks and slivers and bits of black lead underlying the mirror.

"So she loves you, does she?" Julian inquired of the unconscious gunslinger he was attending. "Well, that explains everything, doesn't it? And, at the same time, nothing at all."

Hastily, Julian examined his patient. Then, after applying pressure to slow the bleeding, he dragged over the cot and hoisted the man onto it.

Once he'd settled the inert form there, Julian plucked his cell phone from his shirt pocket with bloody fingers and dialed 911. At some point he would have to explain who the man was and where he had come from, but there was no time to work that out now.

"Julian Drury, here," he said briskly, holding the phone between his ear and his shoulder while he rolled up his shirtsleeves with swift, practiced motions. "I'm a doctor and I'm at—hell, I don't know the address—it's Keighly Barrow's place. A man has been shot."

He'd forgotten how small the town was.

"I'm sorry, Doctor," said the woman on the other end of the line, "but we don't have an ambulance here. I'll send Dan Ferris over right away; he's the acting sheriff."

"Tell him to hurry," Julian barked, holding the phone against his ear with his shoulder because he needed both hands to stem the cowboy's bleeding. There was every chance the bullet had struck a main artery. "And call Las Vegas for a helicopter. This man is half dead already!"

"Did you shoot him, sir?"

"No," Julian said, looking down at the man who had

supplanted him in Keighly's affections. He was ghost-pale, whoever he was, and mercifully still unconscious. "Damn it, get off the line and get me some help now!"

"Are you armed, sir?"

Julian uttered a curse. "No," he said. "I am not armed." He disconnected the call with the tip of one bloodied thumb and tossed the telephone aside. It went clattering over the marble floor. "Hold on, cowboy. Hold on."

A gasp in the doorway made Julian turn his head.

He saw a dark-haired woman standing there, wearing bluejeans, a white T-shirt, and a denim jacket. *Amazing,* he thought, *how much you notice when you're up to your elbows in blood and gore.*

"Hand me my bag," Julian snapped. "It's right there, beside that chair."

She obeyed him. "Who are you? What—what happened here?"

Julian held a spouting artery shut with his right thumb and index finger while he plundered the bag with the other hand. "My name is Julian Drury. As for what happened, you wouldn't believe me if I told you," he said. He'd gotten a clamp out of its sterile packet and fitted it to the artery, and the bleeding slowed. "Go and find some blankets," he said. "And a pillow."

She came back with the requested items at the same time that the erstwhile sheriff burst in and flipped on the overhead lights, half blinding Julian.

"Good God," he bellowed. "What's going on here?"

Julian sighed inwardly. He was still pretty busy, and it would take the rescue people a while to fly up from Las Vegas—if they had been summoned in the first place.

"There's been a shooting," he said tersely. "Obviously."

"Where's the gun?" the sheriff demanded.

"Oh, for God's sake," snapped the woman, "can't you worry about that later?"

"No, Miss Stephens," the lawman said, squatting down

247

to watch Julian at frantic work. "It's my job to worry about it right now."

"Did that idiot dispatcher of yours send for a 'copter?" Julian asked.

"Yes," replied Dan Ferris. "That idiot, who is also my wife, put a call through right after you hung up. They're on their way."

The arrival of the emergency medical team was dramatic. They landed just down the street, on the high-school football field, and were met by the helpful Ms. Stephens, who led them back to Keighly's house and the waiting patient.

"What's his name?" Ferris asked, as the cowboy was hoisted onto a litter, hooked up to a portable IV, and whisked away.

Julian started to follow, and was stopped by Ferris.

"They'll take care of him," he said. He was a burly man, with a good face and a full head of red hair, just beginning to go gray. "What's his name?"

"I don't know," Julian said.

"Darby Elder," Ms. Stephens said, in an odd, musing tone.

From there, they went to the police station.

People streamed down the stairs of the saloon, in through the door, bringing light and noise, but Keighly remained slumped in front of the mirror, her temple resting against cracked glass, her palms stinging with splinters.

Women, clad in once-bright dressing gowns and wrappers with wilting feather trims, clustered around her, put her into a chair. She had no conception of time passing, but presently Will appeared, crouching before her, and the lamplight turned to the muted, dusty dazzle of sunshine gone astray in a dark place.

Gently, he removed the tiny shards of glass from her palms, one by one, and applied some kind of antiseptic

248

that made them burn. Something in his manner must have kept everyone else at bay, for Keighly was conscious of a clear circle of space around them.

"Tell me what happened," her brother-in-law said gently, wrapping her palms in clean bandages, which he secured with small knots. "Where is Darby?"

Keighly swallowed. "That man——Duke Shingler——he shot him." She didn't look, but she was aware of the body, and the murmurs of those who were there to gather it up onto a litter and carry it away.

"So Darby was wounded when he left here," Will prompted evenly. Carefully.

She raised her head, full of misery, and gazed deep into his kind, intelligent eyes. She could never explain this to him, or to anyone else in Redemption. There was simply no one who would understand.

"Yes," she said, though she was sure Darby was dead. "He's gone."

Will was plainly puzzled by her answer, but he didn't press her for more, not then. He knew, as Keighly did, that Darby would have had no reason to flee, and that he'd have taken her with him if he had.

He glanced back over one shoulder at the mirror and then raised himself to his feet.

"I'll take you on home," he said quietly. "And don't worry, Keighly. We'll find Darby, Simon and I and some of the hands. We'll look after him."

Keighly nodded numbly, though of course she hadn't the faintest hope that Darby's half-brothers could track him. He was gone, beyond the looking glass.

She allowed Will to lift her into his arms and carry her out of the Blue Garter Saloon. Simon had just arrived, one arm in a sling but otherwise ready to do his part. He drove a buckboard, and Will raised Keighly carefully onto the seat. The gray mare she'd ridden to town was tethered to the back of the rig, but there was no sign of Darby's gelding. Maybe the animal was behind the saloon.

When Destry was found, as of course he would be, the mystery of her husband's inexplicable disappearance would be compounded.

Covering her face with both hands, Keighly wished with all her heart that Shingler's bullet had struck her instead of Darby. Simon patted her shoulder awkwardly and then, at Will's terse instruction, turned the small wagon toward the ranch. Will rode alongside, explaining the situation to his elder brother as best he could.

Keighly, in her torn and filthy dress, with her hands bandaged and a horse blanket wrapped around her shoulders for warmth, contributed nothing to the conversation, and it was only later, when she was tucked into her bed at home by Manuela, that she realized the rain had stopped.

❦ CHAPTER ❦

16

At 3:15 A.M., no wiser than he had been when he first detained them for questioning, Dan Ferris released Francine and Julian.

"You knew the victim's name, Miss Stephens," Ferris had pointed out doggedly, over and over again. "You called him 'Darby Elder.'"

"I was in shock," Francine had replied, just as persistently. "I don't know why I said that. I have no idea who he is."

Finally, they had been told not to leave Redemption without his permission and returned to the Barrow mansion in a squad car.

When Julian had taken a badly needed shower and changed his clothes again, he came downstairs to find Francine in the kitchen, making coffee.

"I didn't think either of us would be able to sleep anyway," she said.

Julian sighed and shoved a hand through his damp hair. "You're probably right," he answered. "But I admit I figured you'd be gone by now."

She turned her back on the chortling coffee maker and leaned against the counter, her arms folded, her head tilted slightly to one side as she studied him. "I take it you're the ex-boyfriend," she said.

Julian was mildly stung, though he didn't show it. "You take it right," he said. "And you have the advantage, because I don't have any idea who you are. Even after we spent all those hours being grilled together at the sheriff's office."

"Keighly and I are friends."

"Excellent," Julian said, opening a cupboard and jerking out two cups. "Maybe you can explain to me what's going on around here."

"You saw her, didn't you?"

Julian lowered his head for a moment, as close to weeping with discouragement and frustration as he'd been years before, as a surgical resident, when he'd lost his first patient. A nine-year-old girl named Mandy.

"It's okay," Francine said gently, laying a hand on his back.

He looked up, met her eyes. "Is it? I saw your Darby Elder shot tonight, on the other side of the mirror. And Keighly was there, too. She tried to save him."

"Sit down," Francine said, gesturing toward the camping table and two lawn chairs in the center of the room.

Julian sat, mostly because he was too tired to stand. "I'm going to ask you again, Ms. Stephens. What do you know about this situation?"

She poured coffee for them both, brought it to the table, smiled sadly as she set the cups down. "I can answer some of your questions," she said.

"What's the smile for?" Julian asked, none too graciously. "You and I may still be charged with a crime, you know."

"I was thinking that Keighly has interesting taste in furniture," she replied. "She must have bought this stuff at the hardware store. And we aren't going to be charged with anything. If the sheriff could have arrested us tonight, he would have done it. He knows he couldn't make it stick, without a weapon, not to mention a motive.

MY OUTLAW

When the forensics people from Las Vegas go over the ballroom tomorrow, they won't find a trace of gunpowder—or anything else to tie us to the shooting."

Julian took a sip of his coffee. It was blessedly strong. "You watch too much television," he said.

She laughed. "I know," she answered, "but I'm right. Wait and see."

"Talk to me," Julian prompted.

"The mirror in the ballroom is apparently some sort of window to the nineteenth century," Francine said. And after that, the story only got more outrageous.

It ended with her leading him to the trunk he'd seen earlier, showing him the photographs and articles inside.

Julian rubbed his eyes with a thumb and forefinger, studying a photograph of Keighly in a wedding dress, standing behind the man who had been evacuated that night, unconscious and barely breathing, to a hospital in Las Vegas.

For all either of them knew, Darby Elder, Keighly's husband, was already dead.

He couldn't bring himself to read the crumbling articles or sort through all the various keepsakes. It hurt too much to think of Keighly loving someone like that, and then losing him. It broke his heart, just remembering the look on her face as she'd tried to come through that mirror in her grandmother's ballroom.

Julian went to stand facing the fireplace, one hand moving lightly, appreciatively, over the cool stone of the sculpture.

"This is her work after all," he whispered.

Francine came to stand beside him. "Yes."

"Is there any way we can help her?"

She sighed. "I honestly don't know."

Keighly returned to town later the same day, under her own power, paying no heed to Manuela's protests, or Betsey's. She would not be turned from her course.

A solemn Pablo escorted Keighly, his beautiful dark eyes watchful, his jaw set. He was a small protector, but a fierce one, and no one who saw him could have doubted his devotion to his mistress. It was clear that he would have died for her, if that proved necessary.

Will and Simon were already at the marshal's office when Keighly arrived, leaving Pablo outside with the horses. At her entrance, the two mens' heretofore spirited conversation died an instantaneous death, and they gaped at her in surprise and, in Simon's case at least, exasperation.

"What are you doing here, Keighly?" he asked.

"I came to tell you that's it's useless to look for Darby. You'll never find him."

Will approached, took Keighly's arm, and ushered her to a chair. "If you know where Darby is," he said gently, "you've got to tell us. He's hurt, and nobody's going to blame him for killing Duke Shingler, if that's what you're worried about. It was obviously self-defense."

Keighly closed her eyes for a moment. "I don't know where Darby went," she said quietly.

"But you claim it's useless to look for him?" Simon prompted. "How can you be so certain of that, if you don't know where he is?"

"He's—" Keighly paused. "He's dead." The newspaper articles had predicted it, after all. She just hadn't guessed that it would happen in quite this way, that Darby would fall through the mirror when he was shot.

Dear God, was he lying in a pool of blood on her grandmother's ballroom floor? How long would it be until someone found him?

Simon ladled water from a bucket into a mug and brought it to Keighly. She accepted it, with trembling hands, and sipped until she felt steadier.

"We've got to find Darby, Keighly," Will said. "He could be hurt real bad, and afraid to ask for help. He's always been treated as an outlaw, and he's bound to think—"

"No," Keighly said, her eyes brimming with tears. "You want to believe he's alive—I don't blame you, because I do, too—but I know Darby is dead. I know it!"

In her mind, she saw Darby's shooting again, saw him stumbling backward, fatally wounded, falling into that bending, liquid glass, to be enfolded and finally swallowed by it. It had all taken place in a few seconds, and yet Keighly remembered it as a lengthy epic, recalled every horrible, gruesome detail.

She would, she supposed, for the rest of her life.

"Why are you so sure Darby is dead?" Simon asked again, quietly. Reasonably. He would be a good marshal, if he managed to stay alive long enough.

Keighly didn't answer. She just sat stiffly in her chair, fighting back tears.

"Leave her alone," Will said finally. "She's been through enough."

Simon ignored him, though his voice was still gentle. "Why did you come back to town, Keighly? You don't really think Darby is dead, do you?"

"I said to leave her alone," Will repeated. He didn't raise his voice, but the words had sharp edges, honed to cut clean and deep.

"It's all right," Keighly said. "I came to Redemption, Simon, because I hoped I was wrong, thinking Darby was dead. I hoped my husband would have been found by now."

Simon stepped back as Keighly rose out of the chair, evidently knowing that if he tried to help her, she would fling off his hand. She didn't want to get into the habit of depending on any other man besides Darby, but especially not her brother-in-law, the man fate had so arbitrarily chosen as her future husband.

"Thank you," she said, and walked bravely out of the office.

Pablo followed close on her heels as she crossed the muddy main street of town and entered the Blue Garter

Saloon without so much as a moment's hesitation. The new owner, who was due to arrive from back East any day, would find his business in a state of upheaval.

The women were leaving, Oralee included. The saloon was stacked high with trunks, boxes, crates, and hatboxes and bustling with activity.

There were bloody clumps of sawdust where Duke Shingler, her husband's killer, had fallen, but Keighly's attention was on the mirror. Or what was left of it.

The glass threw back a distorted, broken image of Keighly herself, rather like a puzzle with its pieces improperly aligned, but there was no sign of the world on the other side. Perhaps this passage between the nineteenth century and the twentieth had closed forever, and there was no way to return.

What did it matter, if she and Darby could never be together again?

Keighly lifted her chin. She couldn't give up; she didn't dare. She had the baby to think about.

"Come home, Mrs. Elder," Pablo pleaded gently, taking her arm. "Please, come home. Perhaps Mr. Elder is there already, waiting for you."

Keighly didn't think that was so, but she could see no point in remaining in that awful room, where the scents of gun smoke and blood mingled with those of sweat and sawdust, stale cigars and cheap whisky. The memory of what had happened there was simply too vivid; she saw it unfold over and over again before Pablo led her outside.

He ran to fetch her horse from across the street, and knew better than to help her mount. Simon and Will rode behind Keighly and Pablo, at a discreet distance, determined to stay close by. She found that fact both comforting and vexing, at one and the same time.

Darby had not returned to the ranch in their absence, in the way she had once found herself in an upstairs bedroom at the Triple K; Keighly hadn't dared to believe he would. All the same, she searched the small house they'd shared, room by room, and was disappointed when she didn't find him.

She didn't sleep that night, couldn't sleep for wondering about Darby, praying that, if he was alive, he was safe, and if he was dead, he was at peace. She sat upright in a chair until dawn, holding one of his shirts pressed close against her chest, too stricken to weep, too frantic to pace.

Finally, she put on a gauzy dress Darby had liked, sent Pablo to the barn to have a buggy hitched up, and drove back to Redemption. This time, the Blue Garter was locked up tight; Keighly got the key from the lawyer, Jack Ryerson, and let herself in to stand at the harp, idly stroking the strings as she stared at the broken mirror, waiting.

Nothing happened, except that, for a fraction of a moment, she felt insubstantial again. As though she were made of fog and vapor and would dissipate into nothing under the heat of the sun. She did not precisely care if she vanished or not; her only goal was to be with Darby.

And probably, that was impossible.

Pablo waited until she was ready to go home again, and then he took the reins of the buggy and drove back to the ranch without speaking a word. He'd been a little boy before the shooting; now Keighly's tragedy had made him a man far before his time.

Darby knew what had happened even before he opened his eyes. He remembered Oralee climbing down off the wet roof of the Blue Garter and flagging him down in the street, sobbing out that Duke Shingler was holding Keighly captive inside, that he'd meant to kill her and all the others. Will might have been some help in the situation, being a fair shot and a good hand with his fists, but he'd already gone home to look in on Betsey and the kids.

Darby recalled going in through the back way, Shingler knocking Keighly to the floor, the exchange of gunfire, the searing tear as the bullet pierced the flesh of his chest and exploded inside. He remembered falling backward, through the glass, but after that, there was only pain.

"Hey," a female voice prodded gently. "You awake?"

Darby raised his lids, with some effort, and focused on the face above him. A pretty woman was bending over him. "Where's—Keighly?" he ground out.

"Not here. My name's Francine."

An anguish far greater than that of being shot gripped Darby's spirit. "Where am I?"

"In a hospital in Las Vegas," she answered. "You've been here five days now."

"I need to get back to her," he stated, speaking slowly and carefully, lest his strength fade before he got it said. "Back to Keighly. Make sure she's—all right."

"Keighly wasn't hurt," Francine said, and he believed her. She bore a strong likeness to someone he knew, though he couldn't think just then who it was, and her touch was gentle as she raised his head and put a cup of cool, fresh water to his lips. "She's bound to be pretty worried about you, though."

Darby frowned. The woman was wearing peculiar clothes, and there was a dazzling quality to the room that was utterly foreign. Strange machines surrounded the bed. "This is—her world?"

Francine nodded. "Such as it is."

The place wouldn't be much, he reflected, without Keighly in it. He looked down, saw the bulky bandages on his shoulder, then took in the glaring lamp beside the bed and the fixture overhead, shining so brightly that it hurt his eyes. "You took care of me?"

"Dr. Drury did some fancy sewing before the paramedics came," she said. "He's downstairs, exchanging accountant-speak with the business office."

Darby wished the woman would speak English.

"The police, insurance, things like that," she said, smiling. "It's been tough, trying to explain where you came from. Lucky Julian's a solid citizen and I come from the illustrious Kavanagh family."

He stared up at her, stunned. "You're a Kavanagh?"

"Yes, although my married name is Stephens. My great-great-grandfather was Simon Kavanagh."

Darby gave a low whistle. "I'll be damned," he said.

"Probably not," she said. "You seem like a nice enough guy to me. Now, can you suggest a way to get word to Keighly that you're okay?"

"You know about that?" Darby asked. He'd been starting to drift off, caught in a swirling eddy of pain and despair, but her words had snagged his attention. "About our being separated and everything?"

"Oh, yes," Francine answered. "Keighly told me."

"And you believed it, just because somebody told you?"

She grinned, and he saw then how much she resembled Etta Lee, Simon's daughter.

"There was proof. Newspaper articles. Gravestones. Even photographs."

"That mirror—is it here, in this place?"

Francine shook her head. "It's in Redemption. This is Las Vegas."

Darby immediately tried to raise himself off the bed, she pressed him gently down again. "Oh, no you don't, cowboy. You're in no condition to go anywhere right this minute. The tissue in your shoulder needs a few days to knit itself back together and, besides, you'd never get out of here without being nabbed by a nurse."

He didn't have the strength to resist her edict, or he would have done so. Instead, he just laid there, feeling as frustrated and helpless as a blind kitten trying to find a teat. "I can't stay here," he said.

"I know," Francine told him, smoothing his blankets. "When the time comes, Julian and I will do what we can to help you."

A dark-haired man appeared in the doorway.

"I'm Julian Drury," the man said, coming to the bedside and looking down at Darby with an unreadable expression. He didn't offer his hand, which was fine, because Darby was too weak to shake.

"Am I supposed to know you?" Darby asked, not unkindly.

The doctor shook his head. "I guess not. Keighly and I were friends once, and I thought she might have mentioned me."

Darby felt a pang in the region of his heart. Here, then, was the lover Keighly had mentioned, cryptically, on one or two occasions. The one he suspected she'd once expected to marry. "Darby Elder," he said, and then gasped because a sudden flash of pain took his breath away.

"Time for more medication," Drury said. "Francine, would you mind getting the nurse?"

Francine hurried out, and Drury pulled up a chair. "Tell me about Keighly."

Darby ached, and not because he'd been shot. He wasn't whole without his wife, and if he couldn't find his way back to her, he didn't know what he'd do. "I'm not sure I want to answer that," he said, with some difficulty. He felt as weak and dizzy as a spinster in a tight corset.

"You saved her life," Drury said, as if he hadn't spoken. "That bastard, whoever he was, meant to kill her, once he'd finished you off."

Darby swallowed, remembering. Jesus, he'd never been so scared as when he'd thought Shingler was going to turn and shoot Keighly where she lay, sprawled in the sawdust on the floor of the Blue Garter. "You saw what happened?"

Drury nodded. "In the mirror. The force of that bullet you took knocked you backward through the glass."

"I think I went through more than glass," Darby observed ruefully. His shoulder felt as though Dr. Bellkin had subjected him to his hot-poker remedy, the way he had Simon. And, years before that, Angus, too. "If you'd help me out of this place, maybe I could go back—"

"That can wait," Drury said.

Darby wasn't sure that was true, but he couldn't make it all the way to Redemption under his own power, not yet, so he had no choice except to bide his time. He held his tongue.

"Keighly is happy back there, in that other world? That other time?" the doctor persisted.

Darby thought of how he and Keighly had laughed and cried together, how they'd made love and argued and laid plans for a family and a life. "Yeah," he said. "She was happy." It wasn't lost on him, even in his current state, which bore an unfortunate resemblance to the morning after a drinking binge, that in the strictest terms of reality, Keighly was long dead. So was Angus, and Simon and Etta Lee. Will and Betsey and their tribe of little boys.

Christ, the knowledge was almost too much to bear, all at one time like that.

"You'll take good care of her?" Drury persisted. A woman in a short white dress and an odd hat came in, with a needle. She filled it from a vial as she stood beside the bed.

"If I can get back, yes," Darby answered. "What is that?"

"Something to make you sleep," said the strange woman.

"I'm trying to wake up, here, not go to sleep." An instant after he'd spoken, a the needle pricked his arm. And an instant after that, Darby lost consciousness.

Again and again in the coming days, Keighly was drawn to the shattered mirror in the Blue Garter Saloon. In the meantime, Simon and Will and men from the town and the ranch searched high and low for Darby, and found, as she had expected, no trace of him.

There were all sorts of theories, of course: He'd been

captured by Indians. He'd grown weary of a wife and a ranch and gone back to drifting. The Shinglers had buried a chest full of Wells Fargo gold someplace in the mountains of Mexico, and Darby knew where.

Keighly paid no mind to the gossip.

She was too caught up in her own suffering; she barely ate or slept. She just watched, and waited, and hoped, all the while knowing that fate had finally had its way.

Then, a full week after Darby's shooting, the skies opened, as if in sympathy, and a torrent of rain descended, hammering at the tin roofs of the town, turning the streets to mud eight inches deep, and taking out both the telegraph wires and part of the railroad tracks that linked Redemption with the rest of the world.

Keighly had let herself into the empty saloon, and she sat alone at a table near the mirror, staring into the broken glass. Mourning.

The lightning was blue-gold, and it flashed right into the saloon itself, like some dancer in a crackling costume, forcing even Keighly to notice it. She watched in quiet amazement as the room became blindingly bright and then, just as suddenly, as dark as the deepest mine shaft in Nevada.

Keighly cried out, in something made as much of excitement as fear, got to her feet, and was thrust to her knees again. She couldn't see, had no sense of up or down, let alone right or left, and nothing had any substance or any texture.

She screamed again, a hoarse cry that hurt her throat, and then she fainted.

A night and a day had passed, by Darby's reckoning, before he was strong enough to haul himself off the bed, and even then he landed on his knees. It was dark, and a desert rain was pounding at the windows, cooling and cleansing the unmoving air.

He stayed there, on the floor, breathing deeply, trying to

gather his strength. He didn't know where Francine and Dr. Drury were, and he didn't care. As for the nurses, well, they'd kept him in that room as long as they were going to; he had to get to the mirror somehow, try to make his way back to Keighly.

After a while, he dragged himself as far as the doorway. That depleted his strength so badly that he had to lean against the wall for a good five minutes, waiting for his heartbeat to slow down enough that he could breathe. Then, using all his will and all the resources of his soul as well as his muscles, Darby thrust himself laboriously forward.

The hallway outside shifted and pitched before him; he clung to the doorjamb until he could be fairly sure he wasn't going to pass out. Then, using the wall for support, he began to move with excruciating slowness along the corridor.

None of the nurses were in sight, but as he passed an open area, he recognized Francine Stephens sitting in a chair. She saw him and jumped to her feet.

Darby didn't dare speak, but with his eyes, he begged her not to betray him. He was, by that point, utterly desperate, and his strength was failing fast.

He didn't have any to spare for arguing.

Francine hesitated, then came over and took his arm. She was slender, but sturdy, and she provided suprising support.

"Come on," she whispered. "I'll take you back to the mirror."

Darby never knew how he got out of that hospital without passing out cold, but with Francine's help, he did. She loaded him into a sleek version of the motor cars he'd seen in newspapers, back in his own time, and they sped out of the parking lot.

The late twentieth century didn't come as a complete surprise to him, because he'd seen a few pictures on the box in the corner of his room, while one of the nurses was in his room making up the second bed. He'd glimpsed buildings like the ones they were passing, all lit up, with big windows, like eyes, crowded inside, and louder than the Blue Garter on Saturday night.

He hated the whole place.

"How do you stand it?" he asked. "All the noise, all the people?"

Francine chuckled. "It's all in what you're used to, cowboy."

He tilted his head back then, exhausted, and dropped off to sleep.

When he woke up again, they were in front of a big white house, and it was raining.

"You can't go around in a hospital gown," Francine announced, after she'd helped him drag himself inside.

"Where's that Dr. Drury?" Darby asked. "He was about my size. Maybe he's got some duds I can borrow."

"Duds?" Francine echoed, and grinned.

"Clothes," Darby scowled. He wasn't up to cheerful conversation.

"Julian's gone back to L.A.—Los Angeles. He has a medical practice there. But he might have left something behind." They labored into the ballroom, and Francine deposited Darby in a chair against the far wall. "Sit tight," she said. "I'll check out the clothes situation."

Darby leaned back and closed his eyes. Lord but he was tired, and he ached in every part of his body.

Francine returned empty-handed. "Sorry, there's nothing here except a pink chenille bathrobe, and I don't think it's you."

There she went, talking gibberish again. "I'm going back," he said. "I don't care if I'm naked."

"You practically are," Francine pointed out as he stood, wobbling, and made his way as far as the cot in the middle of the room.

He felt a breeze where there shouldn't have been one. "I'll just rest awhile," he said, lying down.

"You do that," she answered.

When he woke up, all the lights were out, and rain pounded at the windows like ten thousand little fists. The lightning spilled into the darkness, pushing the gloom in upon itself, while thunder rocked the skies overhead. Through it all, as a faint, barely discernible melody, Darby heard the whisper of harp strings.

Sweat soaked his hospital gown and glistened on his face and hands as he pushed himself up off the cot and climbed awkwardly, precariously, to his feet. Every movement sent new pain pulsing through his body. He bore it because beyond it—maybe, just maybe—lay the shining possibility that he would find Keighly again. It was all he wanted; all he asked of life or fate.

The song of the harp, discordant and yet beautiful, held him upright. Darby groped toward the mirror, not daring to hesitate even for a moment, propelling himself forward by sheer willpower.

Finally, as the storm reached an earsplitting crescendo, he felt the surface of the mirror with his hands. In that moment, the long chamber suddenly seemed to blaze with light, and Darby blinked, momentarily dazzled.

After a few moments spent catching his breath and gathering his forces, Darby stared into the glass. The lightning poured in again, and he saw that the mirror on that side was whole, utterly unbroken.

His knees gave out and he slid down to the floor, powerless to hold himself upright. Blackness rose up around him, at once smothering and merciful, and swallowed all his senses in a single gulp.

When Keighly awakened, she was lying on the ballroom floor of her grandmother's house, with Francine kneeling beside her.

"Where is Darby?" Keighly cried, as her friend helped her carefully to her feet. *"Where is he?"*

There were tears brimming along Francine's dark

lashes. Unable to answer Keighly's desperate question, she merely shook her head.

And Keighly cried out, in protest, in pain, in unutterable sorrow.

Francine supported her as best she could as they mounted the stairs.

Keighly lay on the small bed in her childhood room. Her grief was torturous; she wailed with it, and simple words would not comfort her.

Francine went out of the room, and a short while later, a doctor came, and gave Keighly a shot. She slept, and dreamed terrible dreams.

She didn't know how much time had passed—would perhaps never know—when Julian arrived. After a whispered consultation with Francine, he administered an injection that made Keighly drowsy.

They all knew that the calm she exhibited was false and, as such, temporary.

"Damn it, Julian," Keighly rasped, her throat still raw, "I'm *pregnant,* and you've given me a drug—"

Julian sighed and thrust a hand through his dark, rumpled hair. "I doubt that a light sedative could do you nearly as much harm as throwing a screaming fit," he said. "Take it easy, Keighly. Francine and I are not enemies—we're on your side."

Keighly felt the sting of shame. Even though her rising hysterics had not been entirely voluntary, there had been an element of railing against fate. "Where is Darby? What happened to him?"

Francine sat down on the side of Keighly's bed and took her hand. "Julian saved his life, Keighly," Francine said quietly. "But Darby wanted to go back to you. He was in the hospital, in Las Vegas, and I—I brought him back here—" She paused and blushed, glancing at Julian as if for support. "I thought he would sleep, so I left him alone. But the next morning, when I came in to check, he was gone."

Keighly closed her eyes, even as sickness welled up inside her. "And he went through the mirror."

"We didn't see it happen," Francine said quickly.

Julian went into the bathroom and came out carrying a cold washcloth, which he laid on Keighly's forehead. "Try to stay calm. Between the three of us, we'll get this sorted out somehow."

"Did you see anything?" Keighly demanded, clutching at his arm. The sedative was already pulling her under; she was fighting the effects, and she was losing. "Please, Julian—anything you can tell me—"

Francine and Julian exchanged a look. Then Julian spoke.

"I saw you in the saloon, Keighly. And I saw the shooting."

"You were there, then—that's what Francine meant when she told me you saved him," she said, as a more coherent understanding what must have happened finally penetrated her confused state of mind. "Thank God you were there, Julian."

"Sleep now," Julian said, and smoothed her hair back from her forehead.

It was old Herb Wallace, sneaking around hoping to find a bottle before the new owner showed up, who found Darby Elder blacked out on the floor of the Blue Garter Saloon, bleeding slightly through the bright new bandages on his chest and wearing a paper nightie. Or so Darby was told when he woke up at the Triple K several hours later.

Simon stood on one side of the bed and Will was on the other, while Angus loomed at the foot.

Darby was getting damn tired of lying around like an invalid while people made pronouncements over his supine body, but his only real concern was Keighly. "My wife," he said, first thing. "Where is Keighly? Is she all right?"

Will and Simon exchanged one of their looks.

"Well?" Darby snapped, but he was beginning to know. And he hoped to hell he had it wrong.

"We aren't sure," Simon told him reasonably. He dragged up a chair and sank into it as if he were a hundred years old, and instead of in the prime of his life. "Pablo saw her last. Said she was in the Blue Garter Saloon, just sitting there in a chair and staring into what was left of the mirror. There was a storm, and Pablo left her to look after the horses. When he got back, she was gone."

Darby closed his eyes. It couldn't be so, he thought, but he knew it was. He and Keighly had missed each other somehow. She was in her century, and he was obviously back in his own. Maybe, he reflected miserably, that was the way things were going to stay. After all, it wasn't usual for a person to travel through time. *This,* her being there and him being here, was what was usual.

"Duke Shingler?"

Angus went to the bureau and came back with a snifter of brandy. "Dead," he said. "And good riddance. Here, have a swallow of this. It'll make you feel better."

"Nothing is going to do that," Darby answered, but he took the glass and threw back its contents before turning his gaze to Simon. "Now I suppose I'm wanted for killing that son of a bitch."

"You aren't wanted for anything," Simon replied. "Everybody knew it was self-defense. Which isn't to say that more than a few people aren't suspicious over Keighly's disappearance. What do you know about this, Darby? There's something you're holding back, and if we're going to help you, we have to have the truth."

"You can't help me," Darby said. "Nobody can."

Will opened his mouth to argue, and Simon got ready to ask another question.

Angus silenced them both with a gesture. "Leave him alone," he said. "Just leave him alone."

* * *

MY OUTLAW

Keighly sat numbly in the airline window seat beside Julian, staring at the blank video screen a few rows ahead on the ceiling. Francine was on the aisle, reading a magazine.

It had been three weeks since her return from the nineteenth century.

While Keighly was recovering her strength, Francine had stayed with her almost constantly, while Julian flew back and forth between Nevada and California as often as his surgical schedule would permit.

Keighly had made several frenzied attempts to get back to Darby, and all of them were in vain. The mirror in her grandmother's ballroom would not receive her, nor would it surrender the man she loved.

The night before, she and Francine and Julian had spent hours going over the contents of the trunk, and Keighly was still deeply shaken by what they'd found—which was nothing at all, except for a few old hair ribbons, a collection of once-colorful advertising cards, and some journals kept by one Etta Lee Kavanagh, spinster. The diaries had made no mention whatsoever of Darby or of Keighly. The existence they described was, in fact, an arid one, a long, empty life, void of all but the most fleeting joys. Etta Lee had died a wealthy woman, at a very old age, but the task of carrying on the Kavanagh name and fortunes had fallen to her younger brother, Timothy, and Will's four sons.

Francine's photocopies told another story, but they were worthless, now that the course of Darby and Keighly's personal history had been changed. Mere dreams, caught on paper during a brief flash of truth, before dissolving into nothingness again.

"Keighly," Julian insisted quietly. "Eat something. For the baby, if not for yourself."

Keighly looked at the food on the tray table before her, swallowed a wave of revulsion, and reached for her miniature plastic fork with all the grace and eagerness of a robot.

"Why are you being so nice to me?"

"Because I'm your friend," Julian answered.

He was indeed a friend, and so was Francine.

One day, Keighly hoped she'd have the heart to be grateful.

❧ CHAPTER ❧
17

As she stood in the small entryway of her long-empty Los Angeles apartment, Keighly once again had the sense, stronger than ever, that she was not a whole person, but a mere reflection of some distant, more solid self. She wanted to bolt, to simply run and run until the last wisps of her image had been brushed away by the wind, but there was the baby to think about. The child needed her.

"Maybe it would be better," Julian said quietly, stepping through the doorway behind her, carrying one of her bags in each hand, "if you stayed at my place. Francine will be there as a chaperone, after all."

Francine, who had become very close to Julian, was at his apartment then, nursing a tension headache.

Little wonder, with all the three of them had been through of late.

Keighly looked back at him, shook her head. Julian had been kind, and she owed him a great debt; he'd very likely saved Darby from bleeding to death after the shooting and, with Francine's help, he'd taken care of Keighly herself. "This is my place," she said. "I belong here as much as anywhere."

But they both knew she did not—her place was in the nineteenth century, with Darby.

Julian carried the suitcases into the bedroom and then joined Keighly in the small kitchen, where she was filling the kettle to boil water for tea and the super-strong instant coffee she knew he drank whenever he wasn't scheduled to perform surgery or on call. They'd often joked, in the days before Keighly's last visit to Redemption, about his caffeine dependency.

"Sit down," Keighly said softly, inclining her head toward the little English pine table under the sunniest window.

Julian sank wearily into one of the chairs. "How can you be sure you're pregnant?" he asked, watching her.

Keighly glanced at the small magnetic calendar affixed to the refrigerator door. Three months had passed since she left the twentieth century, but in the nineteenth, nearly five had gone by. There seemed to be little or no correlation between one place and the other, timewise.

"I could raise my shirt and prove it," she said, in a lame attempt at a joke. Having set the kettle on the burner and turned up the gas, she joined her friend at the antique table. They'd bought it together one Sunday afternoon, at an auction, back when they'd planned to marry. How long ago that seemed. "You and Francine seem pretty serious, or am I wrong? It's none of my business, of course, but I have a sort of proprietary interest, like some kind of Fairy Godmother."

Julian looked beleaguered for a moment, and a bit uncomfortable. He needed a shave, and his clothes, always so impeccable, were rumpled. "We're serious," he said, at length, with a sigh. "But don't ask me where things will go from here. She has a ranch in Nevada and a business in Chicago and a son in Vermont. If that didn't make matters complicated enough, well, there's the fact that my practice is here."

Keighly smiled. Behind them, the kettle thrummed as heat surged through the water inside. "Don't blow this, Julian. Don't let logistics spoil your chances to make a life with Francine. You need more than medicine."

272

Julian grinned and raised an eyebrow. "You aren't the least bit jealous, I suppose?" he teased.

"Not the least bit," Keighly answered, smiling back as she squeezed his hand. "I want you to be happy, Julian. And Francine, too. You both deserve every good thing there is to do and be and have."

"But if you don't get back, you'll be alone—"

The kettle whistled, and Keighly rose to attend to it. She made a cup of coffee for Julian, just the way he liked it, and poured boiling water over tea bags placed in the bottom of her favorite china pot. "I won't be alone," she said presently, returning to the table with his cup. "I'll have the baby."

"Keighly—"

She carried over the teapot and a cup, saucer and spoon for herself. "I am going back, Julian," she said, looking squarely into his eyes. "I don't know how I'll pull it off, or when it will happen, but I can't live here, in this time and place. I just can't."

He reached out, squeezed her hand. There was anguish in his blue eyes. "Sweetheart, don't you think you should just let go of that—that episode—and move on?"

Keighly's hand trembled as she poured her tea, added sugar, and stirred it in. She and Julian were good friends—in their case that was so much better than being lovers—but she couldn't quite bring herself to tell him that she intended to liquidate her assets, donate almost everything to various charities, and move back to the house in Redemption. There, while waiting for a chance to return to the nineteenth century, and thus to the man she loved, she intended to live quietly, sculpting and reading, while her child and Darby's grew within her.

"You've been a fine friend," she said, skirting the issue. "Thank you."

Julian stared into his coffee, perhaps debating whether or not it would do him any good to try persuading her to stay in L.A. "I took you for granted for a very long time," he said, when at last he met her gaze again. "I am so very sorry about that, Keighly."

She smiled. "I was as much at fault as you were. Maybe I even encouraged you to treat me that way, unconsciously at least, so that I could keep some distance between us." Keighly paused and sighed, her fingers warming where she held her cup. "Still, don't make that mistake with Francine," she said quietly. "You could have something really special with her, but not if you keep her at arm's length."

He nodded. "I know. And you have my word, Keighly. I'll do my best to get it right."

Keighly felt compelled to defend Julian against his own self-directed criticism. "You didn't do anything so terrible before," she pointed out. "I was the wrong woman for you, and you were the wrong man for me. Nothing either of us could have said or done would have changed that."

"You certainly seem convinced that Francine and I are right for each other."

"Yes," Keighly said, without hesitation. In spite of everything else that had been happening, she'd felt the sparks arching between her friends, and she'd been pleased by the development. While they might have seemed an unlikely pair at first, Francine and Julian had similar interests, and both had recently discovered that they needed more out of life than what their successful careers gave them. "I'm certain."

Julian finished his coffee, checked the refrigerator and cupboards, and gave his medical opinion—there wasn't enough food in the apartment for a mouse to live on, let alone a pregnant woman who needed a more than ample measure of tender loving care. He would send his housekeeper over with provisions, he said. In the meantime, Keighly was to get some rest.

She took a shower as soon as Julian had gone, then put fresh sheets on her bed and collapsed, tumbling into a deep sleep. She awakened after dark to hear the cozy, happy noises of cooking coming from the kitchen. The scent of some spicy tomato sauce filled the air.

Keighly got up and pulled on a robe over her short nightgown.

The stereo was playing softly as she passed through the living room, with its small terrace and sparkling view of L.A.

Julian, clad in bluejeans and a sweatshirt, was in the kitchen, trying to help but mostly getting in the way, while Francine, wearing similar clothing, put together a pasta dish of some sort.

"Am I invited to this party?" Keighly asked, smiling.

They'd been laughing together, over some small and probably intimate joke, and Keighly's appearance surprised them both. She felt tenderness toward both Julian and Francine, as well as a certain benign envy. They were together, after all, while she and Darby were separated, perhaps forever, by a chasm of time and mystery.

Francine put down her spoon and came over to hug Keighly. "How are you feeling?" she asked.

"Miserable," Keighly responded honestly. "But I must be gaining ground, because that pasta really smells good. I'm starved."

They had salad and Francine's special tortellini, with garlic bread and Chianti. Keighly skipped the wine, drinking mineral water instead.

"You people are going to have to stop fussing over me like this," Keighly said, feeling stronger after the meal. Julian rinsed the plates and silverware and put everything into the dishwasher while she and Francine chatted at the table. "You said it yourself, Dr. Drury, I need to get on with my life."

Francine and Julian exchanged a look.

"So, what's the plan?" Keighly asked quickly, because she didn't want them to start lecturing her further. They'd made their case already, and she was weary of the subject. "Are you going to move to Redemption, Julian, and become a country G.P., or will you, Francine, come to L.A. and set up a new advertising agency?"

Francine glanced at Julian. "I'm moving here," she said. "I'll set up an agency, but I'll probably work from home for a few years."

So, Keighly thought, they'd talked about the future since her discussion with Julian that afternoon, laid plans for it. She was more than pleased.

"We're hoping to have children pretty soon," Julian added shyly. Another look passed between Francine and Julian, tender this time, and definitely wired for high voltage.

Keighly resisted a strong urge to weep, so deeply, so poignantly, did she miss Darby in those moments. "I'm really tired," she said. "I think I'll go back to bed."

"We'll finish cleaning up and I'll call in the morning to see how you're doing," Francine assured Keighly, squeezing her hand. She frowned thoughtfully and added, "Would you like me to stay here tonight?"

Keighly shook her head. She needed to be alone, and what Francine really wanted was to be with Julian. "I'll be fine. Thanks, both of you, for being so kind."

Julian kissed Keighly's forehead, and then Francine hugged her.

She was asleep in her bed, dreaming of Darby, before they locked the front door behind them.

A month passed before Keighly had closed her gallery and dispersed most of her money. She was physically healthy, and her pregnancy had been made official by a home test kit and, subsequently, one of the best OB-GYNs in Los Angeles, Dr. Jennifer Salanders, a colleague of Julian's, but the feeling that she was slowly fading out of existence never left Keighly, day or night. An unshakable sadness had settled over her, and her deepest fear was no longer that she would never return to Darby, but that she might not survive at all. She didn't want to leave her child alone in the world.

For that reason, she had her will redrawn and, with their permission of course, named Julian and Francine, who were to be married at Christmas, as the baby's legal guardians. The request, though they granted it without hesitation, had worried the prospective parents for obvious reasons.

Keighly continued to go through the motions, getting up in the morning, eating a good breakfast, gulping down prenatal vitamins, taking a long walk, and then attending meetings and appointments during the day. She usually had dinner with either Francine or Julian or both in the evening, depending on whether one or both were available, and fell into bed early.

On the morning of her last day in California, representatives of a shelter for the homeless came to carry her furniture downstairs to a truck. Both Julian and Francine were present; Julian had stopped by to make sure Keighly didn't lift anything heavy, and Francine was going to accompany her back to Redemption, both to help her friend settle in and to take care of some business of her own, on the ranch.

"This is not a good idea," Julian said, for the thousandth time. "There is no furniture in that great, echoing mausoleum you call a house." He was gathering steam. "You'll wind up living like a hermit, Keighly, lying on some cot in front of that bloody mirror, waiting for something to happen!"

Keighly smiled sadly at the image of herself as some kind of modern-day Miss Havisham, wandering through once-grand rooms, becoming more and more eccentric with every passing day. "I'll be working, Julian," she said, to reassure him. "And it isn't as if I'll be alone."

"Francine is an ad exec, not a doctor."

Francine gave her future husband a look. "I can dial nine-one-one, Julian," she said sweetly. "Besides, Redemption has a good paramedic team, and the local GP might not have Dr. Salanders' glowing credentials, but he's delivered a couple of hundred babies in his time."

"Let's go," Keighly said. Now that she was actually ready to go back to the house in Redemption, she felt a certain urgency. "We'll miss our plane."

Julian locked the apartment door, promising to leave the key with his secretary, as agreed, so that the real-estate agent could pick it up. He drove Francine and Keighly to the airport in a meditative silence, and once they'd arrived, he said good-bye to Francine with a lingering kiss, then turned to Keighly.

He took her upper arms gently but firmly in his hands and gazed deeply into her eyes. He started to speak, and then sighed instead, gave her a peck on the forehead, and turned to walk away.

The flight to Las Vegas was uneventful, and Keighly passed it in a sort of reverie, as she had before, when returning to L.A. with Julian. The weakness she felt was alarming, though not at all physical, and because Keighly didn't know how to explain it to Francine, who would be concerned, she didn't mention it at all. Things were simpler that way.

By the time they left the Las Vegas airport in a rented car, with Francine at the wheel, Keighly was light-headed. She laid a hand to her abdomen and prayed that whatever happened to her, the child would survive. Keighly wanted the baby's happiness and well-being even more than her own, but she sensed some sort of strange shifting process going on, both within and without.

"Are you all right?" Francine asked, glancing at her passenger as they drove onto the freeway that would eventually pass through Redemption.

Keighly wished she knew the answer to that question. "I'm holding on," she said. It was the closest she could come to telling the whole truth. In actuality, her soul seemed like some invisible balloon, bobbing at the end of a long, fraying thread, ready to break free and float away at any moment.

"I don't like the way you said that."

She sighed. "You wouldn't understand if I explained. Hell, *I* don't understand, so how could anyone else?"

"Try me."

A tear slipped down Keighly's cheek. She had not been aware that she was crying until then. "I feel as though I'm not real, Francine," she blurted out. "I can move and think and all that, but at the same time I'm somehow *insubstantial*, like Peter Pan's shadow. And it scares the hell out of me."

Francine pulled the car over to the side of the road and flipped on the emergency blinkers so they wouldn't be rear-ended. "Why didn't you tell me this before, or Julian?" she demanded.

"Because it sounds so crazy, I guess. I'm not sick, Francine, and I'm not crazy. It's as if I've fallen through some celestial crack and, trust me, there's nothing you or anyone else can do to help me."

"What about the baby?"

"That's what scares me most," Keighly confessed, drying her face with the backs of her hands. "If something weird happens—and we both know that it could—where does that leave my child? In some void, between dimensions?"

Even Francine, for all her intelligence, couldn't answer that one. She gave Keighly a close look, then sighed and pulled back out onto the freeway.

The semi-truck, moving at high speed, cut them off just outside Redemption, catching their front bumper and dragging them along in tandem for a horrifying interval, while the tires of the rental car screeched and smoked on the pavement.

Francine fought the spinning wheel, but in vain, and Keighly sat rigid within the confines of her seat belt, both hands clasped to her stomach in the attempt to protect the baby in her womb. Neither of the women cried out; there wasn't time.

Another deafening crash shook them, and then they were spinning in the center of the road, while other drivers in fast-moving cars tried desperately to avoid them.

"Baby," Keighly said, in a whisper, as darkness descended to enfold her, "I'm sorry. I'm so sorry."

Francine was dazed, but not unconscious. As far as she could tell, she had no broken bones or other serious injuries; just the usual cuts, bruises, and shattered nerves. All around, she heard the sound of falling metal and smelled burning rubber, and it seemed as if those horrific moments in which the accident took place went on and on.

At last, she managed to turn in the glass-sprinkled seat to look in Keighly's direction.

What she saw made her wonder if she'd been hurt after all; a brain injury seemed most likely.

Keighly was fading—*fading,* like a ghost in a movie.

"No!" Francine cried, and reached for her friend, but her hand went through Keighly's shoulder and struck the seat behind. "Keighly, don't do this—don't go—"

Keighly smiled at her, peacefully, though there was intense sorrow in her eyes. She was watery now, like an image projected on mist, and though her mouth moved, Francine did not hear what she said.

Francine began to weep, and then to sob. By the time a state trooper and one of the passersby tugged open the car door and asked if she was all right, Keighly had vanished completely.

"It's all right, ma'am," the trooper said gently, squatting beside the car. "We're going to take care of you now. It's all over."

The man beside him squinted, scanning the ruined

interior of the car. "I could have sworn there was some-body else in here with this lady," he said.

Francine shook her head. "No," she said, her throat tightening around more tears. "I was traveling alone."

"What happened?" Julian asked, when he reached Francine's private hospital room in Las Vegas that night. She'd insisted that she wasn't hurt, but the doctors on duty had wanted her to check in for twenty-four hours of observation, and Julian had backed them up by telephone.

Francine put her arms around Julian's neck, clung to him for a long time. "Keighly," she whispered, when she could find the words, and the courage to make herself say it. "Keighly is gone. She disappeared, Julian."

He went to the door of her room and closed it, then returned to Francine's bedside, frowning. "What do you mean? Did she get out of the car and walk away?"

"No," Francine answered, shaking her head, which began to ache something fierce in protest. "Julian, she *vanished,* like so much smoke. She'd been telling me that she didn't feel real—the word she used was 'insubstantial,' I think."

"God," Julian rasped, thrusting a hand through his hair. He wasn't as perfectly groomed as he liked to be, due to the rigors of the trip, but Francine only loved him more for the fact. "Of course she was real!"

"I'm not so sure of that," Francine ventured, sinking back into her pillows. "There is so much we don't know, Julian. People have always thought that the flesh was more genuine, somehow, than the spirit, but isn't it possible that the soul actually *creates* the body to suit its purposes, instead of just entering at conception or birth or whenever?"

Julian intertwined his fingers with Francine's and touched his forehead to hers. "You've lost me. I'm a pedantic fellow, without a mystical bone in my body." He kissed her lightly, tenderly, on the mouth. "Have you telephoned your son?"

She smiled at the thought of her conversation with Tony, and nodded. "He's coming to L.A. next month, to spend a month. You don't mind, do you?"

He smoothed her hair. "I'll force myself to share you," he said. "Thank you, Francine Stephens."

"For what?" She was honestly puzzled.

"For not dying. I couldn't have borne it, after waiting for you so long. Now, get some rest, please. I'll be right here if you need me."

Francine closed her eyes, a slight smile of contentment settling on her lips. There was still the mystery of what had happened to Keighly, and she knew they would probably never solve it, but she had her theories.

Oh, yes. She had her theories.

Making the transfer—and Keighly knew it was permanent this time, by the sheer intensity of the experience—turned out to be a genuinely weird experience, although once the first shock had passed, Keighly wasn't afraid. After an initial fit of terror, she felt the most extraordinary calmness descend into that crumpled, broken rental car.

She had seen Francine, as if through some clear, gelatinous material, but had been unable to touch her, unable to speak.

Then, suddenly, Keighly found herself spinning, faster and faster, like a cyclone. Light scattered around her in blazing, beautiful sparks, and then there was a painful crash, and Keighly was abruptly aware of having hands and feet again, not to mention a head and all the other accompanying parts of the human animal.

She hadn't imagined the crash landing, either, she thought grimly. This was reality, and the proof was that she hurt in every bone and muscle.

She groaned.

"Keighly?" The voice was familiar, panicky and female, but Keighly couldn't quite place it, and she was afraid to open her eyes. "Keighly, are you all right? Can you move?"

She made herself raise her lids, and was stunned to find Betsey Kavanagh stooped beside her on the wooden floor where she, Keighly, lay sprawled.

"Where am I?" she asked. It was a stupid question, but there it was.

"Why, darlin', you're at the Triple K. Looks to me like you took a little tumble down the stairway."

The Triple K. Keighly's heart practically stopped, then soared high on a great updraft of hope. She raised herself slowly, carefully, to a sitting position. She was back in the nineteenth century.

"Where's Darby?" she asked, fearing the answer.

"He's upstairs," Betsey said, with a frown. "You know, what with everybody disappearing around here, I'm starting to fear for my good sense. First Darby vanished, and then we found him and *you* were gone. What's going on in this place?"

Keighly made a bubbling sound, half sob and half laugh, and scrambled to her feet. She was a little shaky, but otherwise okay, as far as she could tell, and still clad in the pantsuit with the loose-fitting jacket that she'd been wearing when she and Francine had been in the car crash, more than a hundred years in the future.

"I'm sure there's a perfectly reasonable explanation," she said, dusting her hands together. "I just don't know what it is."

Betsey took in her sister-in-law's garb with wide eyes. "I've never seen a woman wear clothes like that before," she commented. "Why, Will would have a fit and fall in it if I wore trousers." The appeal of that prospect was already taking visible shape in Betsey's expression. "If I just altered a pattern meant to fit one of the boys—"

Keighly gripped the newel post for a few moments,

barely able to keep herself from bolting up them, two at a time. There was the baby to think about; she couldn't afford to be hasty or careless. And yet she had to see Darby, wanted that with her whole being.

He was, she knew, the reason she had returned.

"I'd better get word to Simon and Will and the others that you've turned up again," Betsey said, with happy resignation, starting off toward the front of the house. "They've been turning the whole state of Nevada upside down, looking for you. Don't you go disappearing again, now!"

Keighly laughed as she climbed the stairs and, at the same time, she cried. She'd been through a lot of profound changes since she'd parted ways with the twentieth century, but she was back now, in the same world with Darby. And she was no longer a mere projection, but a solid, flesh-and-blood woman.

She found her husband in one of the guest bedrooms, standing at the window, his back to the doorway where she stood. He wore a bulky bandage under a loose shirt. "I told you before, Bets," he said, without turning around, "I don't want anything to eat, so just take whatever you've brought and go away."

Keighly closed the door softly. "I think you might enjoy what I've brought," she said.

Darby stiffened, then turned on one heel to stare at her. *"Keighly?"*

"I'm here, all right. And I'm staying."

He had been holding a china mug in his good hand, and it fell to the floor then and shattered, as the glass of the mirror had done not so long before, when Duke Shingler had shot him. They both flinched at the sound.

Darby narrowed his eyes, staying where he was. "I guess I'm probably dreaming," he said. "But I sure as hell hope you won't wake me up."

She crossed the room, put her arms around Darby, pressed herself close to him, breathing in his scent, delighting in the fierce hardness of his unapologetically male body. "I love you," she said, and kissed him. "And I am definitely not a dream."

He gave a ragged sigh that rent her heart and dropped his forehead so that it rested against her own. There were tears in his voice, if not in his eyes. "God in heaven, Keighly, I thought I'd lost you and the babe forever. I didn't want to go on living, but I couldn't think of a good way to die, either."

"I would never have forgiven you if you'd done that," she said, and took his hand. "Come with me, Mr. Elder. I'm wanting a proper reunion and, unless I miss my guess, so are you."

He chuckled and drew her even closer with his good arm, crushing her against him, nearly overwhelming her with the sweet force of his kiss. While he bolted the door, a few moments later, Keighly stood trembling in the middle of the floor, her eyes burning with happy tears, her body burning with something quite different.

Darby returned to her, cupped her chin in his hand, and gave her another knee-melting kiss. It was a good thing he guided her to the bed and gently lowered her to the mattress, because she would not have been able to stand on her own.

"You plan on telling me, Mrs. Elder, exactly what happened?"

He was standing beside the bed, looking down at her, consuming her with his gaze. "The truth is," she confessed, almost breathless as he began moving the odd clothing she wore, unwrapping her as though she were some infinitely precious gift, "that I'm not sure. It's all starting to slip away, to seem like a dream, or a story I heard a long time ago, as a child—"

Darby kicked off his boots and stretched out beside her on the bed to bare her breasts and fondle the one easiest to reach. "Don't leave me again," he said, and it was at once an order and a plea.

Keighly gasped as he bent and took her nipple greedily into his mouth. Their lovemaking made it even harder to remember what had taken place. There was something about a mirror, and she'd been in some sort of terrible accident with a friend . . .

Or had she really only been dreaming?

Keighly gave herself up to her passion and that of her husband, and soon they were joined, fused by a fire all their own, and for the time being, nothing else mattered in all the universe.

They lay breathless when it was over, half-dressed, their bodies slick with perspiration. Keighly felt as though she was floating, but it wasn't a frightening sensation, merely one of utter satiation and complete contentment.

"You are no gentleman, sir," she said, when she could manage to speak. "Seducing a lady in the middle of the day."

Darby laughed, low in his throat. "You're lucky we weren't in the general store when we met up. I might have had to fling you onto the yard-goods table, throw up your skirts, and have you right there." He paused, and the amusement went out of his amber eyes, replaced by confusion. "But then, you aren't wearing skirts, are you?"

"Right now," Keighly said, hedging, "I'm not wearing much of anything, thanks to you."

He hoisted himself onto an elbow, took the waistband of her discarded slacks between two fingers. "Trousers," he said. "What the devil were you doing wearing a man's clothes?"

Keighly truly wanted to explain, but the fact was, she didn't exactly *know* where she'd gotten the pants and coat she'd had on when she woke up on the floor at the foot of the stairs, with Betsey bending over her. It had something to do with the that place she'd been before, and had wanted so badly to leave.

"I was hoping you could tell me," she said, "because I don't have the faintest idea. I must have hit my head when I fell."

"You fell?" Darby was sitting upright now, the better to examine her. "Were you hurt?"

"Did I seem like I was hurt, Mr. Elder, just a few minutes ago, when I was thrashing on this bed and carrying on like a high wind on a stormy night?"

His concern gave place to a smile. "Maybe you struck your head," he said, after a moment's consideration.

"Maybe I did." She took his hand and laid it over her breast. She liked the feel of his hard, callused skin against her softest places. "I guess you'd better tell me what *you* recall, and fill in the blanks."

"I recall," he said throatily, beginning to kiss her neck, "that the first time I laid eyes on you, you were sitting beside a mirror, holding a doll in your arms. I thought you were the prettiest thing I'd ever seen in my life. We didn't see each other again, for a long while." He was working his way down over her collarbone, and she shivered with anticipation. "Then one day, you were back, a woman grown and even more beautiful than you'd promised to be."

"But where did I come from?"

Darby squeezed her breast, brushed the already-taut nipple with his lips, in preparation for taking it full into his mouth again. "You really don't remember?" he asked drowsily.

"No," she confessed, on a gasp. Her hands were locked behind his head now, pressing him closer. Closer. She supposed she should be scared, because suddenly her whole past, except for loving this man, had evaporated from her mind.

Darby ran his tongue lightly around the morsel that strained toward him, even then. "You rode into town on the stagecoach one day," he said. "I was just coming out of the feed store. We took one look at each other, and it was love."

"Love," Keighly whispered, and she believed him. There was no reason she shouldn't. Absolutely no reason at all.

❧ CHAPTER ❧
18

Keighly found the journal, composed in her own handwriting, three weeks after she'd fallen—or *thought* she'd fallen—at the base of the stairway at the main ranch house. They'd returned, she and Darby, over Angus's protests, to their own place, and she had been working hard on the sculpture of Darby, which she clearly remembered starting, and was covered in stone dust and sweat. Meaning to have a sponge bath and put on a clean dress before dinner, she was rummaging through her lingerie drawer when her fingers brushed the sturdy leather cover.

It wasn't so much the finding of a volume in her drawer that startled Keighly; the jolt seemed to come from within, not without. The stir of recognition made her bring the book out of its apparent hiding place and flip it open.

If seeing her own penmanship was a shock, reading the first entry was an even greater one. As Keighly read, she found that the lost memories were returning, one by one, and dawdling, but all trudging stolidly along the pathways of her mind.

Keighly made her way to a chair near the window and sank into it, brow furrowed. She'd written the journal in fits and starts, determined to set down an accurate and comprehensive account of what had happened to her.

Everything was there, from her first sighting of Darby Elder in the mirror of her grandmother's ballroom to Darby's shooting in the Blue Garter Saloon.

There, the entries ceased.

Keighly had set out to record her travels in time, lest she forget and be caught unaware by destiny. Sitting in that chair, she remembered all she had so easily and so conveniently forgotten. Was there still reason to be afraid? Darby had indeed been shot, as predicted, but, thanks to Julian and Francine, he'd survived his injuries and returned to the nineteenth century. Keighly's thoughts turned to Garrett, the son she and Darby were supposed to have together. Would the boy still be born into a fate that included a fatal bout of scarlet fever?

There was no way to know, of course. Perhaps the child within her was Garrett, perhaps not. Like every other woman who bears a child, she reflected, she would have to take her chances.

Keighly shivered, recalling the accident on the freeway outside modern-day Redemption, and, though vaguely, the strange transformative experience that had followed. She might have learned so much, if she and Francine had reached the house and been able to go through the articles and other items in the trunk, but of course they hadn't gotten that far.

Keighly sat for a while, coming to terms with all of this, then put the journal back in its hiding place and proceeded with the planned sponge bath. She was in the parlor, reading, when Darby came in later and, not seeing her, went past her to enter the bedroom, there to wash off the grime of a day's ranch work and put on fresh clothes.

When he entered the kitchen, some minutes later, where Manuela had laid out a meal of roast chicken, mashed potatoes, and green beans boiled with bacon, Keighly was waiting there for him.

"You look especially beautiful," he said, and kissed her.

Keighly tried to steel herself against her husband's charms, which were formidable. "You lied to me," she accused. They were alone, as Pablo and Manuela and the ranch hands had dined separately.

He drew back her chair and nodded for her to sit down at the table. After a moment's hesitation, she acquiesced.

"What?" Darby asked, looking as innocent and open-faced as Will usually did.

"You said we met when I got off a stagecoach, and we didn't. I found my journal, Darby. The one I wrote before Duke Shingler shot you."

He sighed, pulled out his own chair, and sat. "Oh," he said, and reached for the platter of chicken.

"Is that all you're going to say? 'Oh'?"

"I had my reasons, Keighly."

"Like what?"

"I didn't want you to remember, and commence worrying again. We've got a new start, after all—I've been cleared of any guilt where the Shinglers were concerned, and Will and Simon and I have decided to work the Trip K as a three-way partnership, now that Angus has finally agreed to retire officially. You and I have a baby on the way. I guess what I'm saying is that we ought to look forward from now on, Keighly, not back."

She sat gazing at her husband. He'd known he was slated to be shot to death at the Blue Garter, and the news hadn't particularly shaken him. She couldn't remember if she'd told him about Garrett, their son, and the scarlet fever that might take his life—if so, she hadn't recorded it in the journal. And she didn't intend to mention the matter now, just in case. Because she was keeping secrets herself, she couldn't exactly blame Darby for doing something similar. His motive, after all, had been to protect, not to deceive.

"You're right about part of it. Looking forward, I mean."

MY OUTLAW

They began to eat, alone in their rustic, spacious kitchen.

"Simon has met a woman," Darby announced, midway through the meal.

Keighly dropped her fork, delighted. That news might be even better than it appeared to be on the surface, for it could mean that Darby would not die young of some accident or malady, leaving Keighly to wed his brother. "You might have mentioned that first thing, Mr. Elder," she scolded, beaming. "What's her name? Where did she come from? She can't be anybody from Redemption because Betsey would have told me—"

Darby was grinning. "How can I tell you, Mrs. Elder, if you keep rattling on and on like that?"

Keighly bit her lower lip, fairly squirming on her chair, and waited in an agony of excitement.

Darby drew the matter out, taking a second helping of mashed potatoes and adding a ladle full of gravy before going on. It was all Keighly could do not to kick him under the table.

"Her name is Thora Downing and she is a lawyer from San Francisco. Came to town yesterday, on board the stage, and hung out her shingle right across the street from Jack Ryerson's office. Of course, Simon, being the marshal and a good citizen in the bargain, eager to see the town grow and prosper, went right over there to introduce himself and explain that she'd be more suited to the schoolmarm's job, which just happens to be open. She chased him out and threw a potted plant after him when he went, and he vows God never fashioned a more wicked woman."

Keighly laughed and clasped her hands together, barely able to contain her joy. "He's crazy about her!" she cried.

Darby's grin widened. "Sounds like it," he agreed.

Francine got out of the hospital the day after she was admitted. She'd been right in her initial self-diagnosis: she wasn't seriously hurt. On the other hand, she had suffered severe shock, and every muscle in her body ached, as did the bruises that covered her arms and legs, stomach and shoulders.

Julian took her to the ranch house at the Triple K, because that was the nearest place, and almost drove her crazy with his incessant fussing and coddling. Finally, ensconced on the couch in her study, with the TV playing a soap opera, she ordered him to leave her alone for a little while.

He subsided into an easy chair and was soon comically absorbed in the medical drama being played out on the small screen. Only when the telephone rang did he finally stir, reaching for the cordless on the coffee table and barking out, "Yes!" His expression altered subtly; he had obviously forgotten the soap opera. "Yes, of course we'll talk to you. Fine, then. We'll expect you directly."

Julian hung up, gazing somberly at Francine. "That was Dan Ferris," he said. "He wants a word with us about Darby Elder's disappearance from the hospital."

"Took him long enough," Francine said, unconcerned. It had, after all, been a month since Keighly had followed Darby back to the nineteenth century, hopefully never to return.

"Don't worry," Francine said confidently. "Keighly could be anywhere, and as far as the law is concerned, Darby has been dead for more than a century. Dan Ferris is just doing this so he'll look good when the real sheriff gets over his gall-bladder surgery and comes back to work."

"Nevertheless," Julian said, "he wants to question us, and he's asked a Miss Minerva Pierce to meet him here. Who, pray tell, is she?"

"A friend of mine, and Keighly's. Prepare yourself, Dr. Drury. Miss Pierce will almost certainly look at you askance, at first anyway. You see, she knows you as the troublesome ex-boyfriend who wouldn't go away."

Julian flushed. "Well, that's flattering."

Francine smiled sweetly. "Not to worry. Now that you've changed roles, and become the man who came to dinner and stayed for a lifetime, you'll be forgiven."

"What are we going to tell the police?"

"The truth," Francine said, with more confidence than she actually felt. "That we don't know what happened to Keighly." A thought struck her. "There might be a way we can find out, though."

"What?"

"The trunk. Every time Keighly alters history, the contents of her trunk are changed, too. By examining the things she saved in that chest, we might be able to piece together what happened to her. Tomorrow, we'll go to the graveyard and see if she's finally buried beside Darby."

Julian put a hand through his hair, something he did more and more frequently these days. Francine had already made up her mind to wean him off caffeine.

"I'm not sure I can deal with that—seeing a headstone with Keighly's name on it."

"It's chilling," Francine admitted. "But I want to know that all of this wasn't for nothing, Julian. Before we officially make this ranch our vacation retreat and head back to L.A. to get married and move into our new house, I need to find out whatever I can about Keighly. She was my friend."

"Mine, too," Julian said sadly. He sat down on the couch beside her, squeezing her against its back and looking like a forlorn little boy. "You're the one I love, Francine, and I never want you to doubt that. But I cared about her, and I want her to be okay."

Francine hugged him, kissed his Aramis-scented cheek. Maybe after the replacement sheriff had gone, she would lead Dr. Julian Drury upstairs to her room and make mad, passionate love to him.

"Keighly knew you were her friend, Julian," she said gently. "She was so grateful for all you did to save Darby and help her tie up all the loose ends of her life in L.A."

"How's that going to look to the police, though?" Julian asked.

Francine sighed. "My guess would be that they'll investigate thoroughly, and find out that Keighly closed her bank accounts and liquidated her other assets before she vanished. They'll most likely decide that she wanted to turn up missing, and in a way, they'll be right."

Twenty minutes later, the acting sheriff arrived with two nervous deputies and Miss Minerva Pierce, the town librarian, who had brought along a briefcase and a casserole dish filled with some delectable mixture of tuna, sauce, and noodles. After the lawmen had put their routine questions and left, Francine, Julian, and Minerva sat in the kitchen, consuming the supper the latter had brought.

When that was done, and Julian had rather awkwardly loaded the dishwasher, the spinster librarian set her briefcase—which the police had eyed curiously but never asked about—on the bare tabletop. She opened the locks with simultaneous, flourishing motions of her thumbs and raised the lid.

"I presume," Minerva said, addressing Francine, "that since you mean to marry this man, you've told him at least some of the story?"

Francine caught Julian's eye. "He knows all of it."

"I've brought the photocopies of the documents you found in Miss Barrow's trunk on that first occasion," Minerva said. "First, however, you must catch me up. From what the police said, I have concluded that our favorite time-traveler came back to this century, at least briefly."

Francine nodded, feeling shaken as she relived the accident, and Keighly's unearthly vanishing act, yet again. It was an experience she would never forget, of course, and there were only two people she could discuss the matter with, now that Keighly was gone. Julian and Minerva Pierce.

She let Julian describe Keighly's latest, and probably

last, visit to the current century; his version of the story was condensed but accurate. He even mentioned Darby's shooting, and told how he and Francine had patched up the wound in the ballroom of the Barrow house.

Minerva's eyes were wide as she listened to the tale. "I suppose the trunk is there—at Keighly's place in Redemption."

Regretfully, Francine nodded. "I'm sure the police are watching both doors. If any of us attempts to get inside, they'll decide we were involved in Keighly's disappearance."

"Nonsense," Minerva scoffed pleasantly. "They haven't the manpower to watch that house or any other for very long. This is a small town, after all. I'll stop by there myself, tomorrow morning, and if anybody asks what I'm doing, I'll simply say I've come to collect the library books Miss Barrow neglected to return. Do either of you know where she keeps the key?"

Julian looked a bit sheepish. "In the rim of a plant pot, on the back porch. Geraniums, I think—or at least the remnants of them."

The librarian rolled her eyes. "Nobody to speak of bothers to lock their doors, here in Redemption, but you'd expect it of a young woman from L.A. What you wouldn't expect is for her to be so silly as to hide keys in such an obvious place."

"Keighly was more conventional than she would ever have admitted," Julian said, and Francine reached out and squeezed his hand lightly. Then she got up and searched the drawers of her desk until she found the instant photographs she'd taken of Keighly's gravestone, some time ago, when Keighly had first confided her story.

"Minerva, your idea is a good one—you've lived in Redemption all your life and nobody is going to suspect you of anything, even if you walk right into Keighly's house in broad daylight. So you find the trunk and bring back whatever's inside it. Julian and I will go to the cemetery first thing in the morning, and compare the gravestones that are in the Kavanagh plot now to the ones in these pictures."

Julian frowned. "If the past has been changed, and thus the relics of it, wouldn't the copies and photos reflect that?"

"I've thought about this a lot," Francine said, "and I don't believe so. The copies are essentially an imprint of the reality that existed at the moment we made them. The same is true of the gravestones. The former indicated that Darby Elder was shot to death in the Blue Garter Saloon in 1887, and the central message of the things in the trunk was that his wife, one Keighly Barrow, married his half-brother, Simon, a few years later, and bore him several children."

Julian closed his eyes. "I guess I understand."

Francine smiled at him. "Don't worry, darling. We'll guide you through it, one step at a time. Won't we, Minerva?"

"I say he either keeps up or waits in the car," said Minerva, in a slightly peevish tone, though her eyes were twinkling. She began to gather her papers and put them back into the briefcase. "All right then," she went on briskly, a few moments later, "it's decided. You check the cemetery, and I'll head for the Barrow house. We'll meet at the library at ten o'clock sharp to compare notes."

"I'll see you to your car," Julian said, rising as Miss Pierce rose.

She gave him another look, one that indicated she might be reassessing him. "Thank you," she replied.

Keighly Elder came to term on a warm afternoon in May, while she was swinging happily in a hammock in the sideyard of the Triple K ranch house, her bare, swollen feet propped on pillows and her hair tumbling about her face in curls. Etta Lee sat in the fragrant grass nearby, reading aloud from a book of fables.

Suddenly, Keighly's enormous belly contracted, and

she gasped, clutching it with both hands. The fan she'd been waving languidly under her chin fell to the ground and closed with an efficient click.

Etta Lee dropped her book and sprang to her feet. "Is it time?" she asked, sounding both horrified and thrilled. "Are you going to have the baby? *Here?*"

"I'd prefer," Keighly gasped, trying to raise her ungainly person from the hammock and finding the task impossible, "to give birth in the privacy of the house, since I'm obviously not going to make it home. Run and get Gloria and your grandfather, sweetheart. Then send Pablo for Manuela—and to find your uncle Darby. I believe he and Will are branding over near—" Another pain seized her in a cruel grip. "—over near Cherokee Butte."

Etta Lee ran toward the house, shrieking as if she'd been scalped, and within moments, Angus and Gloria came hurrying from one direction, while several ranch hands dashed in from the corral. Keighly was still foundering in the hammock when they arrived.

Angus shooed everyone but Gloria away, barking at the men, "One of you find my son—damn it, which one do you think?"

Childbirth was a female's province, but it took both Gloria and Angus to hoist Keighly onto her feet. When they'd managed that, they hustled her toward the house.

"This is not going to be fun," Keighly said, as another pain took her into its grasp, threatening to crush her pelvic bones.

"No," Gloria replied. "But for this pain, there is a reward."

With considerable effort, the two alternately shoved and dragged Keighly up the rear stairway and along the hall to the room she and Darby used when they stayed at the ranch. There, working with speedy grace, Gloria divested Mrs. Elder of her clothing and put her to bed.

297

"I want painkillers," Keighly hissed, "lots of them. And I want them right away!"

"Hush," said Angus, who had politely turned his back during the undressing process. "I once had a wound cauterized with a hot poker."

Having reminded her of that, Angus made ropes of twisted sheets and tied them to the bedposts, like the reins of some ludicrous wagon, so Keighly would have something to grasp and pull. In the meantime, murmuring reassurances, Gloria bathed her forehead with a cool cloth.

The pains got progressively worse.

Keighly had managed to put much of her past out of her mind over the last few months, but now, as she lay in childbed, she remembered hospitals and hypodermic needles filled with lovely drugs. She'd seen a PBS special about the Lamaze method once, and tried to recall how to breathe.

"I don't want to do this," she gasped, when the contractions subsided for once.

Betsey had arrived, and was bending over her, looking knowledgeable. Angus had been banished, although Gloria was allowed to remain. "I guess you should have thought of that a few months back," Betsey said, not unkindly. "Don't worry your head, Keighly. It's bad when it's happening, but you get over it fast."

"You'll—pardon me—if I don't find that—comforting?"

Betsey laughed. "Sure," she said. "If you'll pardon me for the things I'm going to be saying about Will the next time I'm in *your* place."

They already had the four boys and a baby girl named Louisa. "You can't be—serious?" Keighly huffed. "You're not—?"

"I am," Betsey said. And she actually looked happy, that fool.

Another pain struck, hard, and Keighly screamed long and loud. When she sagged back onto her pillows again, her throat was raw and she was drenched in sweat. And those, of course, were the least of her complaints. "I'll never do this again," she whispered. "I swear I'll never, ever—"

"You go right ahead and believe that if you want to, honey," Betsey told her indulgently, tossing back the covers and bending to perform an intimate assessment of the situation, "if that makes you feel any better." To Gloria she said, "Fetch me some hot water and cloth, if you will—this baby's about to pop out like a shucked pea, and I'd better be ready to catch it."

Keighly screamed again, her back arched high off the bed. She heard Darby in the hall, and there was a repeated thumping, as if he was flinging himself against the door. He bellowed her name, and the sound of a scuffle followed.

"You locked him out?" she choked, during the brief rest that followed the agony.

"Darby? He'd just be underfoot," Betsey said. "He can come in when we're through with our business, Mrs. Elder, and not before."

Keighly felt herself rising with another contraction, and she clawed at the bedclothes and sobbed, too tired to scream again. "I can't—"

And then, suddenly, there was one great, terrible pain, followed by a sensation of violent release.

"But you have," Betsey said, with pride. "You and Darby have a daughter, Keighly." Gloria had returned with the water, somehow getting past the frantic man in the hall without admitting him, and the baby cried as her Aunt Betsey cut and tied the cord and then quickly washed her.

The little girl was bundled in a blanket and resting in Keighly's arms, five minutes later, when Darby was at last allowed to enter the room.

He practically ran across the floor, then stopped suddenly a few yards from the bed, as though afraid to get too close.

"Come and see your daughter," Keighly told him

299

gently, feeling so full of love and pride in both her man and her child that she must have shone with it.

Darby approached slowly. When he stood near enough, Keighly turned back the thin blanket covering the infant's face.

"Good God," Darby said, in a combination of pity and horror. "She looks just like Angus!"

Keighly laughed. "That's temporary. I hope."

"They're all pretty ugly for the first few days, anyway," Betsey said, on her way to the door. "Congratulations, both of you."

"What are we going to call her?" Darby asked, studying the baby with as much fascination as if there had never been another child born, ever before, anywhere on earth.

"I sort of like Harmony," Keighly replied softly. She'd been considering the name for a long time, but she hadn't suggested it to Darby before that moment. Even then she wasn't sure how he would react.

He searched Keighly's eyes, as if he suspected that she was joking, and plainly saw that she was serious.

"I'd like that," he said. "And I want her middle name to be Kavanagh, if that meets with your approval."

Keighly leaned forward and kissed him to show that it did. Her joy was overwhelming then, because this baby wasn't Garrett, the child doomed to perish of scarlet fever. She and Darby had beaten fate on two counts, if not all around: he wasn't going to be killed in the Blue Garter, and little Harmony, please God, would stay healthy all her life.

"I love you, Darby Elder," she said.

"And I love you," Darby answered. Then he bent down and laid the tenderest of kisses on the sleeping baby's tiny forehead. "And you, Harmony Kavanagh Elder. And you."

Two months later, Simon married Thora Downing in the parlor of the Triple K ranch house, with his father and brothers to stand up for him and a glowing Etta Lee for a bridesmaid. Thora was an intelligent woman, as well as a beautiful one, and she fully intended to continue her law practice even after her marriage to Simon. That she would be a good wife as well, no one doubted, including Simon, although he would have preferred that the new Mrs. Kavanagh stay home like most other women of her time.

Etta Lee adored Thora, and the two had been close from their first meeting. Etta Lee told everybody who would listen that she wanted to be a lawyer, just like her new stepmother, and Keighly, for one, fully expected her to achieve that goal and any other she might set for herself.

As soon as Simon and Thora had left on their honeymoon trip to Denver—Etta Lee was staying with Will and Betsey, as usual—Darby took the first opportunity to grasp Keighly's hand and lead her toward the house.

"What are you doing?" she whispered, as he pulled her through the kitchen to the back stairs.

"We're having a wedding night," Darby said, as though she'd asked a stupid question.

"Do I have to point out that this was Simon and Thora's wedding, not ours?" Keighly asked, but she felt a sweet warmth unfolding in her belly all the same. She and Darby had not made love since before Harmony's birth. "Besides, it isn't night, it's still the afternoon."

"The least we can do is help celebrate," he said, grinning. "A person would think you weren't happy for my brother and his new wife, Keighly Elder, the way you're trying to stall."

He led her up the back stairs and into their room at the Triple K.

Keighly was flushed with excitement. "Oh, I'm happy all right," she said. Manuela was looking after the baby, so she and Darby might have as much as an hour to themselves. "An occasion like this calls for merriment."

The small room was full of spring sunlight and silence, and the delicious scent of fresh apple blossoms. Keighly drew in her breath when she saw that the bed was mounded with soft, pink-white petals, and turned to look up at Darby, to see if he'd known.

He winked mischievously, but there was a certain air of cautious hopefulness about him, too. Her reaction was plainly important to him. "I wanted things to be romantic," he said, and he was serious now. "After all, it's sort of our first time."

Keighly put her arms around Darby's neck and stood on tiptoe to kiss his mouth. "It's fabulously romantic," she assured him. "I couldn't love you more, Darby Elder, than I do right at this moment."

Darby returned her kiss, in a leisurely, teasing way, but with growing urgency. Finally, a little breathless, he drew back. "You make up for every bad thing that ever happened to me, Keighly—you and our baby."

She slid his fancy coat off his shoulders, tossed it aside, then began undoing his string tie. "I was a ghost until I met you," she replied. And it was true, in a sense. Ironically, it was only after her marriage to Darby that she had really become her most genuine self. Her artwork was flourishing, she had a life of the mind and spirit that had been undreamed of before, and her husband and child each gave a new and quite distinctive texture and depth to everything she did, thought, and felt.

Darby shuddered slightly and leaned back against the door of the bedroom as Keighly began unbuttoning his shirt, kissing the hard, hair-covered flesh beneath as she bared it. He endured her teasing as long as he could, then caught her gently but firmly by the shoulders and set her away from him to kick off his boots and unfasten his belt.

While Darby worked the long row of buttons on the bodice of Keighly's rose-colored satin gown, she boldly opened his trousers and set him free of them. He groaned as she closed a hand possessively around his staff and he bent to bury his face in her neck even as he pushed the dress down.

302

MY OUTLAW

There were a few awkward moments while they grappled with what remained of their clothes, and then Darby and Keighly stood beside their bed of apple blossoms, naked and unashamed, Adam and Eve before the Fall. That world, that room, was their Eden, but there was a difference. They would not be driven out, ever, and they both knew it.

They kissed, yet again, and then Darby laid Keighly tenderly on the mattress, the petals making a velvet-soft cushion beneath her. And rather than falling to her immediately, he stood, in stricken silence, admiring her, making her feel, by his regard, more beautiful than any goddess.

Darby parted Keighly's legs, raised her arms high over her head and wide, but there was no force in the motions, only the profoundest reverence. Having arranged her so, with her hair, now grown to her shoulders, fanned out upon the blossoms around her face, he began to explore her with light, caressing passes of his fingertips.

Keighly trembled, grasped the rails of the headboard, and submitted.

Darby's touch became more and more intimate as the moments went by; he made tantalizing circles around her breasts, the peaks of which had already hardened in anticipation. He stroked her ribs, her belly, her thighs and knees and even her feet.

Keighly began to grow feverish, so badly did she want her husband, but she knew much more would be required of them both before true satisfaction was achieved. Although he had been known to seduce her rather quickly when he found her in a private place, Darby was not generally a man to be hurried, when it came to making love to his wife.

Today, he was in fine form.

He found the tangle of moist curls at the joining of her legs and brushed over it so lightly that Keighly moaned aloud.

"In a hurry, are you?" Darby asked, in a sleepy tone.

Keighly shook her head from side to side, but they both knew she was lying. She could have received him then, joyously, but it was not to be. Not yet.

Darby laughed and parted her legs a little further, so that he could kneel between them. He raised her knees and sat on his haunches for a long time, fondling Keighly, taking delight in the small, choked cries she gave, in the involuntary upward thrustings of her hips. At last, he slid two fingers inside her—she gasped a senseless welcome—and leaned forward to take slow suckle at her breasts, one after the other.

A fine sheen of perspiration covered Keighly's skin from hairline to toes. She groaned as Darby first increased the pace of his teasing, then slowed it down again.

Finally, she grasped his head in both hands and pulled him to her, for a desperate kiss. And in so doing, she turned the tide of that sweet, fierce battle, for when her tongue entered his mouth, Darby too was caught in the grip of a desire that could know only one end.

He entered her with a single thrust, forceful and at the same time gentle, and still their mouths were locked together, as inexorably joined as their bodies yearned to be. Very slowly, they moved as one, like a fine bow flexing and unflexing. As the urgency increased, so did the meter of their lovemaking, until at the end the ancient dance was fierce, almost violent, in its tempo.

Then, at last, they reached the devastating, glorious zenith of their union, crying out in one voice, clasping each other as they submitted to an elemental power that was greater than both their wills combined. When they were finally released, they fell together to the bed of blossoms, now dewy and bruised and more fragrant than ever beneath them, and struggled to regain their breath.

A long time passed, during which they lay entwined, their hearts beating in sync, Keighly's head tucked into the curve of Darby's neck. The light changed at the windows, and they could hear the sounds of wagons and buggies leaving, the voices of the guests bidding one another farewell.

Keighly gave a contented sigh. "It's happened again," she said.

Darby raised himself, slightly, and looked down into her face. "What?" he asked, sounding just a touch on the nervous side.

Keighly smiled. "We made another baby."

"How can you know something like that?"

"I did before," she pointed out. "Remember?"

Darby kissed her lightly, his eyes shining with love and pride and joy. "Yes, Mrs. Elder, I remember. Are you scared? You raised hell when Harmony was born, you know."

"Yes, I am and I did," Keighly said, holding back a smile. "And I probably will again. The point is, none of that will matter when I hold our son or daughter in my arms."

"I've mentioned, haven't I, that I love you?"

Keighly laughed and threaded her fingers through his rumpled hair. "Yes," she said. "Mention it often, won't you?"

The trunk stood in a far corner of the attic in the old Triple K ranch house, covered by a large quilted cloth the movers had left behind. Francine hadn't been near it since that morning five years before, when she and Julian had risen at sunrise to drive to the cemetery in Redemption.

They'd found the Kavanagh plot right away, of course, but there hadn't been any need to compare the gravestones with the photos Francine had taken when the adventure first began. The monuments showed that Keighly and Darby had lived to a very old age, as husband and wife, and died within four months of each other. The name on the stone next to Simon's was that of a woman named Thora, and the markers of a large tribe of descendants surrounded theirs. There had been no graves for any children of Keighly's.

At ten that same morning, Julian and Francine had driven to the library, as agreed the night before, to meet with Miss Minerva Pierce, who had collected the contents of Keighly's trunk—the same chest she was looking at now, with tears in her eyes.

Inside were several albums, stuffed with photographs, birth announcements, marriage certificates, old letters, and other memorabilia. The trio of investigators had soon learned that Keighly and Darby had produced six living children, all of whom had grown to adulthood, married, and had babies of their own. Gone were the articles that had proclaimed Darby's death in the Blue Garter Saloon, and although Keighly's letters indicated that she had miscarried twice, no son of theirs had ever died of scarlet fever.

Now, heavy with her own child, hers and Julian's, Francine raised the lid of the old chest and looked inside. She was happy, so happy, in her new life, with Julian and their young daughter, Samantha, and the rewarding career she was building for herself in Los Angeles. Her relationship with her eighteen-year-old son, Tony, was a warmly affectionate one.

Francine longed to somehow communicate all this to Keighly, who had been her friend for such a short time and still touched her spirit in ways that no one else ever had. She couldn't help thinking that she wouldn't have Julian, and all that had come to her through him, if it hadn't been for Keighly.

"Thank you," Francine said, running her hand over the loose lining of the ancient trunk. "Thank you for everything."

It was then that she felt the slight bulk beneath the tattered cloth. Carefully, she tore it away, and an envelope of powdery ivory vellum toppled out.

Francine's heart quickened as she picked up the letter for, in faded and familiar, if spiky, handwriting, it bore

306

her name. She was trembling, her heart pounding, as she carefully opened the envelope and took out the single page inside.

It was dated May 1, 1910.

Dearest Francine,

I hope you will find this, and that your life is as rich as mine has been. My only regret, truly, is that we couldn't pursue our friendship. That's impossible, of course, with more than a century between us, and now that I'm an old woman, I can be pretty certain that I won't be venturing so far forward in time ever again.

Darby and I have been incredibly happy. We've known our share of troubles and tragedies; everyone does. But we always had each other, and that made all the difference.

I could ask nothing more for you than I've had, with my Darby.

I trust that, if you've looked through the albums, which I kept up partly for your sake, you know we named our youngest daughters, twins, Juliana and Francine. It was the best way we could think of to honor you.

They've torn down the old Blue Garter Saloon, or most of it, at least, and a fine new structure is being built on the site. One day, of course, I will walk into the ballroom in that very house, and see Darby, reflected in the mirror. Then, perhaps, the whole thing will start all over again. Do you suppose that time is really a circle? I've long since stopped trying to work out what happened; we'll probably never know.

Please give my love and appreciation to Julian and to Miss Pierce. I don't know what I would have done without all of you.

May God bless . . .

> *Keighly Barrow Elder*
> *D & K Ranch*
> *Redemption, Nevada*

Also available from

Linda Lael Miller

The Bestselling
Springwater Seasons Series:

Springwater

·

Rachel

·

Savannah

·

Miranda

·

Jessica

·

A Springwater Christmas

LINDA LAEL MILLER is the beloved bestselling author of more than fifty novels, of which more than twelve million copies are in print. Most recently she received acclaim for the *New York Times* bestsellers *Courting Susannah* and *One Wish*, for her enchanting medieval romances *My Lady Beloved* and *My Lady Wayward*, written under the name Lael St. James, and for her tales of life and love in the fictional towns of Springwater, Montana, and Primrose Creek, Nevada. Her most recent Springwater novel, *Springwater Wedding*, is available from Pocket Books, and her next novel of Primrose Creek, *The Last Chance Café,* is coming in hardcover. Ms. Miller resides in the Scottsdale, Arizona, area. Visit her Web site at www.lindalaelmiller.com.